Praise for
FIND ME IN THE STARS

"Larimore's ability to engulf a reader into a tale... is brilliantly done... The development of the characters and the story is rich, with believable situations, elegant descriptions, and powerful themes woven into the narrative."
~ The Historical Fiction Company
5-star Award of Excellence
Book of the Year Award Honorable Mention 2023

"Thoughtful, gripping, totally transports you to another time in a way few other stories do."
~ Michéle Callard, author of the *The Bear and the Basque, The Wolf's Legacy, and Born Under the Wrong Sun.*

"Larimore's blend of impassioned love and well-researched history is a tour de force. The struggle of a Huguenot man and a free-spirited holy-woman healer to reunite transports readers from the mystical mountains of France's Cévennes to Switzerland, then London, in a lushly told tale that ignites the senses and feeds the soul."
~ Rozsa Gaston, author of *Margaret of Austria* and the *Anne of Brittany Series*

"The tensions among faith, love, and survival keeps readers eagerly turning pages... Larimore masterfully transports readers to the mysterious, mountainous region of southern France... Against the backdrop of religious persecution, Larimore weaves a tale of ordinary people who embark on a perilous journey in search of hope and freedom... an emotional journey that lingers long after you've turned the last page... If you're seeking an immersive experience that will touch your heart, this book is a must-read."
~ Keira Morgan, author of the *Chronicles of the House of Valois*

"Such immersive, atmospheric writing that I was immediately invested and intrigued with the historical world. Authentic to the history while still keeping a rich, engaging fictional narrative at the focus."
~ Netgalley review

"I... was swept into this beautiful story of romance, persecution and journeys. Larimore is a fantastic storyteller; creating believable places such as treacherous mountain passes in the dead of night, scenes of rural France and 17th century London, which hook the reader from the start. A touching historical novel written with finesse."
~ Netgalley review

"The author skillfully weaves fictional and real-life characters and events into an exciting story, setting it within a vivid background that immerses readers in that time and place... a suspenseful story grounded in history, with characters they can root for, as they reveal both their foibles and their strengths."
~ C.L.R. Peterson, author of *Lucia's Renaissance*

"Lush descriptions that immersed me in the scenes... while I might have come into this book with a thorough grounding in the history of French religious persecutions, the gut-punchingly personal details made all the difference in a story..."
~ Janet Wertman, author of *The Seymour Saga Trilogy*

Also By
JULES LARIMORE

The Muse of Freedom: a Cévenoles Sagas novel
Book One in the Huguenot Trilogy

FIND ME IN THE STARS

A CÉVENOLES SAGAS NOVEL

JULES LARIMORE

Mystic Lore Books

Map Brushes by K.M. Alexander

Identifiers: Ebook ISBN – 979-8-9864488-7-9

For more books by the author, event requests, or bulk purchases visit www.juleslarimore.com.

First edition published in the United States by Mystic Lore Books, 2024

ref·u·gee

A person who has been forced to leave their country in order to escape war, persecution, or natural disaster. Origin: early 17th century (originally denoting a Protestant who fled France to seek refuge elsewhere from religious persecution): from refuge + -ee, influenced by French réfugié 'gone in search of refuge', past participle of réfugier, from refuge.

"Freedom is a heavy load, a great and strange burden for the spirit to undertake. It is not easy. It is not a gift given, but a choice made, and the choice may be a hard one. The road goes upward toward the light; but the laden traveler may never reach the end of it."
~ Ursula K. LeGuin ~
The Tombs of Atuan

"When you part from your friend, you grieve not; For that which you love most in him may be clearer in his absence, as the mountain to the climber is clearer from the plain."
~ Khalil Gibran ~
The Prophet

CONTENTS

HISTORICAL DETAILS

To ground you in the era, see the Author's Notes for some historical details on France and the Huguenots of the Cévennes Mountains in the late 17th century.

Place name spellings
during the late 17th century

Genouillac ~ Genolhac
Mont Lauzère ~ Mont Lozère
Spittlefields ~ Spitalfields

London
Paris
Loire River
FRA
CÉVENNES
MONT LAUZÈRE
CHAM DES BONDONS
Knights of Saint Jean
Les Bouzèdes
menhirs
aven de Malaval
Espagnac
Genoüillac
U TARN
Le Villaret Inn
Quéza
GORGES DU TARN
Pont de Montvert
Dominican Prieuré
Castelbouc
Florac
MONT BOUGÈS
Mijavols
Chambarigaud
GÉVAUDAN
Château de Cougoussac
SE MEJEAN
La Baume Dolente
Château de Portes

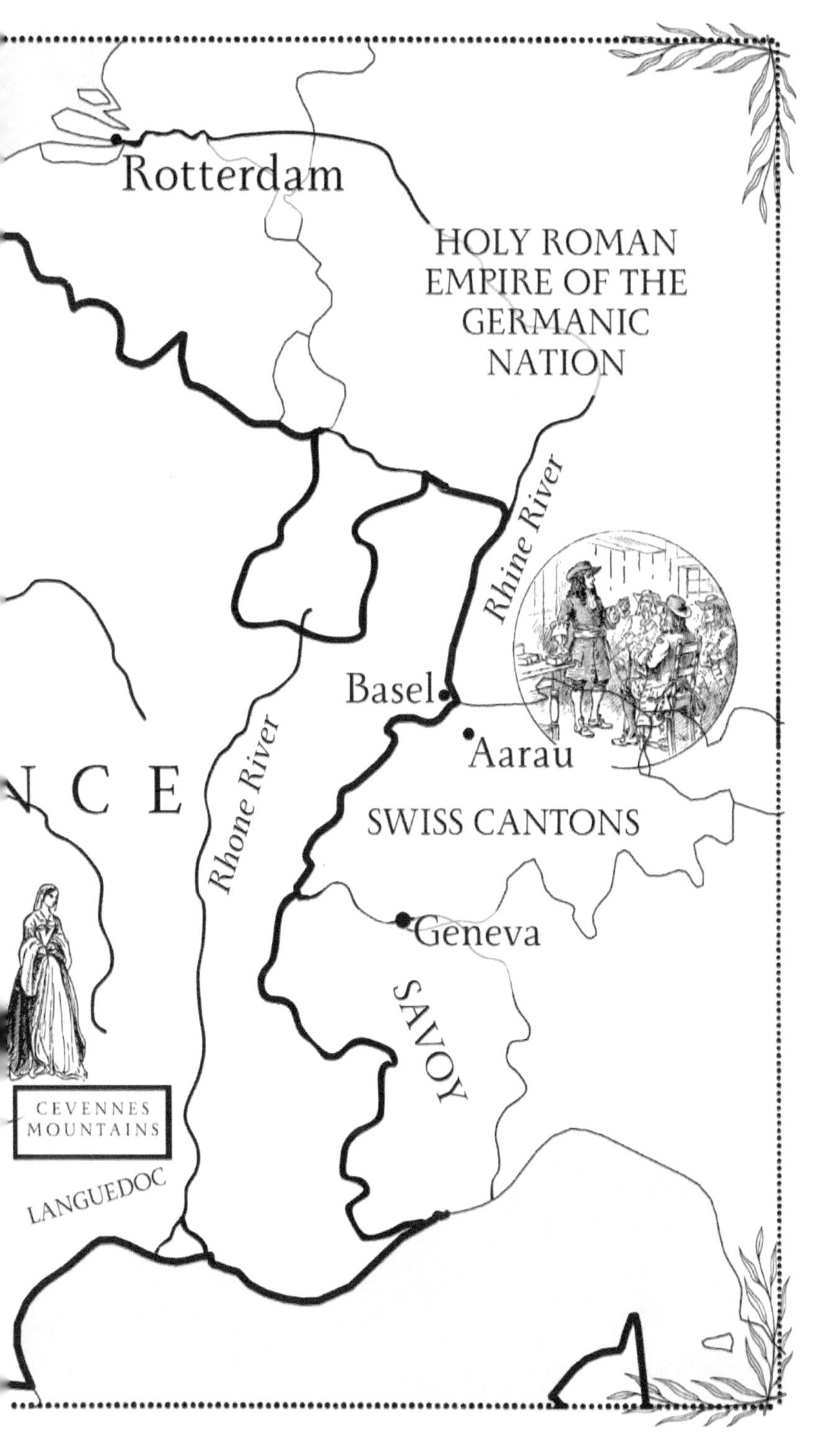

Rotterdam
HOLY ROMAN
EMPIRE OF THE
GERMANIC
NATION
Rhine River
Basel
Aarau
SWISS CANTONS
Rhone River
Geneva
SAVOY
N C E
CEVENNES
MOUNTAINS
LANGUEDOC

PART ONE

CHAPTER I

FLIGHT OF THE DOVES

AMELIA

22 September 1697 ~ Evening
Les Bouzèdes Hamlet, Mont Lauzère, Gévaudan, France

O ne by one, stars emerged in the darkening sky, yet the trembling young woman still clung to the sight of Jehan BonDurant and his spirited band of refugees as they departed in search of hope.

Despite the heaviness shrouding her heart, Amelia Auvrey sat high in the saddle of the magnificent Andalusian mare that Jehan had entrusted to her care and stared at the distant lantern lights. Like tiny fireflies, they flickered, then disappeared into the somber embrace of Mont Lauzère's forest.

A silent witness to the exodus, Amelia tried to quell her remorse as every vital spark of her essence yearned to call out after Jehan. She wiped salty tears from her face, then laced her fingers into the gentle mare's silken mane, taking comfort in the warmth and rhythm of Luisant's pulsing lifeblood.

A sudden wind whistled up the steep mountain cliffs, the pungent scent of pine smarting her nose, sharpening her senses. Leaves tinted by the colors of oncoming autumn ripped from the trees and swirled around her. The veil she wore fluttered like a bird before a storm, its tiny embroidered stars dancing on a sea of azure silk. It loosened from her waves of chestnut hair and lifted just out of reach, disappearing into the night sky.

The sharp wind turned cold and stung her cheeks until she lowered her head. She wrapped her cloak tight and shivered—the air waking her to the reality that she had just watched the love of her life leave on an unknown odyssey to a foreign land.

Think on it no more, for it is done, she tried to tell herself. Knowing their love had been ill-fated from the start made it no less painful, so she struggled to restrain her weeping.

Then, amidst ragged breaths, she thought she heard a faint whimper from below. A slight nudge against her foot turned her focus to the golden eyes of her loyal wolf-dog, Romulus. Set deep in a thick white coat, they glinted in the moonlight.

She leaned forward and rested her head against the horse's neck while stroking the soft fur between her dog's ears. Fatigue gripped her limbs and fixed her eyes as she gazed out at the indigo mountains that had sheltered her people for centuries, keeping them hidden and their secrets safe. Yet new threats were on the rise daily. Threats that might imperil them all.

"Mademoiselle Auvrey."

Amelia's heart lurched, and she spun around in a start, the fierce winds having muted the hoofbeat of the approaching horse.

"I have your veil."

The pounding in her chest slowed as she recognized the reassuring voice of her protector. The Hospitallers' eight-pointed white cross on Commandeur François Timoleon's black surcoat glowed in the moonlight over his tall physique. Even in the dim light, she could make out the creases on his furrowed brow. And, in his outstretched hand, her veil waved like a pennant in the wind.

She could not bring herself to speak. Even as the gusts diminished, her mind raced. Her burning eyes returned the Commandeur's worried look with a vacant stare.

The beating of an owl's wings against the night air distracted her attention from Timoleon and her sullen thoughts, drawing her gaze upwards to the heavens. To the brilliant stars and shining silver moon. She sighed in a breathy, wistful melody. Unlike the lanterns, at least the lights in the celestial sphere would never be extinguished—the only balm she could find for this bittersweet parting.

She tried to persuade herself there was no cause for sadness. After all, it was she who had encouraged Jehan, the young noble apothecary from Cougoussac, to leave their Cévenole homeland in search of Eden.

He needed to find a sanctuary where he was free to practice his healing arts and live according to his own spiritual beliefs. But, above all, where he could evade capture by King Louis XIV's Intendant Basville and his dragoons. Their hunt had been fueled by Jehan's attendance at the clandestine Huguenot assemblies of the Children of God. And by his alleged complicity in their plans to rebel, even though the accusations had been entirely false.

Amelia huffed at the very thought of it. Jehan would never be one to resort to sedition or violence. But the risk of arrest and enslavement on a galley ship still loomed large and was a risk he could no longer ignore. Although it would be a perilous and illegal journey out of the country, she had deemed it safer for him to depart, for she knew it offered hope for a peaceful existence.

Yet now, her certainty wavered. As she ran through the reasoning for Jehan's departure, no amount of logic would lighten her heart. He had become her dear friend, working alongside her at the assemblies to provide healing for the mountain folk while championing tolerance and compassion.

Her very *dearest* friend, there could be no denying. No one had gotten close to her heart in the way he had.

Biting her lower lip, she considered his journey ahead. It weighed on her like a heavy early frost, leaving her frozen, icebound, powerless, and left to face a desolate winter ahead with only memories to warm her heart.

Commandeur Timoleon cleared his throat. "Mademoiselle? Are you well?"

An ample, dark beard framed the benevolent face of this courageous man who had consented to shelter Amelia and her grandmother at his Knights of Saint Jean outpost—their saving grace amidst the resurgence of persecutions and instabilities that plagued the Cévennes again. Amelia glanced at the Commandeur, her fears reeling in her head. What if her presence were to bring trouble upon the Hospitaller community? Was it worth the risk?

She reminded herself that Timoleon had committed to the task without hesitation. They had made an agreement; it was a fair exchange for Amelia's much-needed assistance in the commandery hospital, using the special healing skills passed down through her family for generations.

She took a deep breath of the chill air, grateful that she had come to feel at home in the Knights' hamlet on Mont Lauzère over the past few weeks. But doubts still filled her thoughts. She took the veil from Timoleon and hastily tucked it into the pocket of her cloak. "I am not certain I did the right thing . . . giving Jehan so much hope."

"What is it you always tell us about the power of our words?" asked Commandeur Timoleon.

Ever the voice of reason, Timoleon could be counted on to keep her from veering too far off course. A steady, patient man whom both Amelia and Jehan respected for his dedication to peace and equity throughout the commandery's vast land and lease holdings. She valued Timoleon's friendship. For each year, he and his knights had provided safe escort while on pilgrimage to Marie de Magdala's cave at Sainte-Baume.

She drew another long breath and centered herself, relieved by Timoleon's reminder to lean on the wisdom from old tomes in her family's cottage library. Recalling her favorite saying from the ancient teachings, she cleared the emotion from her throat and recited it aloud, her composure returning. "A person can conjure what is feared by simply uttering the words, so we must choose our words wisely. Yet if we speak our desires with the utmost faith, they can come true. 'Tis the essence and magic of prayer."

As the wind grew wild again, Commandeur Timoleon nodded and raised his voice. "Exactly. Let us hold our thoughts on a safe and successful journey for Jehan and the others. Perhaps one day you will join him."

Upon the Commandeur's words, Amelia's body tensed, every muscle as taut as a hunter's bowstring. She closed her eyes, not knowing if the tension was caused by the bitter wind or by regret for allowing her free-spirited beliefs to hold her back from fully loving Jehan.

In her youth, she had dedicated herself solely to the Divine, committing to chastity and refusing to take vows or adhere to any specific doctrine. Though she knew in her heart, her commitment was just as much to her independence as it was to God. She had tried but could never fathom an obligation to marry and bear children. For she might die in childbirth, just as her mother had. Or raise a child only to see it become a rebel, like her Huguenot father, committing violent acts—that would never be the answer to the freedom he sought—and then dying for the cause.

Her mind vacillated again as another powerful gust left her unsteady in the saddle. Was it a prophetic wind telling her to cue Luisant and race after Jehan? From the first day they had met, she had felt a mysterious connection to him. And now she was coming to realize the immense depth of the abiding love that had grown between them.

She longed to be close to him but could not see her way to giving him what it seemed he desired. No, she had done the right thing. Encouraging him to leave and find his Eden was the only way he would truly be free. But how could she ever be free of her own yearning? Or free of the guilt she felt for leading him to believe she might join him one day? It would tug at her and bend her will like the trees around her, leaning in the tempest, looking for support.

The Commandeur pulled his hood up as the winds continued to wail. "If you are ready, we should be on our way. The hour is late, and we have patients who will need tending in the morning." He clucked to signal his horse, then called out to the dog, "Romulus, come."

Amelia gently squeezed her calves against Luisant, cueing her forward. Yes, the patients. That is how she would free herself of the yearning, and perhaps, one day, of the guilt. Keep her hands and mind busy. At least until another nightfall would come, and she would look to the heavens to find Jehan. For, no matter the distance, they shared the same night sky. And it was there, in the millions of winking stars, that they had promised to meet.

CHAPTER 2

IN SEARCH OF REFUGE

JEHAN

**22 September 1697 ~ Late Evening
Mont Lauzère To Naves, France**

Theirs was a diverse assemblage of refugees, setting out by moonlight on sturdy mules over rugged mountain *drailles*. Two women and seven men, some young and some old. Huguenots, *nouveaux convertis* Catholics, and Roma. Some whose whispered voices trembled with desperation and others whose eyes sparkled with excitement for the journey to new and wondrous places. Yet, for now, Jehan BonDurant could only place his feelings somewhere in between.

In the months leading up to his decision to leave, his friend Amelia's encouragement and love had allayed his trepidation. But here he was, less than a league from his departure point, and misgivings were already creeping in.

He reached into the pocket of his *justaucorps*, to the resettlement project pamphlet she had shared; the course parchment against his fingers seemed a striking contrast to the gentle peace and abundance described in the Isle d'Eden proposal. He longed to find a place such as that, without all the strife and division caused by years of persecution. A place to start anew and be free to practice his healing arts as an apothecary.

Jehan pushed his mind to focus on the other blessings in this departure. He let out a huge breath and looked heavenwards, reminding himself he would no longer be at the beck and call of André BonDurant—his older cousin and apprentice master who had a rather controlling nature.

But the constant grating of the mules' hooves against rock provoked Jehan's thoughts back to the struggle he had faced in making the choice to leave. He cherished his majestic Cévenole homeland and his beloved horse, Luisant. And he cherished Amelia. Leaving the country meant leaving them all. He stared at the stars above in the night sky, knowing the ache of longing would only increase with time. *Ame, my heart, my soul.*

She had spoken a vague promise of hope that, if she were to lose her grandmother to illness or the wrath of time, she might endeavor to join him in Eden. Yet, now it only confused his feelings. He had already once reconciled with the fact that she was a free-spirited holy woman, committed only to God, and may never give him the kind of love that would feel complete. How long could he hold out his heart? Even if she were to join him, how would it be if she were to refuse him as a lover again?

Jehan gritted his teeth and huffed resolutely; he must stick to his instincts. He would let Amelia's inspiration spur him on, enlivening him at the prospect of a better future, but knowing it might be with, or without her.

He breathed in the cooling night air, and studied the stalwart band of traveling companions ahead of him on the narrow draille, wondering if they would fully accept him. He had every desire to embrace their differences. Yet would they reciprocate?

For many years he hadn't quite fit in, having felt torn between indoctrinated Catholic leanings—brought about by his forced upbringing in a Dominican prieuré—and his Huguenot family's Protestant convictions. His parent's determination to retain their faith, against the King's orders, was the precise cause of his captivity at the prieuré for nearly eleven years. And there, he had been converted and left with the disreputable status of *nouveau converti*. The Protestants didn't trust him. The Catholics didn't trust him. So he gravitated toward other outsiders.

Among the travelers, he knew he could count on his elderly cousin, Moyse BonDurant, and the Roma couple, Syeira and Manfri, but would the other three refugees and the guides understand his dilemma?

He watched the others ahead weave around switchbacks on the precarious, rock-strewn path; mule and human becoming one being, ghost-blue moonlit outlines swaying side to side like pendulums. They were difficult to discern in the dim light but he could make out that the lead guide, Massip, was downhill, followed by the other six refugees—Syeira, then Manfri, then just ahead of Moyse, were two fledgling men and a woman of a similar age.

Jehan had missed mention of names of the last three; the group having set off in such a rush for fear of dragoons spotting them. He had only caught that they were hatmakers under the employ of a Monsieur Malbois, who was already in the Swiss cantons, and that they would be a part of the Calvinist refugee colony headed by Jehan's uncle, Pasteur Barjon.

Turning behind to Stéphane, the guide stationed in the rear, Jehan asked. "Can you tell me the names of the three hatmakers?"

"I don't know all of their names, but there will be plenty of time for that later . . . after we reach our first stop."

When Jehan's mule began to dawdle, sniffing at heather and foraging among the rocks, the whispering voices of the others faded into the darkness ahead. He clucked and nudged it with his heels, but the mule would not budge, yet he needed to keep pace. And a watchful eye on Moyse.

It had only been a month, after all, since the older man had injured his wrist in the extreme Cévenol episode—the storm that had flooded the gorges, rivers, and lowlands, destroying properties including two of Jehan's mills, and taking several lives.

"Give her time for a mouthful," said Stéphane, "then she'll move on."

While the mule lingered, Jehan asked the young guide, "Did you have family or friends injured in the great storm?"

"No, but a farm nearby lost several structures in the flooding." The fresh-faced, golden-haired guide spoke in a voice that was as gentle and delicate as his features. "I was told you requested our escort just afterward."

"I did," Jehan replied. "With most of the bridges destroyed, I thought it created the best opportunity to escape the country. Ever since the King's dragoons returned from the Grand Alliance war front, his Intendant Basville has been assigning regiments to the Cévennes to resume persecutions. And I was told my name is on a list of malcontents they are in search of."

"I see. Yes, with the bridges out, travel through these high mountains is nearly impossible for mounted troops. This is certainly the right moment." Stéphane reached out and patted Jehan's mule on the rear. "Come on there. You've had enough now."

The mule scarcely moved, but in a gust of wind, Jehan's long dark hair hurtled about his face. He pushed it back, wishing he had tied it in a queue, then turned again to Stéphane, raising his voice a little over the sound of rustling leaves. "My apologies. This mule is certainly not as cooperative as my Luisant."

"I understand, Sieur BonDurant." Stéphane's tone was mild and consoling, but a bit hard to hear as the strong breezes whistled through the trees. "We all wish we could take our horses, but they would only end up injured on these rough drailles. 'Tis good your friend Amelia will look after your Luisant."

A few more clucks and the mule finally understood it was part of the pack, but Jehan's mind remained on his beloved horse. She had never required this persistent nudging to continue forward the way this stubborn mule did.

For two years, Luisant had been his constant companion—ever since the day of Jehan's release from the prieuré on his eighteenth birthday. He would miss their adventures together.

Memories of their first journey to the cities swept in with the fallen leaves that whirred around him; the same journey that had left him tormented by new realizations about the brutality of the King's minions in their pursuit of a forced state religion. Jehan's shoulders tightened as he recalled it. 'One King, One Law, One Faith' read the leaflets posted throughout the land.

The political divide created among families and friends by that very policy had become abundantly clear as Jehan had traveled through Alais and Uzès. It had left him bewildered as to why the King could not, or would not, recognize that his policy of intolerance was destroying the solidarity he demanded and driving good, productive citizens out of the country.

As the mule settled into a steady, sure-footed cadence, Jehan's remembrances drifted to the more sensual impressions of that first adventure with Luisant, and his worries over his current situation eased a bit.

It had been the Uzès market, with its colorful display of local herbs, spices from the Levant, luscious fruits, and a trail of exotic odors that had elevated his passion for the healing arts. That day had a profound impact on him, igniting a fascination with medicinal plants and spices, their distillation and manipulation, and with seeking the most effective remedies for the infirmed, leading him to purchase the apothecary bag he now wore strapped across his chest.

Jehan's hand glided over the supple leather of his bag, reminding him of the hours he spent with Metayer Benat, the skilled steward of his Château de Cougoussac estate, perfecting the design of the strap to ensure a comfortable fit. Jehan's reminiscence carried him back to their workshop, to the shoes they had made and the sturdy custom saddlebag they had collaborated on as well.

A sudden realization sent his thoughts swirling so fast he could barely focus. *The saddlebag*! It was still attached to Luisant's saddle, and he'd carelessly left the Huguenot medallion inside. *Amelia could face grave trouble over it.*

Fingers of guilt and regret clenched his throat. That medallion, inherited from his father, was as much a curse as a help. It had gained him admittance to secret Huguenot assemblies but if the King's dragoons found it on Amelia, she could be arrested, possibly even locked in the Tour de Constance for an eternity. How could he leave her with that very real threat of danger looming?

He could not restrain himself, the dread pushing his thoughts to obsession, and shouted to the shadowy figures ahead, hoping the lead guide would hear him. "Massip. I must go back. Massip, can you hear me?"

Jehan's mule struggled to keep its footing as Stéphane rode up alongside and grabbed the sleeve of Jehan's justaucorps, whispering straight into his ear. "Stop your shouting. Have you lost your mind? Or just your nerve?"

Stéphane let go but continued in a low voice. "You will need every *ounce* of nerve if you keep shouting and calling attention to us. There might be dragoons or militia creeping about in the forest. We believe them to be far off, nevertheless, you know as well as I, sound carries through the gorges."

At the mention of dragoons, Jehan's hand instinctively moved to the hilt of his light rapier sword. "But I have endangered Amelia, so I *must* go back," he insisted.

"No. We cannot," Stéphane said, shaking his head. "Besides, she seemed perfectly fine under the protection of the knights from the Hospitaller commandery when we left Bouzèdes."

"But we've only gone a short distance. It won't take me long. I just need to . . ."

The guide promptly laid his hand over Jehan's mouth and stopped him from saying more.

Stéphane's soft skin and pleasant scent penetrated Jehan's nose, calming him slightly. *Odd, that a man's touch would do that.*

"We *cannot* go back," Stéphane persisted.

Jehan observed the kindness in the young man's clear blue eyes as they reflected the moonlight, but his countenance was most serious, the brow of his pale forehead furrowed with worry.

The choice to leave the country was in motion, and it was clear that Jehan's panic would only endanger the others. Amelia had taught him that releasing his fears would be the only way to find freedom in life. But despite her wise words, fear was tenacious, and it continued to hold its grip, eroding his confidence. He had no way to know for certain if Amelia would find the medallion in time, nor how the perilous journey ahead would unfold. But he would have to keep faith and envision only favorable outcomes, often easier said than done. Already, he missed her guidance.

⁓

23 September 1697 ~ Before Dawn
Seigneurie de Naves near Les Vans, France

Jehan took a deep breath of cool night air, catching the scent of forest soil and pine, trying to keep himself alert as the weary refugee group neared their first destination. The guides had promised it was not far now to the Naves hamlet stop, a safer place than nearby Les Vans to rest when dawn broke.

The lantern lights had grown faint and eventually sputtered out, and the moon had set, leaving a slow-moving wheel of bright stars that made Jehan think of his promise to Amelia—to meet her in the stars. He wondered if she was sleeping now, or perhaps about to rise. As he listened carefully, he heard night sounds over the steady clopping of mule hooves; the nightingale singing out over the incessant music of crickets strumming their tiny legs, the scrabble of animals about the forest—likely fox and polecats chasing field mice, or roe deer swiftly evading wolves.

Without warning, Moyse brought his mule to an abrupt stop.

Jehan jerked on the reins and rocked back in the saddle, struggling to prevent a collision that might send them all—men and mules—careening down the steep mountainside.

With his heart racing, the fright stuck in Jehan's throat for a moment before he could speak. "What is it, Moyse?" he panted.

"My back," he said, leaning side to side. "I can surely use one of your special cures."

The three hatmakers ahead of Moyse began to murmur. One of them halted his mule and turned toward Jehan.

"And my angry rump needs something, as well," he jested, wriggling about in the saddle.

The two young men burst into nervous laughter and the mademoiselle joined in.

Jehan twisted his mouth into a grimace, taken aback by their bawdiness.

From further up the line, Syeira and Manfri giggled. "A little dancing is the best cure for that," she said.

"Hush!" ordered Massip, and the laughing ceased.

"Let's move on now," said Stéphane, keeping his tone milder than Massip's.

Jehan did not find humor in the situation either, but perhaps it was their anxiety that stirred up the crude taunt. Of course, his rear could use a rest, too. Yet it was his shoulders that ached most from the extra weight in his clothing, making him feel nearly as old as Moyse.

He dared not mention his own pain to avoid any hint to the others that he carried gemstones and extra coin sewn into the seams and hems of his overcoat and justaucorps. It had been the only way to bring at least some of his assets, beyond the meager amount a local traveler would carry in their purse. He resolved not to fret over how long it would last him and trusted that André would forward money as agreed from the false loans they had arranged.

"I have willow bark powder," Jehan said to Moyse. "Can you wait till we reach our stop?" If it could wait, he would slip some powder in his own drink as well, without the others noticing. "We may never get these obstinate creatures moving again should we linger too long."

"I suppose," said Moyse. "If you also do one of those special charms of yours. The one Amelia taught you . . . where you lay your hands on and chant a prayer."

No more than a few thousand *pieds* down the draille, the stars began to fade as a faint pink glow tinged the inky sky. Cockcrow was growing near as the group slowed on a grassy knoll in the hills above a hamlet.

"Why are we stopping?" asked Moyse, stretching with a hand on his lower back. "Are we to sleep on the hard earth?"

Massip dismounted and led the mules into a staggered circle to prepare the group for instruction. "We have reached Naves, our first stop. I need everyone to be extremely quiet as we descend into this valley. And be sure you keep your false passports on your person at all times."

Jehan patted his breast pocket, assuring himself he had not misplaced his, while the others checked for theirs.

"Look closely down below, just beyond that cluster of trees." Massip pointed toward the faint outlines of the structures below, to a large *maison-forte* or modest château—it was hard to tell in the weak light—and several smaller buildings clustered around it. "If you can make it out, there is a grange just behind the largest structure . . . which is the maison belonging to a local *seigneur*. We shall dismount here, lead our mules through the field, and avoid the main roadway by entering through the rear gate. This place is your safe haven during the day. The owner will provide all your accommodations, but since we shall always travel by night, I need you to rest first to accustom your bodies. You will break fast only after you've had a good sleep."

"Will we have beds?" asked the young woman hatmaker as Stéphane assisted her off her mule. "And chamberpots?"

"Mademoiselle, your basic needs will be met," said Massip, his impatience apparent in his flippant tone. "Though this maison is *no* inn." He scowled as his eyes flashed around at the group. "Anyone else take issue with your accommodations?"

Jehan pinched his lips together and glanced at the others, some shaking their heads to indicate they had no qualms and everyone of them now as silent as the trees.

"Fine then," Massip said. "After we get the mules settled in the grange, I shall take you to the sleeping quarters. And, for your safety and the anonymity of the seigneur who owns this place, you must not leave that chamber till I tell you it is safe."

Jehan followed the other refugees inside the grange, the light rustle of straw beneath hooves and feet the only sounds to be heard.

Stéphane carefully pulled the heavy wooden door shut behind them. It moaned a little, but not enough to rouse anyone outside of the isolated *seigneurie*.

Massip located a lantern on a hook just inside, then pulled a flint box from his pocket and ignited a flame in a sudden burst of bright yellow light.

The light blinded Jehan, leaving only a field of white before his eyes. He reeled his head away, hoping it would soon dissipate.

"You're later than expected," a man's voice growled from the shadows.

Jehan blinked several times to see. There, stepping into the flickering lantern light, was a massive man holding a farrier's hammer.

A gasp came from the mademoiselle and she stumbled backward, landing in Stéphane's arms.

Massip took the big man aside and whispered to him for a few moments with their heads nodding in some sort of agreement. The man apparently meant no harm and proceeded to tie up the mules while Massip signaled the group to follow him through a side door and into the maison.

It had been a long night, nearly ten hours over dangerous mountain heights. And Jehan was eager to lie down, be it on a wool-filled mattress or straw pallet, it mattered little. As long as he could relieve his shoulders of the weighty coins hidden deep inside his clothing, and set aside the dagger and heavy sword dangling from the belt at his hips.

CHAPTER 3

THE HEART'S MALADY

AMELIA

23 September 1697 ~ Midday
Hospitaller Commandery, Mont Lauzère, France

After a restless night of worries over Jehan's departure, Amelia woke to find her grandmother still asleep, and wondered if perhaps she had kept her awake with all the tossing and turning.

Trying not to rouse her Menina Elise, Amelia crept softly out to the chapel for contemplative prayer. But, after a few hours, she found that her humble entreaty and deep meditation did little to recover her joy.

Still unsettled, she ambled down the long passageway back to her chamber, grateful that at least the sturdy granite walls of the commandery's 13th century *manoir* house offered her considerable peace of mind. Built with ancient stones, kin to the *menhirs* scattered throughout the Cévennes, the stronghold stood ready to protect against the tempest of persecution that had only been forestalled until bridges damaged by recent floods could be rebuilt.

When she returned to her chamber, Menina's bed was empty. Thinking her grandmother had gone off to the privy—since she claimed her plump little body did not fit comfortably on the chamber pot—Amelia strode past the high-back upholstered chair that faced the fireplace and over to the tall windows where the late morning light streamed through diamond-shaped leaded glazing.

The spacious chamber that Commandeur Timoleon had assigned to her and her grandmother pleased Amelia immensely because this window looked out from the second floor across the commandery's holdings. From just below, the sweet fragrant scent of ripe apples drifted in on a breeze, delighting her nose, and the cheerful call of the mountain birds lightened her mood.

But her new residence was still a far cry from her snug little cottage in the forest, where she could take one step out the door and feel the bare soles of her feet upon the warm, moss-covered earth.

Amelia sighed thinking she should no longer dawdle at the window, but get to her chores instead. Despite the warm summer days, her grandmother chilled easily, thus it was time to kindle the fire.

She turned back round, then drew a short breath, surprised by what she saw—Menina was there in the room after all. From the angle where Amelia stood, she could see Menina's hand draped over the arm of the high-back chair. She stepped closer to find her grandmother was asleep again and, in her other hand, she gripped her old rosary beads.

Amelia could not recall, even once, seeing Menina Elise use rosary beads. They had hung on the wall in her cottage as a way to protect her rights, but she never used them.

Although Menina had been baptized in the Catholic tradition, she had shunned the religion ever since her son, Amelia's father, had been killed for standing up against unjust restrictions on practicing the Reformed faith. In spite of that tragedy, Menina continued to publicly declare obedience to the Catholic church for fear of losing her right to practice as the village *sage-femme*, or worse, being tried for witchcraft.

"Menina," Amelia called out in a gentle voice, but her grandmother scarcely roused. "Menina, is there something wrong?"

Through half-lidded eyes, Menina gazed up at her. "Please help me back to bed, dear. I need a bit more rest this morning."

Amelia's throat tightened as she held her grandmother's feeble arm, supporting her waning weight until they made their way across the room and settled her into bed. While Amelia carefully draped a woolen shawl over Menina's shoulders, she studied her grandmother's hands—scarred and mottled from years of harvesting herbs, they trembled as she reached for Amelia's face.

"Tell me, dear," her once proud jolly voice, now weak and raspy. "Are you worried for your Jehan? Your eyes are so very red."

Amelia tried not to give power to her anguish by giving it voice. And she certainly did not want to trouble her grandmother with it, so she avoided a direct answer. "You know he is not mine, Menina," she said with a weak giggle. "He is his own person, as am I."

The sky outside began to cloud and darken, and the chamber grew too dark for a proper examination, so Amelia lit the taper candle on the bedside table. She held it briefly so the light cast on her grandmother's eyes while searching for signs of some malady beyond the apoplexy she had suffered the prior year. The withered skin that shrouded them had come from decades of laughter and days in the bright sunshine. But a dark blackish ring had started to form around the hazel irises, a sure indication the commandery food was disagreeable for Menina's constitution.

Amelia moaned in regret—if only she'd had time to gather the family's recipe book before they fled their home, then she could be sure of the correct cure. As she set the candle on the table, she wanted to ask her grandmother what she'd recommend.

Menina had always been the teacher, just as all the mothers and grandmothers before them in a long line of sage-femme healers. But she did not want to alarm Menina, knowing her recovery might be hindered should her mind become stressed.

Closing her eyes, Amelia tried to recall the herb for this condition, this imbalance in the humors, but a sudden scuffling outside the room distracted her. She looked up to see a dim glow down the long passageway. It grew quickly into a burst of lantern light leading the way for the attending *frère*.

He entered the room balancing a bowl and an enormous wedge of fine wheat bread upon a carved wooden platter with intricate silver handles. From the pungent aroma, Amelia suspected it was spiced boar stew—something her grandmother never would have eaten at home.

Giving him no more than a moment to catch his breath, Amelia asked, "Frère, have you examined Menina Elise's urine this week?"

"Well, no, mademoiselle. Is there a need that I am not aware of?"

Amelia waited for her grandmother's response.

Menina smiled with a drowsy nod. "We should examine it. I have been a little tired of late," she said as she closed her eyes.

Amelia took him aside and whispered, "I would be grateful if you would analyze it once a week, as a precaution. Kindly let me know should you detect any sweetness. And thank you for this costly bread. We are honored that you indulge us as though we are *noblesse*, but we are simple people, and it is not so healthful for my grandmother since she is unaccustomed to such foods. She should take only the brown barley or rye bread you serve to the field workers . . . and avoid the rich meats."

"The kitchen has a good store of lentils. I shall ask that they add some to a simple broth."

"Very good. And fresh greens. I shall go out for sorrel and other herbs tomorrow and bring enough for all the residents. We must fortify before the snow arrives."

The frère handed her the platter, then bowed slightly and left the room.

She set the food on the bedside table and pulled the desk chair over.

"Is that my potage, dear?" Menina leaned toward the bowl and sniffed.

Amelia held the bowl while her grandmother wrapped her shaky hand around the spoon. She studied Menina's face, thinking of all the precious knowledge she had passed on. Surely her grandmother missed her herb garden and the cottage library filled with old tomes as much as Amelia did, and perhaps that contributed to her slow decline.

Even after just a few weeks, the limitations of living within the commandery were certainly affecting Amelia's own disposition. The village painted a bucolic picture, but she felt trapped within the bounds of its defensive walls.

The more her mind dwelled on it, the more her heart called out for the freedom of the forest and for the cottage but, most of all, for Jehan who had made those special places feel complete.

She longed for all the moments they had spent in the majesty of the trees and among the woodland creatures, meditating to the sounds of the brook and the wind and the birds, the hours in the cottage studying the old tomes on medicine and philosophy, the touch of Jehan's hand as he helped her turn a page, causing a shiver that flooded her body with desire and making her question her vow to celibacy. She longed to discover the other sensations she might have felt—had she not refused his gentle advances. Heaven on earth might have been found in his arms, but he had so faithfully honored her commitment to God alone.

"I'm done now," said Menina, jolting Amelia out of her yearnings. "You can set the bowl down."

Amelia stared at her own outstretched hand, cupping the bowl, then shook her head to bring herself back to the moment.

"I can see it, dear. You *do* miss him."

Amelia parted her lips, but no words came out. Not sure what to say, tears pricked at her eyes. She had been trying to shut out the worry, the heartache, to lock away her feelings in a tidy little place. Love would only make her weak and vulnerable. She set the bowl on the night table, then pulled her knees to her chest, hugging them with her arms.

"You two are more in love than any two people I've seen in all my days. When he gets settled, you should go to him."

"But . . . no, Menina. I would never leave you."

"One day, you will need to leave me behind. You sacrifice yourself for me, for your God, for the mountain people, but one day you will need to take care of your own heart." Menina patted her hand. "You go now. I know Commandeur Timoleon wants you to stay within the commandery walls, but you can at least take some air with the dogs."

Amelia took in a deep breath, trying to drive out the despair filling her lungs. She knew she must envision a potent dose of courage to fill its place. It was the only way to subdue her growing fears. How could she espouse the benefit of letting go of fear if she, herself, were not capable of it? Menina was right—to be out of doors would do her good.

She stretched her legs out from under her faded blue linen skirts, then went to the armoire where she kept her few belongings. Her gown was now so worn that it mattered not if she bothered changing to a work tunic.

It had been weeks since she'd gone out gathering—since before she had come to stay with the Hospitallers—so she checked her herb pouch for what she required. The small tools for cutting, the strips of linen for wrapping plants and roots, the hempen twine for bundling; all in was in good order.

Sudden as a shooting star that opens the darkness, it came into her mind—*Galega. The goat's rue. Of course.* That was the herb that should balance Menina's humors.

Just as Amelia turned to see her grandmother had fallen fast asleep again, sunlight lit the room, warming her back and nudging her on out. She hastened out through the door before the sun could, once again, slip behind the morning's dismal gray clouds.

Straw flew aloft, motes dancing on narrow light beams as the two great wolf-dogs tousled about the stables, the horses snorting and whinnying in protest. The old gray and white cat the knights called Barn Boss hissed at them from the open doorway.

"Romulus. Remus. Settle down." Amelia kept her tone commanding and serious, but the dogs brought a smile to her cheeks just the same. Certainly, they were feeling as restless as she, none of them being accustomed to the confinement or the constant chattering of people about.

She patted her leg and then pointed to the spot next to her. "Come. sit."

Romulus was the first to obey. He quickly came and sat at her feet, his bright golden eyes peering out of a mound of snow-white fur. Remus had more of the look of a wild wolf with his mottled gray fur and a temperament to match so, as usual, he paced for a few moments, hesitating before he minded her.

Amelia leaned over to tousle the fur on their heads. "We shall head out in a wink. I promise."

Jehan's horse began nuzzling her shoulder. She turned and brushed back a tuft of Luisant's dark mane and finished securing the bridle. Then she untied the herb pouch from her belt and, when she opened the saddlebag to lay it in, something deep inside—light in color against the dark leather—caught her attention.

Her eyes widened to see in the dim light. She reached in, grasping at something made of linen with a bit of lace. As she fumbled around, a small object fell out of the cloth. She released the cloth back inside, then clutched at the object. Her hand closed around the hard little thing, discovering it had a cord attached.

As she brought it out of its hiding place, she knew exactly what it was—the Huguenot medallion, the one that had belonged to Jehan's father. She brushed her fingers over the smooth silver surface, her touch heating the soft metal as it rested in her hand, then slipped the cord over her head and pressed the medallion to her heart, holding it close as though she were embracing Jehan, feeling his energy course through her, feeling his love.

She lifted the medallion in front of her eyes, enjoying the simple details of the old silver piece. Cast in a domed oval shape, it was pierced through with an equal-sided cross and the outline of a descending dove, a thin black film of tarnish clinging to the edges.

The cross was much like the one the Hospitallers wore on their surcoats and had carved into stone boundary markers scattered across their vast landholdings on Mont Lauzère. The dove, she easily recognized as the ancient symbol of the Holy Spirit.

The medallion's worth was immeasurable—far more valuable than its weight in silver. For when she and Jehan had attended clandestine assemblies of the Children of God, often in caves or barns, he had employed the medallion to gain entry.

She recalled the suspicion they had faced for their devotion to aiding the ill and injured rather than partaking in worship. Thankfully, Amelia's friend, Jean Cavalier, had vouched for her, but Jehan had been required to show some form of fidelity. Each time they encountered the assembly sentries, he would quickly flash the medallion, then return it to his pocket. It was one of her many memories that would bind her to Jehan forever.

She tightened her hand around the silver piece, wanting dearly to keep it as a token of Jehan's love and their time together. Amelia's breath caught in her throat as a realization abruptly struck. Her conflicting emotions colliding inside, her body stiffened in wariness—the medallion would have the opposite effect here. Instead of relieving suspicion, it would likely prove dangerous to have in her possession. The commandery received frequent visits from devout Catholics who might immediately call her out as a heretic, implicating her in the uprising the Children of God were planning, just as Jehan had been.

Surely, he had not intentionally left the medallion behind. The slight tarnish told her it had been hidden away for some time. She had to conceal it quickly, so she reached into the saddlebag for the linen cloth. As she pulled it into view, she could not restrain the sharp intake of breath when she saw it was Jehan's *cravate*.

The beating in Amelia's chest quickened. Holding the cravate to her nose, she inhaled deeply, taking in the scent of his leather saddlebag, his olive oil shaving soap, his intoxicating musk. *This* she could truly cherish and keep with her, always and forever.

She quickly wrapped the medallion back inside the cravate and buried it deep in the saddlebag below her herb pouch. Then she led Luisant from the stable and whistled for the dogs to follow.

Amelia came down hard on her knees at the base of an oak, then removed the small trowel from the herb pouch and set the pouch aside. She had hoped to find the goat's rue in this small ravine near the commandery, the closest spot with any shade.

The soil here was rich and moist, with a stream flowing year round and enough trees to protect the tender plants from harsh summer sun or early frost. She could not understand—the rue would be plentiful back in Menina's garden in Castlebouc, but there was none here to be found. Absolutely none. Not even a few strays brought in by birds or on the boots of a wanderer. She pinched her lips together in frustration.

There was a bit of watercress in the shallow water. Though it was not the best remedy for what ailed Menina, it would have to do. But first, the medallion would need to be hidden.

She could not think over the distractions, the birds flitting about, the horse noisily lapping water from the stream behind her, and the dogs barking and splashing about. The sounds of nature usually filled Amelia with peace, but in this moment, they completely rattled her nerves. She had lost her center since she had left her little cottage in the ancient forest near Castelbouc.

Inhaling deeply, she closed her eyes, letting the incredible magic of that place fill her mind while she hummed an old canso that always brought her close to Spirit. She swayed to its tune, and it brought the calm back into her being, melting her taut muscles.

It was time to say yet another goodbye. She unrolled the cravate, lifting the lace edges one at a time, cradling the medallion gently in the fine white linen. Touching her forefingers to her lips, she kissed them, then laid them gently on the precious silver piece that held so many remembrances, some quite frightening, but many quite extraordinary. After digging a shallow hole in the earth, she placed the medallion inside, brushed the soil back in, and covered it with a large rock and a bit of lichen.

She wrapped the cravate around her neck where it would stay, Jehan's incense, his very essence, penetrating her soul.

CHAPTER 4

FLEE LIKE MIST FROM THE TEMPEST'S MIGHT

JEHAN

24 September 1697 ~ Mid Afternoon
Naves Hamlet near Les Vans, France

As dawn broke, Jehan and the other refugees had crowded into a large sleeping chamber at the Naves *maison de seigneurie*. Arranged in the manner of a monastery hostel, the room housed rows of small beds with wool-filled mattresses that left little space to walk. Even so, it had been far more comfortable than the regional inns, where the standard was three or more to a bed.

When Jehan awoke, it was with renewed vigor. Curious about what the day would bring, an excited restlessness coursed through to his very core. With most of the others still in a deep slumber, he slipped on his boots and began arranging his few belongings.

He reached under the bed for his satchel where he had stored it for safekeeping, along with his sword, dagger, and apothecary bag. Placing it upon the bed, he unfastened the buckle and opened the front compartment, then pushed aside the small linen foodstuff sac that Biatris, his cook at Château de

Cougoussac, had packed. He pulled out a small block of olive oil soap, one fresh linen square, and his razor, and set them on the bed in hopes of at least a hasty *toilette* later. But with the men and women all together in the same room, he wasn't sure how he'd have the privacy for it.

For now, his concerns lay in the condition of the grapevine rootstock cuttings and the mulberry seeds he had also packed. One day, when he eventually settled, they might provide supplemental income via the wine and silk making trades.

From the top of the main compartment, he lifted out a small folded square of waxed linen and peeled back the folds. Finding the mulberry seeds intact, he took a long breath, then closed the little bundle and set it on the bed.

Further down in the satchel was his cloak, carefully wound around his precious rootstock. He unwrapped the cloak to expose the thick layer of slightly damp linen protecting the cuttings. All seemed well when he peeked in, no signs of sprouting or rot, but there had barely been time for either. *No need to fret.* He took another long breath and reminded himself, as long as they did not get too wet, or too dry, they should be fine.

The chamber door latch abruptly rattled and the door swung open.

Massip leaned in. "Time to arise and get some food in your bellies," he alerted them.

Jehan slid his satchel back under the bed in preparation.

Syeira sat up and jostled Manfri until he opened his eyes. She tidied her white blouse and vivid red striped skirt, then took her *dihklo* and jewelry from her satchel and put them on. Her traditional gold bangles jingled and clinked in a high, clear pitch as she draped her red coral beads around her neck.

Massip put a hand on his hip and shook his head at her. "You might as well be wearing sheep bells. Take those off those bracelets and keep them off till we are in Geneva. Put them somewhere they won't make noise."

Moyse groaned and pulled the woolen blanket over his head. The ten hour hike over mountain drailles had tested the older man's endurance. Thankfully, the willow bark powder had taken care of his back pain and sufficed for the other's ailments as well, sparing Jehan from openly demonstrating the use of special prayers and laying on of hands. He never knew how people would react to the ancient methods, most having become reliant on the convenience of tinctures and pills.

"I concur with him," said one of the two hatmaker brothers as he pointed at Moyse, then rolled over and shut his eyes.

Just after they had arrived and settled into the sleeping chamber, this younger of the two brothers—the one who had made the poor jest about his rear end—introduced himself as Jacques Isnard, and his brother as Daniel.

In the next bed over, Daniel sat up and began smoothing his hair and brushing wrinkles from his breeches.

Jehan's eyes drifted to the empty bed next to the Isnard brothers. Their companion, the young mademoiselle, had slipped out when they first arrived and must not have returned. The room had a reek from all the bodies and a full chamberpot, so perhaps she could not stomach the odors.

His own belly paid no mind to the stench but beckoned for food with a loud rumble, so he was not about to tarry. As they had traveled through the night, he had judiciously rationed the bread and nuts from his foodstuff sac—saving most of it for unforeseen moments ahead—so now he needed nourishment. He rose and made his way around the neatly ordered rows of beds and over to the door.

"Follow the passageway here to the right." Massip motioned in the direction he was to go. "'Twill take you straight to the *salle basse*, the servant's hall, where the seigneur receives his tenant farmers and field workers. But don't expect to see the seigneur today."

Jehan left the crowded sleeping quarters and followed the nutty scent of freshly baked bread as it drifted through the passageway, mingling with other spicy, pungent aromas. A shaft of midday sun spilled out the door of the salle basse and onto the well-worn stone tiles. He peered in to see it came from a high, narrow embrasure window, recessed into thick stone walls that supported a great vaulted ceiling.

As he stepped into the room, it became clear how this ancient fortified structure served refugee groups well. The stout granite block walls were able to contain their voices, while at the same time keeping intruders out.

At the far end was the cookery where a woman tended an iron pot hanging from a trammel hook inside a head-high hearth. She didn't look up as Jehan entered, too intent on the tasks within her sultry domain.

Nearer to the door, a communal dining area was furnished with a substantial oak table capable of seating at least a score of people. Yet, at the moment, it was nearly deserted. Only Stéphane and the mademoiselle from the hatmakers' group sat side-by-side on one of the long benches, empty platters and bowls set before them. They leaned together in an intimate exchange of soft words. Stéphane's golden curls danced around his face when he laughed, and the young woman reached up and tenderly brushed them back.

"Oh . . . good day, sieur," Stéphane said as he looked up from the *tête-à-tête.* "Did you have a chance to formally meet Mademoiselle Anne Broussard last evening? Anne, this is Sieur Jean Pierre BonDurant."

"'Tis Jehan, if you please. I use the old Occitan variation in honor of my grandfathers before me. I met your other companions, the brothers Jacques and Daniel Isnard. However, you left the dormitory before we had the pleasure. And. . ." Jehan raised his brows to signal his curiosity without prying. "I don't believe I heard you return."

She looked from under her eyelashes and smiled. "You are quite observant, Sieur Jehan. After our rough journey, I could not tolerate that foul-smelling room or to lie my weary body on those lumpy straw mattresses. Not when Stéphane offered to share a feather bed."

"Is that so?" *Quite bold, this one.*

Jehan found it interesting that she used little discretion about sharing a bed with a man she'd just met.

From her conservative appearance—hair hidden under a white coif and simple black woolen gown—he would never have suspected she was the sort. He was trying not to judge the situation. Trying to practice tolerance, in all ways, just as he and Amelia had exposed to others. But he felt his face involuntarily twist awry in disapproval. The Dominican codes of moral conduct, that had been so much a part of his upbringing in the prieuré, left him struggling on this account.

"'Tis not what you may think," said Stéphane. "Anne and I have known each other for many years. We keep our relationship to ourselves and would be grateful if you would not mention it to the others. It might stir up a hornet's nest."

Jehan decided it best not to debate or inquire further. Whatever their reason for hiding their relationship was none of his affair. He studied the joy written on Anne's face, her skin aglow, her cheeks and lips blushed with a rosy hue. She may as well enjoy the companionship, and the luxury, while she could. He knew not every night on this flight from danger would be so comfortable.

"Well, you are radiant this morning, mademoiselle. So it must have been a pleasurable rest you had."

Anne lifted her chin a bit and said, "If you keep it to yourself, we shall tell no one of those questionable healing charms your cousin spoke of." Her voice held no threatening tone, nor the honeyed tone of one trying to get her way. It seemed like a simple negotiation.

Jehan heaved a breath in frustration. This being in close quarters with strangers was already proving to be challenging for all.

"I shall not speak of it, but regardless of my discretion, the others are bound to catch on should you continue to rendezvous. I would not presume your absence went unnoticed by them, either."

A clattering of boots on stone suddenly echoed down the passageway, and Jehan turned to see Massip leading the rest of the group into the servant's hall.

"Take a seat, everyone, and I'll have the cook serve your meal," Massip instructed. "Afterwards, we'll need to discuss the route we'll take at nightfall."

Over the next hour, the new acquaintances chatted with hopeful excitement as they ate a robust stew, pleasingly sharpened with unfamiliar spices. Jehan was glad for the unexpected camaraderie that came so easily among them, knowing this sense of community and solidarity would be essential to carry them through the challenging days ahead.

"We've had an uneventful first day," said Massip as he poured a bit of the watered wine. "But don't expect they will all be this way. You need to be prepared for what might lie ahead."

"Please, enlighten us," said Jacques Isnard, in a snide tone.

An urge came over Jehan to assess this brazen chit of a man. He peered around the others, looking to the far end of the bench where Jacques sat with his brother, Daniel.

Jacques' well-groomed appearance suited him well for his new position at Seigneur Malbois' atelier boutique in the Swiss cantons. Yet what about Jacques' childish manners? This tone he projected, and his behaviors, like the jest he'd made when they were on the draille, would not be appreciated in a fine boutique setting.

Jehan sighed and dropped his shoulders. To preserve the peace and his own patience, he realized he couldn't take this whelpish dandy too seriously.

Syeira leaned in from between her husband, Manfri, and Anne Broussard. "What Monsieur Massip says is true. We cannot possibly know what might lie ahead." Her *baxtali*, that special joy for life the Roma expressed, was now replaced by the same serious face she possessed when Jehan first met her, telling fortunes at a *soiree* in Genouillac.

"Can be no worse. . ." muttered cousin Moyse, his mouth stuffed with food. He wiped breadcrumbs from his lips and continued, ". . .no worse than the torture we've witnessed at the hands of the dragoons."

"Make no mistake. It could be worse," Massip avowed. "Falsified passports and fleeing the country without legal documents are punishable crimes you are all guilty of. In the event you are apprehended, you will be imprisoned or forced into slavery on the galley ships. The King's Intendant Basville does not discriminate between young or old, women or men, rich or poor. And if you resist arrest, you will likely find yourself tethered to the wheel or at the end of a rope."

If the patina on the two pistols holstered on Massip's belt wasn't evidence enough of his experience, then his features certainly were—nails blackened from gunpowder, chin-length hair that must have been the color of the sun in his youth but had gone drab with the gray coming in, brooding eyes set over a scarred cheekbone. Jehan had been told Massip was not yet thirty, but his hard living had added years to his appearance.

"There are several stops planned, some more dangerous than others. Some are at other seigneuries sympathetic to your cause, but at other stops, you may be required to sleep in a grange or a cave. There is one stop . . . after we cross the Rhone River . . . that will be at an inn near Crest. 'Tis quite comfortable but, by far, the most dangerous. Most of our stops are properties of sympathizers who mostly want to remain anonymous. So, I need to repeat what I warned you about this morning. Stay to the areas where you are directed. *No more* wandering."

Anne let out a breath that she seemed to be holding and turned wide-eyed to Stéphane.

Jehan watched Massip's eyes to see if they landed on Anne, but instead, they scanned each face at the table as he continued. "On the third night, we shall reach the outskirts of Le Pouzin. That's where we'll ford the Rhone."

Fear flashed in Moyse's eyes. "Ford the Rhone! How is an old man like me to do that?"

"The water will be low this time of year," Massip assured. "The river valley has not suffered from the great storms as did the mountains in last month's Cévenol episode. And I've not lost a traveler to the river yet."

Yet. That was no sort of reassurance to Moyse, or any of the hatmakers, by their expressions. Only Syeira and Manfri showed little reaction, for they had forded numerous streams and rivers in their travels. Jehan knew he must keep his own focus away from fear, remaining stoic and courageous for Moyse's sake.

"Is there no bridge?" Moyse said, clasping his hands together.

Massip rose from the table, then came to lay a hand on Moyse's shoulder as though he hoped to calm him, but his voice only filled the air with more intrigue. "There is just one bridge for many leagues. Pont-Saint-Esprit. But it is heavily guarded. The risk is far greater there. The crossing at Le Pouzin is the safest place, I assure you."

As Massip divulged more information, he steadily circled the table, pausing to engage with each of the travelers, his gestures emphasizing the importance of every detail.

Jehan regarded the faces of his new companions. Regret tugged at his thoughts as their visages brought on memories of smiles and the tears on the faces of loved ones he'd left behind in the Cévennes—many who had no choice but to stay and who endured even greater hardships than any person in this motley group of refugees ever would. Like the impoverished shepherds and carders of the mountains, who wanted nothing more than to practice their faith in peace. And Amelia, who might have left, had it not been for her grandmother.

Jehan raked a hand through his hair as the guilt caught up with him again, gnawing at his determination to keep his eyes focused on peaceable horizons.

As he stared at tiny flecks of dust dancing in the sunlight from the embrasure window, he realized there was nothing he could do to change the past—or the future. All he could do now was focus on the present and do everything in his power to ensure the safety and well-being of himself and his fellow travelers.

25 September 1697 ~ Sunset
Grotte above Ardeche River, France

The refugees rested through the daylight hours, shoulder-to-shoulder, in a grotto tucked into volcanic cliffs above the Ardeche River. Their breathing producing a dissonant symphony of sounds, and even the slightest movement or stirring rippled through the mass of bodies.

In a fitful half-sleep, Jehan shifted against the rough stone wall. He tried not to disturb Moyse, who lay to his side. The crowded space and thoughts of Amelia were not the only matters making it difficult for him to sleep. Even if there had been more room, the secret treasury lining Jehan's justaucorps would have, nonetheless, prodded and annoyed him.

He pushed his mind to focus on the good in the situation. The cool damp environs of the grotto had been a blessed relief from the late September midday heat, and its remoteness brought some comfort amid the danger they faced.

Someone began shuffling about, so Jehan lifted the brim of his hat and peeked one eye open. The glaring daylight that had hindered his slumber during their first hours in this abandoned troglodyte abode now softened to an orange hue that painted the walls of the grotto's narrow entrance and attached itself to Stéphane's features as he stood nearby.

After hours of trying to rest, Jehan knew movement would surely be of more benefit for working the stiff places out of his bones and muscles. *Better than staying put*. So he rose to join Stéphane.

Jehan looked around for their lead guide but he appeared to be missing.

"Massip?" He whispered.

Stéphane tipped his head in the direction of the opening. "He's outside."

When Jehan peered out, he could see Massip readying the mules.

Stéphane stooped down and struck his firesteel against a sharp-edged piece of flint with a click, click, shooting sparks at the unspun flax in his tinderbox. He held the burning tinder to a candle inside his lantern. Slowly, light pushed back the walls of the grotto, revealing an array of eerie shadows.

He sat back on his heels and looked at Jehan. "We should take nourishment from what we each have in our satchels before we set out."

Jehan nodded, then began to carefully step around the Manfri and Syeira.

Curled against Manfri's chest, Syeira rubbed her eyes and sat up. She pulled her raven-colored braids forward, then straightened the dihklo wrapped around her head.

Once Stéphane started to rouse the others, there were a few soft moans as they gathered their belongings. But after all of

Massip's accounts regarding the terrors that might befall them, they were largely enduring the stop in the dank gloom without complaint.

Jehan returned to his spot at the rear of the grotto and seated himself on the cool stone floor. He removed the foodstuff sac from his satchel and tore a large piece of bread from the loaf inside, then broke it into smaller pieces. After handing some to Moyse, he leaned around him to offer a piece to Anne.

"Were you able to rest, mademoiselle?" Jehan asked.

She did not answer as she took a few hairpins from her pocket and laid them on her skirts. She stared at the fire and removed her coif, revealing hair the color of new copper. Smoothing and tucking several loose strands, she pinned and arranged them back into a *chignon* as best she could.

"Thank you." She took the bread and nibbled at it for a bit.

Between rapid chews, Moyse mumbled something that sounded vaguely like an echoed thank you.

Anne's gaze returned to Jehan. "Pardon, Sieur Jehan. I am not yet myself. I barely slept at all. I have much to grow accustomed to. I wish not to be a burden to any of you, so I must not share my suffering aloud."

Jehan took a drink of water from his *costrel*, then offered her and Moyse a few chestnuts and figs.

He let his voice sink to a whisper as he leaned close to Anne. "Did Stéphane tell you not to share your sufferings?"

She nodded from under her lashes and opened her hand to take the nuts and fruit—a hand that must have held a thousand words she longed to speak. He studied Anne's features, the fiery hair, fair complexion, and long legs that were in no way similar to Amelia's petite frame and chestnut hair. Jehan had yet to know what Anne's true sufferings were, and he suspected it had less to do with an uncomfortable place to sleep than it appeared.

He picked up his sword belt and secured it at his hips, then took up his satchel and apothecary bag.

"Well then, sustenance will surely help you gain the courage to bear your sufferings," said Jehan. "And the moon . . . she shall shine brightly again tonight, sending her energy and strength . . . our own 'night-sun' that will show us the way ahead."

26 September 1697 ~ Early Evening
Chomérac, France

Their journey from the grotto the evening past had been peaceful. And its reward the next morning, a good rest and a feast of a meal in pleasant quarters at a farm near Chomérac.

At this point along the route, the treacherous terrain of the mountains gave way to rolling hills and plains and towns, making a mule pack at night an all too obvious site that might tempt clergy and reward-seekers into making a report. Since the mules were to be left behind, restoring the travelers' vigor and their moods had been of utmost importance to keep them nimble and alert.

Immediately after sunset, Jehan and his companions moved out again in their usual order, this time on foot, following Massip along the tracks of a rutted farm road toward a river crossing near Le Pouzin. The soft melodies of a nightingale gave Jehan a moment to ponder all that had been revealed while at the farm. It was most impressive, what he had learned.

An entire network of people and places existed throughout the realm that were available to aid refugees from the King's persecutions. Massip explained that funding for it came from the far reaches of the globe—from those who held compassion for the oppressed of any creed, or from those who wanted to strengthen the position of the Protestant faith. Mostly English and Dutch nobility competing for philanthropic pursuits.

All was quiet along the road until they arrived at the signpost for Le Pouzin. But as they turned onto the main road, hoofbeats and rattling clamored in the distance. They looked at each other in a quandary since they could not yet see who might be approaching from around the next bend in the road. Likely a quartet of horses pulling a carriage or coach, by the sound of it.

Daniel Isnard ran up to Massip and grasped his arm. "What do we do?"

"Nothing. Just keep walking but form groups. As though you are friends heading to the tavern. 'Tis best you show no reaction."

Jehan could feel his throat tighten and ran a hand through his hair. Moyse hesitated and swayed, appearing as though he were about to lose his balance, so Jehan gave him his arm. Stéphane lent a hand with Moyse, and Syeira and Manfri fell back to walk alongside them.

The noise grew louder until lantern lights emerged from around the bend, creating an aura of light around the three hatmakers and Massip as they led the way ahead.

Jehan inhaled deeply, trying to maintain an impassive expression, but Moyse's trembling was unsettling. Within moments, a grand carriage rushed by them, horses at a full canter.

"Don't turn around," said Stéphane.

The blood pulsed through Jehan's temples as they waited for the hoofbeats to fade into the night.

Once it was quiet again, Stéphane spoke out. "Whoever it is, they must find themselves too important, and this band of peasants too undignified, to bother with us. By the looks of that fanciful carriage, they surely don't need any blood money."

Jehan chuckled to himself at the good fortune in that. Allowing himself to find some humor eased the tension, and the pulsing that hammered through his head gradually ceased.

Massip veered off the main road down a moonlit path, and they all scurried to keep up. Soon they were deep in silvery reeds where a chorus of croaking frogs surrounded them, and the musky breath of marshland filled Jehan's nostrils with the smell of fish and algae and wet earth.

In an abrupt movement, Massip stopped in a small clearing, then pulled a coil of rope from a satchel. "You may not desire your boots to get wet," he said as tied the rope around his waist, "but keep them on. The marshes are home to the *Vipère* snake."

Anne gasped and leaned her head around the others as if searching for Stéphane.

Syeira put a hand on Anne's shoulder and said, "They are likely to slither away when they hear us."

"Scared of us, they are," added Manfri, animated hands and face aiding his limited grasp of the French language.

Tiny moonshadows formed across Syeira's nose as she wrinkled it. "And the silly things don't even know how to strike with their mouth open. The greatest danger they pose is their dreadful scent."

As Massip began tying each of them to the rope, forming a long chain, he continued his instructions. "Ladies. 'Twill be best if you bring your skirts up between your legs and tie them."

Anne's face pinched together, a gruesome look in the dim light, the shadows magnifying her dissatisfaction.

"Do not give me that look, Mademoiselle Broussard," Massip grumbled as he cinched the rope about her waist with an abrupt tug. "If your skirts are caught in the current or snagged on a rock, it will pull us all under. Now . . . for those of you who do not have satchels with back straps, place them on your heads to keep them dry as we cross. And keep silent as we move out."

Moyse clutched at Jehan's arm and muttered. "You should go on without me."

"Moyse," Jehan said softly, looking deep into the old man's eyes. The rising moon reflected there would give them light to see, but it also increased the risk of being spotted. He knew he had to give Moyse some courage, some hope. "As long as we take our time, it will be fine. As we cross, let us keep our minds on the warm hearth and splendid companionship we shall find in the company of my Uncle Barjon's community."

Moyse nodded again and again and again as though the motion would help him convince himself.

Massip finished securing everyone to the rope while they positioned their belongings.

Jehan knew leaving his sword at his hip would make the crossing cumbersome. As he removed the belt and secured it atop his satchel, he heard one of the Isnard brothers tittering and grunting.

He looked up to see Jacques Isnard elbowing Daniel while he brazenly ogled the women. Jehan's gaze followed theirs to Syeira. She had lifted the front of her skirts, exposing her bare legs to just above her knees.

A heat prickled his neck when he watched her reach between her legs and pull the back of her skirts through and up, tucking them in at the waistline. He could feel the intensity of Manfri's angry stare, so he closed his eyes and turned away, feeling shame for looking at another man's wife in that way—for looking at his *friend* in that way.

He clutched his forehead. *I must stop myself from lapsing into these reactions.*

But just as he opened his eyes, there was Anne, timidly raising her own skirts. She paused, then turned her head and looked away. She seemed frozen, hesitating to follow Syeira's lead.

Jehan's eyes moved down the length of Anne's torso, fixating on her exposed lily-white shins, luminescent in the moonlight. The heat at his neck moved lower through his body—the same way it had one night when he'd laid in a shepherd's *cazelle*, entwined with his beloved Ame. Yet this sensation he felt now had none of the same sweetness and deep love he felt with

Amelia. And it seemed more urgent, more difficult to control. Restraining himself that night in the cazelle had come from his vow to expect nothing more from Amelia than friendship. However, there was no such vow with Anne.

He licked salty beads of sweat from his lips as he noticed Stéphane heading toward them.

"'Tis not a time to be modest," Stéphane said to Anne while pushing Jehan away.

Jehan straightened and inhaled to calm his excited state, then tightened the strap on his apothecary bag until it was nearly choking him. He needed to get control of his desires, elsewise he'd get himself into trouble the way he nearly had with his cousin André's wife, Lucrèce, a few years before. For one raised in a prieuré, he surprised even himself at his inability to avoid the cardinal sin of covetousness.

After Massip slung his gun belt over his shoulders and gave the signal, they moved on. Carefully, a few steps at a time, they came closer to the gentle lapping sound at the river's edge, but it was hard to see through the thick reeds.

Jehan felt the ground beneath his feet soften, then heard the splashing of mud and water, his boots sinking and sticking with each step. A trickle of water spilled over the top of his boots as they moved past the reeds and out into open water. Silver moonlight flickered in wavering bands over the water, giving an allure to the gentle river that brought a flood of memories.

Days spent with Amelia by a brook in the forest were the happiest days of his life, and now he had left that all behind. His head reeled with confusion and doubt. Would the Eden he'd set out in search of be any safer than if he'd had the courage to stay?

The water saturating his boots and feet brought him out of his questioning, the discomfort forcing his mind to the present. There could be no faltering now. His future lay ahead and he had to stay open to God's messages.

A few more steps and the river was waist-deep. He could feel the tug of the current and was thankful for the extra weight of the coins, but his boots grew heavy on the slippery rocks at the river's bottom, making it hard to resist the drag.

The rope at his waist suddenly jerked, and Moyse yelped as he slipped under the rushing water. Jehan reached for his cousin's arm. But Moyse flailed about so much he had trouble getting hold of the old man.

Jehan pulled furiously on the rope and cried out to Daniel Isnard, who was at risk of going under with Moyse. "Secure your feet and pull your end taut, then up."

They worked together, hand over hand, moving closer to Moyse. Jehan clutched the rope so tightly the skin on his palms burned, but he felt a surge of strength pushing him on. They managed to bring Moyse up from the water, coughing, spitting, cursing. Jehan wrapped an arm around his back and righted him.

"Take a minute to breathe and steady yourself." Jehan said as he planted his feet in a wide stance against the current, holding on to Moyse until they both regained their breath.

Massip looked back at them, and even in the moonlight, Jehan could read the grimace that etched the guide's face.

As they reached the far side, the water shallowed, and the reeds grew thick again. The frenzied splashing of their boots as they rushed toward the shore startled some nesting ducks. Squawking and quacking, they took flight, setting off scores of other waterfowl hidden away in the reeds. Jehan's chest tightened. It was a sure way to draw attention if the shouting hadn't already.

While the birds were making their desperate noises, Massip used the cover of the mayhem to speak to the group.

"I want absolute silence from here on out," he said, his tone commanding and curt. "No talking, no moans or gasps, no crying out. Should you have pain, bear it."

Jehan clenched his jaw as his frustration with Massip mounted. Their guide seemed to dole out his plan in bits and pieces as though too much information might overwhelm some of the refugees. But withholding details only infuriated Jehan. It was like the information denied him about his Huguenot parents while he was forced to live in the Dominican prieuré. His father's arrest and his mother's deep sorrow over losing her children, all because of their Reformed faith, had come as a great shock to him after their death.

Not being forthright in life always had the potential to cause even more damage. To Jehan, Massip's strategy seemed nothing less than careless, and he wasn't sure how much respect he could maintain for the man.

"Massip, will you please keep us informed of our planned movements? Had I been acquainted with the lay of the river . . . where it would be at its deepest, the current the strongest . . . I may have been better prepared to assist Moyse."

"If I shared every detail, half of you would turn and run toward home with your tail between your legs." Massip put his hands on his hips and huffed. "But that would certainly lead to capture. So then . . . here it is. We'll take up here on dry land for a short distance and head as quickly as possible along the tributary river, the Drôme, which is a mere trickle this time of year. We'll cross and pass through a small wooded area on the edge of Livron-sur-Drôme. When we reach the frontage road, we'll duck into the back side of the mariners' inn. We'll have time to dry off and they will supply us with food."

Late Evening
Livron-sur-Drôme, France

The moon hung low, sending shards of pale light through the woods along the Drôme River. The refugees' sodden clothes and boots made darting out of the trees and across the frontage road into Livron cumbersome and dangerous.

As Jehan clutched Moyse's arm to prevent another fall, his ears filled with the pounding of his heart and his head ached with worry. He realized some of his belongings were likely ruined during the mishap in the river. But his worry was not over his spare clothing in the satchel or about the bit of stale bread and chestnuts still remaining. It was for the grapevine rootstock and the mulberry seeds and the important documents deep within his pockets; his certificate of Catholic conversion and the false passport meant to convince any dragoons they encountered of his nouveau converti status. *And the medicines*!

Dread tried to pull him down in a sudden falling sensation as he prayed that the tinctures and powders in his apothecary bag were not corrupted, safe in their tiny glass bottles. But there was no time to stop and check on any of that now. They were only possessions. As long as he and his companions stayed safe, that was all that mattered, and to do that, they had to keep moving.

An urge came over Jehan to pull his old rosary out of the satchel and say a prayer—a tenacious habit from his childhood indoctrination by the Dominicans that taunted him at times like this. He needed to focus on Amelia's teachings instead, and not let his fear get the better of him. They were so close now, and they would make it if he would just hold on to that vision.

One at a time, they crossed a footbridge over a mill canal while Stéphane guarded the rear, hand on his pistol, eyes scanning the streets. They followed a path behind a series of old buildings, reverberating with lively singing and murmuring voices, occasionally interrupted by shouts or raucous laughter.

Through the windows, golden candlelight glimmered, offering a message of warm welcome.

Massip led their sodden refugee group to a rear door and knocked in a distinct rhythm or cipher. He waited. Several minutes seemed to pass, so he repeated it, louder this time. The sound of wooden sabots clapping across a stone floor could be heard through the door. Then the unbolting of a series of locks. The door cracked open and firelight spilled out in a wedge across Massip's face. He whispered in response to the low grumble of a man's voice. When the door opened, Jehan's height allowed him to see over the heads of the others, and beyond, to a kitchen where a woman sat at a large table, scraping turnips with a knife.

"Come in. Quickly, now," said the woman as she stood. "We must get you some dry clothes."

She reminded Jehan of Biatris, the kind-hearted cook at his Château de Cougoussac, slightly stout with a rosy complexion, yet this woman's hair was the color of golden river sand.

Once they all crowded into the kitchen, the man whose voice they had heard emerged from behind the door. The brawny fellow was close in age to the woman and wore the sleeves of his chemise rolled high and taut over his generous biceps. He appeared robust enough to fight off any fool who might cause trouble.

"Follow me," he said, his sonorous voice resonating off the stone walls of the room.

He led them down a hallway and through a locked door to two adjoining windowless rooms. The man stoked the fire in the larger room until it was bright and warm, then went to a cupboard and rummaged through while the refugees huddled near the fire.

"Massip, what are we waiting for?" asked Jacques Isnard in a loud, shrill voice, shaking his head and rolling his eyes. "I see no beds. And where is our meal?"

"Keep your voice down," Massip said with a glowering stare.

The man set out five soldiers' uniforms, several other sets of dry clothes, nearly a dozen thick socks, and a stack of woolen blankets atop a table.

Massip picked up the uniforms and began calling out names. "Sieur BonDurant. You shall be Lieutenant."

Jehan's shoulders tensed, and he stepped back. He could not give up the clothing he wore, or he'd be giving up his funds. No, he would have to refuse if it meant he'd be leaving his own clothes behind.

"Why me? I have no experience as a soldier, let alone as an officer, and I doubt I can purport myself appropriately."

"You are the only one who possesses a sword to demonstrate your nobility." Massip laid the uniform across Jehan's shoulder, then tossed the remaining clothing at the others. "Stéphane will be Cadet. Daniel, Jacques, you and I shall be foot soldiers."

"What do I be?" Manfri asked, his brow pinched with disappointment.

"You and the mademoiselles will be our captives, but all of you will dress as men."

Manfri huffed and put an arm around Syeira.

After handing the brawny man a purse full of jangling coins and sending him on his way, Massip began passing out the woolen socks to each of the refugees as he explained the ruse. "If we are stopped, Sieur BonDurant will say that, on their way to Lyon, he and his men came across these Huguenot heretics. Stéphane will take over from there, saying we are delivering them to the Tour de Crest fortress dungeon. But we'll actually turn off a side road just before the fortress and head to a guest house in the hills. We shall shelter there throughout the daylight hours."

Massip snapped his fingers. "Change. Quickly. We must arrive there before dawn."

Stéphane walked over to assist with the distribution. "The women will need dry linen for binding for their breasts," he said.

Jehan decided he needed to assert himself with Massip. "I prefer to wear my own clothing."

"Look," said Massip. "We all need to play a part."

Wearing an intimidating scowl, Massip leaned in close, causing Jehan to instinctively recoil, his muscles tensing in readiness to defend himself.

"Don't think you are so clever, BonDurant," Massip said as he wagged a finger at him. "I know you are carrying money and so would any thief. You give yourself away with those odd bulges and the way you carry yourself."

Jacques grew a sardonic smile and began whispering to Daniel.

Massip turned to the others. "Be sure to take your own clothes with you. At our next stop, lay them out to dry promptly, then we will change out of the disguises after we've had some rest."

"We need to at least have a hot meal before we head out," demanded Jacques, voice low, but still saturated with an air of entitlement.

Massip's face grew fierce. "Your payment for this journey does not afford you luxury accommodations. Discretion is far more costly than you may realize. The cook will send us off with provisions, and you'll need to ration those over the next three days until we cross into Savoy."

Jacques groaned, but Daniel put a hand on his forearm to quell his demands. "Remember brother, we decided we are determined to endure even the galleys or death, rather than renounce our Reformed faith. So we must place our reliance in God to give us that endurance. We should be grateful for the warm clothes and *any* sort of nourishment we are offered."

A smirk grew on Jacques face and he rolled his eyes, but at least his brother's lecture silenced him for the time being.

Jehan thought about his part in the masquerade as he removed his justaucorps and waistcoat and rolled them neatly into his satchel. Going over the role in his mind—down to every response, to every potential scenario he could think of—he decided it would not be such a difficult task after all. But explaining a hefty satchel full of clothes may be. He would need to stay confident and commanding, and if confronted, feign a display of indignation.

Lost in the play-acting going on in his head, it took him a moment to realize that Stéphane had joined the women behind a drape in the adjoining room. Jehan's thoughts scrambled to understand. Perhaps Stéphane was only showing them to the room.

Someone lit a candle, and the dark outline of their figures emerged upon the drape. The two shadowy forms removing skirts and chemises were surely Syeira and Anne. So the figure in hat and breeches had to be Stéphane.

Yet why would Syeira undress in front of him? Jehan's stance grew restless along with his confusion. He hastily changed his own clothes, pulling his chemise over his head in time to watch Stéphane shed the last bits of manly clothing, revealing the outline of what appeared to be a more feminine shape—narrow at the waist, hips wider than usual. Jehan tried to control his brow as it furrowed with surprise.

Stéphane spoke in a hushed voice to the women, so Jehan leaned an ear in their direction.

"The binding is simple," said Stéphane. "Mine is drenched and will need to be replaced, so I shall demonstrate."

He is wearing a binding?

Something was amiss. Only slightly obscured by the translucent drape, Jehan could detect their guide unwinding long strips from around his chest. As Stéphane reached for the uniform, Jehan had no doubt about what he was seeing—the outline of two perky breasts.

Sudden disbelief caused his heart to lurch into his throat, and he looked away. Shadows told no lies and had revealed the fragile truth of Stéphane's true identity.

Now it was apparent why Stéphane and Anne tried to keep their relationship a secret. And why Jehan had felt such comfort—an attraction even—with Stéphane's kind ways and delicate features that first night on the mountain drailles.

Syeira came out from around the drape, outfitted in the manner of a craftsman, or possibly a merchant. She was tucking her colorful traditional Roma clothing into her satchel as she moved past Jehan.

He leaned over to her and whispered. "So you knew? And Manfri?"

She mimicked his discreet tone. "We've both known since Anne pulled me aside the first night. They began as friends, looking for a way to avoid marriage to a man and, along the way, they found true love. We all seek freedom, so there should be no shame in it."

"Yes, I agree. Yet, had I known, I would have done a better job of watching after her . . . I mean . . . Stéphane."

Syeira tilted her head, shaking it with a mirthful smile playing on her lips. "*He* can look after himself just fine. Stéphane wants us to always refer to him as a man. No matter what."

"I hear my name spoken." Stéphane came out from behind the drape, smartly dressed in a crisp, bright blue uniform, accompanied by Anne looking like a poor, forlorn shepherd boy, hair hidden inside a woolen cap. Stéphane saluted when he saw Jehan. "Lieutenant," he said, dropping his usual tenor voice a bit deeper.

Jehan returned the salute with a broad grin. "Cadet."

Stéphane and Anne were not the only ones to avoid a relationship or marriage with a man. The risk of death during childbirth was enough to cause many women to find any number of reasons for evading it. Amelia had her reasons, too, and her solution was to live a chaste life as a mystic holy woman. Jehan wished that their love had been enough to make it otherwise, but all hope for that was slipping away.

These two women had found their answer when they found each other. Jehan wholeheartedly agreed with Syeira that each should be free to choose their own path, without interference, without judgment. It made him happy that Stéphane and Anne had found love.

Nearing Midnight
Crest, France

By the time the group approached the city of Crest, the moon was setting on the horizon. The brightening sea of stars in the night sky winked at Jehan as they sporadically disappeared and reappeared from behind long fingers of gathering clouds. It was as though Amelia were there, sending him courage and love. *She must be thinking of me.*

He felt her presence in his heart and in his soul, in a strange vibration that coursed through him, even as the stress of the dangerous journey to the Swiss border consumed his thoughts.

An unsettling feeling washed over him, as if she were in distress. He paused, trying to read it. *No, not distress. A warning.*

He thought he could hear a faint clattering noise arising in the distance, but he looked around at the others in their group and none seemed to notice.

Jehan turned to Stéphane, who took up the rear, as usual. "Did you hear that?"

Stéphane shook his head.

As they moved on, the houses grew closer together, but there were no lights to indicate that any of the residents were awake.

Even so, Jehan was sure he could hear something. His breathing became shallow as he focused his eyes, trying to seek out the source. The sound increased little by little, but distinctly, into the clopping of hooves and the rattling of hard timber wheels against the roadway.

"There." Jehan whispered over his shoulder to Stéphane.

He gestured with a quick dip of the chin. "Yes. I hear it now. We shall regroup into the planned formation and stage the arrest if someone comes near."

Jehan thought perhaps he was overreacting, and it was only more late-night revelers, like the drunken mariners they had passed as they were leaving Livron. But something didn't feel right.

They continued on, the Tour de Crest looming on a rise in the distance, while the sounds grew more clamorous with each step toward the city.

"They're getting closer," Jehan said.

Stéphane whistled the soft call of a nightingale, and Massip responded. Jehan knew they must be preparing for the charade. He glanced ahead again, but with the darkening night and a bend in the road, it was hard to discern who might be approaching.

When they came nearer to the heart of the city, they found lanterns here and there, swaying over the streets on heavy rope suspended between houses; a precaution that many dangerous cities had installed in recent times. Far ahead of them, the sporadic glints of light served their purpose well when the source of the noise moved through their path. It was dark figure on horseback, still so distant it seemed small and unmenacing. But just as it slipped back into the darkness, another swiftly emerged into the light, followed by what appeared to be an entire troop of mounted soldiers in blood red uniforms and trailing fatigue caps, with a horse-drawn cart of captives.

Dragoons. There could be no doubt.

The atrocities Jehan had witnessed at the hands of dragoons in the Cévennes were engrained upon his mind, their indelible mark impossible to erase. He straightened and stood tall, preparing to take on his new role and fortify his courage.

Massip turned to the group, signaling them to draw close. "Follow me. Quickly."

Jehan could not understand. Hadn't the plan been to fool anyone who confronted them?

"I thought . . ."

Massip cut him off. "Our first tactic is avoidance."

Jehan and Stéphane took up the rear again as the refugee group slipped into the shadows of a back alley. They hastened over uneven cobbles when, suddenly, Daniel tripped—his left knee cracking against the stones before he could brace the fall. He let out a loud yelp.

Moyse stood wide-eyed, looking between Daniel and the threatening sound of rapid hoofbeat back out on the main road. The others turned around, the darkness unable to conceal the alarm written on every face.

Syeira took a few steps toward Daniel until Massip grabbed her arm and growled, "Do not stop. Jacques, get him up. Now!"

"Let go my wife," Manfri hissed under his breath, moving his face within inches of Massip's.

The tension and fear was hurdling them all toward hysterics. Jehan ran his fingers through his disheveled mane, feeling racked with torment to see these good people come unhinged.

Jacques tugged at his brother's arm, but his slight frame was not robust enough to lift him. Blood began seeping through Daniel's breeches.

Jehan swiftly knelt and rolled one leg of the woolen cloth, finding a large abrasion. A knot was already forming under the skin. But with the ghastly noise from the dragoons reverberating through the city, he knew a treatment would have to wait.

Jehan grumbled to Jacques, "Take him from under his shoulder. I have this side."

Together, they got Daniel to his feet. They staggered along in the gloom, Daniel's limp hindering them, while the others were disappearing into the dark alleyway ahead.

Jehan looked back to see Stéphane still covering them from the rear, then hesitated for a moment, worried by the newly discovered secret that their young guide may be more frail than Jehan had realized.

"Keep going," Stéphane said, giving Jehan a thrust with his elbow.

It nearly knocked the breath out of him. He felt a sneer reflexively emblazon his face, and he spun his head around. Stéphane pushed at him again and, in that moment, Jehan could see the dragoons down the long alleyway.

He gasped, holding his breath. Then released it as he saw they were passing by. They continued to travel the main road; black shadows of man and beast outlined by the street lights, their short blunderbusses poised. One of them shouted, but Jehan's heart beat so loudly he couldn't make out what the soldier was saying, and he wasn't about to wait to find out.

"Jacques. Lift!" Jehan urged.

In moments, they had Daniel flying above the cobblestones and caught up with the others.

A shot was fired. Then another. But this time, Jehan did not look back.

The refugees darted into the darkness through a maze of back streets, then up a passageway too narrow and tight for men on horseback, until the dragoon's noise faded. They moved through a garden where the city gave way to the countryside. When they came to a stone wall, Massip, Syeira, Manfri, Anne, and Jacques all clambered over and into a pasture.

"Drop down," Massip ordered.

Stéphane held back and carefully assisted Moyse over. Jehan cupped his hands for Daniel to step into with his good leg, then boosted him up while Jacques pulled him from the other side. Once the others had safely landed, Jehan and Stéphane vaulted over the wall and dropped behind it with the others.

Jehan's chest almost ached from the exertion, his heart beating like a mallet against his ribs. He looked at Stéphane. "What happened? I don't hear them anymore."

"They were shouting about one of their captives escaping. I fear they may have shot and killed the person."

Jehan clutched his forehead, praying they had seen the last of those maniacal dragoons.

✥

27 September 1699 ~ Dawn
Vercors Massiff, France

By dawn, Jehan and the refugee group made it upland into the Vercors Massif, to the ruins of an old fortified château. By God's grace, they had escaped. For now.

Moyse's breathing was ragged as he folded onto the ground and stretched out flat, Jehan and the others collapsing next to him.

Massip stood before them. "Everyone, keep quiet and lay your damp clothes out on the rocks. It is too great a risk to go to the guest house as planned, so we shall rest here for a while."

"Are we safe here in this ancient crumbling structure?" Moyse asked. "It doesn't much resemble a stronghold any longer."

"I assure you, we will. As long as you don't wander out near the cliff edge where you could be seen from below. This place was abandoned precisely because there was so little threat to this remote mountain location."

Jehan surveyed the surrounding area, certain it was the right environment for a medicine chest of natural remedies. Straight away, he set out to seek cures for Daniel's injury. After traveling at night for so long, it was good to see by the light of day as he foraged the nearby meadows, finding juniper berries, calendula flowers, and sage. They made a fine poultice to treat the swelling and bruising, using the spare linen binding to hold it in place over the wound.

The group portioned out some food and ate, savoring each bite with expressions of thankfulness, then rested against the sun-warmed stones of the old château, lulled to sleep by the soft breeze and birdsong.

Upon rising from their rest near midday, they shed the disguises for their own clothes, leaving them tucked behind a small pile of rubble.

Jehan was happy to be traveling by daylight again, taking in endless vistas of pastoral plateaus and mighty steepled peaks—God's special church in this land that touched the heavens. Goats and sheep dotted the landscape between stands of evergreens lining the long, upward-climbing mountain valley.

As nightfall approached, temperatures dropped and wood smoke settled in the valley. The pleasant aroma reminded Jehan of home, calming his worn nerves. An early snowfall began to dust the mountains with a biting cold that slipped through the seams of his clothing.

Massip and Stéphane had the group pause and instructed them to tie the donated woolen blankets around them like a cloak. It helped to cut the persistent wind blowing in from the south.

Jehan's hands soon grew numb, so he planted them deep inside his pockets, nervously fingering the coins hidden within the lining.

Moyse murmured prayers for their endurance while they pushed on through the night with little other talk amongst themselves; cold stiffening joints and slowing them, wet snow clinging to their lashes, making it difficult to see the way forward.

After a few hours, the snow abated, but clouds of fear and frustration hovered over Jehan. They stopped to rest and burrowed in their satchels for the last bits of food, finding little there. Exhausted and missing his home, and Amelia, he felt dispirited. His chest became hollow and heavy. The miles between them were growing and the vision of her magical hazel eyes set against silken skin was already leaving him.

Yet, just as his hope dimmed, the moon rose over the treeline and beckoned like a distant star into the holy land. With a cleansing breath, he bolstered his resolve and vowed to himself to stay a source of encouragement for the others. They *would* steadfastly push forward—on to the place of their destiny—only one more night's journey to the safety of Savoy.

CHAPTER 5

ON THE THRESHOLD

AMELIA

30 September 1697
Hospitaller Commandery, Mont Lauzère, France

As Amelia climbed the rise toward the commandery's threshing grange, she pinned her veil to secure it against the wind. Then, retrieving Jehan's cravate from her pocket, she draped it around her shoulders, ensuring it was tucked securely into her bodice. She leaned her head toward her shoulder and inhaled deeply, taking in his scent. The rousing musk that lingered on the soft linen set her heart to beating like the wings of a hummingbird in search of nectar, and it quickened her pace as she strode.

Up the dusty road ahead, the sound of clanking chains and creaky wheels filled the air as a team of oxen toiled to pull a cart laden with sheaves of wheat. The boy leading them motioned her around. She lifted her skirts, dug her toes into the soil, and sprung forward, making haste to pass. Dodging several squawking chickens, she darted up the ramp to the grange.

Immense doors on each end of the building had been propped open to welcome in the wind and sun. Just inside, other boys were unbinding sheaves and spreading them about the floor, while several men and women flailed the stalks to separate grain from husk.

The miller stood by at the opposite end of the grange, overseeing the workers as they sang out a time-honored harvest song. It was a beautiful ritual to behold; flails rhythmically swinging up then whistling down with a blow, all in rapid succession, the older women moving in with pitchforks and brooms to rake up the grain and load it into the winnowers' baskets.

Amelia's face lit into a smile when she saw how the winnowers worked those enormous baskets—woven into a flat roundish form with handles, enabling them to master the strong wind to do their bidding as it blew through the grange. Generations of ingenuity had been handed down from their *Gabali Celtae* ancestors into this mesmerizing dance that had shaped their culture for centuries.

She took joy in the harmony of it all—their voices and their movements—but she couldn't just stand by and watch without aiding them in some way. Surely the miller had a task for her. Yet, if she entered from this side, she risked interrupting the work, or worse, getting caught in the swing of a flail. It would be easier to reach him by circling the outside of the grange, so she retraced her steps back out the front door and ran around the great stone edifice.

When she stopped at the foot of the rear ramp to catch her breath, someone in the distance shouted out her name. She turned but, with the bright sun in the midday sky, she could not make out the group downhill near the Hospitallers' manoir house. As she shaded her eyes with her hands, she could see it was Commandeur Timoleon with three young women she did not recognize. So she swept up her skirts and took off running toward them.

It was a wonderful sensation of freedom. Flying, soaring down the hillside through the golden late summer grass and heather.

She sorely needed the release. If she couldn't scamper safely through her beloved forest near Castelbouc, at least the grounds of the commandery were hers to roam unrestrained.

She slowed her pace as she grew nearer, taking long, deep breaths to still her wild soul and present herself with more composure.

"Mademoiselle Amelia. I am pleased for you to meet our new novices." The Commandeur motioned to the dark-haired girl on his right. "Mademoiselle Griselle from Causse de Sauveterre."

Amelia nodded to the girl, a woeful sight with matted raven hair, threadbare clothing, and skin darkened by many days in the sun. She seemed close to fourteen years of age, the time of womanhood and quite late to be joining as a novice. But by the grim, brooding expression on her face, perhaps she was still under her age of emancipation, and her consignment was not of her own volition.

"You come from far away, Griselle. Welcome."

"And Henriette." Timoleon held a hand toward the tall, slender, burgeoning woman near the same age as Griselle, with bright blue eyes and flaxen hair neatly pinned under a white coif.

Henriette rested her hand on the shoulder of the small girl next to her. "And this is my sister Jacquette. We are from Pont-de-Montvert."

There was no mistaking that the two were sisters. Were it not for the difference in their height and shape, and the six or seven years difference in age, Amelia would not be able to tell them apart.

"They lost their mother a few years ago and have been pleading with their father to join our order." Commandeur Timoleon raised his brows and rolled his eyes toward Jacquette with a chortle. "Most especially Mademoiselle Jacquette here."

The tiny girl stepped one foot forward and raised her arm high. "Yes, so I can be a *chevalière*! My *père* is gathering papers to show we are noblesse. I want to ride like the wind into the Holy Land and be a great protector," she exclaimed.

Amelia smiled, thinking of the joy this strong-minded, brave girl would bring to the community. "Are you ladies ready to take a vow of chastity, as have I? Perhaps one day the women here will outnumber the men and, perhaps, the good Commandeur will let you take on some of their roles." Amelia gave Timoleon a congenial grin as he stood silent, holding back his amusement at her proposal, eyes wide and smiling.

"What I would like the ladies to concentrate on first . . . before we discover the roles they are destined for . . . is perfecting their skills in the kitchen, and spinning and weaving. These are the most vital and revered tasks any Hospitaller can take on, second only to our devotion to God."

Griselle stepped closer to Amelia. "I don't know if I want to take the vow. I only know I want to heal people." The look in her dark eyes was almost one of desperation as she reached out toward Amelia. "Commandeur Timoleon says you possess much knowledge on herbs and medicinals. I want to be the best healer in all of Gévaudan."

"We cannot keep Amelia much longer," said Timoleon. "She has a guest waiting in the Great Hall."

Amelia could not imagine who it would be. "A guest?"

"Our friend, Monsieur Cavalier."

"Cavalier! Does he have word from Jehan? It has been barely a week. Could he have made it to the Swiss cantons already?"

"No. 'Tis too soon to hear any news. Yet he brings us word on what is going on outside of the safety of our commandery. From what he speaks of, it is more important than ever that you young women only leave the commandery on assigned errands. And that you are escorted by at least one of my knights at all times."

"Of course," said Henriette.

Little Jacquette stood at attention. "Yes, most certainly!"

As Amelia turned to leave, Griselle clutched at her sleeve as though grasping for her last hope, a mere tadpole struggling to pull itself up onto the shore. "Wait . . . promise me you will be back soon. I want to learn your secrets."

Amelia pulled her arm gently away. "Yes, later. I must go for now. Cavalier and I have much to discuss."

She rushed toward the manoir where two knights were stationed outside the main entry. Even from a distance, it was an imposing remnant of the original Gothic construction, topped with hoodmolds forming repeated arches with pointed apexes and, above that, hung a stone lintel carved with tracery and the Knights' crest with the eight-pointed star. As Amelia approached, one knight opened the heavy oak door suspended by elegant iron brackets and she nodded to him in respect as she entered.

The clacking of her boots over the hard granite floor echoed through the foyer, announcing her eagerness. She halted at the broad doorway leading into the Great Hall, anticipation pulsing through her.

Cavalier stood before the leaded colonette window festooned by the Knights' colorful standards on either side. Staring out toward the orchard, an aura of gilded light framed his figure, his long wavy locks as golden as the sunlight. His visage reminded her of the illuminated panels of Archangel Michael from the old tomes in her cottage library.

"What news, my friend?" Amelia called out from the doorway.

He turned toward her, the dignified features of his vernal face etched with shadows of worry. She could not understand what motivated him to take on the responsibility of caring for the Children of God so early in his life, yet he carried the burden well. Although two years shy of his age of majority, he was a man by Amelia's standards, emerging as a leader and protector, wise beyond his years with both the strength and compassion that comforted the people.

"It becomes worse again," he said solemnly. "My uncle tells me the persecutions are as bad as the Revocation years . . . when I was not old enough to remember. There must be something asleep in my memory about those times that drives me on."

Amelia's heart raced. "Tell me, Cavalier. What is it? What has happened? I thought, with the bridges out, the dragoons could not make their way into the mountains."

Cavalier began to pace the room. "While waiting for the rivers to recede, they discovered new routes. We get reports that the soldiers are ravaging homes, carrying off all they can sell. . . furniture, books, grain. . . mostly to the priests who buy the spoils dirt-cheap. They tell the people they will ruin anyone who does not go to mass."

Trying to contain her emotions, Amelia pressed her teeth against her lower lip. She had already seen the zeal of Cavalier's Huguenot friends, Mazel and Rolland, while at the Children of God assemblies, and knew they were planning a rebellion. Their forbidden worship services in the forest had elevated Intendant Basville's commitment to rid the Cévennes of those who would not conform to the King's religion. And since word of their plans to revolt had leaked out to Basville's spies, it had only increased the man's rage and savage tactics.

These latest raids must have been like salt in the Huguenots' wounds. The loss of their temples to the King's edicts and their loved ones to imprisonment already had them teetering on the edge of a breaking point. One that could only result in tragedy for Cévenol people of all faiths.

"Are your friends still going through with their plans? Is there no other way?"

"They are preparing," answered Cavalier, "convinced it is the end times and they should follow Pasteur Jurieu's command to fight."

Amelia squeezed her hands together to stave off her frustration. "Why do they follow the orders of a man who hides in the safety and luxury of Rotterdam? He insights their base instincts to survive only to serve his own agenda."

"There are some who will flee the country instead," said Cavalier.

"That seems the wisest solution," Amelia said as she relaxed her hands. "No good can come from violence. As enlightened souls, we should be past this 'eye for an eye' reaction."

Cavalier's gaze moved to the window again. "While that is true, many have not enough coin to flee."

"Or, like myself, have other reasons to stay, and choose to sacrifice their freedom instead." Amelia languorously shook her head, understanding there was no clear solution. "And you? What do you plan to do?"

"I am considering leaving for Geneva, but not right away. Whenever I meet the others at Les Bouzèdes and see the hoards of weapons, I realize they are in a stupor of their own fear. And lately, when the Spirit comes on them, they carry on even more about taking up arms in the name of God."

Amelia took a breath and sighed. "I can never believe that is truly the word of Spirit . . . to commit acts of violence. I am glad to hear you have your doubts about joining them. And I thank you for coming all this way to share the news." She paused when she heard soft footfall and noticed movement out of the corner of her eye.

Cavalier's brows drew together. He leaned close to Amelia and whispered, "Who is that watching us?"

She turned toward the foyer where Griselle peered in from around the doorway. Seeing her creeping toward them, Amelia knew she had to finish her talk with Cavalier quickly.

"A new novice. Not to worry," she said softly, resting a hand on his shoulder. She studied Cavalier's eyes. They were reddened with dark circles around them, but thankfully the irises gave no signs of disease.

"I see the melancholy in your eyes. Should you need some time away from the affrightment your friends stir up, I am certain Commandeur Timoleon will welcome you for some sanctuary. Fear can be very powerful, but with a respite and some of my herbs, you can chase that fear away."

She could hear the novice's steps growing louder as the girl continued into the room unbidden. In moments, Griselle was standing just behind her, the girl's breathing heavy and impatient.

Amelia took her hand from Cavalier's shoulder and stepped aside.

The girl nearly jumped between them and curtsied to Cavalier.

"Am Griselle from Causse de Sauveterre. I can heal your melancholy. And my cure is much stronger than herbs." She leaned her head to one side, gazing intently and trailing a finger over her lips.

Cavalier looked at Amelia, raising his eyebrows with a wry smile on his face.

"I am not sure what I'd be in for if I stay." He shook his head and took a deep breath, then with a nod, he said, "But I shall consider it."

Amelia wondered what life would be like for the Hopsitaller's community with this eager, yet feral, addition to the novices. What a wayward, vulnerable soul Griselle seemed to be, so much like herself when she, too, was but a youngling. Perhaps Commandeur Timoleon could be a better influence than Griselle's own family.

CHAPTER 6

FETTERED FREEDOM

JEHAN

**1 October 1697 ~ Afternoon
Republic of Geneva**

Following two grueling days of trekking the mountains, their muscles throbbing and bodies depleted, the refugee group found temporary respite in a farm cart laden with bales of wool. Though it gave time for blisters to calm, it was a desperate attempt to avoid being discovered. The suffocating stench of unbathed bodies concealed under greasy, unscoured sheep's wool, heads and elbows incessantly thudding against the wooden floorboards, was nearly intolerable but Jehan knew the situation could be much worse.

The group managed to evade the Pont sur le Guiers border guard, who'd been passed out in a drunken stupor. But once they safely crossed out of France and into Savoy, and rose from the dregs of their confinement, the grumbling began. The ordeal had been so utterly disagreeable that they heartily concurred to share the extra expense of a coach.

Massip did some scouting around the villages just beyond the crossing and easily located a coach for hire. With Jehan covering Moyse's share, the group hastily boarded.

Eager to see what lay ahead, Jehan took the seat alongside the coach driver, and they moved swiftly on through Savoy toward the Republic of Geneva.

Some hours after passing through Annecy, the clouds finally gave way. Jehan angled his head toward the sun, filled with gratitude for the long-awaited touch of warmth on his face. He smiled, knowing that their destination was close at hand.

As the driver gradually slowed the coach and stopped on a rise, a flurry of other refugees traveling in carts, carriages, and on foot pushed past them. The location afforded a stunning view of the most magnificent walled city Jehan had ever seen.

"There she is," said the coachman. "We call 'er the Protestant Rome. Lots of those philosophical sorts in the city these days."

Geneva. Jehan filled his lungs with the crisp afternoon air and sighed. "Splendid."

Set at the edge of a vast lake tucked between rolling, verdant hills and majestic mountains, the city's grandeur evoked the very essence of the mythical Eden he'd envisioned. A multitude of spires and towers reflected in the sparkling waters of the Rhone and Arve Rivers, and beckoned to all to enter through its bustling gates. He didn't need to go further than this beautiful city. Here, he could stay closer to France, closer to Amelia.

As the coach continued on toward the city, Jehan contemplated a plan to stay in Geneva and forgo his uncle's offer to join the colony in Aarau. He had to make a choice of his own free will, even if it displeased Uncle Barjon. They approached a queue at the south gate, and Jehan could see the guards were requiring paperwork. He turned back to Massip, who sat on the rear bench.

"Do they need our passports?"

"They want your letters of attestation."

"Attestation of what?" Jehan asked.

"Of your Protestant faith."

Jehan swallowed hard. Had he come all this way only to be denied entry? Although he had a growing interest in the Reformed Calvinist faith of his forefathers, he had never denied the Catholic faith after being converted by the Dominicans as a child. He had fled France to escape the violence. And to avoid conscription into the King's militia, where he'd be forced to fight against his friends and neighbors. And especially for freedom of conscience, no matter what spiritual path he chose. But now, was he to be forced into yet another singular path? Why had his Uncle Barjon not mentioned this in their correspondence over the past year?

"'Tis not something I have, this attestation." The words caught in Jehan's throat.

Massip waved a hand. "Do not worry yourself, Sieur BonDurant. Since you are Pasteur Barjon's nephew, that will count for much. I'll take care of getting you the required paperwork to enter the city. We each must obtain a *Passa* that allows us to stay for one night, but one night only. Then we'll continue by boat to Aarau and join your uncle's colony."

Amelia's tender smile and the mesmerizing, mutable color in her hazel eyes came into Jehan's mind. "I would prefer to stay in Geneva. It would be far easier for my friend Amelia to join me here. I have my own money."

Massip's expression hardened, and he shook his head. "I am sorry. Money does not buy everything. Geneva will welcome us for a brief stay. But because of food shortages, those who are not citizens must move on."

Jehan's shoulders melted under the disappointment.

3 October 1697 ~ Afternoon
Aarau, Swiss Canton of Bernese Aargau

Jehan grimaced from the tight hold Pasteur Barjon had on his arm as he directed him through the door of Aarau's Reformed *Stadtkirche*. He didn't much appreciate being treated as if he were an insolent schoolboy and huffed as he shook off his uncle's grip.

Next to the two well-dressed gentlemen who accompanied them, donning perruques and plumed hats, Jehan knew he looked no more than a pauper in his torn and dirt-laden justaucorps, so he wondered if his appearance influenced the harsh treatment.

"Sword off. Now," barked Uncle Barjon as he opened the weapons house cabinet. "And that old dagger, too."

Jehan had never recalled his uncle being so inhospitable, though it had been many years since they had seen each other. Since the year Jehan was forced to live with the Dominicans—the same year the Reformed Calvinist pasteurs, including Uncle Barjon, were banned from France. And much had changed in both of their lives since that time.

The walls of the church, whitewashed and rigid as starched linen, burned Jehan's eyes as he entered from the afternoon gloom outside. The austerity of the church was a stark contrast to the breathtaking Catholic *cathédrales*, with ceilings adorned in golden stars on a sea of blue. Or compared to the majesty and mystery of the forests where the Children of God assembled for their own version of Calvinist worship.

"Uncle, can I not have a meal and some rest before we perform this ceremony of yours? It has been a long and arduous journey to get here."

"You must do this *now*, or you risk deportation *and* my reputation. You are the only one in your group who dared show up here without holding letters of attestation to the Calvinist faith . . . except for your Roma friends who will have to move on, anyway."

"What? I thought this was the land of tolerance. You are telling me I must avow to a faith that I am yet still exploring. And now you say Syeira and Manfri are not welcome here?"

"'Tis our way." Pasteur Barjon pointed to the pulpit. "Stand there. Messieurs Malbois and Brochet shall witness."

"All the same . . . 'Tis not what your bible teaches, Uncle," Jehan said as he stepped up. "As the elect of God, you are told to put on tender mercy and kindness."

"Ha!" croaked the Pasteur. "So you *have* been practicing the Reformed faith."

"Only acquiring knowledge. I attended a few of the secret prayer meetings held by André's wife, Lucrèce, back in Genouillac. But most of what I learned came from studying with my dearest Amelia, in her library, where I read as many tomes on religion and philosophy and medicine as I had time for."

The Pasteur grunted with disdain, waving a hand and shaking his head as he went to a small side table. He opened a registry book, then a bottle of ink, picked up a quill, and began penning a statement of some sort.

Jehan did not want to cause trouble, but everything was happening so fast. He wasn't sure what the face of the Reformed faith would look like in this huge, stripped-down structure where one's every move, every thought, every intention would be judged by a massive congregation and a rigid consistory. Over the last year, he had found solace in the small meetings Lucrèce had organized, but he could already tell how very different his uncle's version of the faith would be.

Pasteur Barjon brought the registry to the pulpit. "Jehan. Are you quite ready?"

Jehan hesitated, glancing between the two gentlemen standing on either side. One solemnly nodded, but the other gave a welcoming smile. Perhaps there were some men with heart here, after all.

Yet this did not at all resemble the freedom Jehan sought, and it filled the air with the heavy scent of righteous confinement. This was the day he had waited for, had traveled hundreds of miles for, had suffered for—all this way, and his spiritual path was *still* being dictated to him.

His unsettled stomach hardened as he leaned toward the pulpit and read the notation.

> *The 3rd of October 1697, Seigneur Jean Pierre BonDurant, apothecary, presented himself in front of us, claiming that he was extremely affected by the fault he committed in his youth, which was to attend the worship of the Roman Catholic Church; showing his repentance by asking God to forgive this sin and after he claimed that he would live and die in our Holy Religion, he was admitted into the peace of the Church and to participate in the Holy Sacraments. He signed this present deed along with us: Henry Malbois and Pierre Brochet, both hat makers who took refuge in the town of Aarau, and undersigned by myself:*
>
> *Barjon*
> *refugee Pasteur*

Pasteur Barjon held out the quill, but Jehan stepped back, feeling a sinking sensation. His chest began to tighten, drawing him into himself, making him feel smaller, insignificant, unworthy. It was not the first time he'd been accused of committing a sin that he was not guilty of.

"The choice was not mine to attend the Catholic church. You know as well as I, Uncle, that I was a mere child when the

Dominicans took me, and they forced me to convert. This goes against my morals, and the convictions that brought me here, to make an oath that is untrue."

The more affable of the two gentlemen spoke up in an empathetic voice. "Tis not that we believe you were responsible for your sin but, in our eyes, participating in the Catholic worship is a sin even if forcibly practiced. And certainly, you want to profess the true and perfect Calvinist faith."

"'Tis merely a formality," said the Pasteur. "To keep you safe here amongst us."

For a man of God, he seemed more about practicality than morality. Only time would reveal his true predilections.

Jehan was not sure he would ever find a perfect faith. He had yet to understand the tenets of the Calvinist faith. What if he were to end up questioning them as much as he did those of the Catholic religion?

He could see impatience growing in the men as they became restless. His uncle cleared his throat while the terse gentleman tugged at the cravate that was pressing against his neck.

Jehan's mind raced through the outcomes. He was running out of options if he wanted to live in this peaceful and orderly land. *Peace*—that had also been what he sought. He did enjoy the singing of psalms, so he may be able to compromise on this required vow in order to learn more about their practices. But would Amelia? He sorely missed her already and very much wanted her to join him. Yet she had declared she would vow only to herself and to the Holy Spirit. Perhaps it was unrealistic—absurd, even—to think she would ever leave her homeland, or for him to expect freedom in every aspect of life and still be able to live in harmony with others.

Jehan's uncertainty ran deep, so he looked again into the eyes of the men before him and bolstered his choice with an even deeper breath. He pushed his hair away as he took the quill and bent over the registry, hoping he would not regret this later.

4 October 1697 ~ Dawn
Aarau, Swiss Canton of Bernese Aargau

The dawn could not come soon enough for Jehan, so he pulled back the thick bedcover, heavy with an abundance of wool filling, and tried to move about without waking Moyse. He took his writing supplies from his satchel, tiptoed to the small table, and lit the rushlight candle.

He would need to word his letter to Amelia carefully. Although she had seen much in her two and twenty years, she may never consider joining him were he to paint a picture of the treacherous conditions he had faced while fleeing France. And there must be no mention of his own name in the letter, in case it was intercepted. If the officials learned of his departure, they would seize his properties, so the story his cousin André had agreed to tell was simply that Jehan was off in the Gorges du Tarn, healing the sick.

Jehan moved the candle closer to the parchment to dispel the darkness and began.

4 October 1697

> *Dearest One, I pray this letter finds you in good spirits and your grandmother in good health. I write in haste to send you news of our safe arrival in our destination city. And to warn you to take heed should you come across the silver medallion I left behind in my saddlebag. You know its purpose, so I shall make no mention of it here. You might*

prefer to hide it well away. But it is a double-edged happenstance in that its value will provide the means to travel when you are ready.

Though my new city is farther from you than I truly wish to be, you will be pleased to know it is in an idyllic land in a broad valley below sweeping foothills and surrounded by the sort of forests and wild places we both love. I am afraid I must discard my grapevine rootstock and mulberry seeds for they became riddled with mold after a river crossing, but I shall find others to purchase when the time is right.

The walled city with ringed streets is not overly large and is situated on a rocky outcrop above a broad, gentle river. ˜Tis as ancient as our Cévenoles cities, but the residents here have reconstructed many houses in recent times. You would delight in the splendid way they have embellished the gable eaves with flowers and arabesques, angels and dragons, crests and cartouches of all sorts. Dachhimmel is the word for it in Alemannisch, the Swiss Germanic dialect spoken here, and I am certain it will bring much gaiety to the cold winter months.

Syeira and Manfri are captivated by the city with its colorful, clean, and orderly atmosphere. Yet I fear they will not be permitted to stay. I am saddened to share that tolerance here takes a narrower path than I would have hoped.

The Swiss have been quite generous to French refugees, providing aid and relief from taxes while the craftspeople and merchants establish their workshops, but only to those who avow to be servants of the Calvinist faith. I did not agree at first to take their pledge, and it has troubled me to know it is counter to our desire for direct knowing and for seeking the common thread that runs through all religions and creeds. But later I learned the authorities are trying to prevent pauperism and fraud, so I must comply with their requirement if I am to be permitted to stay.

Funds raised by the city and from the immigrant residents' own "Bourse Francaise" provide for housing. Moyse and I have an apartment in a rather large hostel near the temple, or Stadtkirche, as they call it, in the language here. The hostel provides these apartments for Pasteur Barjon and his family, along with other families of higher rank or profession. His wife, Dame Bernadine de Tourtoulon de Valobscure, being very much younger than he, has blessed their family with many children, seven in total if my count is correct, whose names I hope to learn after a few more days.

The craftspeople and weavers and such are provided quarters in the old St Ursuline monastery until they can save for their own apartments. I am fortunate that I do not need to rely on charity, or perhaps they would force me to move on. I shall, someday, find a place of my own where you can join me. Perhaps a cottage in the forest, beside a beautiful brook.

Mon Ame, my beloved, I wish my requirements here allowed me more time to dwell on you in this letter. And I wish to God you were coming in through the door at this very moment... that I could hold your hands and linger in the beauty of our togetherness. My heart bids me evermore to love you and, if you command me to keep true to you wherever I go, I shall most gladly comply.

I recalled this from our divine days of reading and study in your library, and it holds the truth of my heart. "Absence lessens the minor passions and increases the great ones as the wind douses a candle and kindles a fire."

Know that I laid awake these past several nights while in the wilderness, looking to find you in the stars, and always, always, hoping you will meet me when I find our special Eden.

Your devoted and loving friend

The Saturday market had not yet opened, the breaking daylight just piercing the shadows below the cheerful eaves, but the street buzzed with vendors as they pulled in their carts and assembled their colorful canopies. Jehan wanted to find Monsieur Giraud, the bookseller, before the man was too busy with patrons, so he hastened through the commotion, scanning the area for Giraud's familiar face. Over the past year, he had become the family's most reliable method for exchanging letters between France and the Swiss Republic, so surely he could deliver Amelia's letter to the Knights of Saint Jean Commandery.

"Jehan. Jehan. Wait for a moment."

Jehan recognized the voice and stopped. It had to be Syeira. He looked around to see that she and Manfri were trying to catch up to him.

Both breathless and carrying their satchels filled with the few belongings they owned, they threw their arms around Jehan.

"We could not leave without farewell," Manfri said.

Jehan returned their sad embrace and could see Syeira's eyes were red from crying.

"'Tis beyond belief that they are putting you out already," Jehan said. As he shared their anguish, his breathing became heavy and erratic, his nostrils flaring as outrage and indignation coursed through him.

He caught a glint of golden hair out of the corner of his eye, then felt a warm hand on his shoulder.

"We all decided it was best to leave before trouble started."

Jehan spun around. "Stéphane! Not you and Anne as well."

Like the others, they were also loaded with satchels and ready to depart. The injustice of it all tightened Jehan's neck. He could feel the veins bulging and throbbing under his skin.

Stéphane squeezed Jehan's shoulder with a firm grip. "Yes, dear comrade-in-search-of-freedom. We have all decided Rotterdam will be more accepting of us."

Anne stepped up on the opposite side of Jehan. At the same moment, she and Stéphane planted a kiss on each of Jehan's cheeks, then broke out in laughter.

He heaved a calming breath and noticed the smiles returning to Syeira's and Manfri's faces.

"Thank you for being our friend without judging," Anne said. "It means so much to both of us."

Jehan's heart felt a bit lighter knowing they appreciated his acceptance. It elicited a gentle smile on his lips. He stood resolute in his values and he wanted them to know it. "We all deserve respect and love, and you have both from me."

Stéphane patted his hat onto his head and put an arm around Anne. "May God keep you safe and bring peace to your days."

"And to you, as well," Jehan said, slowly tipping his hat to each of them, as though the ritual might ease the farewell.

Jehan watched the foursome of wandering souls make their way through the vendors and out the upper tower gate while the smile on his lips faded. The bonds they had forged during the trials and challenges they had faced together would *never* be broken.

With their departure, Jehan was left with only Moyse as a friend, but his cousin's adherence to the Calvinist faith made him an unreliable confidant. Perhaps Jehan needed to cultivate new acquaintances—kindred spirits—who could provide consolation and understanding while he struggled to accept yet another spiritual path that demanded conformity.

PART TWO

Mystic Lore Books

CHAPTER 7

YULETIDE PRESENCE

AMELIA

21 December 1697 ~ Winter Solstice
Hospitaller Commandery, Mont Lauzère, France

As Amelia descended the manoir's ancient stone staircase to join the Yuletide preparations, she tried to herd her unruly thoughts. She found it odd—a second letter had come from Jehan, this one written mid-November, but the tone was rather different from the first. She fingered the rough parchment, folded deep within her pocket, that had arrived hidden inside the lining of a small, embossed leather-bound book.

Jehan's first letter, written upon his arrival in Aarau, had expressed a deep love for her. Even without his physical presence, those words had lifted her for days.

Now, this letter was pragmatic and practical, speaking of his difficulty in finding work as an apothecary and still having trouble remembering all the names of Pasteur Barjon's children. And he never once acknowledged her own heartfelt letter from late October, where she had shared her deep sadness over their parting.

Amelia's mind reeled with torment over the reasons Jehan seemed so cold and distant. Her vision blurred as she fought back pent up tears. She knew she must shift her thoughts.

Perhaps he simply had not received her letter before he wrote again. Or perhaps it was of her own making, and she needed to be more forthright about the deep love she held for him. Or could it be that his feelings had changed?

As her body started to ache for him with that familiar sweet pain, she became distracted and stumbled on the next step, abruptly jolting her to her senses. She grasped the bannister, pausing to regain her composure, then continued downstairs.

When she stepped onto the upper landing and turned toward the lower flight of stairs, she found Henriette standing at the bottom with an armful of fresh holly cuttings and evergreen boughs, her pleasant face and congenial smile bathed in a warm, radiant glow.

"Mademoiselle Amelia," Henriette said with polite nod. "We have completed the lighting of the candles."

Henriette's cheerful nature brought Amelia out of her brooding straightaway and prompted her to inquire about the knights who'd gone out in search of a yule log.

"Do the men return soon?"

"I believe so. But since they are not yet here, perhaps you could help me dress the balustrade."

"Certainly," answered Amelia.

The two of them went to work, interlacing a garland of boughs over and around the stout stone banister. Even Henriette's long arms were not of a length to reach around the huge balusters, so Amelia took the garland from her once it was halfway through the opening.

The heavy entry door creaked open and a gust of wind whistled in, rippling their veils and the skirts of their tunics, and sending an icy chill across Amelia's ankles. She descended the stairs to meet the foraging party, her heart jumping in expectation of what they might have found.

A flurry of snow swirled in just ahead of six knights, who tugged a massive log with ropes tied around its girth. The crisp, moist air and a pungent scent of pine filled the room. Amelia could sense life returning to the stark foyer, blessed by God's gifts from Mont Lauzère's forest and the solstice that carried the promise of the returning light.

"You see! You see what they do," shouted Griselle as she ran in from the Great Hall.

Commadeur Timoleon took his time as he followed her in.

Griselle bounced about, pointing at Henriette. "They must stop. These are pagan traditions."

"These are *our* traditions, Griselle." The Commandeur replied with a smirk—an expression Amelia had never before seen on him.

As the men dragged their yule log toward the Great Hall, scraping it across the stone floor and leaving small heaps of melting snow, the Commandeur motioned Griselle aside.

"I realize your father, with his fervent Reformed convictions, is the one who instilled this notion in you. However, we always have, and always will continue with our yuletide celebration. 'Tis how we thank the Lord for bringing the light, and for the remembrance of Christ. There is no sin in that. And it is your choice whether you participate or not."

Henriette hastened down the stairs and began picking up the small branches and pine needles trailing across the floor, then scampered outside with her head down.

Wanting to reassure Griselle, Amelia drew near to her. "It lifts our hearts, and our infirmed recover faster when the mood is bright and hopeful," she said as she placed her arm around the girl.

But Griselle vigorously shrugged it off.

Amelia pinched her lips together, fighting the urge to react. "You may find it worthwhile to join the others after Vespers in the traditional custom of sprinkling wine on the yule log and offering a prayer. 'Tis how we burn out our old errors and misdeeds. How we let them go, and start anew."

The girl looked up at her with a frown, and her chin began to quiver. Amelia wanted to reach for her again. To hold her and hug away the fright or guilt or whatever it was that was distressing the girl so. She took a step closer, but Griselle abruptly pulled away and stomped off toward the Great Hall on the heels of the knights.

Despite the tension created by Griselle's unrestrained emotions, the festivities and rituals of the evening had been joyous for most. Even Menina had come to listen to the tin whistle tunes and watch the young novices dance in delight. But Amelia's head pounded from the stress and excitement. So she excused herself early from the activities in the Great Hall to retrieve her herb box for making a curative tea.

She took a rushlight from a table in the foyer and then started to climb the stairs, but something tugged at her skirts. She looked down to see one of the holly branches had snagged a spot in the loosely-woven blue linen. *Yet another flaw to be mended.* Her life was beginning to feel so full of making repairs of one sort or the other that it seemed there would never be time to sew a new gown.

Once she climbed the stairs and headed down the long passageway to her chamber, Amelia's taut shoulders relaxed and her mind began to clear of concern over Griselle.

Reaching the depths of darkness at the far end, thoughts of Jehan filled, not only the void in her mind, but every inch of her being. As if he walked alongside her, Amelia clearly envisioned his smile, his azure eyes, his strong physique, and recalled his inquiring mind and quick wit. A wave of love surged through her as she felt his gentle, protective spirit. It drew her to him in a way no other could. She needed time with him. Time alone.

She considered the *solar*—the usual place of activity when there were no celebrations. Where the women gathered to embroider in the warm sunlight that spilled through the many windows or read by the crackling fire. She retraced her steps to the other wing where it was located and, fortuitously, found it empty.

The dark room was serenely lit by a half moon streaming subtle light beams through the oriel window, painting the shadows with a subtle blue light. She could see the moon was in the waxing phase. Had winter already passed, it would have been time to sow plants that grow above ground, just as she had taught Jehan the past spring. Perhaps it was a sign. A sign to bring her feelings above ground, out into the light of day.

She slipped off her boots and climbed onto the soft cushion in the window seat. The aroma of lavender inside the wool stuffing wafted around her as she settled into place. Leaning her head against the window frame, she peered out through small leaded panes of glass that gave an ethereal, dream-like quality to the night sky.

A single cloud moved across the moon, blocking all but a faint aura of light. In the darkness, the trail of stars across the night sky suddenly brightened, and she felt it again. His presence. The connection. There, in the stars.

Tomorrow, she would write again and bring her deep yearning for him into the open, revealing the depth of her love. Perhaps one day she could join him. Perhaps he loved her enough to wait. If he truly loved her, he *would* wait. Years even. Yet, even if he did not stay true to her in the physical sense, there could be nothing that would sever their profound connection.

CHAPTER 8

FORBIDDEN CURES

JEHAN

5 January 1698
Aarau, Swiss Canton of Bernese Aargau

Jehan stood before the bureau in his apartment and peered into the table mirror, closing the last few buttons on his blue wool serge ensemble. It was now the only respectable clothing he owned after his escape into Aarau, but he was determined he would make do until he secured employment or else received funds from his estate in shipments from André. After over three months in Aarau, the uncertainty of either dictated that he remain frugal with the assets he had.

He stared into the open armoire next to him, at the bedraggled gray justaucorps hanging there that had served as his traveling clothes. Its sad state—every stain, every tear, every drop of perspiration that clung to its threads—told the story of the daunting and arduous escape from France. Though Jehan could no longer wear it in refined company, or any company for that matter, it still served as a noble disguise for his secret cache of money—the best substitute for a bank or strongbox he could think of.

He poked a finger through the stitches of the lapel and hooked it around an *ecu*, pulling it from its hiding place, then dropping it into his purse. Turning to the mirror again, he ran a comb through his thick dark hair, then donned his hat and left his apartment in search of a bakeshop.

When Jehan set out into the wintry day to wander the busy streets of Aarau's old town, he found the recent snowfall muted the usual noises and brightened the dull day. The scent of wood smoke filled the air, masking the aromas of bread and pastries that may have otherwise led the way. Street workers maintained orderly paths next to the buildings using horse-drawn iron wedges, but there was not much they could do about the long icicles looming dangerously from the broad eaves four and five stories high.

Jehan passed by a few bread shops, but they did not specialize in the sort of sweets he had in mind. After circling the city center once round, he decided a little guidance would be of benefit.

A tall, well-dressed young woman approached, her body hidden behind the bolts of silk brocade and wool serge she carried. But Jehan could see she wore a cape of expensive black velvet with a matching hood lined in the finest pleated linen, generous enough to show off the Alencon lace and golden curls in the *fontange* assembly mounted on her head.

"Pardon, mademoiselle." Jehan tipped his hat. "Can you tell me where I might find a shop selling the *gâteau des rois?*"

By the woman's bewildered expression, she clearly did not understand him. She glanced around as if looking for answers.

"I know not this," she replied in an attempt to speak French.

The back of Jehan's neck grew taut, and he rubbed it to dispel the annoyance he felt with himself. In the three months since his arrival in the city, he had mastered no more than a few words in the Alemannisch dialect spoken here. At times like this, the new language and the unfamiliar way of life vexed him, making him miss his homeland and his beloved Amelia all the more. He would much rather be sitting with her by the fire in her library, learning the ancient languages from the old tomes.

The thought of ancient languages gave Jehan an idea. The manner in which this young woman adorned herself—in the latest French style, a luxury not accessible to all—suggested she might possess a level of education and familiarity with Latin.

"Epiphania," he said as he brought his hand to his mouth and mimed eating.

The young woman giggled, her bright blue eyes animated and mischievous. "Ohhh . . . Epiphany galette. No?"

"Yes!" Jehan was relieved she understood. He wanted to complete his shopping and return to the apartments straight away. His little cousin, Louis, lay ill, and the Epiphany cake could be just the thing to cheer the lad up a bit.

"You need *Dreikönigskuchen*," said the woman. "'Tis not same as gâteau, but is for Epiphany. Look for *Konditorei* shop. They make the sweets. Next cross street," she said, pointing ahead, then cocked her head and looked him up and down, seeming to judge his appearance. "I am Udine Schuler. You come visit me at Meister Lemieux's boutique for new fashions." She clicked her tongue twice and shook her head. "This ensemble you wear . . . the serge fine quality, the blue good with your eyes . . . *noch*, for Frenchman, you very behind on *a la mode* fashions."

Jehan's face heated from embarrassment despite the cold air.

"Are you *Herr* BonDurant?" she asked. "All the ladies speak of you."

"Yes. 'Tis me," he answered, bowing deeply to hide the grimace he made.

What sort of talk had transpired about him? Was it only about his lack of fashion sense? He had put his desire for that aside a few years earlier when investing funds in his family's near-derelict estate was far more important. But here, with an abundance of French immigrant merchants, it seemed everyone except the staunchest Reformed and the peasant farmers wore the expensive courtier fashions.

Jehan looked at the young woman's gloved hand. He could not tell if perhaps she was unmarried and had motives beyond wanting to sell him expensive clothing. Either way, he would agree to call on her—he had motives of his own. He was tired of his lonely existence in this city. Calling on her at Lemieux's boutique might finally gain him a friend and improve his language skills.

"It was a pleasure, Mademoiselle Schuler," Jehan said, tipping his hat. "I shall gladly come for a visit after Epiphany. I am most *certainly* in need of something new, or at least a little mending on something old."

With few people of his own age in the hostel, Jehan had become a friend and mentor to his twelve-year-old cousin, Louis, teaching him which herbs and flowers could be utilized for healing. But, recently, the boy had taken to his bed with an ague, rales in the lungs, and a consumptive cough.

Jehan headed down the long hallway of the Barjon's apartment with Louis' mother, Dame Bernadine de Tourtoulon, who was a kind woman in stark contrast to her controlling husband. He carried his apothecary bag and the Epiphany galette, wrapped in a linen cloth, while sifting through his mind for the best proportions for a mustard plaster treatment.

Dame Bernadine pointed to the third door on the left. "This is Louis' bedchamber. Thank you for coming, Jehan. With so many children to look after, I am happy for your help." She sighed and smiled with a doleful expression as she closed the door. "I shall leave you to your work."

He set his apothecary bag and the galette on the bureau next to washbasin then approached Louis' bed. Brushing the boy's hair from his forehead, he sensed significant heat under his fingertips.

"How are you feeling today, Louis?"

Louis tried to clear his throat. "Like I am on fi . . ." The boy coughed, cutting his words short.

"On fire?" Jehan asked as he peered into Louis' eyes, looking for clues about which illness afflicted him.

The boy nodded and pushed out his bottom lip, looking like he might cry.

"Don't fret, my little cousin," Jehan said. "I have cures for this sort of thing."

The wall sconce candles cast barely enough light as poured fresh water from the pitcher into the basin and washed his hands.

He took a small wooden mortar and pestle from his apothecary bag, along with mustard powder, a few pinches of wood spurge powder, flour, olive oil, and water, and blended them into a thick plaster.

Jehan turned back to the boy. "Would you please unbutton your chemise?"

Louis started to do as Jehan asked, but had to pause halfway through with another bout of coughing that echoed off the paneled walls.

"Do you need help?" Jehan asked, handing him a linen handkerchief from a stack on the bedside table.

Louis wiped his mouth on the linen, then pinched his lips in determination. "Just two more buttons," he said as he finished and pushed back his chemise.

As Jehan spread the plaster over little Louis' chest, he explained the ingredients and properties. Then, while he let the plaster take effect, he kept the boy occupied with stories of the escape from France.

In a short while, Louis' cough eased and his breathing became less strained. Jehan leaned his ear close to the boy and could still hear a small crackle, but there was most definitely some improvement.

He knew it was time to remove the plaster before it irritated the Louis' skin. "Do you feel any prickling or stinging?"

"It tickles a little."

Jehan cleaned off the plaster with a damp linen towel, thinking of what more he could do to ease the the boy's discomfort. "Did you know our minds also play a part in healing?"

Louis' brow lifted in curiosity.

"Yes, indeed they do," Jehan assured in a playful tone. "So it is time to lighten our spirits. First, we shall chase the miasmas from the room."

He jumped up, then pulled back the heavy brocade draperies and opened the window a bit to let in what little light and fresh air the winter day offered. "But I shall make sure you stay warm enough."

Jehan went to the fireplace and took up the poker, prodding the hot coals until a few sparks burst into steady flames.

He sat back on the bed and reached into his apothecary bag again, to a compartment deep within, and brought out an old cross that Amelia had given him for healing. He had never used it before, but it might entertain Louis after three long days in bed. And with the Barjon's maidservant, Madame Saigne, out of the room, it seemed like a good time.

Jehan held the silver piece from its plaited leather cord so Louis could see. The simple, equal-sided cross glimmered in the candlelight.

"What is that?" Louis asked in a weak voice. "Am I going to die?"

"No, no, Louis. You will be better soon."

"I've never seen a cross such as that before."

"'Tis quite a special piece. From the times of the Merovingians. With words to help you heal. Words and prayers have great power, so we must learn to choose our words carefully."

"Please read them to me." The boy's eyelids grew heavy.

"You will need to open your eyes, Louis, so you can see the blessings it contains." Jehan pointed to the edges as he continued, knowing he had to keep the boy's mind focused. "You see how these words are etched around the perimeter? The letters spell out *'ha brachah dabarah'*. They are ancient Hebrew for 'I speak the blessing'. 'Tis the same as a prayer to the Holy Spirit."

Jehan turned the silver cross over to reveal a list of words Amelia had etched there, meant to encourage him on his journey. "And on the back are the words you will meditate on. First is faith . . . faith that you will be well. Then courage . . . have courage to work with Spirit to send the illness out from your body. Next is good health . . . envision yourself recovered and strong. And then there is success . . ."

The boy clapped and giggled. A smile came to his face as he pointed to the last two words on the cross. "And with success, I shall feel . . . joy . . . and . . . love. I shall be well!"

Jehan's heart swelled to see the boy's face brighten. "Yes! Now, let us pray the *Pater Noster*."

The door creaked open and Madame Saigne shuffled into the room. "Sieur BonDurant. Has he recovered? I heard him laughing."

"We are working on it. There has been notable improvement."

"What is the cure you are using?" she asked.

Heavy footsteps echoed in the hall, and Pasteur Barjon appeared in the doorway alongside Madame Saigne. "What is this? What are you doing to my son?" he demanded.

"I just completed a simple poultice to ease the breathing." Jehan began to feel the blaze of his uncle's scrutiny. "Your wife gave me permission to treat him."

"Look, Papa." Louis took the cross from Jehan and twirled it around from its cord. "Jehan has an ancient magic cross. And it is helping me to heal myself with words. 'Tis like praying."

Barjon's eyes widened and he snatched it away. "'Tis nothing more than an evil pagan symbol. There will be no more worship of amulets and charms in my house," he bellowed, startling Madame Saigne, who cowered and stepped out of his way. "My son needs a professional physic, not some novice sorcerer apothecary committing heretical acts."

Pasteur Barjon's chiding flailed at Jehan's tender spot, and the pasteur knew it.

Jehan raised a hand and squeezed his forehead, the tension in his temples matched only by the sinking feeling in his chest. Was he truly qualified to heal the ill since, in truth, he had not even an apothecary's license? Everything he had learned had been taught by his cousin, André, or by Amelia and her grandmother.

Nevertheless, Jehan had seen the effectiveness of the cures he administered, time after time. And his uncle could see for himself how well Louis was healing. Perhaps more explanation would calm the pasteur—or only vex him further. Either way, it was worth the risk to try.

"You do not seem to understand, Uncle. The cross is simply a means to direct one's thoughts in prayer, not an idol to be worshiped or an evil symbol of some sort. 'Tis much the same as a rosary, though I know you think a rosary to be sinful as well."

Barjon's eyes grew black with fury as he stood speechless for a moment, his lips pinched into a harsh, thin line.

Jehan thought about the last remaining vestiges of his Catholic upbringing that were still in his apartment, buried in his satchel, and realized it would be prudent to discard them as soon as he returned. The old rosary and certificate of conversion he'd carried with him out of France to safeguard against arrest might only bring more false accusations and seething condemnations from his uncle, blinding him to all understanding or compassion. Even so, those items would be Jehan's only means of returning to France if he ever chose to.

The pasteur crossed his arms and took the same fortifying breath he used before every sermon. "If you were not family," he said, gritting his teeth, "I'd ask the Consistory to have you thrown out of our colony. *You* do not seem to understand. Calvin believed in the total depravity of man. That we are miserable sinners, born in corruption, inclined to evil, and incapable by ourselves of doing good. And you are becoming an example . . ."

Jehan interrupted before his uncle could continue. "What *I* believe is that we are each capable of great things when the Holy Spirit calls us to be of service for good. And who do you suppose is meant to set all of us miserable sinners on the right path to salvation? Would that be you, Uncle?"

"Well . . . yes. I am the tool God uses to draw you to Him, a vessel that He has already prepared. It is impossible for you to come to Christ without God acting first. Only by following our community rules will you be put on the right path."

"Yet, I thought your Calvinist concept of predestination said we do not have control over our salvation. I do not understand how you have determined that God works through you and that you now have control of my salvation on his behalf. What proof do I have of that?"

Pasteur Barjon grew red in the face, looking as flustered as a hen with a brood of ducks. "You verge on denial of predestination, and for that, you could be banished."

Louis reached an arm out from under the bedcover. "Papa. Please do not let them banish Jehan."

"I shall do what I can since he is my sister's son, but Jehan, you truly try my patience. You've caused enough trouble already by taking our religion so lightly that you attend the Stadtkirche only when it pleases you."

"Uncle, I professed your faith in that confession you had me sign, and I participate in the sacraments weekly. What more do you require?"

"An upright life," the pasteur barked, his eyes black and penetrating.

"How more upright can a person be? I tend the sick at the hostel without compensation while I seek employment. I contribute to collections for the needy and cover all my expenses to the household. I do not spend my time in taverns, I dress modestly, and I am even celibate as a monk."

His uncle's disrespect and righteousness was stirring a blinding urge in Jehan to rebel. He had been *no* servant to the persecutions in France, and he would be *no* servant to Pasteur Barjon.

He huffed and cleared his throat, then stepped closer to his uncle, lowering his voice. "But all my virtuous living may soon change. Your rules stifle the people and push them further away from you. Have you not noticed how your attendance has dropped?"

"Well, I . . . I." The pasteur stumbled over his words, then balled his fists. "I shall admit, I have, but *that* is another matter altogether. Regardless of what my wife tells you, you *must* stay away from my son. You are *forbidden* to practice healing. 'Tis not my rule, but is one of the conditions we agreed to when we were granted permission to stay here."

"But Louis needs treatment to heal." Jehan's stomach hardened at the thought that Barjon would leave his son to die.

Pasteur Barjon scoffed, "Oh, he'll not go without treatment. But we are required to use a local physic. He'll stick to standard practices, and none of this dark sorcery gibberish." The pasteur wagged a finger at Jehan. "What you need to worry your head about is finding a trade in couture manufacturing, or you'll be required to leave our colony."

Jehan knew then and there, what he truly needed to find was another place to follow his passion for healing. But, in the meantime, he would not let his uncle dictate his entire life.

Without saying a word, he hastily rinsed out the mortar and pestle in the washbasin and packed up his bag. He picked it up the galette from the bureau and handed it to Madame Saigne. "This is for tomorrow. After the Epiphany celebration."

She smiled and took it in her hands. "Is it what I think?" she asked, lifting the linen wrapping to peek inside.

The pasteur reached for the galette, but she pulled it away, rebuking his attempt. "There is no harm in a galette, Pasteur Barjon," she complained defiantly.

"How *dare* you, woman! I shall have you in court for disobedience," Barjon shouted. "That galette is just another pagan symbol that I shall *not* tolerate."

"Papa. Pleeeease," Louis begged, pulling back his bedcovers and struggling to sit up. "Please let us keep it."

Jehan could not stand by and watch this abusive behavior. He took the galette and darted away from his uncle, who snatched at it. But the old pasteur was too slow as Jehan sidestepped him and darted to the hallway door.

"Do not worry, Louis, there will be other sweet treats," Jehan said, resolved to hide the cake in his apartment and bring it back to Louis' mother once his uncle left for the Stadtkirche.

"And . . . Madame Saigne," Jehan said, taking pity on the poor, trembling woman. "I shall be your witness should Uncle do you the injustice of taking you to court over this."

Jehan let out a breath as he left the room. Had he just guaranteed his removal from the colony? If so, it no longer mattered. He had seen many forms of intolerance in his life, but the hypocrisy in his uncle's intolerance was verging on madness.

8 March 1698
Aarau, Swiss Canton of Bernese Aargau

The stench of dung and damp wool in the marketplace was stronger now that winter was passing, and the snow had begun to melt. Jehan carefully navigated past a deep puddle and made his way to the side of the bookseller's market stall. He hoped the latest delivery might include a payment from assets he'd divested before leaving France.

Monsieur Giraud heaved a small oak strongbox from his cart, and it emitted a muffled jangling as he lugged it over to the linen-covered display counter. He dropped it with a crash that sent dust specks dancing in the sunlight, then turned his head and sneezed.

"Another shipment from your cousin, André," Giraud said as he inserted a key in the iron lock. "And this time . . . he's sent more than just a letter." He lifted the lid, revealing a collection of small books neatly organized inside, then chuckled. "And herein lies a wealth of knowledge."

"I can tell by the jangling, the wealth is not only in the knowledge," said Jehan, tempted to laugh with Giraud, but he held back, eyes scanning the clamorous street around them. "Tell me, how is it you can transport all these coins without being detected?"

"The soldiers get lazy. They have grown so accustomed to seeing me over the years, that they only take a quick look inside the boxes and caskets, and never bother to sift through the contents. I must apologize for the delay in delivering this. The roads have been impassable in places the past few months." Giraud removed his hat and scratched his balding head. "So how do you fare now that you are settled?"

"Since I find my services as an apothecary are forbidden here, I recently began work as a shoemaker. 'Tis a skill I acquired a few years ago, thanks to my *métayer* at Château de Cougoussac. The work helps me forget what a sad winter it has been."

Giraud's eyes widened in an inquisitive manner. "What has happened?"

Jehan paused for a moment, hesitating to share the entire painful story of Louis' death, but he knew it would benefit him to talk to someone, anyone. And he trusted Giraud.

"I lost my young cousin to a *certain* physician's ineptitude."

Rage started to pound in Jehan's ears like a distant drum, growing louder each moment as he recalled the days leading to little Louis' death.

"'Twas a local physic . . . whom I shall not name. The man insisted on treating Louis with antimony and bloodletting. I had the boy all but recovered. Yet after a few weeks of that outdated torture, my poor cousin weakened and passed on to the Creator."

Jehan's hand twitched as he fought the urge to cross himself. The old habit, learned under the auspices of the Dominicans, was *still* so hard to break.

"I am very sorry. May I offer my condolences."

Jehan removed his hat and heaved a long sigh. It calmed his nerves a bit, but did nothing to rid him of the heavy guilt he carried.

"I wish I had demanded that Uncle seek a different medic. But since I was banished from the Barjon's apartment and keep to my own apartment because of the animosity that lingers, I was not aware of the boy's condition until after that feckless man had killed him."

"He banished you? But why?"

"My uncle accused me of sorcery."

"Tis' absurd. I know your good reputation and I am confident you would not involve yourself in such practices." Giraud reached out and put a hand on Jehan's shoulder. "I always say, should the people we love be stolen from us before their just time, the one sure way to have them live on is to never stop loving them."

The melancholic Black Bile ran deep in Jehan but he fortified against the tears that pricked his eyes.

"Thank you, Monsieur Giraud. That is a truth to hold dear. Little Louis *will* live on in my heart." Jehan cleared the lump from his throat before he continued. "Have you anything more for me? A letter from Amelia, perhaps?"

"Again, I am sorry, Sieur BonDurant. I have nothing. You have written twice now, have you not?"

Jehan hung his head and nodded slightly, unable to answer directly. He had hoped for better news to lift his spirits during his mourning. Instead, rejection spread through him like a tumor suffocating his spirit.

Giraud tapped a fist to his lips, then held up his forefinger. "I can only think that someone must be intercepting them, since I personally deliver the book shipments to the Commandery's contact at Pont-de-Montvert market."

"Who would that be?" Jehan asked.

"One of the novices," Giraud said pointedly. "If you bring me another letter before I head back to France, I shall hand deliver it to Commandeur Timoleon and inquire about Mademoiselle Amelia. Surely, she will write to you in return. Though it may take some months for me to make the trip there and back again."

"I am grateful for all you do for my family," Jehan said as he handed the bookseller the agreed payment of twenty livres to cover the books, the strongbox, and the extreme risk. "And I am heartily glad for this chest of coin, since I am not sure how much longer I can stay with my uncle's colony. But I do not know where I might go if I leave, since the Swiss require an affiliation."

"Perhaps you will think of returning home? There is news of a new edict authorizing the return of French Reformed Protestants on condition they convert to Catholicism within six months."

"At this point, I would gladly return home. Yet that edict does nothing to relieve my obligation to join the militia. I *refuse* to fight against innocent victims of the King's persecutions." Jehan heaved a long breath as the sour taste of dread filled his mouth. "What the King really wants is a return of the money that is pouring out of the country."

He looked to the sky, cluttered with clouds that began to block out the sun. How he wished he could talk this over with his dearest Ame. She would help him sort out his thoughts.

"I shall write to Amelia and bring the letter to you tomorrow."

"And you will stay put in Aarau till I return again?" asked Monsieur Giraud.

"Most assuredly," promised Jehan.

8 March 1698

My dearest, I long to know God preserves your health and safety, and I truly desire to hear of your welfare. So I write again to tell you that I, myself, am not in good health of spirit, nor of heart. Nor shall I be till I hear from you. No one in this foreign land will ever know the pain I endure as thick clouds constantly cover the night sky, and I search for even one small, glimmering star so that I can find my way to your heart.

My own heart bids me ever more to love you truly, over all earthly desires, and should your reason for not writing be that some harm has come to you, I could never forgive myself for leaving you behind. Should you be well, and you still love me, even merely as your friend, I ask that you find a way to reply.

I have nearly lost all hope in discovering our Eden after finding the Swiss cantons to be not at all what I had imagined. There is no more freedom of conscience here than in France. Though punishments are not as harsh, persecutions exist here as well, mostly directed at those outside of the Reformed faith. And my ink would be consumed in its entirety were I to tell tales of the many restrictions. The one that hinders me most, and comes as a great shock, is the restriction on my profession. Because I am French and a refugee, I am not permitted to practice the healing arts, which is my only passion beyond my love for you. I was told to work a trade or leave the city, so instead, I spend my days using the skills Métayer Benat taught, working as a shoemaker.

I cannot bring myself to go further afield without you, as long as I believe you still wish to join me one day. Yet my trust in your continued feelings for me hangs on a thin cord. I fear, before long, I may take leave of my senses, losing all that I have become by lowering myself to those earthly desires that I have resisted because of my love for you. Mon Ame, my soul, if you would only write to me, I would not forsake you.

CHAPTER 9

GRATEFUL FOR THE BEES

AMELIA

**1 May 1698 ~ Morning
Hospitaller Commandery, Mont Lauzère, France**

Amelia sorely missed her times in the forest, and with no word from Jehan since December, she was beginning to think her response to his letter had only pushed him away.

Hoping to bring a little spring cheer to her ill and injured patients—and lighten her own day as well—she placed a enameled earthenware vase of *muguet* on the Infirmaria's center table. She was thankful to Henriette for gathering them and to the knights who had escorted the ever-helpful novice to the woodlands. Perhaps the tiny lily of the valley blooms and colorful vase would dispel her sombre mood.

A soft breeze blew down from the open lancet windows, high above the patients' beds. Until scarcely a few weeks earlier, every window in the Commandery had been locked and shuttered against the rains and snows. And just when Amelia thought she could take no more of the confinement, *Mare Tèrra*, Mother Earth, had not disappointed in her promise of renewal, and the frères had climbed a tall ladder to resume the daily ritual of opening the leaded glass casements.

Amelia lifted her face, letting the warm, fresh air brush across her cheeks, the spring day bathing her in welcome relief after the long, tedious winter. She closed her eyes and breathed deeply, letting the verdant aromas enliven her senses.

The first of May—she could scarcely believe it had been a year since Jehan had visited her cottage near Castelbouc, bearing a bouquet of muguet. The memory tugged at her, reminding her it was time to return and check on her bees.

She approached Commandeur Timoleon, who had gathered with the attending frères around one of the patients as they conducted their morning rounds.

Timoleon looked up from across the bed, one brow raised. "Good morning, Mademoiselle Amelia. What is it?"

"Excuse me, Commandeur. The patients all seem to be settling, though some of their symptoms continue to concern me. I have been treating them with my special honey, but my stores are running low. I would like to make a trip to Castelbouc to harvest more, and to bring back the most useful herbals from my library. Can you arrange an escort?"

The Commandeur folded his arms and pursed his lips. "I hesitate. Surely honey is available elsewhere?"

"The curative properties of honey depend on the flowers that go into their making. My bees have access to the yellow *Aristolochia clematitis*, and so produce a strain that is remarkable against infection. And I know my herbals have more recipes for me to try."

"I suppose it is a necessary risk. I shall instruct my knights to say you are a novice, should you be confronted."

Amelia set her eyes directly on his. "I understand. 'Tis not entirely a fable since I have learned much during my stay here."

"Have the laundress provide you with a novice's tunic and veil, then be ready in the stables after the midday meal," Timoleon instructed. "I shall have two of my strongest young knights meet you there."

Mid-afternoon
Castelbouc Forest, Gorges du Tarn, Gévaudan, France

Warm sunlight filtered through the forest canopy, creating a prism that painted Amelia's little round cottage in dreamlike luminescence. Brambles and ferns cloaked the ancient stone while the moss-covered roof and knotted oak door aided in disguising the small abode from intruders.

She had almost forgotten the magic here in the forest around Castelbouc. The same magic that had once nearly convinced Jehan she was either féerie or Mélusine, the female spirit of sacred waters. She smiled at the memory of it. And at seeing the two typically stoic knights finally relaxing on a boulder near the brook—though their movements were awkwardly restricted by their steel armor and the swords at their hips. They laughed at Romulus and Remus, who splashed about in the water, leaping from one small pool, then another, over sparkling elfin cascades, and up to the next pool.

With her band of protectors nearby, Amelia could go about collecting the honey in peace, but first, she would gather the herbals she needed. She took her satchel from the pommel and rubbed Luisant's withers as the mare bent to eat emerald clover blanketing the forest floor. Lifting the hem of the oversized black tunic to keep it from tangling in her riding breeches, she entered the cottage.

The one-room structure was just as she had left it, although as she moved about, an accumulation of dust danced sprightly in a wedge of sunlight that squeezed in from between closed shutters. Amelia flung the shutters open, elated to be back in her little library.

As she ran her hand over the leather and parchment bindings of old tomes and manuscripts that lined the concentric shelves, she inhaled deeply and felt steeped in their ancient perfumes—of ink and vellum, of smoke and rain and snow, of spices and herbs and the sandy desert winds of the Levant. She heard the voices of her ancestors who had collected the writings over hundreds of years, encouraging her to take in the knowledge found within.

The warmth of the Holy Spirit radiated through her as she murmured a prayer of gratitude to the knights and Commandeur Timoleon for—at long last—making this visit possible.

She went about collecting a variety of her favorite herbals from the shelves, including an old recipe book left by a man some said to be one of Jehan's ancestors. Amelia ran a finger over the name inked inside the cover. *Yohanan Ben Durant.* The Jew from Aragon. Perhaps the very man who started the long line of physicians and healers in the BonDurant family.

Amelia's grandmother had recounted the legend many times of how this man had escaped into the Cévennes after the Albigensian Crusade, escorting the Trencavel children—heirs to the last Count of Carcassonne. And here in Castelbouc, they had come under the protection of Menina Elise's family for a time.

The features of her grandmother's face, now sunken and hollow from age and illness, drifted into Amelia's mind. *Menina. Poor Menina.* Her languor had increased in recent weeks, compounded by her hopelessness over her declining health.

Amelia browsed the collection of books for something that would brighten her grandmother's days until she came upon the perfect thing—an old troubadour chansonnier.

"Ah ha!"

She packed all the books into her satchel, closed up the shutters, and headed out. As she took one last look, the little cottage seemed to beg her not to leave. *I shall try to return soon*, she promised the ancestors. *'Tis not yet my time to go.*

She stepped out and locked the door, then went to the mare.

"I must still collect the honey," she said to the two knights as they rose and approached her.

The knight with cerulean blue eyes, so similar to Jehan's, gazed up from under his helmet's visor as he kneeled next to Luisant. He interlaced his fingers, holding his cupped hands for her to step into.

"I shall show you the way," Amelia said as she placed her foot into his hands and mounted.

She led them back down the path, past dwarf holm oak trees and craggy boulders covered in lichen, with the dogs staying a few paces behind the horse's heels.

The forest opened at a spot where several terraces held a steep hillside in place. The ancient stonework created level ground for the score of tree-trunk beehives scattered among poet's narcissus and unfurling maidenhair ferns.

Amelia dismounted and left Luisant to graze on wildflowers that grew along the path, then wandered over to the *bruscs*—as Menina Elise referred to the hives in her native *langue d'oc* tongue. The upright hollowed-out chestnut logs—all knotted and bumpy and weathered to a soft gray, and topped with pieces of schist for roofs—were the magical homes for Amelia's buzzing brood.

Her worries began to dissolve into the sweet-scented forest air as she recalled the first day she met Jehan. The day he had come to this very spot, nearly convinced he had arrived at a féerie village. The day his endearing naivete had charmed her, and she had felt a lightness of being as his open heart and open mind connected with hers.

She suppressed a giggle at the memory of the look on his face when he had first seen the beehives. It was true, they did resemble small forest houses belonging to elfin creatures or féerie folk, adding untold delight to the task of beekeeping.

She unloaded her supplies from the saddlebag—the jars and linen coverings, the long-stemmed white clay pipe, a pouch of tobacco for smoking the hives, and the sheer veil to protect her face as she worked. The sound of clinking glass filled the air as she removed the jars three at a time and laid them on the ground before she draped the sheer linen veil over her head.

This ritual to collect the honey was sacred to Amelia, so she paused and grounded herself, hearing the bees' gentle, penetrating hum, taking in the warm, humid aroma of honey and beeswax. Moving slowly, methodically, she removed the schist stone from two of the logs, then gently—so as not to disturb the bees—she placed one on top of the other. Next, she packed the pipe with tobacco, lit it, and waved it over the top log to calm the bees and encourage them to move into the lower log. With the first log vacated, its golden treasure was revealed, its network of combs dripping with rich honey.

She had only three jars filled and loaded into the knights' saddlebags when one of them interrupted with alarm in his voice.

"Wait, mademoiselle." Both knights grasped their sword hilts. "Do you hear that?"

Amelia froze where she stood. She felt it before she heard it. Hoofbeats. Heavy hoofbeats that shook the ground, as though a large number of men on horseback approached in a hurry. She knew before she saw them—it had to be dragoons. No one else would enter this forest at such a pace.

Pressing a hand against her ribs to still her beating heart, she refused to let fear determine the outcome of this situation. She had protection, and she knew neither the knights nor the dogs would back down should she be threatened.

Her muscles tightened as she hardened her determination to finish her task. "'Tis likely Intendant Basville's dragoons. There is no way to outrun them now. Hide in that stand of trees in readiness. I shall continue my work and see if I can reason with them."

"But, mademoiselle . . ."

"Shhhh." She raised a finger to her lips, then waved the knights into the trees to her left, just beyond the beehives. "Let us try before we risk a battle. Stay behind those brambles so they won't see you from the path, but position yourselves so you can see my signal."

They complied but looked at each other, faces distorted with disbelief and doubt.

The noise increased, rumbling like thunder during a mid-summer storm. The dogs began growling and barking.

"Stay," Amelia commanded.

Flashes of red appeared from between the trees. And within moments, the first mounted soldier appeared from around a bend in the path. Then another. And another. Clad in uniforms and trailing fatigue caps the color of brilliant flames. They were far fewer in number than she had imagined, but they were running their horses frantically, causing the immense steeds to kick up earth and moss and fallen leaves in a great tumult.

Amelia stood her ground, holding the pipe with the long stem positioned to double as a weapon. The dogs were barking wildly, ready to attack at her behest.

Charging into the clearing, the dragoons reeled their horses to a stop. One pulled hard on the reins, making his horse snort and stomp as it circled Amelia and the dogs.

She started to shrink away, panic trying to take hold, her mind cycling through the need to stay safe and small. But then she straightened and stood tall, to convince the dragoons—and herself—that she had nothing to fear.

"Where are they?" the soldier bellowed. "Where you hidin' the heretics?"

The dogs snarled, but stayed by Amelia's side.

She opened her mouth to speak, but the words had to be forced out. "I . . ." She took a deep breath, drawing on all her courage to make a show of confidence. "There are no heretics here. But you are disturbing my bees with your ruckus."

"What you say there, *Coquette*? You say you got some sweet honey." His pupils widened like a wolf who'd found its prey as he eyed her up and down. "I'll take some of that."

The pounding in Amelia's ears was deafening and the dogs' growls grew louder. She knew what the hideous brute really wanted. But she would fight with all the might God would bestow to retain her chastity. Seeing the short blunderbuss in the dragoon's belt caused her boldness to waver, her hands to tremble. She had to hold a strong vision and rely on the power of her faith.

Dear God, I trust you will protect my chastity. Let no man ever touch me without my consent.

As she backed away, the dragoon moved his horse closer, cackling and taunting her. She could almost smell the fetidness of his pock-marked face and blackened, rotting teeth.

"Monsieur! I am a holy woman with the Knights of Saint Jean."

Romulus pounced toward the dragoon, echoing her outrage with a fierce barking that caused the man's horse to snort and toss back its head.

The dragoon pulled hard on the reins, trying to keep his horse still. "Holy woman. Hah! It's no matter to the Intendant, so it's no matter to me," he said before reaching down and grabbing her upper arm.

Amelia flinched at the violent pain that shot through her arm. She curled her tongue and whistled. The knights took her cue and charged out from the brambles, swords drawn, and made their way toward her through the maze of beehives. From the corner of her eye, she saw Luisant snaking aggressively toward the attacker and his horse, trying to drive them away. Ears flat against her neck, baring her teeth and squealing, the mare stomped repeatedly at the dragoon's horse.

Time slowed to a crawl. The atmosphere thickened, making her movements seem sluggish as she looked at the dragoon's hand clasped around her arm, then at the pipe in her free hand. "Blessed archangel Michael," she cried out, her voice sounding distant and otherworldly to her ears while she raised the pipe above her head. "Be our safeguard against the wickedness and snares of the Devil!"

In an abrupt shift, time thrust forward as she swung the pipe down, jabbing the stem into the hand of the detestable soldier.

Yelling out in pain, he immediately released Amelia. His horse reared in response and he was flung violently to the ground, where the dogs circled and barked.

The other two dragoons spurred their horses. They headed toward the beehives, charging the knights who'd positioned themselves just beyond, but one of them side-swiped a stump. It teetered and fell as the dragoons slowed, trying to work their way through the hives, but another crashed to the ground. Within seconds, bees flooded out in swarms, angrily assailing the malicious riders and their innocent steeds. The men foolishly swatted at the bees, only incensing them more, and giving the knights every advantage without needing to strike a single blow.

Amelia's attacker tried to regain his footing. Her heart lurched, and she backed away. But her brave dogs wasted no time in driving him into the mayhem of buzzing and stinging and shrill cries of agony.

Amelia knew it was her chance. The knights and dogs shielded her while the bees completed their task of mercilessly sabotaging the dragoons.

She swiftly tucked the hem of the tunic into her belt and ran to Luisant. While grabbing the pommel, she flung herself up and into the saddle. Even before she could squeeze her thighs against the mare, the horse took off in a gallop. Amelia fixed her eyes on the path back to Castelbouc and held tight, the dogs at the horse's heels, the Knights following just behind, leaving the dragoons helpless against the swarms.

❧

Early Evening
Hospitaller Commandery, Mont Lauzère, France

From her seat at the writing desk, Amelia rubbed her throbbing temples and peered across the bedchamber at her grandmother. Menina relaxed in her favorite chair, enjoying the troubadour cansos with a broad smile and the fire's warm glow lighting up her face.

It was good to see her happy again, so Amelia could not bring herself to shatter that happiness by sharing the day's horrifying experience. The terror of the dragoon's attempt to violate her would be too much for her grandmother's weak heart. It was enough that she had already suffered great loss, first with the death of her husband and then her son. The fear of losing her granddaughter, as well, might take Menina's life before her time had truly come.

Desperately needing to share her feelings, Amelia wished she could be with Jehan—laying her head on his firm shoulder, feeling his warm breath brush across her forehead. He was the only one she had ever felt truly safe with. The only one she could open up to. But the notion was futile and lamenting did no good. All she could do now was put her words of pain and rage to paper and pray that the bookseller would finally come again to market after the long winter.

Amelia opened the desk drawer where she had left Jehan's cravate while changing into her novice disguise. She draped it around her neck and leaned her head down, seeking his scent. After so many months, it had grown fainter, yet it lingered still, and that gave her at least some comfort.

She wrote in haste so her grandmother wouldn't notice and inquire about the letters' contents.

Once finished, she quietly made her way down the passageway to the novices' chamber and knocked on the door. There was a quick patter of little feet and the door opened to the beaming face of little Jacquette.

"Amelia! Have you come to teach us about the herbs?"

Amelia patted the girl's nightcap. "I wish I had time for that, but I need to fetch some soup for Menina. Neither of us has yet eaten, and besides, I see you fine ladies are in your nightclothes, nearly ready for bed."

Henriette came to the door and put an arm around her little sister. "You do have a most serious look on your face, as if it is time for our studies."

Amelia forced her unwilling lips into a smile and said, "I have a letter, that is all. Will you be going to market next?"

"Yes," replied Henriette. "'Tis my week to go, but I am not sure if the bookseller will be there."

Over Henriette's shoulder, Amelia could see Griselle sitting on her bed, legs tucked up under her chemise. The girl hugged her legs, then rested her chin on her knees, glowering across the room. Taking a short breath, Amelia tried to still her reaction. She'd had enough confrontation for the day, and despite the empathy she had for Griselle, tonight was not the time for discovering what aggravated the girl so.

"If Monsieur Giraud is not there, please return it to me and we shall wait until he comes again."

Chapter 10

Chaos and Fury

Jehan

7 June 1698 ~ Mid-afternoon
Jehan's Apartment, Aarau

At long last, it had come—the first letter from Amelia since Jehan had arrived in Aarau eight long months ago. His heart bounded, knowing she was alive. He could scarcely wait for the privacy of his apartment chambers to unwrap the small book covered in parchment that concealed her correspondence.

Monsieur Giraud had arrived at market after his travels back to France, bringing Jehan this latest book delivery along with another small strongbox from André. The bookseller had profusely apologized for the delay in returning, saying he had picked up Amelia's letter from the Hospitaller's novice, Henriette, at the Pont-de-Montvert market the first week of May, but an increase in dragonnades had forced him to shelter at a local inn for a time.

As Jehan made haste through the hostel's long hallway, the bookseller's news of more persecutions created a tempest of worry that tumbled over and over in his mind. He unlocked the apartment door and, on his way to the bedchamber, uttered a quick prayer for Amelia, and his family, and all victims of the dragoons' dreadful acts. Then he stopped and raised his eyes to the heavens.

"Merciful God. I thank you for seeing this letter here safely. And I pray you will let Amelia make her way to me . . . soon."

He placed the strongbox atop his bureau then ripped through the parchment finding Giraud had chosen a small book of devotional sonnets to conceal the letter. It seemed to hint at containing what his heart most desired, a message of Amelia's devotion to their love. He took his dagger from the bureau drawer and ripped the lining with abandon, not concerned over the damage he caused. His fingers fumbled—clumsy, shaking—as he cracked the seal and unfolded the letter, leaning it toward the window to read by the gray, overcast daylight.

1 May, 1698

I intended to write to tell you of life at the commandery, but then a most horrid thing happened to me today. I can only share my feelings concerning it with you, as you know me best. I was nearly violated by a hideous dragoon as I collected honey from the hives near my cottage. The man cared nothing for the nun's garb I wore, showing no respect for my vow of chastity. My most sacred chastity. The one thing most important to me. Thanks be to God that I was under the protection of two valiant knights. I was most grateful that they assisted me, but worried senselessly the entire journey back that they might attempt the same. 'Tis all the more reason for me to stay locked behind the commandery walls in the women's quarters, safe with the others who have taken their vows to join the Order of Saint Jean. And you, my friend, should be happy you are far away from the madness here.

Stay far away. Go find that peaceful Eden and do not look back.

Jehan crumpled the letter and tossed it to the floor. His nostrils flared as he drew long, steady breaths, trying to calm himself. Confused and embittered, he paced the room, not knowing what sparked the greatest anger—the guilt that assailed him for not being there to protect her, or the sense of betrayal. The very first reply from Amelia, and she spoke of protecting her chastity, above all, without a single mention of her love for him.

Had he been tolerating his unhappy life here for nothing, laboring fifty hours a week as a shoemaker with hands now stained and blistered, and staying in Aarau for no other reason than to wait for her? And now her old promises to join him felt like nothing more than a ploy to rid herself of his desires and overtures.

Hoping some fresh air would help him think more clearly, he stepped over to the armoire and took out the lavish red velvet cape he'd purchased from Udine at Lemieux's boutique, throwing it around his shoulders. As he peered into the table mirror and tucked his lace cravate into his waistcoat, the apartment door creaked open.

"We missed you again at worship," Moyse called out as he shut the door behind him and came into the bedchamber.

"'Twas necessary to meet Monsieur Giraud at market for a shipment."

Jehan reached into the armoire for his sword belt and fastened it under his justaucorps at his hips. He removed the dagger and the sword, and while sheathing them, he watched the wrinkles on old Moyse's forehead grow deeper as his eyebrows pinched together.

"I've not seen you take out your weapons since we've arrived. I thought you knew the church consistory's moral tribunals frown on that."

"Thieves and beggars *everywhere*!" barked Jehan, not in a mood to explain his actions. He took a deep breath and rolled his eyes.

Moyse fell silent. He took a seat by the fireplace and pinched his chin, dissuaded by Jehan's hostility.

Long moments went by with no words between them, causing Jehan to feel the need to defend his behavior. Yet he hardly knew himself what motivated him other than bitterness for the entire disappointing predicament he found himself in. As though a small, unruly child had overtaken his soul, everything in him cried out to rebel against these restrictions. When he continued his vindication, he couldn't seem to refrain from some bitter sarcasm.

"Have you not heard? As the Pasteur says in his sermons to stir up fear in the population, 'evil lurks *everywhere*!' But I tell you, the consistory is looking in the wrong place, if they are looking to find it in me."

"'Tis not like you, Jehan. You are always the one who sees the good in the world. We are worried about you."

"We? Do you mean to say Uncle Barjon?"

"Well, I am worried that you seem so unhappy here. But Pasteur Barjon is worried for your soul. And for the reputation of his church. You never attend weekday worship, and we rarely see you on Sundays."

Jehan's head began to ache from contempt for Pasteur Barjon's lack of courage. His uncle had sunk low in using Moyse to send his berating message.

Knowing Moyse was only the messenger, Jehan laid a hand on his cousin's shoulder and said in a gentler tone, "The rules of governance say at least one member per household should attend. So since you and I, together, make up this household, I'd say your attendance is more than sufficient for us both."

"Though you know that's not enough to please Pasteur Barjon."

"Nothing is ever enough for him," Jehan said, clutching his forehead to ease the pain. "He can make a request to the church's moral tribunal that I be required to appear, but the worst they can do is admonish me before the congregation. The city magistrates are the ones with the real power."

He took his hat from a hook on the wall. "I'll take my leave now to see Mademoiselle Schuler at Lemieux's boutique. She is to take my measure for a new ensemble."

Moyse rose from the chair and picked up the hem of Jehan's cape, brushing his thumb over the crimson velvet. "'Tis also not like you to desire such finery. Don't know where you get the coin for such things."

"I just received another shipment from cousin André, from the sale of my properties. So my savings have grown. And ever since I started crafting shoes for the *cordonnier*, my earnings have been enough to pay for lodging and food without depleting my cash assets."

Jehan studied Moyse's own threadbare work coat and breeches. "I can pay for new attire for you as well."

"You know the Pasteur would disapprove," Moyse said with a frown. "We are to keep to simple styles. I heard him threaten to turn you into the magistrates for this flamboyant clothing you now wear."

"Once again, Uncle is misleading you if he says the magistrates will punish us for our choice in clothing. Their opinion on the matter is not in alignment with the church. The magistrates *want* us to purchase new clothing, to support the tradespeople. The *couturiers* would be out of business should the entire town wear nothing but gray and black wool with no embellishments. And since most of the tradespeople are French, that would put most of Uncle's congregants out of work. It makes no sense whatsoever."

Moyse raised his bushy brows and nodded in agreement. "Yes. I see your point."

Jehan patted him on the shoulder. "Now then, as I said, I'm off to see Udine. I shall tell her to add your new garments to my account, should you change your mind."

"Udine? You use her forename now?" Moyse shook his head with hesitation, but his judgement was apparent. "Jehan, you are showing such interest in her these days. What about Mademoiselle Amelia?"

Jehan cleared his throat, endeavoring to quell the underlying resentment that would manifest in his words if he were not careful. "She has finally written, and it seems she is to join the Order of Saint Jean, which I do not understand. She always said she would never vow to anyone but the Holy Spirit, so why would she vow to the Hospitallers?"

Moyse's eyes soften with empathy, and it loosened a flood of deep feelings in Jehan that he'd sealed up inside.

"She will forever be my dearest friend," he said, a quiver resonating in his hushed voice. "But I no longer have hope that she might one day love me in the way I love her. It seems certain she no longer plans to join me in the search for our Eden."

"Are you sure that is what she meant? That she would never join you?" asked Moyse. "Perhaps she is simply waiting for you to settle in this Eden place you seek, and then join you."

"I believe that *is* what she meant. She told me to go find my Eden . . . and never look back."

Late Afternoon
Monsieur Lemieux's Boutique, Aarau

Unsure of Udine's intentions, Jehan stood dumbstruck watching her hand move toward his breeches.

She giggled and placed it on his sword scabbard and traced a finger up its length. "*Meine Güte*, Herr BonDurant. *Das* rapier *ist* splendid."

He laughed with her, his taut shoulders melting. Curious and intrigued at where her attentions and his pent-up impulses might lead them, he was glad for the privacy of the boutique's small but well-appointed private salon.

"*Und* now, with new ensemble, you show people your status," she said, then reached over toward a stand brimming with walking sticks and pointed to a rather expensive-looking sort with a brass lion's head. "You should also purchase *spazierstock.*"

Jehan took another long draw of wine from a crystal goblet as she stood behind him holding a long strip of paper, measuring from sternum to spine. It was a bit unsettling to have a woman, other than Amelia, touching him in this way, and was precisely the reason he had stalled in ordering a new ensemble. But now that it was clear Amelia had in mind a future that could not include him, he would allow himself to take pleasure in Undine's forwardness and flirtations.

As she reached around and marked the paper with a graphite stick, putting soft pressure against his chest, his heart rate quickened and he took a long breath. His hands yearned to reach out to the golden curls cascading down her cheeks and set her hair free from its coif.

"Now arm," she said, moving in front of him. She tossed his dark hair back behind his shoulder, brushing the tender skin on his neck, then took ahold of his hand and lifted it.

The spot where she had touched him tingled as if calling for more attention. With each move she made, the aroma of rose water filled the air, reminding him of Amelia's sweet scent. The memory was like a sharp taloned golden eagle trying to light on his shoulder, and still he couldn't take his eyes from Udine's bust, spilling from the top of a tightly fitting stomacher and only slightly hidden behind the sheer silk scarf tucked into it. His eyes followed her long curves, elegant as a swan, to the small of her waist, and he felt stirrings of desire rise through his body.

When Udine finished measuring his arm, she took a cushion from the brocade-covered settee and lowered to her knees. "Inseam," she said, looking up from under her lashes with a coquettish smile.

She pinched the paper measuring strip between her outstretched fingers and moved them close between his legs.

Jehan tried to keep his composure, but his mind fogged with urges. Blood rushed to his natural parts as her fingers brushed them for a quick moment.

He swallowed, trying to regain his poise and force out the words, "Do you not . . . already have my measurements."

She stood and faced him, revealing bright eyes and a playful smile. "I only measure for cape last time. And you adding *das gewicht*. Err . . . heft."

"Heft?" He fought a compulsion to look down at his groin.

"*Ja*. Heft from much drinking."

Jehan took a deep breath. He couldn't seem to control his drinking any more than he could control this craving that Udine stirred in him.

"The drinking . . . it helps me get through my days. I can find no pleasure in the restrictions Pasteur Barjon tries to place over me. And now my dearest friend, who I thought would join me here, seems to no longer have interest."

Udine set her measuring strip on a side table and looked at Jehan with compassion in her eyes. "Others also *unzufrieden* with how Pasteur leads."

"*Unzufrieden?*"

"Not happy. We have group who meet now. Every week. We study new ideas. Perhaps you join us. There is meeting tonight."

"Non-conformist ideas? Are you dissenters?"

"Could say this word . . . dissenters. But many go still to Reformed *stadtkirche*. Some French refugees moved to Brandenburg, but returned. For lack of good wine. And brought back new ideas. They explain better."

"I am ready for any ideas that allow us to choose our own path. Yes, I shall join you."

She laid her hands gently against his chest. His heart pulsed as she rose on her tiptoes and leaned up toward his ear, whispering, "Good, then. I be pleased for time together."

As she began to pull back, her lips lightly caressed his jaw, triggering an impulse to kiss her. He leaned his head down toward her, but the *glockenspiel* outside chimed, and she slipped out from under him.

"Come. We go now," she said, heading for the door.

Lockentopf Coffeehouse, Aarau

Udine threaded her arm around Jehan's and led him through the crowded coffeehouse—filled with trails of white pipe smoke and chattering patrons playing tables games—to a large table in the dimly lit rear corner.

Seated around the table were a dozen or so men and one woman, all dressed in exquisite high fashion clothing, their faces bathed in soft yellow candlelight. They were engaged in ardent conversation that appeared to be fueled by the wine and coffee drinks set before them.

As Jehan and Udine moved in the direction of the table, he leaned close to her and asked, "Are these people also of noble birth?"

"Oh, *nein*. Some work *haute couture* trades, make stockings, hats. One *ist* locksmith, and one make fine swords and daggers with gems. We all earn good money."

Jehan wondered if this group lived by a different set of morals than most in their colony, with their daring clothing and partaking in wine outside of the hours designated by the consistory.

He leaned near to Udine's ear to inquire discreetly. "I see many of the patrons here ignoring Pasteur Barjon's rules."

"*Ja*. We need be free. To live in joy," she said, wiggling up against him. "Is why we meet."

A knot began to form in his belly—his wild imaginings picturing Udine free and easy with this table full of handsome men.

"Who else in this group do you measure in the way you measured me? Or is it all of them?"

Udine's eyes narrowed. "Shush. *Nein*," she said, then pressed her lips together and waved her hand in dismissal.

She took a step closer to the table and interrupted the conversation. "Pardon, *Herren und Dame. Herr* BonDurant joins us. Also from Cévennes, like some of you. Tell him what we discuss."

Jehan tipped his hat. "Yes, I am most interested in your new ideas."

"Well then, welcome, fellow Cévenol," said the eldest man in the group, raising his clay pipe in a salute. From the auburn hair sprinkled with gray that peeked out from his powdered *perruque*, the man appeared to be nearing fifty years. Despite his age, his round face still had a warm, amiable glow.

"Antoine Aigoin, hatmaker, from Ribaute," he said, bowing his head. He moved his free hand gracefully around the table as he made introductions. "Our other Cévenols . . . Luc Dodet, locksmith, and his wife, Elaine."

The couple appeared to be nearing their thirties, just about the age of Jehan's cousin André and his wife Lucrèce, with the same dark brown hair common to Cévenols.

Udine nudged against Jehan's shoulder. "Come. We sit."

They pulled two chairs up to the table, then Antoine continued. "And we have our friend here from Paris, Etienne Roussel. And our young ones," he said, pointing to the three men close to Jehan's age. "Like you, they are eager to learn new religious and philosophical ideas. We have Etienne's brother, Mathieu Roussel. The Roussels are glovemakers. And Constantin Eschalier, stockingmaker. And . . ."

The last young man jumped up before Antoine could introduce him. His raven black hair, dark skin, and deep brown eyes set him apart from the others as he offered a formal bow with a lively flourish of the hand. "Jacques Corbell, at your service, Sieur BonDurant. I am a cutler, should you need to repair that stunning dagger you wear or commission serving pieces for your table."

Jehan dipped his head to each of them while laying a hand over the dagger, hoping not to explain the Moorish and Hebrew engravings.

"We are all equals here," said Antoine. "So now that we've had our introductions, we shall use our forenames. And yours is . . .?"

"Jean Pierre. Yet please call me Jehan."

"Very good, Jehan. We gather here because we believe free will is the most important gift God gives to humanity, allowing us to seek Divine grace as a deliberate choice while still allowing us to remain individuals."

"That is precisely my belief." Jehan let out a long breath with a sigh of relief. There was an expansiveness in his chest that had not been there for such a long, long time. Not since the times he had spent with Amelia, soaking in new knowledge and meditating in the forest alongside her.

The flaxen-haired Mathieu Roussel leaned in, his gray-blue eyes growing large and sparkling with eagerness. "Antoine and Luc and Elaine have recently returned from Brandenburg and have brought ideas both old and new from their great philosophers . . . Böhme, Arndt, and Spener."

"I am acquainted with none of these names," said Jehan.

Mathieu smiled and raised his eyes to the heavens with a wistful expression. "They speak of a mystical union between the believer and Christ."

"I most enjoy their writings on spiritual rebirth and renewal," Elaine added.

Corbell's look was more sullen as he spoke. "What I find most important is the tenet these philosophers teach on the sympathetic and kindly treatment of unbelievers . . . Jews, Saracens, Buddhists, anyone actually, from any faith. And I have heard that the younger Swiss theologians have supported this notion in their lectures, demonstrating how Christianity rejects the use of forced religion."

"That sounds like a most rational tenet. 'Tis sorely needed in our world and is one I can surely stand behind," Jehan said, his voice effused with praise.

"We can no longer abide by the stiff, hair-splitting doctrines of the older pasteurs," said Corbell. "They only create divisions among the people."

Jehan felt Udine slide her hand onto his thigh, and every sensation narrowed to that one point of contact. The heat of her hand radiated up his leg, and he shifted, crossing his legs to stop the progression.

He tried to focus on the conversation, but every time she murmured in agreement with the others or moved her hand, a blaze rushed through his body. His mind longed to follow the ideological discussions and solutions for putting humility and love at the forefront of religion, but his body had other ideas.

The talk continued on to subjects of individual devotion and piety, but when she leaned in closer to whisper something in his ear—her breath warm and moist on his neck—he thought he could take no more. The scent of her skin was intoxicating, and he couldn't resist the temptation any longer.

He stood, sliding his sword belt so that the hilt and scabbard hid his virility. "Twas a pleasure to join all of you tonight. I must take my leave now," he said, then turned to Udine. "I may have left something important at the boutique." He hoped she would understand his urgency and that his inquisitive gaze would be enough for her to read.

She smiled indulgently and rose to join him, entwining her arm around his. "*Ja*, you did. We go back."

They stepped into the fading evening light, a mass of clouds swirling overhead in the balmy summer air. Jehan looked around for the first place that offered some discretion.

"There," he tipped his head toward a parked carriage. He took her hand, and they ran around to the far side of it, out of the street lantern's light, out of the view of meddling passersby.

He pulled her close, no longer fighting the urge to press himself against her. She tipped back her head, and he wrapped her face in his hand, running his thumb over her flushed lips.

A crack of thunder split the air and shook the ground below them.

"Quick," she said, and pulled him in the direction of the boutique.

They rushed along the cobbles as the sky burst forth with a torrent of warm rain, slowing their progress, the wetness of his rain-soaked clothes nourishing the almost painful anticipation.

When they reached the door to the boutique, she turned and flung her arms around his neck, their wet lips meeting in a fiery kiss. She pulled a key from her pocket and unlocked the door in haste. They nearly tumbled into the foyer, kissing as they moved into the salon, hands reaching, grabbing, fondling.

Once in the room, she broke free from Jehan's embrace to bolt the door, then rushed to draw the draperies closed.

While she stepped away, Jehan's mind tried to thwart his body, reminding him he wanted his first time to be with Amelia. But it was never to be, so he threw off his hat, weapons, justaucorps, overcoat, and boots with chaos and fury, scattering them about.

Udine tossed off her coif and spread herself across the settee, raising her skirts high above her ankles. Jehan moved to her and could smell the heady muskiness of her damp hair, making him dizzy with desire. He put one knee on the settee and leaned over her, combing his fingers through her hair, then tracing along her neck, feeling the heat emanating from her. His hands roamed the fascinating contours of her body, and she responded eagerly, her own desire matching his.

She reached up and pulled off his chemise, her hands coaxing, caressing, persuading his breeches to the floor, then she lifted her skirts higher and pulled him to her.

As they moved together, lost in passion and desire, it was as though nothing else existed in the world except for their two bodies joined as one. Jehan closed his eyes and in the moment of release, all his worries, every last thought, disappeared into an abyss. Everything but the angelic face of his true love. He could not keep the words from flowing from his lips. "Mon Ame. Ame, my love."

CHAPTER II

THE WEIGHT OF SECRETS

AMELIA

**6 July 1698 ~ Late Evening
Hospitaller Commandery, Mont Lauzère, France
Infirmiria**

Sporadic moans echoed off the Infirmaria's solid walls, creating the most lamentable sounds Amelia had heard in all her time at the commandery. She and Cavalier paused at the bedside of a young shepherd, one of nearly a dozen Huguenot assemblers who had arrived with injuries. The young man drifted in merciful sleep while novices scurried about, lighting rushlights and candles to provide light to work by.

The sharp smell of blood filled Amelia's nostrils when she leaned over to set a stoneware bowl of clean water on the bedside table.

Cavalier drew close to her and whispered, "He sleeps from exhaustion. The wound is to his arm."

"Is he the last of the injured?"

"For now," he responded as he removed his dirt-stained hat, his long sandy hair falling about his smudged face. He wiped beads of perspiration from his forehead with his sleeve, then gripped the hat tightly to his chest. "I pray the Intendant will stop ordering these dragoon attacks on the secret assemblies.

There was some relief after the incident you experienced in May. But . . . 'Tis worse than ever now. They are ravaging the houses, and carrying off furniture, and grain stores, and even cattle, intent on finding Pasteur Brousson."

Amelia recalled the charismatic Claude Brousson from the first assembly she had attended a few years earlier. It was his encouragement of fanaticism that had the Children of God stockpiling weapons in recent years.

"He is back in the country, then?"

"He is. Defying the edicts that ban all Reformed pasteurs and trying to incite his flock to retaliate against the persecutions. He reminds them daily of the pain and losses they have endured, yet spares not a moment on healing their souls. 'Tis creating a vicious cycle that drives my people to madness."

Amelia knew this sense of madness—a sharp blow that would assail her from nowhere while blending salves or tisanes, or thrust her awake from a sound sleep. The deep wound to her spirit had barely begun to heal since the dragoon attack at her cottage.

She dropped a linen towel into the water bowl and spread another on the table, then assembled her tools on top.

"How did this latest attack happen?" she asked as she rolled back the young shepherd's sleeve to examine the wound on his forearm. Several blunderbuss pellets had grazed his arm, ripping through his chemise and tearing open the skin.

Cavalier stepped closer, peering over her shoulder to observe the wound. "We were fleeing a dragoon raid upon a secret assembly in the woods outside of Florac. Most everyone escaped while our band of sentries distracted the dragoons. We scattered up a cliff, too steep for their horses, to a ledge. But there simply was not enough tree coverage to prevent injuries. We had to lie still and deceive them into thinking they had killed us all. Then it was a matter of waiting them out." He paused and scuffed a boot on the floor. "Augh! I should have done a better job at protecting my people."

Cavalier's exclamation caused the young shepherd to stir, but he did not open his eyes.

Amelia placed a hand on Cavalier's shoulder. "'Twas a very brave effort, and it is to your merit that these people made it here in time. There has been some blood loss, but they should all recover."

Cavalier spread his arms open and looked toward the heavens. "Thanks be to God!"

The jubilation roused the young shepherd from his dozing. He blinked a few times and cleared his throat. "'Twas *your* courage that got us here, Cavalier."

Amelia steepled her hands together, hoping to give her friend some reassurance that his efforts were of worth. "Yes, thanks be to *you*, my friend. For the Holy Spirit needs a willing heart to inspire such courage. Your work is done for now, and you can get some rest. The frères will arrange for a bed in the dormitory."

"Are you sure you don't need my help?"

She saw worry in his fatigued eyes and knew he needed a task. For his equilibrium, if nothing else. "It would be of great benefit were you to seek solace in the chapel, where you can pray for your comrades."

Cavalier nodded, then made his way out, his steps labored and weary.

Amelia felt around the shepherd's wounds as gently as she could. "A few of these pellets are lodged in the tissue. I shall need to remove them."

"*Deman es dolor?* Pardon . . . will it be painful?" The young man's chin quivered as he spoke.

"I understand *langue d'oc*, should it be easier for you."

He shook his head as tears of anguish glistened in his eyes.

"'Twill not be nearly as painful as if infection takes hold." She reached to the bedside table and filled an earthenware mug from a squat, dark-glass jug of wine. "Here, my friend, fortify. Then bite on this," she said, handing him the wine and a small wooden rod.

She wrung the water from the linen towel and cleaned the crusted blood on his arm. Using a long-handled probe with a sharp, hooked end, she carefully removed several pellets. At each extraction, the young man flinched, groaning slightly as he bore down on the rod.

"There," she said. "The hard part is done. Now I am going to blend a honey poultice for pain and inflammation. "'Twill do a fine job of keeping the wounds from festering."

While Amelia worked, the novice, Griselle, came by with a basket of new linen towels she had woven, laying one at the foot of each patient's bed.

Amelia laid a hand on the girl's basket to stop her. "Would you please leave me a few more? I shall need another to clean off this poultice later."

Griselle slowly pulled away, her brooding eyes not meeting Amelia's, then tossed a handful of towels on the bed. She clenched her teeth and hissed, "I saw the two of you," hurrying off before Amelia could make sense of her words.

"What? Grise . . ." Amelia clucked her tongue in frustration, knowing she had no time to chase after her.

She thought for a moment. *The two of you? Ah, Cavalier.* The girl had always seemed quite jealous over him. Even so, surely there was something more that troubled her.

Amelia turned back to her work, laying on the poultice, then coiled a strip of linen bandaging around the young man's forearm, pausing to place a word amulet with ancient *charakteres* and prayers under the last layer.

The wound wasn't very deep, but the terrors the young shepherd had witnessed made his hands tremble, so a prayer for healing his courage and spirit, as well as his body, was needed. She held her hands just above the area of the injury and silently mouthed the ancient Hebrew words for 'I speak the blessing', then recited the *Pater Noster* out loud, hoping the young man would feel God's presence.

She was so focused on her task that she did not notice Commandeur Timoleon until he stood beside her.

"I ran into Monsieur Jean Giraud, the bookseller, while in Pont-de-Montvert this morning. He arrived a few days ahead of market."

Amelia's heart leapt. Months had gone by since she had received a letter from Jehan. The fête for Saint Jean's day had come and gone. And she had made her annual pilgrimage to Sainte-Baume for the celebration of Marie de Magdala, safely escorted by Timoleon and his knights, and still there had been no word.

"Did Giraud have a letter for me?" she said as she hastily wiped her hands on a clean towel.

"No. However, he inquired about your well being. He tells me he's received only one letter from you to deliver in all these months, and wonders if that's the reason Jehan stopped writing to you. I thought you had written him several times."

"I have. Three times now. I do not understand." Amelia bit her bottom lip while her thoughts froze. The room seemed to close in, becoming a blurry outline. She gripped the towel to her breast while thoughts of betrayal swept in, the fear trying to push her off course.

"I . . . I gave them to Griselle to take to market. Except for the one, which I gave to Henriette. Do you think Griselle could be giving them to the wrong bookseller? That might endanger us all."

Commandeur Timoleon narrowed his eyes and held his chin between his forefinger and thumb. "I know of no other bookseller who will hazard coming up to the mountains. 'Tis more likely that she failed to deliver them. You should speak to

Griselle. Since we have no answers as of yet, let us not make our troubles worse by fretting before we know what they are."

Timoleon's steady, confident voice reassured Amelia. She knew she could not let her thoughts go down a destructive path. In spite of that knowledge, it was easy to see evil everywhere while living in a land where fear and intolerance had taken over.

She took an anchoring breath. Surely, there were answers. Surely, Griselle had meant no ill will.

"Yes. Your wisdom holds an important truth, Commandeur."

"'Tis you who preaches the power of our words, mademoiselle. I am simply reminding you of your own wisdom."

"Your stoicism is to be admired. Thank you for keeping me on course," Amelia said, bowing her head in appreciation. "I shall have a talk with her then. Perhaps Monsieur Giraud is simply forgetting."

"I believe she will appreciate your attentions. We still have a big task at hand with so many wounded, so I shall find one of the frères to relieve you while you speak to her. I suspect she is simply keeping the letters for herself. But should that be the case, it will *not* be tolerated."

"I realize there must be consequences," said Amelia. "But perhaps it could be an opportunity for her to learn from her mistakes . . . if the punishment is not too harsh. I believe there is something deep troubling her."

"Very well. Inform me if you find any reason that I should be involved," he said as he turned toward the refectory.

Amelia scanned the room for the girl, checking at each of the patient's bedside, until she heard the scrape of metal against metal. She turned to see Griselle in the doorway, pulling back the heavy, woven wool curtain.

Amelia murmured to herself, "She must have heard us."

The girl hesitated in the doorway and turned back around, her face gone ashen with dread. Amelia motioned to Griselle, but she flinched and quickly drew the curtain back across the iron rod. As the curtain stilled, the rough gray-brown hem of her tunic protruded against the deep red brocade—a telltale sign that she still hovered just outside the Infirmaria. Either she was afraid of being punished, or wanted to eavesdrop, or both.

Novices's Dormitory

Griselle backed against the wall near her bed. "I told you already. I gave your letters to the bookseller, just as you asked," she said, defending herself in a loud, indignant tone that echoed through the novice's dormitory. She folded her arms across her chest, lowering her head and glaring at Amelia.

"You have nothing to fear, as long as you are truthful," said Amelia. "Even if it takes you a bit to recall the truth. Should you have something to confess, it is best you share it with me. I shall ask the Commandeur not to punish you, and you can pray for God's grace and forgiveness."

Griselle pinched her lips together and shook her head, not saying a word. Her dark eyes were like a lead casket trying to conceal her true thoughts. But Amelia could see behind the stubborn face to the scared little girl who had likely faced something painful and horrifying.

Amelia took a step closer and held out her hand. "Griselle, no one here is your enemy. We all risk the wrath of the Intendant and his blundering dragoons, Reformed and Catholic alike. Let us be grateful that we live together, here in this stronghold with the knights, and work hand-in-hand to stay safe from our common enemy."

Griselle raised her head a bit, the apprehension still fixed in her eyes but her arms loosened their defensive grip across her chest. "You would still let me work with you?"

Still? Was it a sign that Griselle had committed some sort of misdeeds? It was not yet clear to Amelia if it concerned the letters. She realized her own inaction tinged the situation. She had been promising the girl more lessons in the healing arts, but had been distracted by her sadness over Jehan's departure and tending to Menina Elise.

A wave of guilt tightened Amelia's chest as Griselle stared at her with a deep sadness in her eyes. She could tell the girl was not ready for confessions, so perhaps showing her what trust looked like would help her understand its rewards.

Amelia stretched out her hand again and signaled. "Come with me. I shall show you how to blend the honey poultice. We have nearly a dozen wounded patients who need it to prevent infection, and I cannot keep up. I could use your help."

Griselle's dark eyes brightened. Her face grew luminous and tender, transforming her into an entirely different creature. Perhaps all the girl needed was a purpose and a little love. With so many ill and injured to tend to, Amelia knew she had to let go of the worry over Jehan's letters.

CHAPTER 12

REFUGEES MUST GO

JEHAN

7 February 1699
Lockentopf Coffeehouse, Aarau

Jehan leapt over a vast, foul-smelling puddle murky from animal dung, just one of many that deluged the streets of Aarau since the onset of February. He questioned if any living thing could thrive in this dismal climate. So wet and cold, it certainly contributed to the lingering darkness that pooled inside his disenchanted heart.

With this relentless icy rain, he could never seem to control his convulsive shivering. Despite the tallow and beeswax coating on his boots, the water seeped in, day after day, chilling his toes until they were numb. And his fanciful cape did little to keep him dry. He much preferred January's clear days after an evening snowfall rendered everything crisp and bright. At least his visits to the vibrant, scintillating Lockentopf coffeehouse offered a respite from the dreariness.

He quickened his pace through a driving rain that pelted his back, narrowly arriving at the coffeehouse in time for his weekly meeting with his non-conformist friends.

Stepping inside, he removed his hat and cape, then shook off the rain that was making a muss of his fine clothing.

He was grateful for the heat that promised to dispel the chill in his bones. It radiated from the blazing hearth and the generous candlelight and the bodies of patrons packed in every corner of the room. Thankfully, the penetrating aroma of coffee drinks and pipe smoke dulled the abhorrent odors often found in a crowd.

He secured his belongings on an empty wall hook and saw Jacques Corbell—'the Raven', as Jehan had fondly dubbed him for his dark blue-black hair—waving from their usual table at the far end of the room. Their friendship always made for a bright spot on dreary days. The young cutler's unwavering way of welcoming everyone made Jehan's life in Aarau more tolerable—alongside these thought-provoking meetings invariably followed by a descent into sinful oblivion with Udine.

As Jehan made his way through the chattering patrons, Mathieu Roussel chuckled loudly and crowed across the room, "You are late, BonDurant."

Mathieu, the younger of the two Roussel glovemakers from Paris, had also become a good comrade. And the three often met between the weekly meetings to pass the long winter nights.

When Jehan approached his freethinking friends, their faces aglow from the table's stout candle, he saw Daniel Isnard from the refugee group was also in attendance.

Jehan bowed his head. "Daniel Isnard. It has been a long while."

"Pleasure to see you, Jehan." Daniel dipped his head in return. "Perhaps we'd see more of one another if my brother and I had our own apartment in the grand hostel with you, and the Pasteur, and the other noblesse."

The inequalities in the colony's housing assignments did not make Jehan happy either, but he knew Daniel had a respectable room at Monsieur Malbois' hatmaking atelier, far better accommodations than those on the last rung who slept in dormitories at the old Ursuline monastery. Jehan could let himself feel disdain, but could not let himself feel guilt over a policy which he had no control over.

"Believe me . . . living in an apartment so near my uncle has its drawbacks. So, have you come to open your horizons on spiritual and philosophical teachings, or just to escape the confines of your room at Monsieur Malbois' *chapellerie*?"

"Both. Malbois is still not happy that Anne Broussard left with Stéphane and the Roma couple, so to this day, he takes out his vexation on us."

Jehan looked around the table, realizing that Udine had not arrived. Their trysts had become such an intoxicating habit, yet they meant little to his heart. Even when he tried, he could never evoke the same deep love that he still held for Amelia.

He considered discreetly asking after Udine, but in truth, he would be happy to settle for some pleasant conversation with the others.

"We are ready to start," said Antoine Aigoin, adjusting his powdered perruque. "Jehan, where is Udine?'

A flush heated Jehan's face. He floundered for a moment, surprised and somewhat embarrassed that Antoine had come to think of them as a couple.

"Pardon, but I have no knowledge of her whereabouts," he mumbled, hoping the penny-royale tisane she'd requested to bring on her menses was not making her ill.

Jehan held his sword close to his side so he could edge his way around the table to where Luc Didot and his wife, Elaine, sat. Surely she would know more about Udine. Jehan came to stand behind them and leaned in.

"She has been delayed, Jehan," Elaine whispered before he could ask his question. "But she is well."

Apparently, his relationship with Udine was no longer the secret he had thought it to be.

"She may not attend tonight since Lemieux is keeping her rather busy as of late. You do realize . . . we must keep our employers happy," she said, raising one eyebrow then gazing at her husband.

Jehan was not at all sure what she meant by that, but there was no time, nor the privacy, for questioning Elaine, so he moved around past her and took an empty chair between Corbell and the stocking maker, Constantin.

Antoine placed a hand on his chin for a moment and scanned everyone at the table. There was a look of deep concern on his usually jovial face. "We've important news this evening." He paused and looked around again while taking a draw on his long-stemmed white clay pipe.

Etienne Roussel grumbled, "Out with it, Antoine."

Antoine pursed his lips, then spoke slowly, as if trying to choose his words carefully. "The Swiss officials announced just today that with the widespread harvest failures . . . many of the French must be prepared . . ."

Etienne huffed at Antoine's delay. "Prepared for what? Tell us!"

"To . . . to move on . . . by July."

"What?" Etienne pounded a fist on the table.

Elaine and Constantin both gasped, and a general mumbling around the table grew louder.

Antoine's mention of '*many* of the French' puzzled Jehan, and he wondered if any of the others had heard it. "Who, exactly, must move on? You said *many*, but you did not say *all*. How will the officials determine which of us is to go?"

"Those who have the means to support themselves, without working, may stay. Those who have set up manufacturing businesses . . . the atelier and boutique owners . . . will be awarded special status as residents and be allowed to stay."

Loud rumblings of discontent interrupted Antoine. He inhaled deeply, letting out a huge breath of frustration as he spoke over them. "Please, let me finish. Those of us who are highly skilled in these manufacturing trades and earn a good living will be allowed to stay. The dressmakers, hatmakers, stocking makers, shoemakers, watchmakers. But should a Swiss citizen come along who has the same level of skill, we may be asked to leave."

Jehan's pulse quickened. Unlike his friends, the officials would not consider him a highly skilled shoemaker, since he had less than a year's experience. He poured himself a glass of wine to steady his nerves while his mind spun off on all the worse scenarios. Likely there were many Swiss citizens with far more skill that could replace him, so he'd soon be without steady income. The officials could not banish him immediately, as long as he still had means to support himself—but at some point, his assets might run out.

He took a drink of wine, and then two more, settling his immediate reaction. He reminded himself it mattered little if he stayed in Aarau. With Amelia no longer planning to join him, there was no need to stay close to France to wait for her. He may as well travel to the far reaches of the earth and explore new places where tolerance and peace were a way of life.

Etienne tilted his head, and a corner of his mouth lifted into a wry half smile. "You have not mentioned the pasteurs. Most of them rely on charity. What about Pasteur Barjon?"

Antoine said nothing at first, packing more tobacco into his pipe and lighting it with the candle before he responded. "Essentially, anyone who cannot support themselves without aid is being asked to leave. Old men, widows and their children, the sick, the unskilled or uneducated. And yes, Etienne, Pasteur Barjon as well. Which I see makes you rather pleased."

"Does," Etienne said with a slow, contented nod. "I think even the Swiss would find his rules too restrictive had he been their pasteur."

Mathieu Rossell leaned his arms onto the table to join the conversation. "Now that the money from his wife's family has run out, the locals are saying he and his family are just a brood of worthless mouths to feed."

Jehan felt his stomach cringe a little. He did not care for his uncle's oppressive restrictions, either, but he would never call his uncle's family worthless. Each and every one of his cousins and their mother were dear to Jehan, despite only seeing them in passing.

"Well . . ." Etienne began. "I don't think I'll stay around, just the same. I still hear talk of Lord Galway's resettlement project in Irelande and rumors of something called the Carolana project."

A gravelly voice came from over Jehan's shoulder that he recognized.

"That Irelande project has come to an end."

Jehan turned in a start. The once golden hair had gone even more gray than Jehan remembered, and a new series of smaller scars now intersected the large one on his cheekbone. But it was unquestionably the tenacious refugee guide, Massip.

"I thought you were back in the Cévennes for the winter," said Jehan.

"I dared not stay after the Intendant's men captured Pasteur Claude Brousson and had him executed."

Jehan's shoulders tensed at the shocking news. The others passed incredulous looks with animated eyes, and Elaine touched her fingers to her parted lips, displaying utter shock.

With Brousson gone, Jehan wondered what it would mean for the Cévenol Huguenots, since the pasteur had been the one pushing them to take up their weapons. Would they quit stockpiling arms, or fight in retaliation? It had to be nearing a tipping point, if it hadn't already. It made Jehan thankful to know his beloved Ame was safe at the Hospitaller commandery.

"I must say, I never expected to learn any of *this* news tonight," said Daniel Isnard. "I thought we would talk about new manners for connecting with the Divine."

"None of us did," said Antoine. "When did it happen, Massip?"

"Early November, just as I was returning."

"So, what has caused the Irelande project to end?" asked Etienne.

"I've heard told," said Massip as he pulled up a chair and leaned an elbow on the table, "that despite the donations and funding to aid the refugees, Lord Galway found the lack of open land an insurmountable obstacle. There is not one inch of land which does not belong to someone, whether as landlord or tenant."

"In this vast world we live in, there must be someplace where land is available," Jehan said.

Massip nodded in agreement. "You are still seeking your Eden then, are you?"

"I am," Jehan replied. "I feel it in my core that there must be a place where freedom to choose is an absolute tenet for all men and women."

Massip stood and pushed in the chair. "I shall keep you all informed if I hear of any new resettlement projects. And please do likewise. I need to see that my wife is safely moved on to a new home. She's been told she has little value as a cook for the hostels, since they will be shut down soon."

"Agreed," said Jehan. "I, for one, will be alert to any new opportunities."

Jehan thought of how much had shifted in all of their lives in one short day and of the choices they would each be forced to make. He was determined that his own choice would reflect his hopes—and not his fears.

CHAPTER 13

TAINTED TRUTHS

AMELIA

1 March 1699
Hospitaller Commandery, Mont Lauzère, France

It had been a dark and endless winter at the Hospitaller's manoir after the news of Pasteur Claude Brousson's execution. Driving mists had caused the walls to run damp and seep like the tears that trickled down the faces of the peasants and shepherds mourning his death.

After Yuletide, when the frosts and snow had stiffened the grasses and hardened the earth, Brousson's followers had also hardened their hearts, growing more resentful and inclined to join the young people in their brewing rebellion. When they came to Amelia seeking cures to relieve their sorrows, she tried as best she could to reason with them that their intentions of malice and violence could never be the answer.

As spring approached, the Intendant's passion for ridding the land of Huguenot pasteurs seemed to be quelled, and a fragile peace returned to the Cévennes mountains, allowing people to move about safely once again and bringing hope to many.

The day had finally come when the snows melted and Timoleon agreed to let Amelia make a trip to market, unescorted. Eager to set out, her lifeblood quickened and coursed through her veins. She drew up the voluminous hem of her faded blue linen gown, gathering it into her belt, and mounted Luisant. Then pressed her thighs to the mare's side, goading her into an ambling gait.

Along the small path toward Pont-du-Montvert, the warming days had signaled spider orchids and fern fiddleheads to poke up through the mossy soil. Clutching the reins in one hand, she held her veil tightly over her unbound hair with the other while chestnut strands fluttered about and tickled her face. Her cheeks lifted into a smile, the first in quite a long time, as she watched Romulus bounding alongside, weaving in and out of the trees and taunting her to follow with his wild yips. Inspired by the early season songbirds, she hummed a merry troubadour canso.

The renewed sense of freedom lightened Amelia and made space for recalling blissful moments in the forest with Jehan. For months, she had refused to let her mind linger on thoughts of him. But with spring nearly here, she could now hold on to the hope that Giraud would soon arrive from his usual wintering at home in the Hautes-Alpes—and he'd come bearing a letter from Jehan.

Amelia slowed Luisant upon entering the small ravine where she had buried Jehan's Huguenot medallion long ago, hoping a visit here might rekindle the connection she so dearly missed. The clouded winter skies had been preventing her from seeking it in the stars. And his cravate—still worn around her shoulders and tucked into her bodice nearly every day—was no longer enough to keep her feeling close to him. She untucked it and pulled it close to her nose. His musky scent barely lingered, nearly vanquished by her rose water baths.

Perhaps a prayer with the medallion would provide the binding force to bring Jehan's energy into her being again.

Luisant tossed her head and whinnied as though she were encouraging Amelia.

"So you think this is the spot, do you?"

Amelia slid down off the mare, then dropped to her knees at the base of a large oak. With no trowel or tool to dig up the medallion, she had to make do. She brushed away two winters' worth of decomposing leaves and began scooping the rich soil with her bare hands until she caught a glint of silver peeking through.

She grasped the medallion and held it high, whispering a prayer for their love to return, its gentle words tingling upon her lips. Once finished, she began singing another ancient chanson, this time *d'amour*. She barely had two lines completed when Romulus interrupted with his growling.

The great white wolf-dog was sniffing the air and staring toward a distant bush that emitted a rustling sound. Likely, it was only a fox. If it were anything more dangerous, she trusted Romulus would chase it away. She watched as his ears pulled back and the fur on his tail stood on end.

"Romulus," she said softly, trying to calm him.

But he lowered himself into a defensive posture, poised to attack the intruder.

At once, her shoulders tightened and her mind spun with memories she had tried to bury. Flashes of the dragoons came into her imagination. Or were they real? *No, no. It cannot be.* She hugged her arms around herself and rocked back and forth, her rapid, shallow breaths gripping like a vise inside her lungs. Frozen with fear, her eyes affixed to the quivering bush. She began praying for courage, for the strength to fight off whoever or whatever was watching her.

Abruptly, the movement stopped. Romulus relaxed. Her breathing slowed a bit.

Then the padding of small feet could be heard, diminishing into the forest, as the animal, or perhaps a small person, tread off down the path.

Amelia focused, trying desperately to bring herself back to a state of calm. She wrapped the cravate around her shoulders again and took several long, deep breaths. It was helping her nerves, but her thoughts were still disturbed and muddled. She drew a few more slow breaths while she pondered about what to do next, then decided it best to lay the medallion to rest again in its earthen vault.

She buried it deep in the rich humus. Then, as she sprinkled leaf fragments and tiny twigs across the bare ground, she asked Spirit to use this precious food to bring new life to the soil—and to the bond between her and Jehan. Though their connection was no longer as intense and undeniable as it once had been, she trusted it was only in some bewildering state of hibernation, waiting to awaken again.

Pont-du-Montvert Market, Mont Lauzère, France

Amelia tied Luisant to a tethering ring near the inn, then loosened the hem of her gown from her belt and crouched down to stroke Romulus.

"My fierce protector. Keep watch over Luisant for me."

As she tousled the long white fur on the dog's head, he tried to lick her hand.

"Stay. I shall be back soon."

She bounded up, the anticipation of a letter from Jehan the only thing now on her mind, and headed across the road to the marketplace.

After pacing the riverfront square back and forth several times, she could not find Giraud. It was a small market, so if he were here, she would have found him by now. Disappointment abruptly slammed her like a blow to her stomach. Fighting back tears, she kept walking but dropped her head.

Amelia knew she had set herself up for this pain. By praying in the forest to renew her attachment to Jehan, she had left herself vulnerable again. Now she must pray for the fortitude to set aside her expectations in order to make it through the day.

She seemed to be attracting odd looks and whispers from a few women here and there, so she stood tall and ventured over to a textile merchant's stall.

As she ran her hand over the fine wool serge cloth and the silk damasks and brocades, she wondered if it was the frantic pacing that had attracted so much attention or if they had noticed her despair. Many townsfolk likely knew of her reputation as a healer, so she hoped their gossiping was over some favorable testimonial from one of their friends.

Amelia moved on toward another stall specializing in Pelardon goat cheese, but more women gathered, inching nearer to her, staring and pointing and covering their mouths as they talked. Their whispers began to sound like the hissing of snakes. As she glanced from the corner of her eye, their faces seemed to depict more malevolent intentions than she had dared to imagine.

She ignored their glares as she stepped up to the stall and bowed her head in greeting to the merchant, a middle-aged man dressed in the simple attire of a farmer. "Good day, monsieur."

"Mademoiselle." The man tipped his hat to her. "You are the woman assisting Commandeur Timoleon at the Infirmaria, are you not? I've heard wonderful things about what you've done for our people."

"Yes. 'Tis me," she said, wondering now if she had been letting her fears get the best of her all morning. Perhaps the women intended no ill will after all.

"What may I offer you today?"

"I shall take two of the small rounds, please," she said, gesturing to the wrinkly, white-skinned cheeses.

As the man began wrapping them in clean linen, he leaned toward her and spoke quietly in a taut voice, "I must tell you. These women have been saying some unkind things about you, so I would not linger too long."

Amelia wrinkled her forehead in confusion and tilted her head. She wasn't quite sure how to react and hoped he would explain.

"There was a girl here telling everyone she believes you a witch."

Stunned by this news, Amelia's limbs grew heavy. She realized she should heed the man's warning and leave, but she was weighed down by the dread that someone had seen her in the forest—digging in the dirt, the medallion, the prayers, the cansos.

She knew she must stand firm in her defense. "There is no truth to that. None whatsoever." Amelia quickly scanned the area, her eyes landing on a group of women near the fountain that she recognized. "I have treated many of these people. How could they believe I would ever practice dark magic?"

"I take you at your word, mademoiselle. I am acquainted with Timoleon, and he would never tolerate evil enchantments at his commandery and . . ." He stopped mid-sentence, his eyes widening. "Something is afoot."

Amelia heard the growing sounds of a distant commotion and spun around. There was some sort of disturbance near the Le Rieumalet bridge where a crowd had gathered.

"What is it?" she asked the merchant.

"Can't tell yet, but that's the direction of Abbé du Chaila's house. He has been on a rampage lately, trying to take over where the Intendant left off." The merchant shook his head and clucked his tongue. "Such a vengeful old snake."

Amelia remembered the cautionary tales her Menina would tell of this priest who'd recently been appointed Inspector of Missions. He was an odd man who passionately hated women and was always on the hunt to find one he could drag into his cellar to torture as a heretic.

A shrill voice could be heard over the murmuring that Amelia thought she recognized, but it was too far off to be certain.

Then a man's screeching shouts startled the doves roosting in the clock tower. "Clear the way. Now! Out of the way."

The birds took flight in a savage fluttering above the crowd, drawing Amelia's eyes upward.

"Look," exclaimed the merchant, pointing toward the rabble.

She turned and could see the crowd parting on the ancient stone bridge. The head of a thin, hard-faced man with long, straggly, stark-white hair became visible. As he crested the high arch of the bridge, his black ecclesiastical robes confirmed it was the Abbé.

"Du Chaila! You must go, mademoiselle."

Amelia hesitated. She had done no wrong, and she was *not* under the rule of this tyrannical Du Chaila. But then she saw Griselle scampering along behind him. Amelia drew a sharp inhale. *Griselle?* Could she be the one who reported her? The one who was hiding in the bushes? This could only mean grave trouble, and Amelia had no intention of seeing the inside of this crazed Abbé's cellar.

"Go," the merchant urged again, waving her on. "I've heard the monster wraps his captives' hands in wool steeped in oil then lights them afire. You can't let him do that to you!"

Amelia shuddered, then took in a slow, deep breath, determined to replace her fear with a dose of courage. It gave energy to her leaden limbs. She unpinned her veil and tucked it into her pocket—hoping she'd be mistaken for a local maiden—then darted over to the inn.

Her fingers fumbled with the reins as she struggled to untether them from the ring. While she was loosening them, she peered over Luisant's back and could see the crazed Abbé heading her way.

"Romulus," Amelia said, pointing toward Du Chaila. "On guard."

The dog's haunches were instantly up. His upper lip curled, baring his teeth in a loud snarl. As the Abbé approached, Romulus crouched and slowly advanced on him.

Once Amelia managed to release the reins, she wasted no time, grabbing the hem of her skirts and swiftly mounting Luisant. Looking over her shoulder, she saw Romulus begin to circle and snap at Du Chaila, forcing him to halt. She shook the reins hard, and the horse responded to the queue, urgently bolting into a wild gallop and taking a wide berth around the tumult.

As she and Luisant scrambled up a steep mountain draille, Amelia whistled for Romulus. She would be forever grateful for her fierce protector. He had saved her life on many occasions, but now she would need to count on Commandeur Timoleon to untangle this dreadful mess Griselle had gotten her into.

❧

Hospitaller Commandery, Mont Lauzère, France

Amelia huddled outside the door of the novices' dormitory, fighting a natural urge to let bitterness and resentment rule her thoughts. Her jaw tightened as she resisted, reminding herself Griselle was yet a child, and one who had suffered some terrible trauma at that. Trauma so great that she still refused to reveal the details to anyone.

The two knights guarding the doorway were exchanging nervous looks, while inside the room Commandeur Timoleon stood with feet planted in a wide stance, blocking Griselle from leaving.

"I believe you have been lying to us, Griselle. Men," he said, raising a hand over his shoulder and signaling the knights to enter the room. "Begin the search."

Griselle's breathing was harsh and uneven as she continued to defend herself. "Wait. What are you looking for? I did *not* lie. I saw her digging up a silver medallion."

"The story you told the Abbé was certainly a fanciful version of the truth," said the Commandeur. "There was no evil in what Mademoiselle Amelia was doing. I have known her since she was a child, and I assure you, she is no witch. 'Tis you who should be punished for your sins."

"Me?" Griselle said, contorting her face in disbelief.

"Yes, you. Not only have you been bearing false witness against Mademoiselle Amelia, but I suspect you have also not been truthful about the missing letters."

A slight rise of Griselle's eyebrows suggested her surprise. Amelia wondered if the girl's mind had been so set on pointing the accusatory finger that she never imagined it would turn back around on her.

With a hand nervously clutching the door frame, Amelia watched as one of the knights began going through a small trunk by the window, while the other crouched on the floor near Griselle's bed. He reached under and swept his long arm along the floor, then retrieved a dirty linen satchel from the dark recesses next to the wall.

Griselle's eyes tightened, and her face flushed. "Those are my things. No, no, don't!" She grabbed the satchel from the young knight before he could stand.

The Commandeur stepped over and tugged at it while trying to pry her hands loose. "I shall send you home immediately should you continue on this way."

Her hands still locked on the satchel, the girl froze as soon as the word 'home' spilled from Timoleon's lips.

"Argh! Let go of it, or . . ." he cried out in a burst of anger, wagging his finger near Griselle's face.

She dropped the satchel and wrapped her arms over her face, cowering behind them. "No Papa. Please, no."

"I am not your Papa," shouted Timoleon. Then his brows arched in a look of sudden recognition, and he heaved a growling breath of frustration. "Your father promised me you would give us no problems, yet your evil ways are now the bane of my duties. Makes me wonder what depraved things he did that instilled such wickedness in you."

Griselle looked up at him with wide, mournful eyes, and her lips began to tremble. It was clear the idea of going home to her father terrified her.

Amelia stepped in through the doorway and tried to swallow past the lump building in her throat. She'd heard told that some fathers got away with maltreatment of their children and wives—another reason she had resisted the notion of marriage—and it was becoming clear that must have happened with Griselle. Amelia's life was now at risk because of the girl, but how could she remain incensed at a child who was a victim of abuse and misguidance? Was this another test laid before her by God?

The Commandeur placed his hands on his hips, a gesture sure to prod the girl into defeat. "I can protect Mademoiselle Amelia from Abbé du Chaila and the Intendant's dragoons. They have no jurisdiction on our lands. And I can protect you from your father. But who will protect you from yourself, Griselle? You have surely learned by now that, in our Order, lying and deceit are considered sins. Although we no longer affiliate with the Church of Rome, we do follow the tenets of Saint Jean the Baptist, so penance will be required. You will start with an apology to Mademoiselle Amelia."

Griselle's eyes welled with tears that began to stream down her face. She fell to the floor sobbing and buried her face in her hands.

Amelia bit her lower lip. Timoleon's tactics worked well when faced with the enemy, but anything too harsh might only drive the girl further into her protective shell, keeping her angry and dangerous. Empathy flooded through every pore as Amelia watched the girl break down. Love was the guiding principle in all the teachings she espoused and, in her heart, she knew it was the only answer.

She rushed over to Griselle, then dropped onto the cold stone floor beside her. This time, when she threw her arms around the girl and held her tight, there was no backing off, no resistance to Amelia's affections as before.

Rocking the girl as if she were her own babe, Amelia whispered, "I forgive you. We shall set things right. I shall see to it that you need *never* return home, unless it is by your choice."

One of the knights picked up the satchel and peered inside. "Sieur, we've found something." He held out a stack of letters and a small book with exquisite, but aged, fanfare binding.

Amelia's pulse surged with a jubilation she had dared not let herself feel until this. It was from Jehan. It had to be.

Timoleon took the items from the young knight, his stern glare firmly planted on Griselle. He was a tiger trained in battle who had been disturbed from its slumber and his instinct was to attack.

Apprehension about the Commandeur's methods caused Amelia's momentary elation to waver, and a sudden lightheadedness overcame her. She was at a loss for what to do next, so she continued to hold the girl while stroking her hair and wiping tears from her cheeks as her sobs diminished.

Timoleon pinched his chin, glancing toward the ceiling. "Seems it will be necessary for your penance to last throughout the year. Instead of once daily, you will have time for reflection and repentance in the chapel thrice daily. And . . ."

Concerned he may be considering some overly severe punishment, Amelia presented an option before he could finish speaking. "She could learn many lessons from a pilgrimage to Sainte-Baume."

"Hmm. Yes," responded the Commandeur. "Sainte Marie de Magdala has been the mother of mercy for many, and this child sorely needs mercy and grace."

Relieved, Amelia took a deep breath. She knew how much the girl had wanted to join them the summer past. "Griselle, did you hear that? The pilgrimage to Sainte-Baume."

The girl relaxed, responding by burying her face in Amelia's shoulder and returning her embrace.

"But, Griselle, your heart must be available to the Lord," directed Timoleon. "I shall require you to not only pray the Stations of the Cross as we go up the mountain to the cave, but I shall also designate others all along the route."

Amelia lifted the girl's chin so she could look into her eyes. "You will find your way to God . . . as long as you wish it to be so." She laid the girl's head back on her shoulder and mouthed to Timoleon, "Thank you."

He sighed and nodded, placing the letters and book on the bed, and left the room with the knights.

After some time had passed, Griselle raised her head. She wiped a sleeve across her reddened eyes. "Thank you, Mademoiselle Amelia. I promise I shall never do those awful things to you again. You have treated me better than anyone ever has, and I am sorry." A smile lifted her tear-stained cheeks. "And now I . . . I am to go on pilgrimage?"

"'Tis not all happy journeys to travel to Sainte-Baume," said Amelia, loosening her embrace as the girl sat up. "Ten or twelve hours a day over rough terrain on horseback and the threat of road bandits makes it an adventure many are not suited for."

"I had a hard life at home . . . even as a small child," Griselle said, then her eyes brightened. "'Twill be a joy to join you and be of service."

"Would you like to tell me about your life at home?"

Griselle hesitated. Her face grew ashen and as bleak as a winter's sky. "He . . . my father . . . he lied and cheated the other villagers. He was always swilled with drink and hostile. He beat my mother till she nearly died." She sniffled and blinked at the tears that hung on her lashes. "And when I said I would report him, he . . ." Griselle began shaking again, choking on her sobs, unable to speak.

"What did he do?" asked Amelia.

Griselle closed her eyes and shook her head. "Not now. Pleeease."

Amelia could see that confessing her father's sins would do none of them any good. Some truths could only be given up to God.

She gently patted the girl's shoulder. "Very well then. I shall take my letters and leave you to your thoughts."

"Yes, yes. I am sorry. I only wanted to know what it was like to be in love. You will want to read them soon since I think I caused your Jehan much confusion by holding your letters back."

Amelia's breath hitched, and she momentarily forgot to breathe. As she released it, she tried to control the small moan it pushed out. She had to make it clear the girl's actions had not been the right course to take.

"'Tis best you start immediately to set your good intentions by praying for mercy and grace. Commit yourself to it, and it will be yours. And I shall pray that our lives will be free of this strain we've all been under."

She gathered the letters and the book, placing them protectively in her pocket, and went into the passageway where she found the Commandeur waiting.

"Let us talk while I walk you to your chamber," he said.

They moved down the darkening passageway in silence until they were well out of Griselle's earshot.

Timoleon heaved a sigh. "Your commendable ability to forgive could one day mark you for sainthood."

Amelia flushed and kept her eyes focused on the stone tiles as they walked. She had never thought of herself in that light.

"I assure you I am no saint," she said. "Forgiveness is always a struggle for me as much as for anyone, but I've learned it does not serve to carry anger. 'Twill only eat away my soul. Behind these intolerable behaviors some people exhibit, there is pain and suffering. So I must let my desire to help them heal outweigh my instinct for resentment."

"If only we could all embrace that philosophy. I am not so skilled at forgiveness, but I believe myself to be adept at protection." The Commandeur cleared his throat. "And I would like to do more to safeguard you from these accusations of witchcraft."

"Do you know of a way?"

"I do. I am fully aware that you are against taking vows to our Order, but I can write to our Grand Master to request permission for you and your grandmother to be recognized as Dames of Honor and Devotion. This requires no oath or vow on your part, yet it brings an affiliation to our Order with a lifetime of our protection. All we ask is that you to continue your good works in the world. This might not put a stop to the rumors, but at least Du Chaila will be forced to back down."

She swallowed back her apprehension—despite her years of resistance to anything remotely similar to an oath, she knew it was for the best. Hot tears tried to form in her eyes when she stopped walking and looked up at Timoleon.

"I would be grateful for that, Commandeur. You know my desire for independence as well as any, but I recognize the gravity of this situation and would humbly accept the honor."

"Do not worry. You will still have your independence. Yet should you venture outside the commandery walls, you could still face threats. We all desire freedom of choice. But history has taught us that structure, such as we offer here, can prevent disorder. As long as it is for the common good, and tolerance and compassion are at its core."

When they arrived at Amelia's chamber, the door was open and an apricot glow from the setting sun spilled out of the room.

"I shall leave you to your evening," Timoleon said, bowing his head slightly.

Amelia watched him walk off down the passageway, where the darkness gave way to a golden glow as one of the novices flitted about lighting wall sconces.

She turned and hastened into her chamber, her stomach fluttering over the unknown contents of the letters. Perhaps they held some hope, some word, that Jehan had discovered their peaceful Eden and it could save them from the madness that ruled their homeland.

Menina Elise had already fallen fast asleep in her chair by the fire, so Amelia slowly closed the chamber door, then tiptoed to her desk and lit a rushlight candle. She lifted the chair out from under the desk with care so as not to wake her grandmother, then removed the small book and letters from her pocket and took a seat.

As she examined the tiny, pocket-sized book, Amelia's heart raced. "Ah, Utopia," she said without restraint, her anticipation causing her to forget herself.

Menina shifted in her chair and moaned, but did not open her eyes.

Trying to contain her joy, Amelia placed a hand to her lips as she studied the title. *De optimo reipublicae statu deque nova insula Utopia scriptus* by Thomas More. Surely this was Jehan's way of saying he still wanted her to join him in Eden.

While waiting all these long months, the recollections of joyous hours they had spent discussing and dreaming about that peaceful paradise were becoming indistinct, as though she were looking through the waters of the Tarn, swimming against a current that held her back. Perhaps this letter would bring those memories alive again.

She ran her fingers over the little book's deep gilded embossing, then opened it and brushed them across the marbled lining where she detected the letter, concealed within. After carefully loosening the lining's corners, she located it, neatly folded in an interlocking configuration. She removed the letter, cracked the seal, and pulled back the entangled folds to find it had been written nearly a year before. *The 8th of March. So long ago.* She took a deep breath and scanned the words. Here and there, a few lines stood out, and she grew uneasy.

> '. . . *not in good health of spirit, nor of heart. Nor shall I be till I hear from you . . . should your reason for not writing be that some harm has come to you, I could never forgive myself for leaving you behind . . .*'

Amelia's eyes moved down the page, absorbing every sentence, every word.

> '*I search for even one small, glimmering star so that I can find my way to your heart.*'

Touching the ink scrolled upon the parchment, she whispered. "You are *in* my heart . . . *forever*, my love."

She slowed to read the last portion of the letter, making sure to be clear on his intentions.

> '. . . *my trust in your continued feelings for me hangs on a thin cord. I fear, before long, I may take leave of my senses, losing all that I have become by lowering myself to those earthly desires that I have resisted because of my love for you. Mon Ame, my soul, if you would only write to me, I would not forsake you.'*

Jehan's words sounded ever so desperate. It was clear, in her absence, he struggled to resist temptation. Her stomach hardened when she thought of the abundance of enticements in Aarau that most likely flocked to him. After all, he was alluring in so many ways—his deep blue eyes, always alive with curiosity, his sharp mind and playful nature, his tall, virile physique. And, without question, his title and money alone would be enough to attract most women.

But what had instilled so much doubt in Jehan? Amelia's mind flashed to the letter she had written just after the dragoon attack, when she had been racked with fear. Perhaps that had been it. That letter had been nothing more than a rant about being nearly violated, and had likely contributed to the burden of guilt he was feeling. While under the hold of that fear, she had lamented that he should stay far away, and that she would be better off locked up with the novices. But she hadn't meant it. Not in the way he may have taken it. By now, he'd probably received that letter and was thinking she no longer wished to join him. Regretting her words, she laid a hand over her knotted belly.

Yet perhaps her other letters had reached him—the letters that would reassure him of her love and intentions. And perhaps he had written again.

Amelia hastily rummaged through the stack, spreading them across her desk. By their bulk, it had appeared there were several, but there were only two, both with broken seals. She scrambled to unfold them, and her heart sank when she realized they were both letters *she* had written. Undelivered letters Jehan would never see.

There was nothing more from him, and it was little wonder. In all this time, he'd only received that one letter from her, filled with reckless prattling about the dragoons, with no mention that she longed to see him nor of her deep love for him. Amelia bit her lip, but it did nothing to stop the remorse. It was evident now that their communication had not only been thwarted by Griselle, but it had also been muddled by misunderstandings between the two of them.

The realization hit her hard, tears welling in her eyes. After nearly a year, Jehan had most likely given up on her. Of course he had. She had given him reason, time and time again, to think she would only give herself to God.

Her inhales grew shakey, her pressed lips trembled. She folded her hands on the desk and leaned her head upon them, then wept with wild, unrestrained anguish, the day's turbulent emotions tugging her out of the feeble light and toward a very dark place.

CHAPTER 14

THE NEWLANDERS

JEHAN

7 March 1699
Newlander's Meeting, Town Hall, Aarau

Jehan smoothed the rain-drenched leaflet against the wall of
the town hall so Corbell could read the details. "You see,
this meeting with the Newlander's representative is open to all
French refugees."

Corbell pulled his cloak close to his neck and looked the
other way. "I am not interested if it's more persuasion to join
the Brandenburg resettlement project Pasteur Barjon spoke of
last Sunday. Going further north into the Germanic states is not
how we'll escape this miserable weather."

"No, no. Neither am I. I want to go as far away as possible
from my uncle's control. Just look . . . this leaflet is not for the
Brandenburg project but for the Carolana project in the New
World. The one Massip spoke of when he was last in Aarau."
Jehan gave Corbell a firm pat on the back. "Come on now. The
meeting starts promptly at six."

Corbell shook the rain from his hat as he followed Jehan in.
"Let's hope the climate in this Carolana is more hospitable."

Voices echoed down a long gallery from the moment they
entered the building, making it easy to locate the meeting room.

Antoine Aigoin stood near the doorway waving them on. "Hurry, lads. Half the town is here, so there is only space to stand."

The crowd was milling about, searching for seats where they could find them. The high ceilings did little for the odorous cloaks and bodies that smelled of wet livestock run hard into a holding pen.

Most of the free-thinkers' group had gathered in the rear left corner. Alongside Antoine were Constantin Eschalier, Luc Dodet and his wife Elaine, and the Roussel brothers—Etienne and Mathieu. Since Daniel Isnard had not shown up, it appeared he'd changed his mind about the prospect of a future outside of Europe. And it was no surprise that Udine was not present. She had no need or desire to leave her homeland.

Corbell strode over to the group with a smile from ear to ear and took a spot next to Mathieu. Jehan followed, glad his friend was as pleased as he to seek a new adventure—one that might keep his mind away from missing Amelia and away from a life of morals so rigid that he could barely breathe.

Jehan began to feel inexplicably fidgety when he saw the stout, middle-aged man in black liturgical robes step up to the podium. He had not expected the project to be led by yet another pasteur.

The man vigorously cleared his throat and projected his voice, "Welcome, friends. I am Pasteur Borel and I have been sent today by the honorable Sieur Charles de Sailly to share the good news of the Carolana resettlement project. We know you've gone from country to country to find some asylum among your brethren. And now many of you are being told to leave so your jobs can be handed over to the Swiss. You are but poor sheep gathered into a flock who wish only to eat their bread in joy, without being a burden to the refuge countries."

The pasteur paused while the sea of hats and coifs filling the room bobbed in agreement.

A man close in age to Jehan stepped alongside him. "May I take this spot?" he asked in a hushed voice.

"Indeed," Jehan replied with a slight bow of the head.

From the corner of his eye, Jehan noticed the young man reach into his pocket and pull out a graphite pencil and small journal, then promptly begin taking notes. He was certain this young man was not a refugee. His pale milky blond hair and light gray eyes resembled most of the Swiss in the northern cantons; his words had been accented with Alemannisch, and his fine ensemble was not in the French style, though its detailing was impressive. It left Jehan to wonder about the man's purpose for attending this meeting.

Once the crowd had grown silent again in anticipation, Pasteur Borel bellowed out, "The plains of the Carolana colony are covered with lofty trees and lovely orchards of apples, pears, cherries, apricots, figs, and peaches. You will see there, great rivers meandering along on their tranquil, peaceful course, never overflowing the riverbed. And along these rivers, there are fine pastures or lands planted with tobacco, grain, vegetables, and all the necessaries of life. The hills and low mountains have deep forests, pleasant streams, and gentle slopes where fine vines will grow, and doubtless, the wine produced there will be excellent."

Corbell elbowed Jehan. "Sounds like our sort of place, eh? All that fine wine."

"Truly seems like the land of milk and honey," said Jehan. "'Tis the natural beauty and the tranquility that appeals to me most. That is what I discovered in the Gorges du Tarn where Amelia lives, and it is where I would still be were there even the slightest bit of toleration to be found there."

The surrounding crowd took to an excited chattering, so Corbell spoke out loud. "I thought Udine was your true love now."

It seemed everyone had insight into the trysts Jehan and Udine had been having. But those not-so-secret rendezvous had stopped, and he was still not sure of the reason. Perhaps she'd simply tired of his distance and disinterest.

Jehan shook his head and winced. "No, no. You are mistaken, my friend. I take her the herbs she requires, but that is all. Other than that, I've not spent time with her since our meeting over a month ago."

It was a risky thing for them both—that so many people suspected their illicit behavior. Should he stay in Aarau much longer, his reputation would be so sullied he might be forced to go, despite having the means to sustain himself.

"Mesdames and Messieurs. Your attention, please. We invite those of you who still have your basic belongings, who wish the advantage of fertile virgin land, and who prefer peace above anything else, to sign our roster of interest and return here in one month's time when Sieur de Sailly will be here to formalize the agreements."

The young man who'd come to stand next to Jehan waved a hand at Pasteur Borel. "How much will this cost? Even if one has the means for daily food, how do you propose the expenses for the journey be covered? Many of these people cannot afford the river barges and tolls and lodging costs, let alone the ship voyages."

Borel looked down for a moment, his lips pursed, then took a breath and said, "De Sailly will arrange for the funds to be covered by charitable sources." The pasteur's eyes flitted around the room, at the walls, the ceiling, anywhere but into the young man's eyes.

"Are you certain," said the young man, "that this is not a scheme to acquire indentured servants?"

"Uhm . . . well," Borel hesitated and tugged at the snug white linen preaching band constricting his neck. "That is not Sieur De Sailly's intention, I assure you." As he strode toward the door, he clapped his hands together and wheezed, "That is all for today. Be here on the seventh of April".

Jehan had not considered that this might be a dishonorable venture.

He turned to the young man to see if he understood more than he let on.

"Jehan BonDurant," he said, bowing formally from the waist.

"A pleasure. I am Herr Frantz Ludwig Michel," the young man said, returning the gesture.

"I appreciate your concern and caution. Are you seeking a new life in the Americas as well?"

"What I am seeking is an answer to a problem my father faces in Bern. He is a member of the Council there, which has established an Anabaptist Bureau because they . . . they want to enforce religious uniformity."

Jehan's face grew taut, and he took a step back from this Michel fellow. He wanted nothing to do with this man if he endorsed intolerance.

Michel raised an eyebrow, seeming to read Jehan's unease. "Please do not misunderstand me, sieur. I do not agree with the Council. Most do not find the Mennonites' and Anabaptists' views to their liking, and some have gone as far as suggesting imprisonment. However, *I* am looking for a more humane solution."

Imprisonment? Jehan swallowed hard, trying to clear the bitter taste in his mouth. How could leaders be so blind to their own sins?

"The most humane solution would be to allow them their freedom of conscience," Jehan retorted. "But it seems that is not the reality in the Swiss cantons any more than it is in France."

"'Tis true. Nevertheless, you appear the sort who would enjoy adventure. And would gladly leave Aarau to escape all this injustice. I watched how your eyes lit up at the mention of the idyllic, untamed environs of the colonies."

"I am that sort," Jehan said. There was no doubt. His foray into the wilds of the Gorges du Tarn had changed his life forever. "There is something in me which is always in search of a peaceful wilderness . . . a place where I can find my connection to the Divine."

❧

Monsieur Lemieux's Boutique, Aarau

As Jehan pushed open the door of the boutique, he startled at the crisp jingling of a tiny bell. He turned and looked up at the annoying little thing positioned on the upper jamb. It had not been there on his last visit, or at any other time he could recall. Was the purpose of the new addition to announce patrons, or to alert Monsieur Lemieux to Udine's comings and goings at night?

She had been reluctant to join the group at the coffeehouse for the past month, offering a multitude of frivolous reasons each time Jehan had stopped by to bring the penny-royale tisane she requested. But he worried there was something more. Was Lemieux forcing her to work unreasonable hours?

Jehan removed his hat and entered the salon where Udine was fitting a woman in a new *mantua* adorned with lustrous metallic trim and styled to have the appearance of a jacket. "You see, Frau Martin. Much more refined."

"Splendid," said the woman, turning side to side, studying herself in the long mirror. "I am quite late for an engagement and must go at once. Please put it on my account."

Jehan stepped aside as the woman glided past and out the door, setting off the irksome bell again.

"Udine, can we speak?" Jehan leaned out to the foyer for a moment to see if Lemieux was about, but saw no signs of him.

She smiled, her eyes toying with him. "I quite busy, Herr BonDurant."

"Are you feeling well? Any stomach ailments?"

With her hand raised to her mouth, she emitted a muffled laugh. "I no with child. 'Tis why I use herb."

Jehan leaned in close to her. He whispered, yet he could not restrain the urgent concern in his tone. "But why do you need the tisane when we have not kept company for *weeks*? 'Tis too dangerous to use, if you do not need it. Have you had any ague, burning of the throat, muddling of the mind, restlessness, vertigo?"

"No. None of these. I drink only small cup each day." Udine began buzzing around the salon, organizing her supplies.

Jehan's mind could only envision a dire outcome. He refused to be the cause of her ill health, or worse, her death—a distinct possibility if she kept drinking the tisane daily.

He could not let this lie. "Do you not *understand*, Udine? You only need the tisane if you are *actively* coupling." The blood banging at his temples made it hard to restrain his temper.

Udine took his hand and spoke in a delicate tone, "But I am. And with such passion." She smiled and blinked like a satisfied cat.

Her taunting ignited a wave of carnal fury in Jehan that seemed to flow from the touch of her hand to his, and on through his body. He knew it was not jealousy, only the utter frustration of suppressing his longing for Amelia for nearly a year. On one hand, it made him want to kiss Udine, and on the other, he wanted to push her away and be free of her.

"And soon . . ." Udine squeezed Jehan's hand, then let go. "'Twill be no sin."

"How is that?"

"Herr Lemieux's mourning time is now over. And we will marry."

The taut sinew of Jehan's shoulders yielded as he relaxed into gratitude. "Ahh. Now I see."

He had forgotten entirely that Lemieux had been widowed a year past, in the early spring. Udine had mentioned it during one of their rendezvous, but it had been the last thing Jehan wanted to focus on at that moment. It had never occurred to him that Lemieux had hired Udine, a local girl, over one of the French women because he had his sights set to marry and bed her. Perhaps it was a strategy to stay in the good graces of the city magistrates who had been soliciting to replace French workers with Swiss natives.

A sudden lightness lifted the corners of Jehan's mouth, realizing he could depart the country free of any guilt for leaving Udine. The burden he still carried over the wrongs he'd done to Amelia was already more than he could handle at times, and he despised himself for it.

As the relief surged through him, he took Udine's face in his hands and kissed each cheek. "I am quite happy for you, dear Udine. May God bless you with many children and a long, happy life."

Her golden brows arched in surprise, but then a smile crept onto her lips. "You have other true love, do you not? A woman knows these things."

Jehan nodded. The intuitive power of women astounded him.

❧

2 April, 1699
Newlander's Meeting, Town Hall, Aarau

It pleased Jehan that Corbell had arrived early at the town hall. He'd managed to save seats, so this time, their group was not required to stand in the back corner. Over the past month, word had gotten around about the Newlanders' resettlement project, and interest had grown, so he and his friends knew to expect a crowd.

Jehan relaxed onto the long wooden bench, Corbell on one side and Mathieu Roussel on the other. Folding his arms over his chest, he regarded the director of the project.

This Sieur Charles De Sailly certainly resembled a man of success, dressed in the English style in an ensemble of dark red broadcloth with gold braid and buttons finished off with a cravate of fine lace. He carried a feather-trimmed, three-cornered hat that may have crushed his voluminous *perruque* if he were to wear it, and he glanced at a fine gold pocket watch. Yet, despite his appearance, the man's fingers twitched as he gripped the sides of the podium, giving away a certain nervousness or lack of confidence.

As much as Jehan dreamed about an adventure to the new world, after hearing young Herr Michel's concern about indentured servitude at the last meeting, he needed to learn more before committing to De Sailly's terms.

A prolonged silence fell over the crowd as they waited for De Sailly to settle. Many of the attendees had been on edge after the last round of dismissals. In recent weeks, many of the French who worked in the haute couture ateliers were let go, even though their skill levels far exceeded those of the Swiss citizens who were to replace them. Resentment had brought on some primitive behaviors by both sides and it reminded Jehan far too much of the divisiveness in France that he had found unbearable.

"Thank you for coming tonight, Mesdames and Messieurs. I am certain you will want to join our Carolana project, but there will not be room for all, so do not tarry in signing on." De Sailly pointed to the table at his right where Pasteur Borel sat. "Please see Borel here for the necessary papers."

The pasteur was surrounded by orderly stacks of paper and three sets of quill and inkwell, prepared for an onslaught of takers.

"Who goes to this land as a servant, becomes a lord," said De Sailly. "Who goes as a maid becomes a milady, a peasant becomes a nobleman, a citizen can become an artisan or a baron. Those who know the silk and wine trades will flourish there."

To Jehan, he sounded like a hawker peddling his wares and wondered if he should be taken seriously.

But just then, a couple in simple attire rose and scampered up to Borel's table. They appeared to be some of the unskilled laborers from the almshouse at the old Ursuline convent who had nothing to their names. The contracts they were so eager to sign would change the lives of these distressed souls forever, and it was hard to know for certain if fortune would shine on them or not. Unlike Jehan, many of these people could never afford a return trip, so they were sealing their fate on one man's word.

Like a frenzy over the best truffles at market, many of the attendees rose and pushed past those who were slow to decide. Voices reverberated off the coffered wood ceiling in the commotion.

De Sailly was all business, remaining somber as he continued. "Your journey to Carolana will begin by boat passage up the majestic Rhine. You will need to make your way to Rotterdam in early July, where, upon your arrival, our company will reimburse you for your travel thus far. There, a ship will be waiting to transport you to London. You will make your way to one of the French Reformed churches, either Threadneedle or Spittlefields, and the French Committee will arrange for your lodging until the time is right for our ships to set sail for our colony. Once we arrive, you will each be given one hundred acres of land."

Antoine Aigoin leaned around the others seated on their bench, his powdered perruque sliding over his bushy eyebrows. "The man paints such a glorious picture of the New World. If he can offer funding, how are we to say no?" He stood and waved as he straightened his perruque. "Sieur de Sailly. This man of yours, Borel, told us you would be securing charitable donations to pay for our expenses. Is that still part of your offer? And who will be donating?"

"Indeed, it is still our offer," said De Sailly. "I am meeting with delegates from each of the Swiss cantons tomorrow to arrange for them to pledge the funds."

Jehan narrowed his eyes and then turned toward Antoine and the others. "So he hasn't even secured the money. Take heed, my friends. His promises could be bait to have you sign away your freedom."

De Sailly stepped away from the podium and pointed at two young men in ragged clothing. "You two. If you have no belongings of your own, you go to this line."

Mathieu leaned over toward Jehan and Corbell. "What is he doing?"

"Looks as though the poor have a different document to sign," said Corbell.

"Seems suspect to me." Jehan was ready to take the risk of traveling the high seas to a land halfway around the world—he had the means to pay for it, and then some—but he was not about to let his friends be swindled into servitude because of blind enthusiasm.

He nudged Corbell's shoulder to engage him in an inquiry. "Everything has a price, so let us find out what it is."

As Jehan led the way to the registration table, he and Corbell maneuvered around several people who blocked the aisles in their hesitation to join the queues. Upon reaching the table, they found a crowd of individuals eager to sign on had gathered.

"We need to get a little closer," Jehan said.

They maneuvered their way through the people amidst a flurry of animated conversation and heat radiating from the tightly pressed bodies. Corbell stood tall on his toes to see over a stout, older woman. He turned to Jehan with his brows pinched together, creasing his forehead.

"They've printed the blasted documents in English," Corbell said indignantly.

"You read English?" asked Jehan.

"A bit. I see the word 'quittance'. It has something to do with being released from debt."

Jehan squeezed past a couple of small boys who occupied a spot in front of the table. "Pardon, there lads. I need to speak with De Sailly."

He waved to catch the director's his attention. "Sieur, I have interest in joining your company, but I have my own funds, so I shall not sign your contract."

"Fine. Fine, indeed," said De Sailly. "We are happy to have paying clients."

"However, you must first explain, in detail, each of these contracts before any of my friends will sign on. Monsieur Corbell, here, will review them to confirm."

De Sailly heaved a tremendous sigh and looked at his watch again. A long-winded explanation followed.

His company would receive an allocation from donated funds for each individual who signed on—the amount of which was still to be determined. After he had been beleaguered by more questions, he finally admitted the allocations were not likely to cover all the costs. Those who had no means or belongings would be provided for, but would be selling themselves into servitude for however long it took to repay the costs over the allocation amount. Those with some possessions and assets were eligible for an allocation, but they would be required to pay coin or provide a bank note for any expenses over that allocation.

The most unsettling part for Jehan was that the higher the status, the higher the allocation. His lips pressed tight as he fought the urge to shout out in rage at De Sailly. He could not abide by that inequity, but neither did he wish to miss this opportunity to travel with his companions. He thought for a moment, then it came to him.

"I shall go on two conditions," Jehan said to De Sailly. "That our agreement is strictly by our word alone. I shall not sign a contract. And second, that you use my allocation to fund those most in need and keep them from servitude."

"Agreed," said De Sailly, reaching out to shake Jehan's hand.

Jehan grasped the man's hand, mustering the tightest grip possible, intending to convey a clear warning. "Splendid! I am Sieur Jean Pierre BonDurant dit Cougoussac *and* I am an apothecary. Thus, with your system, I have two counts of higher rank, so my allocation should take care of *several* poor souls."

⁂

Late Evening
Jehan's Apartment, Aarau

Jehan watched Moyse speak with great animation as he described how the new life in Brandenburg would be. His cousin was so enthralled that Jehan struggled to tell him he had different designs. He held back, letting Moyse elucidate the preparations Pasteur Barjon had set in motion for his group of followers.

Warm candlelight and promises of better days ahead rendered the elderly man with a youthful glow as he spoke. "And the Elector has promised the funds. We shall each have our own house and be given the materials to build workshops and ateliers. Are you sure you won't join us?"

"You know I don't do well with following Uncle Barjon's restrictions," Jehan said as he poked at the last hissing embers in the hearth.

"But your uncle will not join us right away. He's planning to wait till after his wife brings their new babe into the world. They believe it will come in early June. That will give you time to set up an apothecary business." Moyse put a hand on Jehan's shoulder and turned him so they were looking eye to eye. "And your Amelia could join you there."

Moyse's words caused a tiny flicker in Jehan's heart, yet his head was still in control. "My hope for that is long gone," he said as he mindlessly prodded the embers into a small flame.

But the moment he spoke those words of surrender, the flicker turned to a spark, and his great love for Amelia started to burn through his resignation.

He had to write to her, even if only one last time. Perhaps their love was strong enough that she could change her mind and join him after all. Or that he could let go and live the rest of his days in joy over her happiness as a good sister in devotion to the Holy Spirit. That would be the sort of unconditional love she deserved.

Jehan looked up at Moyse. "I want a life so full of new adventure that there will be no more room for despair. And so . . ." He paused and saw tears welling in Moyse's eyes, making it difficult to say. "I am going to Carolana."

CHAPTER 15

LOVE NEVER FAILS

AMELIA

6 May 1699
Hospitaller Commandery, Mont Lauzère, France

The ceremony in the commandery chapel to receive their recognition as Dames of Honor and Devotion had been brief, with few in attendance. And the Holy Spirit had provided the courage and resolve Amelia had prayed for, guiding her to set her own worries about the ceremony aside and focus entirely on her grandmother.

Amelia had been unaware of the degree of weakness in Menina's limbs until she had roused her from her favorite reading chair to accompany her to the chapel. The shock of it had caused a heavy feeling in Amelia's stomach. She realized she must have been in denial while caught up in her trepidations over the ceremony.

But those worries had vanquished altogether when her thoughts shifted to Menina's condition. Amelia had seen it time and again how choosing her thoughts and words wisely would chase her fear away. "I am here for you Menina, and I am glad we are pledging to the Order to continue good works," she had said before the ceremony. Once she had spoken that dedication, even her fear of being charged with witchcraft diminished.

Although Amelia had once thought her grandmother to be invincible, there could be no better purpose than helping her live out her life comfortably. Healing the infirmed was Amelia's life purpose, after all, and purpose was what she needed most at this time.

As they made their way out of the chapel, she held Menina's frail arm, and step by step, they plodded down the passage toward the stairway.

"You see, child, the oath we took to do good works is no different than what you set out to do on your own," Menina reassured.

"Yes, Menina. You are right."

Menina smiled and put a hand to the black silk sash, embroidered in the Hospitallers eight-pointed white star, that lay across her chest. "Now we have these sashes that prove we are under the Knights' protection, yet you still have the freedom to choose your own spiritual path."

Amelia hesitated to agree. Despite Commandeur Timoleon's policy of tolerance and the new title he bestowed on her for protection, her path still seemed as if it had come to a dead end. Here. Within the walls of the commandery. Even when lies and rumors could be disproved, they lived for a long, long time in Cévenols' memories, and the word 'witch' is one that seemed to carve itself in their minds forever, making it impossible for Amelia to safely travel to her home in Castelbouc again.

All the same, her grandmother deserved some peace of mind. As they took the next careful step, Amelia patted Menina's hand and thought of the bright side. "Yes, and now this official vow of support from the entire Order will allow me to tend to people of all creeds without the threat of arrest . . . as long as I tend to them here in the Infirmaria."

"'Tis a good thing. I could not bear the thought of leaving you to fend for yourself, alone in the woods at Castelbouc."

At times, Amelia thought of taking her chances on her own, just so she would no longer suffer this sense of imprisonment. But she would stay at the commandery as long as her grandmother still inhabited this physical plane and try as she might to delay her inevitable passing.

"What is this talk of leaving me, Menina? You are *not* going anywhere. But I do need to adjust the tisane and your meals to better suit this lethargy."

"Have you seen any *lusèrna* in the meadows yet?" Menina asked. "That should help me."

"The alfalfa? Yes. I saw new shoots in the courtyard last week."

"Shoots and roots. That's what I need, child. Shoots and roots," Menina's sing-song voice lifted the moment. At least she had not lost her merry temperament.

Amelia could not seem to keep the loose ends of Jehan's cravate tucked into her bodice while she kneeled to pick the emerging wildflowers, so she removed it, no longer trying to seek his fading scent, and buried it in her pocket. She looked to the overcast sky that sealed the walls of the commandery courtyard from above, wondering if this was all part of God's design for her.

The task at hand of collecting the lusèrna stilled her mind from her other worries just long enough for thoughts of Jehan to overtake her. She contemplated each twist of fate along the way that had separated them. After his last letter and Griselle's misguided intervention, it seemed their separation would now be forever. With all the misfortune in her life, holding on to hope for their love was harder than she could have imagined, but her resolve was stronger than ever.

She brushed a thumb nervously over the smooth handle of the chestnut basket she carried as little Jacquette came skipping up alongside her.

"Thank you, Mademoiselle Amelia, for letting me be your special assistant." The young girl beamed with joy over being chosen.

"I am very glad to have you along while Griselle serves her penance. I can use a dose of your sunny smile today."

Jacquette brushed a hand over the variety of new spring shoots and wildflowers that grew at the foot of the courtyard's inner walls. "Which ones are the lusèrna? There are so many."

Amelia crouched and thrust a small spade into the soil, releasing a specimen from Mare Terra's nurturing hold. "These," she said, running her fingers over the tender young plant. "Look for the clover-like leaves with the clusters of purple flowers coming on." She broke off a leaf and put it into her mouth. "It has a fresh, nutty flavor."

Jacquette made a wonderful helper, adding three plants in her basket in no time. She paused and looked up at Amelia. "Do you think the Commandeur will let me take my oath to be a chevalière soon?"

"I am not certain. But should you take to memory all that you learn today, I believe it will count as part of your training."

The sun broke out of the clouds, heating the stone wall and brightening the hues of each plant growing before it. Moments later, a long shadow drew over the ground, creeping steadily up the wall. Amelia halted, her muscles tightening with caution. She knew she was in a vulnerable position, but she trusted that no one within the commandery walls would bring harm to her. As she turned her head over her shoulder and looked from the corner of her eye, she saw an aura of sunlight surrounding the indistinct outline of a man. She squinted but could not make out who it was.

"You may need to wait a few more years, Jacquette, for the Commandeur to take you on. But I can offer some training in the meantime."

It had been some time since Amelia had heard that deep, throaty voice. Only a trace of youthfulness still remained, but she would recognize it anywhere.

"Monsieur Cavalier!" Jacquette jumped up and stiffened to attention, her eyes wild with excitement. "Will you please? Will you?"

"I shall. And we'll start with testing your agility. As soon as I have had a chance to speak in private with Mademoiselle Amelia, we shall start with a round of cup-and-ball."

Cavalier had become quite a striking young man upon reaching his eighteenth year, and apparently all the young women found him so, even little Jacquette. She blushed and took a dainty curtsy, her big blue eyes affixed to his face the entire time. But she quickly reverted to her childish ways and began skipping around in circles.

Amelia called out, "Run along and find the game sets. Then report back to Cavalier." As the girl ran off toward the commandery manoir house, Amelia motioned to Cavalier. "Let us visit Luisant."

"I saw the bookseller at market this morning," he said as they strolled along the cart track toward the stable. He drew a folded parchment from his pocket and handed it to her.

Amelia's pulse quickened and her heart dared her to believe it could be true.

"Giraud said it is from Jehan and, if you'd like him to deliver a reply, he will stop on his way through from Florac in two days' time."

She held the letter to her breast and closed her eyes for a moment, letting her intuitive knowing take voice again and guide her feet along the track. A warmth began to radiate through her when she wondered what he might be doing at that precise moment.

As they stepped into the stables, she opened her eyes. Dust motes danced on beams of light making their way through cracks in the gray stone walls. Her cheeks lifted at seeing this sign—the light of grace had, at long last, broken through the darkness in her life.

But then Amelia looked at Cavalier and noticed a pained look in his gaze. She had sensed there was something more than the letter, something disturbing her young friend, and that look confirmed it.

"I hope you have been well," she said. "We have not seen you for many months. I know you are quite proficient in eluding the dragoons, but I do worry."

"I am torn, Amelia." Cavalier's eyes blinked and flitted about as he spoke. "I rejoice in the great happiness I've found in my ardent love for a wonderful young woman. She is Marie Mathieu from Lussan. And, at the same time, I am fraught with fear and sorrow."

Amelia placed a hand over her heart. "I am so pleased that you have found love. But . . . I am perplexed. Where lies your fear and sorrow?"

"Marie is a prophetess. Perhaps the greatest ever. When she is in the state of mystical trance . . . when God is present in her . . . she can turn hearts and minds in a way I have seen no other *inspiré* do before."

Amelia pushed back her surprise that he had fallen in love with a prophetess. In the past, he had seemed wary about the legitimacy of the inspirés, but love had the power to color beliefs in an entirely new way. "I understand now . . . how you could be fearful of losing her, with the Intendants' orders to capture all prophets."

"The vicious cycle continues to worsen. Just after the snows melted, and the dragoons began raiding clandestine assemblies in full force again, the number of prophets, mostly young children, increased significantly. 'Tis as if God is possessing these young souls to serve as martyrs in some ludicrous, violent Apocalyptic crusade."

Amelia wasn't sure what more she could say. There was no assurance of safety for anyone in the Cévennes, since both sides had been known to take up the mantle of persecution.

She held Cavalier's hands in hers and squeezed them in gentle reassurance. "I shall pray to the Holy Spirit and Sophia to stand for you and your Marie, and all those who want to worship in peace. In the hands of a loving God, at least your souls will be safe."

Amelia said her goodbyes to Cavalier, then huddled in Luisant's stall and unfolded Jehan's letter. She stroked the mare's silken, chestnut-colored coat as she read.

Dearest One,

I write to tell you I am now endeavoring to throw off sorrow and selfishness, and to raise my spirits by finding joy in your happiness. Whatever pleases you, pleases me. I confess that I grew angry last year when I received your letter about the dragoon attack. Angry with myself for not being there to protect you, and angry with you for saying you would join the Order. My heart was wounded, thinking you would sacrifice your freedom for the Knights of Saint Jean, but not for me.

Often my eyes would fill with tears, for to direct my heart toward you seemed ruinous. To yearn for you was constant torture—when I could not gaze into your eyes of mystery and delight, when I could not ramble through the forest with you in search of nature's medicines, or sit together with you while studying the ancient teachings, so close that your warm breath on my cheek would set my body to tremble with emotion and desire. The love I feel for you is a fever that can only be calmed by your healing hands. I shall never stop loving you. 'Tis in your eyes where I have always seen my true home. Your soul brings solace to my fire, enough to bring a calm I have only experienced in your presence.

I know full well how audacious my love for you truly is. You who are so high above the baseness of my nature. I sin in loving you—a precious being who strives daily to embrace the Divine—and I have sinned when I am not able to love you. I have abused your trust and kindness by giving up on you and having sought love in another. Yet I did not find it since my soul can love no other but you. So I dare to ask for your mercy and forgiveness. And for you to consider, for one last time, joining me in the Eden that I know is as important to you as to me.

Not long after the Swiss officials announced that most of the French refugees would be required to move on to other lands, an opportunity presented itself for me to leave Aarau and the stringent restrictions of my uncle's colony, for the beautiful colony of Carolana. 'Tis the entire south-eastern area of North America from Virginia to nearly the center of Spanish Floride, and west to the areas occupied as French territory. 'Tis a vast land of beauty and abundance, with forests and fruit trees, and great tranquil rivers.

I do still hope Menina Elise is well, and she is in good hands at the Hospitaller's Infirmaria. The choice to join me will be yours and Menina's to decide. There is still time to write your reply before I journey on to Rotterdam and London in mid-June. The first ship to the colony is expected to set sail in the early spring of next year. If your soul longs to find mine, not only in the stars, but in a land where we shall thrive and flourish, then seek me in London by way of the French Protestant Church of Saint Jean in Spittlefields. I shall write you again to confirm just before I depart Aarau. I beseech almighty God for guidance and safety in whatever choice you make.

The body's sight can sometimes forget, but my soul remembers yours forever. I humbly pray for your forgiveness and send you my enduring love. May it embrace you in peace and joy.

Amelia traced a finger over the gentle curves of the ink inscribed on the parchment. Her breath quickened as she took in the depth of Jehan's devotion in every word. There were no more doubts that her soul longed to be with his. No doubt that she loved him despite his misstep and that, like the Christ, she would somehow find her way to forgiveness. It would be a struggle at first. She was already fighting against her mind as it tried to fixate on what sort of woman he'd been with. But she would pray every day until the love in her heart won out against the jealousy and betrayal she would naturally feel once this elation subsided.

As much as she wanted to be with Jehan, the time had not come. Not while Menina still graced the earthly realm. But now that she knew Jehan's true heart, she would write and fearlessly vow to find her way to him, even if it took years. *I shall not let our love fail.*

PART THREE

CHAPTER 16

AN UNFORSEEN COURSE

JEHAN

6 June 1699
Banks of the River Aar, Aarau

Light broke across the water of the Aar River in tiny flashes, a magical and serendipitous backdrop to the creased parchment Jehan held in his hand. He sat upon the grassy banks and leaned his face toward the warm spring sunlight, thanking God for the blessing of Amelia's letter. He smiled indulgently and read it a second time, imbibing her declaration of love.

1 May 1699

Throughout the winter, I struggled to rekindle the tiny spark that was left of our connection. Although it was there, it had grown quite dim. During the day, the sun blotted out the light of the stars, where we pledged to find each other. And at night, I would look to the sky, laden with thick winter clouds that brought only a blackness as dark as pitch. Yet now, because your recent letter has just arrived, the brilliancy of the stars is so great again that I feel as if I could touch them with my hand.

I was most pleased to read it, in spite of your confession, and I greatly appreciate your concern about Menina. She is in good hands here, although she is not at all well, and I fear she has not much longer on this earth. I am as healthy as ever. However, I must make my own confession—I have yearned to be together with you since long before the day you left, and I have, at times, suffered great melancholy, rendering me into a person you would no longer recognize.

I became even more distressed when I learned two fortnights ago that our connection suffered from interference by one of the novices. I had written two more letters to you that I entrusted to her care, but instead of delivering them, she had hidden them along with your previous letter to me. I could feel your pain in every word of that letter and I could only think that, with all the time that had passed, you would have surely given up on me. I can understand how you thought I'd taken vows to the Hospitaller's Order, but that did not happen. Instead, the Commandeur offered a sensible solution that provides a lifetime of protection without professing religious vows or the Order's Promise. He has graciously bestowed the Dames of Honor and Devotion recognition on Menina and me with a sash bearing the Order's cross.

I can understand how your transgression may have been inevitable. And thus, my heart tells me to take the path of forgiveness and to place my trust in you. I choose to love you because you have held my soul in your heart, no matter what else has happened.

I have but few moments to gaze upon the stars, but when I do, I shall find our connection through that which is greater than ourselves in this physical realm. There may be times when the light is blocked from our view, but our faith in the Holy Spirit and in each other will help us overcome our doubts and fears. Please trust in my love as I shall in yours. I shall not let our love fail over misunderstandings. I vow to you, someday we shall be together, sharing the same view of the sky. Write to me again with a meeting location in London, and yes, somehow, some way, I shall join you there as soon as I am able. I long to be free in a wild place again, where we can relive the moments we shared together.

Your Ame for all time

7 June 1699
Jehan's Apartment, Aarau

Jehan opened the casement window of his apartment in the hostel to view the clamorous activity in the street below.

The 'grand depart' was underway with a melee of horses and iron carriage wheels clattering over the cobblestone streets, with negotiations over the cost of transport, with women and nursemaids calling out for the children to hurry along.

Moyse joined him at the window, whistling a melodious psalm that softened the raucous. "'Tis an exciting time, is it not?"

Jehan took a slow, easy breath, feeling content for the first time in ages. He nodded in agreement, looping his thumbs in the pockets of his justaucorps. "Indeed. We have a whole new future ahead of us."

"Thanks be to the good Lord that we shall finally have houses to call our own when we reach Brandenburg." The joy on Moyse's face withered as his brows came together. "Yet it'd be less worrisome if Pasteur Barjon were traveling with us. I spoke to him, but he says his wife is still recovering from the birth of their little Marie Marguerite."

"I am sure that after bringing nine children into the world, Dame Bernadine will need an extended lying-in," Jehan replied. "'Tis what I would recommend should I be her physician."

"It also worries me that you are planning to take that dangerous path to Rotterdam. Our route to Brandenburg does not take us anywhere near the French-held Alsatian lands, but I'm told . . ." Moyse's down-turned lips pinched together and his voice began to quiver, "there is a long stretch of the Rhine en route to Rotterdam that will put you squarely within the sight of those devils." His eyes pleading, he gripped Jehan's forearm. "Are you certain you shall not join us instead? 'Twill be safer if we all stay together."

A twinge of guilt tightened in Jehan's chest as he saw his cousin's eyes glisten and a tear catch in the surrounding creases.

Moyse had never quite recovered from the mental wound of losing his farm to a destructive Cévenol episode, the greatest storm to batter the Cévennes in decades. Then, even before the rain had ceased, he had stood among the ruins and witnessed a horrific dragoon raid in the village below. The farm had been his life's great work, and he had nothing left—no family, no home—nothing but his devotion to the Calvinist faith.

Jehan took hold of Moyse's shoulders. "My course lies elsewhere, for I must meet my dearest Amelia in London. I have given Giraud a letter just yesterday confirming where to find me when she arrives. As much as I love you, too, Moyse, she and Carolana are my destiny."

He pulled the old man close and hugged him hard. Moyse stood rigid at first, holding his hands in the air, not accustomed to such expressions of affection, but gradually he moved his hands around and returned the embrace.

Jehan released him and went to the armoire, knowing what would lighten the mood. "I want you to have some of my things."

He took his red velvet cape from inside and whirled it around Moyse's shoulders. "There. You are now a man about town."

"But . . ."

"Say no more," said Jehan, waving a hand to stop Moyse's objections. "I have my old cloak to wear and my fine ensemble from Lemieux's boutique. And . . ." He unbuttoned his overcoat and reached into the jangling purse at his waist. "I wish you to take some coin for your journey."

Moyse's eyes widened as Jehan counted out ten *livre*, eighteen *sous*, and the rest of the *deniers*, then lifted his cousin's hand and dropped them in.

"Oh mon Dieu! 'Tis enough to feed me for a year or more. Thank you, thank you."

"At the least, it should be enough for meals and lodging for a few months. You will no longer have charity funds from the city of Aarau to depend on, and I want you to keep yourself healthy and hardy until you can receive aid in Brandenburg."

Moyse looked at him with concern. "Are you sure you do not need this money?"

"Do not worry," Jehan said. "I shall be fine." He knew all would be well as far as funds, but traveling with such large amounts of money could set him up for all sorts of trouble—road bandits, greedy toll collectors, pickpockets. He needed to convert a portion of his money to a bill of exchange just as soon as he could locate a bank or trading company that offered the service. His jaw tightened as he wondered where that might be, since there was nothing of the sort in Aarau. Even asking around about it posed a threat.

"André has sent several shipments of income from my estate, so I have accumulated a good deal. He is happy to do me the service as long as he retains the townhouse in Genouillac. And I am happy to share what I have."

Moyse wiped the sleeve of his threadbare chemise across his eyes, then raised an eyebrow. "Our group is to leave for Brandenburg in a few days. When do you set out?"

"Monsieur de Sailly has told us he will charter a ship out of Rotterdam on the 6th of July, so, by my reckoning, we shall leave mid-month." Jehan patted his old cousin's hand. "There may be sorrow in what separates us, but let us rejoice in what unites us. May we each endeavor to find the individual truth we seek."

14 June 1699 ~ Early Morning
Anchorage Landing, Aar River, Aarau

As Jehan emerged through the city gates and stepped toward the river bank, he prayed for the safe journey of the Brandenburg group just as he'd done each morning since their departure. And now that it came time for his group to depart for Rotterdam, he added a prayer for their safety as well.

In the pink light of dawn, he followed the muffled chattering at the river's edge toting a bulging satchel of clothing over one shoulder and his apothecary bag over the other. He wore his sword strapped at his left hip and his dagger on the right, and had stashed his journal and graphite stick in his pocket. Under his left arm, he nestled the small oak strongbox where he stored the copious coins that would not fit into the lining of his justaucorps, along with a few tiny books on philosophy. His belongings were few, but they were truly all he needed.

When he moved closer, he realized the morning mist over the Aar had disguised and quieted the true intensity of the departure commotion—the anchorage spot was utterly jammed. He gradually made his way through the maze of trunks and barrels and strongboxes and satchels, even a few small pieces of furnishings here and there, until he reached the cluster of people waiting for further instruction.

He stood on the towpath at the water's edge, studying the vessels that were intended to carry all of this—belongings and bodies alike—down the Aar, then on to the Rhine, and all the way to Rotterdam.

Water sloshed and slapped against the half-dozen flat-bottomed boats still tied to the moorings. They were nothing more than *weidlings* used by the fisher people, with narrow hulls about 20 pieds long that had a curvature on each end. They looked as though they could each carry about ten passengers, at most, with some room to tuck a few bits of cargo under benches. There certainly weren't enough of them to carry all seventy-five people who had signed on for the voyage.

Jehan questioned whether the boats could bear the weight of so many heavy items along with the anxious, fidgeting passengers, particularly the excited children. Even if three or four more boats were available, his gut told him this was a huge mistake, and he hoped he could convince the others

Most of the free-thinkers group had arrived and were gathering near Antoine Aigoin. He seemed to be left in charge to negotiate with the boatmen, as there was no sign of De Sailly or his man, Pasteur Borel, to assist.

Jehan approached Corbell and Mathieu Roussel and carefully set down the weighty strongbox.

"These vessels are not our only option," he said to the others. "They are much smaller than the *gabarre* hired by the group heading to Brandenburg. If we take these, we may be forced to leave behind some belongings."

He grasped the button band on his justaucorps and ran a thumb over the concealed coins sewn inside while he pushed back visions of capsizing and being dragged to the river's depths.

"Why is Antoine not considering going overland?" Jehan asked.

"He says he wants to keep the cost down," Mathieu answered.

They all turned to see Antoine nervously puffing on his clay pipe as he struggled to communicate with the boatmen who spoke scarcely any French.

Mathieu reached over and tapped Antoine's shoulder. "Jehan has some concerns, and he has another idea."

Squinting an eye at Jehan, Antoine blew a cloud of rich-smelling pipe smoke from the corner of his mouth.

"'Tis a good thing that pipe gives you an air of authority," Jehan said, fanning the smoke away from his face. "Otherwise, it is worthless."

"Thought you physic sorts used tobacco as a cure."

"We do. In a tisane as a purgative, or to heal a wound by applying leaves. But I am of the opinion that taking smoke, of any sort, into the lungs is not healthful. Yet I do notice it induces energy for a short time."

"Well, what other than my smoking worries you, Sieur BonDurant?"

"I am concerned we are too many in number to safely board these vessels, and the river is not the best mode of transport the entire way, so I have an idea." He pulled his journal and a graphite stick from his pocket and began some calculations. "Factoring in the tolls and additional nights lodging to go by boat, I believe our best choice is to hire coaches or carts for a more direct route to Basel. There, we can locate larger vessels than these precarious fishing punts and continue on the Rhine from there."

Antoine leaned over to look at the computations. "Ah, yes, I see. I am all for saving money with what little I have."

Jehan chuckled and turned to Corbell. "Let us fetch some drivers. It should not take long, and we shall reach Basel well before supper."

14 June 1699 ~ Midday
Basel, Swiss Canton of Basel-Stadt

The ride overland was not the most comfortable, but the caravan of overcrowded coaches and carts did the job of reaching Basel even before midday. To avoid tolls, the drivers let them out beside the moat-bridge at the city's imposing east gate.

"All off at Saint-Alban Tor," the lead coach driver shouted.

Jehan and the other refugees queued outside the medieval walls that went on as far as the eye could see with defensive towers at frequent intervals. He stayed near the front with Antoine—who seemed to be the de facto leader for the moment—and their other friends as they presented their documents to the guards. Jehan's mind began to drift as he waited, imagining this impressive city in the days of Erasmus, the great provocateur of Renaissance culture.

When he approached the tower and handed the guard his papers, he glanced up. Sharp metal points of the portcullis loomed over him, suspended by mere ropes and ready to be dropped at the first sign of danger. An urge to move quickly overwhelmed him. He took his papers and passed on through the tower in haste with the others.

They came out onto a main road lined with half-timbered houses, only to find a second moat-bridge, tower, and ring of protective walls just a few blocks down the street.

Corbell heaved a huge breath. "Gah! They are prepared here for the war to end all wars. I hope we don't have to wait too long at the next gate. I need to find a privy soon."

Jehan chuckled and pointed a thumb in the direction of Etienne Roussel's two sons, who had ducked behind a mule-drawn cart filled with small barrels to relieve themselves. "Looks as though the little ones aren't able to wait."

"Boys," shouted Etienne, grabbing their arms. "That mule could knock you in your heads till you're both clay-brained."

Quite the sight, their party of seventy-five received many nervous looks as they paraded with their possessions across the moat and through the second tower, then on to the Altstadt district, where they'd been told to seek lodging.

Jehan could sense the eyes on them, peering from behind shutters set ajar, as they dodged carriages and sedan chairs and pedestrians in the crowded city center. It was no wonder the Swiss had come to resent French refugees, as they had regularly migrated through their cities in droves since the Revocation.

He found Basel rich in many ways and a world apart from Aarau. They passed by a gothic cathédrale with grand twin spires and sculptures of Saint George and a tiny dragon, and then by a château-like, arcaded city hall with a statue of the Roman founder, Munatius Plancus.

In the central district, they came upon some splendid old coaching inns, but those were priced far beyond the means of many in the group, causing the patience of a few to run short. With a recommendation from a helpful concierge, they ventured across the Rhine bridge to the right bank, where they found more modest accommodations, yet some were still rather unhappy with their options, especially the prices.

Upon arrival at the Rheinhof Inn, the usually soft-spoken Constantin Eschalier nearly started a tussle with the innkeepers's wife.

"'Tis outrageous, madame," he said waving his arms about.

The woman folded her arms across her chest and straightened, stepping into the doorway as if to block him from entering.

"Take up with city magistrates," she said in broken French. "Includes their tax. You fortunate we have two rooms. But for first twenty only. Ten to a room. Others must find another inn. Plenty on this street."

Antoine sighed and turned to break the news to the others. "There is room for only twenty at this inn. The rest of you will need to find lodging in one of the other inns further down the street. Meet back here in the morning at half-past eight," he told them.

Jehan had not calculated for such high taxes on the lodging and felt somewhat responsible. It made good common sense though, being it was a city at the conjunction of three countries and located on a major waterway. The city required funding to maintain its extensive fortifications and, despite what the woman had said, there was little doubt that innkeepers' portions were also overpriced as a result of the high demand.

After they settled into their rooms, Jehan took a meal with Corbell and Mathieu in the dining hall. It was bathed in the mellow glow of candlelight and filled with a steady cadence of murmuring from the guests. But even the comforting smells of ale and wine and the rich *Basler Mehlsuppe* flour soup did nothing to still Jehan's apprehension about how they were to move forward.

He looked at the others, his mouth twisted in thought, then shared his view of the situation. "We need to determine the possible wharves and mooring locations where we can find boats large enough for the group."

Silenced by a large bite of bread and his good manners, Corbell just nodded in agreement.

Mathieu jumped in with his observations. "When we crossed the bridge, I saw only the smaller weidlings and those slipshod cargo barges piecemealed from waste lumber."

Glancing across the room, Jehan noticed Antoine had been busy conversing with the innkeeper for some time. "Maybe Antoine has something worked out," he said as he waved to catch his attention.

After a few minutes, Antoine strode over, accompanied by a short man in stylish but simple bourgeois attire, and introduced him.

The man took a deep bow. "Name is Herr Vermittler," he said in nearly perfect French. "Sounds as though your group can benefit from my services." His brown eyes held an honest look with a hint of compassion. "I can secure three vessels and their captains for a reasonable price plus my fee, but you will also require passports to travel undisturbed past the Alsatian customs fortresses under French control. I have connections who can provide them for you with French government certification."

"A moment please, Herr Vermittler." Jehan pulled Antoine and Corbell aside and lowered his voice. "You realize they will be counterfeit. Acquiring a legal, certified passport is a lengthy process with each individual needing just cause and a signature from the authorities. But what choice do we have? We shall never secure them on our own, and we dare not risk traveling without them."

"Agreed," said Antoine. "'Tis no different from the passports we used to leave France. And should we employ this man's service, we can set out right away."

Corbell gave a quick, decisive nod, and they resumed their discussions with the man. They talked through the details at some length, but Jehan was only satisfied with the arrangement once the man agreed to reduce his overall commission on both the boats and the exorbitantly priced passports.

It was all set, yet Jehan still needed to deal with his strongbox of coinage that he'd perilously wrapped in his cloak and hidden under his bed in the shared chamber.

"One more thing," Jehan said, leaning in close to prevent anyone from overhearing. "I need to locate a bank or trading company that offers bills of exchange."

"Have a bit of coin with you, eh? In the morning, seek the mercantile exchange next to the market. Tell them I sent you. "

"*Danke*, Herr Vermittler. I could not locate such conveniences in Aarau." Jehan slipped him a few sous. "I feel you are a man we can count on for discretion."

"Most certainly. Now, be sure to be at the wharf no later than nine."

15 June 1699 ~ Early Morning
Upper Rhine River

Jehan tucked the bank note securely into a hidden pocket upon leaving the mercantile exchange, and made it with time to spare to the mooring site where the boarding was going smoothly.

Two flat-bottomed gabarre boats, equipped with a central folding mast and sail, were sufficient to transport the majority of the group and their smaller personal effects. He counted fifteen who were seated in the third vessel that was being loaded by shoremen with furnishings and larger trunks alongside barrels of some sort of cargo that must have been commissioned by a local merchant.

Corbell and Mathieu were seated on the benches near the bow, but Jehan's thoughts were scattered and he was not feeling much like crowding in and talking. So he went to an empty bench near a small cabin at the stern.

He stowed his strongbox under the bench and placed his satchel and apothecary bag in front to hide it. Although he no longer worried about the amassed coins being stolen, the box now served a new purpose, protecting the other important possessions—his fine ensemble from Monsieur Lemieux's and the special books on philosophy—yet he had kept the gemstones and banknote on his person, hidden deep within his justaucorps.

Grasping the upper band of his sword's scabbard, he pulled it forward and swung it across the lap as he sat. Still wary about the chance of encounters with French soldiers, Jehan's nerves were on edge, tightening his shoulders. He took a long breath of the morning air and tried to settle in.

The captain gave a signal, and his boat hand set the long punt into the river, pushing hand over hand to move the boat away from the wharf. It creaked as it moved away out of the shallows and caught momentum in the fast moving current.

The other passengers were chattering like chickens, but Jehan did not hear a word they said, his mind slipping into visions of falling into the hands of the French troops. He had to let go of the fear. He pinched his eyes shut and shook the thought from his head, trying to envision the far leg of his journey—on board a ship bound for the New World, with Amelia by his side.

From atop the small cabin, the captain shouted out, "*Bleibt ruhig, Leute*. Be calm, people! You attract French soldiers and *Banditen*. And scare away fish."

Jehan observed the multitude of small boats up and down the river, too numerous to count, and detected grimaces on a few of the fishermen's faces. They surely were none too pleased with the presence of this boisterous group exhibiting serious cases of anxiety. But the refugees soon quieted as the natural beauty of the vast Rhine River enchanted them into a trance-like state.

Ah. Nature is the best medicine of all.

Jehan sighed and languidly dragged his hand through the water, watching the morning sunlight shimmer across the gentle ripples his fingers etched on the surface. Elegant white swans and a variety of ducks drifted by while warblers and buntings sang their cheerful songs.

He looked across the wide river to a white-tailed eagle as it plucked a small fish from the shallows and flew skyward. He studied the ascent, his eyes drawn to a huge ruined fortress castle on the cliffs above.

"You see many *Schlösser* here," said the captain as he navigated with a long wooden oar.

Jehan looked up at the man, his skin withered from time spent in the elements. "Have they been abandoned for many years?"

"*Für* . . . um . . . ten years. On Alsatian side, French King ordered most all *zerstört* during last *Kreig*."

"*Zerstört*. That is destroyed, is it not? Destroyed in the last war?"

"*Ja. Und* land and people not good from war before that. No one here to protect farmers and fishers from *Banditen*. Huh! They are now *die Banditen*."

Jehan could see how the desolation would make the area ripe for thieves and wayward French soldiers looking for a bribe, and his hand reactively moved to the hilt of his sword.

"You in a good place to keep eye out," said the captain. "You strong and have weapons and can fight them off, *ja?*"

Jehan knew he was capable. His intensive training with his seigneurial métayer, Benat, had provided him with the necessary skills. Although he had not used those skills for a few years. He had come close but, by God's grace and his own good wits, he'd manage to avoid any real fighting. He clenched his teeth in determination and inhaled. If a situation arose, he *would* be prepared, but he would always aspire to follow Amelia's convictions to be a peacemaker first.

"Certainly," he said, hoping to reassure the captain—and himself.

By the cast of the sun's light, it was not yet even midday, so there was little reason Jehan could see to stop so soon—no city and no river fortress, either.

"Why are we slowing?" he asked the captain.

"Toll. They are many," the captain said, as he skillfully maneuvered the boat ashore on the right bank.

Jehan could make out an arch of boats ahead, carrying a score of disheveled boys and men. Along with a half-dozen or so men on the shore, they all held long-bows or pistols pointed directly at the refugees.

As the passengers started to mumble and whisper, the noise reminded Jehan of an approaching insect swarm.

The captain shouted out a series of exchanges in a Germanic dialect with one of the men onshore.

"Jehan. What are they saying up there?" Antoine called from the second boat.

Jehan shrugged. The conversation was far too rapid for him to understand.

The captain turned back and waved at the other boats. "*Zehn pro Person*. Ten each."

"Ten deniers?" asked Jehan.

"*Nein*. Ten *sous*. Or six *thaler* or *rijksdaalder*.

The boat hands came around with linen sacks to collect the money while several of the passengers in the second boat complained loudly about the cost. Jehan could hear their captain trying to quiet them. "Only first toll. *Es gibt* many more ahead. You want walk instead?"

It was already clear to Jehan—it would take more time to reach Rotterdam than they had anticipated. And with these toll stops, some of his fellow travelers were likely to run out of money before they arrived since they had counted on De Sailly to pay their expenses. Jehan's jaw clenched as he speculated that the man had intentionally dodged this portion of the travel expenses which, quite likely, could cost more than the voyage to Carolana.

CHAPTER 17

MIDSUMMER FÊTE

AMELIA

**22 June 1699 ~ Fête de la Saint Jean
Hospitaller Commandery, Mont Lauzère, France**

The jubilant sounds of the Fête de la Saint Jean mid-summer festival drifted on the breeze and lifted Amelia's heart as she surveyed the commandery's field from the door of the Infirmaria.

Laughter and singing filled the air as twilight hung on the horizon. Scores of lanterns glimmered as a procession of young men and maidens gathered up wildflower bouquets of fennel, rosemary, foxglove, elderflower, millepertuis, male ferns, and wild roses strewn over rows of long tables, then danced off to the distant bonfire for the traditional ritual.

Despite the need for evermore diligent security, the people remained in good spirits as they celebrated Saint Jean's birth and the longest day of the year, grateful for the respite from their hard labor.

Amelia stepped back inside where the candlelight cast a warm glow on Griselle's smiling face. She had prepared linen bandaging and honey poultice, readied atop a table just inside the door.

"You have done fine work here, Griselle."

The young novice bowed her head. "This should take care of anyone who becomes reckless around the fire."

Amelia stepped over to the table and stood beside Griselle, tucking an errant strand of the girl's dark hair into her coif. She found contentment with Griselle's remarkable turnabout in both behavior and outlook, and it had fostered a deeper connection between the two of them. The girl had done her penance with great devotion for almost four months, and it was nearing a time when she, too, should be rewarded for her hard work.

Griselle focused her warm brown eyes on Amelia's as though she were trying to read the deep emotion inside. "Have you heard from your Sieur BonDurant yet?"

"Not yet," Amelia answered. She looked down at her hands, realizing she had begun absentmindedly wringing them. "He said he would write to confirm his lodging in London. They were to depart Aarau any day now, so perhaps I shall have word the next time Giraud comes to market."

"I do hope you will find him. You both deserve to be free, but I shall miss you dearly, Mademoiselle Amelia." A sad, wistful smile crept across Griselle's lips.

"We still have some time before I go. I shall stay as long as Menina is alive, and I have so much more to teach you. I want to be sure you can read beyond the basic recipes so you can study the ancient texts as well. That is where I acquired much of my knowledge."

Griselle took Amelia's hand. "Thank you. I have prayed that you would still help me with this. I know it will change my life for the better, and I shall always be grateful."

"Studying the people here tonight . . . is a lesson in itself."

"It is?"

"Yes, indeed," Amelia said, as she motioned Griselle toward the open door. "This is a day of freedom for these people, but they must each make a choice about their conduct. Some will get swilled with drink and likely burn themselves in the fire, maybe even knocking someone else in and causing injury to that person as well. Others will use restraint but will nonetheless enjoy the merriment. Freedom is not so much the right to do all that we please, but the opportunity to do what is right. With freedom comes the responsibility to live with love and respect so as to give rise to the freedom of others. If we are not doing that, we shall never be truly free."

Griselle hung her head, but Amelia put a finger under her chin and lifted it. "I think you have come to understand that, haven't you?"

The girl's eyebrows raised, and she smiled, nodding in agreement. "I have. Yet I do still feel so much guilt for the suffering I caused you."

"Do not worry yourself any longer. I have forgiven you, and with your repentance, so has God. Recall what the frères teach you from Isaiah. 'I have wiped away your iniquities like a cloud, and your sins like a mist. Return to me, because I have redeemed you.' I have spoken with Commandeur Timoleon, and he is in agreement that you should have your freedom to join the celebration tonight."

Griselle's eyes widened, and her mouth dropped open. "Do you mean . . . out there . . . with the others?"

"Yes, I do mean out there. With the other young people."

Amelia looped her arm around Griselle's and guided her out through the doorway.

The sweet scent of herbs and pine drifted in on the woodsmoke, and youthful voices rose up and over the flames in an ancient chanson that tumbled in waves to their ears. "Let's go, pretty heart, the moon has risen! Let's go, pretty heart, the moon has risen!"

"You see," said Amelia as she lifted a hand toward the revelers who danced around the great fire. "There is no sin in their merriment. For should the mirth and joy in this world stop, it would be the end times. And those days are far off, despite what some might attempt to prophesy. I know your father would not approve of celebrating Saint Jean or the dancing or the old Celtae traditions, but he has taken his Protestant convictions much farther than most and has used them to cause suffering. His insecurities and fears created his insatiable desire to control others, much in the same way as it has with many Catholic leaders. But when we are in fear, we are separated from God . . . something that I, too, must remind myself of any time I feel fear trying to take me hostage."

Griselle tipped her head down a bit and looked up at Amelia. "Yes. I understand. I have felt that separation and I promised myself I shall not fall into the same patterns as my Papa. Not ever again."

The girl had come so far from where she had started, and was becoming wise beyond her years. Amelia's heart pranced in gladness for her young friend, and her cheeks lifted into a broad smile.

"So go now. Rejoice with the others! Let the essence of the fire burn away your old fears. Celebrate the light and give thanks to the Divine for bringing new hope to your life."

She leaned in closer and took one of Griselle's hands into hers. "This night is set aside to honor the birth of Saint Jean and also to bless the maidens as they enact their fertility rites."

As Amelia continued, she twirled Griselle by the hand in a mock dance, again and again, in time with her words. "You may get swept up by the sweet, spicy, sensual aromas as the young men and maidens wave their bouquets through the fire. But, remember . . ." She paused and looked into Griselle's eyes with ardent concern. "If you want to take your vows to join the Order, you must preserve your chastity. The choice is yours and only your heart can decide."

Griselle lifted Amelia's hand and kissed it. "Bless you, Mademoiselle Amelia." She smiled and curtsied, then broke into a run, past the tables and out to the dancers where she joined hands with them, circling the fire in a joyous dance.

Amelia sighed, feeling relaxed for the first time in many long months and delighting in Griselle's first real day of joy.

CHAPTER 18

BREAKING FREE FROM THE EDDY

JEHAN

23 June 1699
Rhine River near Mainz, Lower Palatinate

Like leaves caught in one eddy after another, the refugees' boats had been detained at some fifteen toll stops over the past week, and by Jehan's reckoning, they were only halfway to Rotterdam.

Although nerve-racking, their encounters with French soldiers in occupied Strasbourg had ironically gone free of incident thanks to the false passports. But they ran into difficulties in several Germanic cities along the Lower Rhine. Each time they came to a city with custom houses, there were rules requiring them to stop overnight, wasting time and money. There had also been more unauthorized toll stops, similar to the first stop out of Basel, manned by farmers and fishermen demanding their share of the river bounty.

Jehan thought it odd the boat captains had insisted on choosing the lodging each night for the group. Though he had no real evidence of wrongdoing, the pieces were beginning to fall in to place—it all seemed part of a grand network, with a payoff here or a cut of the proceeds there, where everyone profited except for the passengers.

With a clear day and a good wind in the sails, they approached the fortified city of Mainz many hours before sunset, and with that, came heated complaints about costs from passengers in the bow. Despite arriving early, they would lose yet another entire afternoon just to comply with the rules to lodge.

Jehan leaned a hand against the small cabin and spoke to the captain. "With all these stops, many here are running short on money and are concerned about making it to Rotterdam on time. Can we simply pay the toll here and pass on through? It would be expeditious to wait to lodge closer to sunset."

"*Nein*. Mainz holds *stapelrecht*. *Die* stacking rights. We must unload. Stack goods for their agents to take to market for three days. And you must lodge and eat and wait."

As Jehan let the news sink in, he bristled, his mounting frustration causing his breathing to become rapid. He had never heard of such an absurd regulation. One night was bad enough, but three nights lodging would completely exhaust the savings of many of the refugees.

He scanned their faces, regarding their expressions. Aside from the worry that wrinkled many brows, the dark shadows that encircled their eyes indicated that most had not slept well. The group had only been offered overcrowded chambers at all the inns, forcing them to put up with snoring and coupling, the stench of chamberpot deposits, and restless children.

To share a bed with six, sometimes eight, and lying crosswise with feet dangling, often meant sleeping with complete strangers. So Jehan had chosen the pallets or trundles instead. Though they were rather uncomfortable, at least there was no threat of elbows or knees prodding him out of a half-sleep. He had the means to sleep like a king if he chose, but he could not bring himself to do so when several others would soon have not a single denier left until they met De Sailly in Rotterdam.

The waterfront at Mainz comprised a long stone wall and wharf from one end of the fortification to the other. Jehan held a hand over his eyes to shade them as he gazed toward the center of the wharf and spotted a low-lying bridge.

"There is no sailing past that bridge," he said. "Not even a small weidling can make its way under that."

"Is how they want it," said the captain. "Prepare to take all off boat," he shouted. "*Kiste* and *die Möbels* also."

An older gentleman sitting on the bench in front of Jehan turned around. "What does he mean?"

"I believe he is speaking of the trunks and furniture."

"But they have watched after them on the other stops. What do we do with them?"

The captain must have overheard, so he crouched to speak to them. "We say farewell here," he said, keeping a kindly tone with the elderly man. "You go to boats on other side of bridge. They take you to Cologne."

Jehan could scarcely believe what he was hearing. "But we paid for passage to Rotterdam. Do you provide a voucher for the next boat?"

The captain blew out a breath, rattling his lips. "You only pay for my boat to Mainz. You must find boat from guild of Middle Rhine to go to Cologne. Then from guild of Upper Rhine to go to Rotterdam."

Jehan squeezed his forehead and tried to think, struggling to contain his anger at that currish swindler, Herr Vermittler. Heat flushed his face, and sweat beaded under his fingers.

The captain of the second boat must have also shared the bad news, since Antoine and a few others stood and raised their voices. Jehan held his breath as he watched all the movement cause their boat to tenuously dip in the water, then rise, then dip.

They would need a plan, and fast. He reached under his bench and readied his belongings for departure.

Just as Jehan stood, the captain slowed the boat, guiding it toward the wharf, all the while his eyes nervously flitting askance. He seemed to be watching for signals from the boat hand who had jumped over to the wharf and began securing the mooring line, but he kept looking toward the second boat.

Jehan's eyes narrowed in annoyance—the crew of the second boat was completely distracted by the continued arguing, and they were letting it drift straight toward where he stood in the stern. His heart lurched. He grabbed the side rail in haste, planting his feet firmly while the boats collided with a violent jolt.

Screams and shouts filled the air as Antoine and a few men who had been standing tumbled onto some of the other passengers.

An elderly man near Jehan fell off the bench, and his wife bent over him and wailed, "Oh, my dear Lord!"

"Steady there. We safe now," the captain said as the boat hand separated the boats with his long punt.

Jehan came to his knees beside the elderly man and helped him back to the bench. He looked him over and saw that the skin on his forearm had abraded.

"Do not worry, Madame. I have something for this."

He pulled his apothecary bag from under the bench and reached in for a strip of linen and a small bottle of vinegar, then promptly began cleaning the wound.

The old man puckered his face, but never let out a single moan.

Jehan made quick work of applying a dressing to the wound, then held a hand over it for a moment while he said a brief prayer. "O God Almighty, Healer of our souls and bodies, we pray that You bless our friend with Your loving care, renew his strength, and restore his good health. In Your loving name. Amen."

"There, you should be mended in no time," said Jehan.

He stood and turned around to see Corbell and the Roussel brothers had disembarked and were standing on the wharf behind him.

Etienne Roussel had his hands on his hips. "So, was this fine mess in your calculations and negotiations?"

Jehan closed his eyes and took a deep breath as he sank in a wave of guilt. Yet he could not take full blame.

"I had no idea."

Antoine stepped up alongside Corbell. "'Tis not his fault. I was also involved in the negotiations and we were both entirely misled."

"I shall confine my role to apothecary from here on out," Jehan said as he reached to assist the elderly couple from the boat. "Nevertheless, we must focus on a solution and remember that our friendship is what will get us through these trials."

❧

1 July 1699 ~ Afternoon
Rotterdam, Dutch Republic

A salty wind struck Jehan's face as he strode through the west gatehouse and onto Rotterdam's west transfer quay, then stopped. He scanned the surrounding waters, checking once again for De Sailly and his ship set for London. For a second day, Jehan and his friends had each taken a different path to search the maze of streets, alleys, ports, canals, and wharfs that made up Rotterdam, looking for any trace of the elusive man, but still to no avail.

Jehan walked down the quay, studying the great vessels tied to the moorings, then stopped halfway, thinking he should preserve his energy. From his vantage point, it seemed to be the same seven ships that had arrived the day before.

Warm, damp air and sweat clung to his skin and clothing, weighing him to the spot where he stood in profound disappointment, and he realized it was time to shift his expectations.

His mind scrambled for answers while he lifted his hat and combed a hand through his hair. He stared out across the Nieuwe Maas River delta, the wind cooling his face as it faithfully blew in from the North Sea and through the ports and canals, clearing the air of the smoke and foul smells. The constant breeze was the perfect fuel for driving the windmills that churned near the dikes in a soothing rhythmic melody—creaking and thrumming and swooshing—that provided an abundant supply of food for Rotterdam's ever-growing population.

Seeing the well-ordered prosperity had Jehan mulling over the plight of the other refugees bound for the New World. Although the peaceful, wild places of Carolana were what most suited him and Amelia, perhaps it would it be more advantageous for some of the others to stay in this thriving and tolerant city. Since it appeared De Sailly had abandoned them, it was time for Jehan to put his own plan in place.

He cast his eyes down the quay looking for possibilities and noticed a few ships flying the British flag where he might inquire. And anchored offshore, where the water bristled with masts, were several Dutch East Indies Company vessels that might be scheduled to stop in London.

As he ventured on toward the end of the quay, the unfamiliar cacophony grew louder with each step—gulls swooping and crooning in low, piercing 'keows', a stow-master calling to his men as they hauled cargo, the wake lapping against creaking wooden hulls, and here and there a ship's bell.

He made his way around a heap of substantial oak seachests waiting to be loaded on a Flemish merchant ship. Just beyond, he noticed a smaller ship he had not seen the day before. His pulse quickened as he questioned whether it might be the ship De Sailly had commissioned.

He moved closer to see it was one of the vessels flying the British flag and was splendidly painted in a golden yellow with a thin black stripe around its girth. Jehan had never seen a royal naval vessel before, but this was certainly magnificent enough to be one.

He held his hand over his eyes to block the bright afternoon sun as they tracked up the masts and confirmed that the Navy's Saint George's Cross pennant was indeed flying. He blew out a long breath of dismay. This could not be the ship meant to transport his group of refugees—but perhaps he could garner the sympathy of the commandeur of such a vessel.

Jehan took a few steps up the gangway, then stopped, thinking about the others who had, thus far, not even arrived in Rotterdam. *But I promised Etienne I would wait.* He backed down to the wharf and scuffed his boot along the brick walkway in frustration.

"De Sailly, you accursed man," Jehan growled.

He could not delay his departure to London much longer, in case Amelia was on her way, yet he found it hard to think of leaving Rotterdam until he knew Etienne and his two boys were safe.

Jehan wrestled with the dilemma over and over in his mind. Etienne, along with nearly twenty other refugees, had separated from the main group at Cologne to go overland on foot, saying they could no longer afford the boats and tolls along the Rhine. Jehan knew the choice had been theirs. After all, he had offered to loan them the fare, but they were too proud for that and feared they could not repay him.

Yet, all that reasoning did nothing to stop the anxiousness that racked his chest. The only thing to do now was to meet his friends back at the fish market and, together, they would stay focused on trying to make heads or tails of what happened to De Sailly.

Before heading back, Jehan glanced up again at the ship.

"Do you need direction, Monsieur?" said a young man regaled in a deep blue justaucorps as he came down the gangway, his polished leather boots tapping along the wooden planks. "You seem to be in some distress."

Jehan regarded the impeccable white cuffs, brass buttons, and ornamental shoulder pieces adorned with gold fringe and some sort of insignia. He realized this was indeed a naval man. However, it was odd that he spoke French instead of English.

"Yes, thank you." Jehan tipped his hat in greeting. "I am Sieur BonDurant de Cougoussac and I am seeking a Sieur De Sailly."

In return, the young man removed his hat and took a deep bow, revealing auburn hair tied neatly in a queue. "Lieutenant Brooks."

"I am surprised to hear you speak French," said Jehan.

"'Tis the most common language in the port cities. I am newly commissioned to the ship for Marquis de Ruvigny, Earl of Galway and Lord Justice of Irelande, who still speaks primarily in his native language."

"Galway. My friends have spoken of him. The one who organized a resettlement project in Irelande?"

"Indeed."

"And he is the Lord Justice? I did not realize it was possible for a Frenchman to attain such a high rank in service to the English."

"Anything is possible. Look at me, a lieutenant at seventeen." Brooks paused and took a long breath. "I do know something of De Sailly's whereabouts."

"Has he been arrested? That would be a well-deserved justice for enticing refugees with his pamphlets and fancy stories, then abandoning them."

"So you are one of the French Huguenots? You certainly don't look as though you need aid."

Jehan huffed, trying to dispel his vexation, and gazed around at the elegant chaos of stately ships as far as the eye could see.

"I can pay my way if I were to find a ship to London. I am simply seeking a land where I can begin anew. But there are many others in our group who cannot afford the fare. So then, what is it you know? Does De Sailly rot in jail?"

"My apologies. Despite the sensitive nature of the situation, you deserve an answer. The truth is, De Sailly came back here after a trip to Aarau with his tail between his legs. He utterly failed to get the Swiss cantons to contribute to the relocation, so Milord Galway sent him back to London to seek funding from the English Relief Committee for Poor French Protestants. Since Milord is one of King William's favorites, De Sailly is assured of their approval. I don't believe either of them thought your group would come on to Rotterdam without De Sailly."

Jehan shook his head in disgust at the presumptions of these men who used refugees like pawns in a game. "This is not right! De Sailly had contracts with most of our group. And we were given a *set date* for the departure. I had a verbal agreement, witnessed by many. He said the funders would offer larger allocations based on one's social status and, on his *word*, he promised to use my allocation as a noble to provide transportation for those most in need . . . to keep them from indentured servitude . . . while I agreed to pay my own way. I am afraid we shall need to report De Sailly to the authorities for breaking his contracts."

Lieutenant Brooks began to open his mouth as if to say something, then pinched his lips together. He blinked slowly and nodded in understanding.

Jehan's cheeks burned with frustration, but he knew he should not take it out on this young man. "Pardon for the outburst, Lieutenant. I do not fully understand your Lord Galway's involvement, but I thank you for the information."

"Well . . . you see, Sieur Bondurant . . . although I am most certain Milord is not aware of these contracts, he is actually the one who hired De Sailly as his agent. He is, in fact, the main force behind the Carolana project. A Huguenot himself, he uses his position to do whatever he can to assist in relocation."

Jehan crumpled his hat in his hands, trying to dissipate his ire. "So, are you saying De Sailly operated of his own accord with the contracts? And your Lord Galway is not involved in a scheme to recruit refugees for servitude?"

"No, no!" Lieutenant Brooks waved his hands. "He is surely *not* one of those vile soul traders. He truly has concern for Huguenots, as does King William. They both want to assist the refugees, but they could not do so publicly. Not after all the funding the King invested in Milord's Irelande project. There has been some mighty criticism from the English subjects about spending too much on his foreign favorites." Brooks looked around, lowering his voice. "I daresay De Sailly has ulterior motives. He lost money on an earlier scheme and must be looking for a way to recoup his losses."

Jehan began to pace, for his anger was not being easily assuaged by ruining his hat. Perhaps the movement would help.

"I may have a solution for you, Sieur BonDurant," said Brooks, as he followed Jehan's footsteps. "I believe it will not take much convincing for Milord to share a ride on his vessel when we set out for London next."

Surprised by the lieutenant's proposal, Jehan stopped his pacing. After all the obstacles he had faced to get this far, he was so relieved he felt like hugging the young man. "Can he take all the others as well?"

"Our small frigate is meant for maneuverability, not large capacity. Perhaps we can take forty or so. I am afraid we only have room in the cargo hold at this time, where the best accommodations we can offer are hammocks. But the journey is no more than a few days."

"We spent the last few weeks crowded into small gabarres over cataracts and past French territory. I have no doubt we can manage a short journey in your cargo hold."

"Very well. I shall speak with Milord tonight. Where can I find you tomorrow morning? Say, half past ten."

"De Buerse Inn, near the bank. Thank you for your kindness, Lieutenant." Jehan removed his hat and bowed deeply, grateful for the good providence of meeting Lieutenant Brooks.

Without delay, Jehan made his way back up the quay and through the gatehouse, following the tidy brick wharfs along the Leeuve Haven canal, past rows of houses and on toward the fish market. He clutched his forehead, not sure how to break the news to the others. Who would go and who would stay? He never imagined the predicament of transporting seventy-five refugees could become so tangled and liable to stir up conflict.

As he walked, a fishing vessel moved alongside him through the canal, the net on its deck wriggling with the morning's catch. He looked ahead and could see the attendant at the first drawbridge stood poised to hoist the chain, so Jehan made a run for it. He dodged a carriage, then a group of stylish ladies who giggled as he passed by. When the decks began to lift, he committed all the strength he had in his powerful thighs, running as hard as he could, his heart pounding in his ears as he watched the void grow. He reached the deck just as it was nearing two pieds wide and bounded across to the other deck. He pressed one foot out in front of the other and slid down to the street just as the deck clanked into its vertical position.

Applause went up from the ladies on the other bank. He waved, then rested his hands on his knees, looking at the precise patterns in the brick pavement while he caught his breath.

"Jehan! Jehan!"

He looked up in the direction of the shouting and saw Mathieu back on the left bank.

"I have news," Mathieu called out. "Meet me at the fish market."

They both made haste back along the wharfs—Mathieu along the left bank, Jehan on the right.

Jehan had two more drawbridges to cross and was grateful to find them both intact. He arrived at the fish market to find Antoine and Corbell standing near rows of enormous fresh pike and baskets of herring displayed along the pavement. He wasn't sure if the sour look on their faces was from the odors intensifying in the summer sun, or if they had also heard the news about De Sailly.

Jehan lifted his arms a bit, realizing sweat had saturated his chemise. He pulled off his justaucorps—no longer worrying about decorum—slung it over his shoulder, and made haste over to his friends.

"It appears you have also learned about De Sailly," Jehan said.

"Oh, we most certainly have," grunted Antoine. "Milk-livered huckster."

Corbell shook his head, then sucked a breath in through his teeth. "We asked around at every blasted inn until we finally found where he stayed before stealing off to London. This city should really post a map of some sort. I became confused with so many ports and canals. Between the shipwrights' port, and wine port, and ink port, and herring port, and a half dozen others, I retraced my footsteps more than a dozen times."

A moment later, Mathieu ran up to meet them. Panting for air, he pulled off his hat and wiped a sleeve across his forehead. "I have good news! Thanks be to God Almighty that my brother and his group have arrived."

Jehan took a deep breath, and they all seemed to let out a collective sigh.

His mind raced through all the scenarios of Etienne's family's state of health. "Was anyone injured? Are they all well? Perhaps I should tend to them? Where are they?"

Mathieu placed a hand on Jehan's chest. "Whoa there, friend. No one is wounded, but most are in a weakened condition. They haven't had much food since they needed coin for ferries. And there was a tumult with some inept bandit . . . a young lad that didn't know what he was up against. But they managed to subdue him without harm to anyone."

Jehan's pulse quickened as his mind pictured Etienne's group in an emaciated condition. "I should . . . I should go to them."

"They are resting at the Walloon Church," said Mathieu. "I shall take you. The pasteur there has offered them shelter and a meal. And he is meeting with city officials to see what can be done. He believes they will offer some aid."

Jehan looked at Antoine and Corbell. "The two of you look as though you could use some rest yourselves . . . and withdraw from this heat."

"You read my mind," said Antoine. "We shall meet at the inn later. We'll need to find solutions to this quagmire De Sailly has left us to drown in."

"Surely, we must," Jehan responded.

As much as he wanted to, he could not yet share the prospect of sailing with Lord Galway with anyone but Corbell. Not until Lieutenant Brooks confirmed the offer.

❦

4 July 1699 ~ Morning
De Buerse Inn, Rotterdam, Dutch Republic

Jehan waited with Corbell in the common room of the De Buerse Inn, shuffling a deck of cards and tapping his foot under the table in anticipation of Antoine's return. Wall lanterns and candles atop the tables glimmered as the daylight that had spilled through the windows just a short time before faded into dusk. Surely, the meeting Antoine was attending with Rotterdam's delegate to the States General would be over soon.

It had been three days since one of the refugees, a Monsieur Cumin, had stepped up to ask the delegate for aid, and Antoine hoped this meeting would finally bring some answers. Jehan felt as if he and his friends were caught in a mill wheel during a flood, and the overwhelming uncertainty of the situation, day after day, had him at his wit's end.

"Can you stop that incessant tapping?" bemoaned Corbell, squinting his dark eyes from across the table.

"Not as long as everything is so unsettled."

"But you said Lord Galway has approved taking up to forty on his ship to London. And we both have money for our own sustenance. So that is what we shall do, is it not?"

"Yes," answered Jehan. "But that won't take care of everyone. I need to know that the request for aid for the others will be honored. I could not leave in good conscience until I know they are provided for. Yet we cannot delay much longer since Amelia may have already received my letter and be on her way to London."

"Do you sincerely believe she could be safely on her way to London?"

Jehan held both hands to his forehead, hoping to relieve the pounding and the misguided anger festering inside.

"I do not know *anything* for certain," he barked. "I cannot even bear to imagine how she might make it out of France. Each time I try, my fear for her life is like a blade threatening to cut out the last remnants of my courage. I *must . . . ,*" he balled a fist and pounded it on the table, causing Corbell to lean away, "find a way to change my view. I have been so embroiled in this sense of defeat, I feel I have succumbed to it."

"I believe we all have, in one way or the other." Corbell pursed his lips and cast his eyes down onto the table.

"Yes, I have noticed even you have lost your usual whimsy."

Corbell straightened, then raised a hand, pointing a finger to the ceiling reminiscent of a pasteur at a sermon. "Let us vow we shall not give in to defeat," he said with exuberance, then cocked his head and bobbed it for emphasis. "We made it alive thus far, so God must be on our side."

Jehan chuckled to see the prompt turnabout in his friend's demeanor. "You are right. Amelia has always told me that we can envision the outcome we desire, and so it shall be done. Going forward, I shall believe in her guidance and have faith." Jehan reached across the table and clasped Corbell's shoulder. "We must trust all will be well in the end."

Antoine burst into the common room with pipe smoke swirling around his head and wearing a smile."We are redeemed," he rejoiced, flailing his arms in the air until his perruque began to slide backward. He pulled it back into place and said, "The States General has agreed to fund us."

On Antoine's heels, Mathieu Roussel burst in with his brother, Etienne, and his two boys. They all clambered onto the bench next to Jehan.

He reached over and patted Etienne on the back, then ruffled the boys' hair. "Good to see you, my friends. I cannot deny, we've been rather worried about you."

"Antoine, tell us more," said Corbell.

"A letter was compiled to tell the States General that De Sailly, the so-called director of the resettlement project, had urged all the supplicants who had taken refuge in Aarau, to go to Carolana where they were to be transported at the expense of his company. Then depositions were taken from several in our group. After a vote, the delegates generously allocated 500 florins to move us to the Germanic States."

"Not to Carolana?" Jehan asked.

"Many of us have decided we are weary of any more danger. Who knows what tragedies might befall us on the sea voyages. And they tell us that participating in the Reformed Church will not be a requirement like it was in Aarau. We can be Lutherans or Jews or Quakers or whatever suits us. So from our free-thinkers group, Luc Dodet and Elaine, Etienne and his boys, and Constantin Eschalier will all go with me. Some of the others, mostly those whose youth still gives them courage or those without families, will go along with you on Lord Galway's ship . . . Mathieu, here, for one."

Mathieu nodded, his flaxen hair glimmering in the candlelight. "Yes, I am more than ready for an adventure to the New World."

Jehan steepled his hands and said a silent prayer in gratitude for the forward progress. And another for Amelia's safe-keeping. Soon he and his two comrades would be setting off for London. One more step closer to his love.

❧

5 July 1699 ~ Evening
North Sea

The onshore winds had eased with the sunset, and Lord Galway's ship slipped out into the open waters of the great North Sea with the horizon darkening to an inky violet-blue. Jehan stood on the upper deck, growing accustomed to steadying his footing in time with the gentle waves that lapped against the ship's bow. He had never imagined how soothing and peaceful the pulse of the sea could be.

The masts and booms creaked as the trimmers set the sails to take them to London. Jehan took in a long, clearing breath. At last, he was on his way.

He circled his head around, in awe of the vast open sky that surrounded him on all sides, having never seen the stars so bright or so great a number. There . . . there in the stars he could be with Amelia. It was as though his love for her had expanded so much that it burst into billions of tiny lights, each with its own hue—red, orange, yellow, green, blue, or white—each with its own unique shimmer or sparkle. Jewels in the night sky that spoke of the abundance of their love.

A warmth radiated through him, creating a euphoria that he wanted to cling to. He could feel her there. Feel her with him somehow. Yet he knew she must still be far away. Still in France, perhaps. And still with many challenges ahead of her.

He spoke to her through his mind. *I am blessed by your guidance, mon Ame, my lovely muse. Your words speak truth. All the courage we need lies within us. Yet we can only discover our Eden if we have the courage to lose sight of the shore. Will you follow me across the waters?*

A soft whistling in the sails transformed into a whisper. "*Have faith, my love, it will bring us together.*"

CHAPTER 19

THE VIGIL

AMELIA

5 July 1699 ~ Afternoon
Hospitaller Commandery, Mont Lauzère, France

Diamonds of mid-afternoon sunlight spilled through the leaded glass window of the bedchamber, warming the floor under Amelia's bare feet as she carried in a bowl of soup. In a darkened corner of the room, Menina was asleep again, but it was high time to get some nourishment into her. She had been hard to rouse for a few weeks and, some days, had slept for more than half the day.

"Cook has made your favorite *bajanac* soup."

"Hmm?" Menina moaned but did not open her eyes.

"Smell how wonderful it is," Amelia said, as she waved the bowl slowly under her grandmother's nose, letting the nutty aroma of chestnuts fill the air around them.

Menina blinked her eyes and shifted. "Oh, dear child. Thank you. I am so grateful for you. Thank you."

Amelia lifted the spoon and blew to cool the thick puree of chestnuts, sheep's milk, and sweet onion before testing it for flavor. It melted like savory velvet over her tongue—sweet and roasted and creamy—that slipped down her throat with a comforting warmth.

"'Tis almost as good as your own, Menina."

Amelia set the bowl on the table next to a stoneware water pitcher and a blue-rimmed glass beaker, then helped her grandmother sit up while fluffing the pillows to cradle her frail body.

"How is that?"

"Good, dear."

Once Menina seemed settled, Amelia sat in the chair next to the bed and lifted the spoon to her grandmother's lips.

"I had a most pleasant dream about your *maman* and papa," said Menina, compelling Amelia to set the spoon back in the bowl. Menina caught her breath, then continued. "Did I tell you your papa came to visit yesterday? We spoke for a long time."

Amelia's shoulders dropped. The thought of her long-departed parents pricked the tender wound that would never entirely heal. She wished with all her heart that they *could* return from heaven. If only she could embrace them both in her arms—the mother she never knew and the father she scarcely remembered.

She observed Menina's placid expression and, with reluctance, recalled the old lore—as the veil between life and death grew thin, loved ones who had passed on would visit the dying to ease their transition. Although Amelia's father could not have visited Menina in body, surely he had been there in spirit. Much the same way Amelia had felt Jehan's presence the evening before as she stared up at a cloudless, bejeweled night sky, a velvet of dark purple filled with pulsing stars. A perfect night sky that brought them close, at last. If she could feel this presence with Jehan, surely Menina could feel it with her loved ones beyond the veil.

"That is wonderful, Menina. Now open up and take a sip of your soup before it gets cold."

Her grandmother smiled and opened her mouth like a baby bird.

Amelia spooned the warm soup as she shared her own experience. "I, too, had a visitor of sorts last night. I was drawn to the Delphinus constellation as I was meditating on the stars, and it was as though I heard Jehan calling out to me. To have the courage to set out across the waters and join him."

"Awh . . . the dolphin has come to protect you . . . and take you to your love, like in the Greek myth."

"Perhaps," said Amelia. "An inner voice told me to assure him to have faith. And that faith would bring us together."

"And it will, child."

Menina gazed at Amelia and smiled in a way she had not seen for over a year. Although her grandmother had become quite fragile, her face now glowed, even in the muted shadows.

She swallowed another sip of soup, then spoke again, her voice becoming ragged and hoarse. "Your papa has the same task as Delphinius. He has come to take me home."

Amelia filled the beaker with water and had Menina take a sip. It seemed her grandmother's time on Earth was coming to an end, although the truth of it was hard to take. She stared down at her lap, biting her lip then pulled Jehan's cravate from her neck and dabbed at a single tear that burned in the corner of her eye.

A light tap came from the open door. Amelia looked up to see Cavalier, his hat tucked under his arm. He carried a bouquet of late-blooming pink orchids in one hand, with his other hand wrapped around a small object of some sort.

"Good day, madame . . . and mademoiselle." Just as he bowed with a flourish, Romulus and Remus pushed their way past him, nearly knocking him off his feet. "Pardon. I know the dogs are discouraged inside the manoir, but I could not bring myself to say no to them. They wanted to see you as much as I."

Remus jumped up onto the foot of Menina's bed while Romulus rolled out across the cooling stone tiles.

Menina uttered a weak giggle. "Our handsome Cavalier. All grown up. I am so happy for your visit."

"I have flowers for our dear Menina." He stepped aside the bed, kissed Menina on the forehead, and laid the bouquet on the bedside table. "And a letter from Jehan."

Amelia squeezed the cravate and held it to her breast with a gasp, her quickening heart daring her to feel excited.

Cavalier handed a folded and sealed parchment to her as he shared the details. "I saw Giraud on his way to market at Pont-du-Montvert and he thought you would want this straightaway. 'Twas Jehan's last letter before he left Aarau."

"Thank you, my friend. Seems you are my steadfast courier of late," said Amelia, as she broke the wax seal. "You look well, and how is your beloved Marie?"

"Yes, I am well, thank you. Marie is taken with great ardor nearly every day now. Many people now ask her to preach to their assemblies in the woods and caves. God must be with her because, despite the long nights and damp conditions, she is as strong and healthful as ever."

Menina raised a shaky hand and pointed. "Read the letter, dear."

"Very well." Amelia opened the carefully entwined folds, too eager herself to be embarrassed over the personal contents it might contain. "6 June 1699," she said. "A month on since he penned this."

"That means he could be in London by now," said Cavalier. "Or at least in Rotterdam."

She scanned the letter. "Yes, yes. It seems as if it does," she said, then read on.

> *Mon Ame, my dearest. Time has passed quickly now that I keep my thoughts on you and the deep connectedness that we, once again, share. It overjoys me to know you are willing to join me. And I believe the timing is for God to decide. I, too, love your Menina and I am pleased to know you will*

stay and take care of her. You can trust that I shall prepare the way for you and hold fast to our designs knowing, 'He has made everything beautiful in its time'.

Our guide, whom I need not name being you have already encountered him, saw us safely to Aarau. And I would trust him to guide you as well. His wife now resides in Rotterdam, so he could escort you the entire way.

When you prepare to depart, please send a letter through the bookseller. He will deliver it to the courier going to Rotterdam, and then it will be sent by ship to me in London. I have written to my cousin and instructed him to provide funds from my estate to cover the guide's fees and your passage through to Carolana.

I set out tomorrow on my journey from Aarau to Rotterdam, then on to London. It is confirmed that we are to go to the Saint Jean de Spittlefields church when we arrive in London and ask for the pasteur, Monsieur De Joux, who will work with the French Committee on arrangements for our stay. Should you arrive in London before we set sail for Carolana, you will find me in the same way. The pasteur will know the address for my place of lodging. We are also told it will take until at least spring of next year before a ship can leave for the New World. Should you not arrive until after we depart, there will be other ships that frequent the route to Virginia or the West Indies with transfers on to Carolana.

I look forward to the dazzling fire in your eyes that now blinds me to all others, and to the day your tender kiss will smooth these lips roughened by the outside world. I pray for your happiness daily, and for God to bring you safely to my side.

All my love

Amelia closed her eyes, feeling a heat burn her cheeks when she thought about his lips on hers. As the fire swept down her length and lingered below her belly, she realized it was far more than simple discomfort over sharing Jehan's intimate words.

"Thanks be to God," Menina called out.

Glad to be distracted from her awkward longings, Amelia tilted her head and looked curiously at her grandmother. "What do you mean, Menina? Do you mean thanks that Jehan has finally left the control of his uncle?"

"Thanks be that you will now go to him. You belong together."

Amelia's shoulders stiffened. "Not just yet."

"Yes, child." Menina tried to wave her hand, lifting it only a bit before it dropped back to the bedcovers. Her inhale was shallow, but she wrinkled her forehead and seemed to will the words out. "Your job is done. Now I can go home to my Lord. Time to call the chaplain for my last rites. And time for you to go to Jehan."

Her grandmother's words made Amelia wince. She was not ready to let go. It was her inner nature, after all, to stubbornly meet tragedy head on. She always tried to hold an unwavering belief in the power of hope, encouraging Jehan, her patients, and the oppressed Cévenol community to share in her conviction. Practicing the healing arts had become her way of focusing on hope, and she was not about to stop now.

"But no, Menina. I cannot leave you and I cannot leave Romulus and Remus either."

The dogs' ears pricked at the mention of their names, but their attention only added to the conflicting emotions that sparred inside Amelia.

Quibbling over this would serve no one. She knew in her heart it was time to let go—time to let Menina be at peace and cross over, knowing her granddaughter would be well loved. If only her strong-willed mind would listen.

Menina gave a languorous, disapproving shake of her head. "The dogs will die if they stay locked behind these walls. Cavalier can take them. They will be free with him."

Cavalier stepped close and spoke softly, "I would be glad to adopt them as my own. Rest assured, they will be in good hands."

"Go." Menina's voice grew weaker each time she spoke. "Go find your love and be happy in your Eden. I am tired and need to rest now."

Amelia took her grandmother's hand in hers—the skin now nearly as transparent as a dragonfly's wing—then stared off for a moment, a vision filling her mind's eye. She could finally see what she had pushed away for so long—her grandmother peacefully, gracefully, shedding her earthly skin for her soul's heavenly ascent.

She held Menina's hand to her cheek and said, "I love you, Menina. I promise I shall go to Jehan."

"I love you too, child." Menina's words came out in a faint rasp. She paused and her eyes gradually shut before she whispered, "I am so grateful for you, dear." A small smile curled her lips as she fell into a gentle slumber.

Amelia slipped her hand from her grandmother's, then picked up the flowers and water pitcher from the table. She walked to her desk, her vision watery and distorted as she held back the tears that welled in her eyes.

"It makes Menina happy that you will honor her wish," Cavalier assured her. "Shall I request that the Commandeur send in his chaplain?"

Amelia took a deep breath, trying to dispel the sadness that had already tightened in her throat. She nodded reluctantly and began arranging the delicate orchids in the pitcher. "Menina will enjoy seeing these when she wakes."

6 July 1699 ~ Early Morning

As Amelia blinked her eyes open, her gaze fell on the stone walls of the bedchamber, already pink with the light of dawn. She stretched and pushed back the bedcovers, peering across the room to check on Menina. Her face was decidedly ashen, the glow from the day before now missing.

Surely a nettle tisane will bring the color back.

Menina had taken provision for her heavenly journey the night before. The chaplain had heard her confession, given the Viaticum, and performed the Extreme Unction. But now, as day broke, Amelia was still not ready to let her go and was prepared to fight with every herb she knew to employ.

Her heart racing, she bound up and scrambled to her grandmother's bedside, but halted a few steps away—there was no usual rise and fall of Menina's chest under the bedcovers. Amelia shuddered. She moved closer and placed her hand before her grandmother's mouth, yet she could detect no breath. Swiftly, she moved it to her neck—no pulse. Then her wrist—nothing.

She took Menina's hand in hers and patted it. "Menina, wake up." Amelia could barely swallow, the panic choking her. "No, Menina. No. Come back."

Amelia placed both hands over her mouth as though holding back her lament would make her grandmother's passing an illusion. The reality abruptly forced the air from her lungs in a long wail that came from deep inside and ripped a dark void in her chest. She dropped to her knees on the floor, hot tears streaming down her cheeks. Overcome by the grief that assailed her, she collapsed her head on the bed, redolent aromas of consecrated olive and frankincense oils invading her nostrils. After a few moments, she became aware of rapid footfall echoing out in the passageway as someone came running.

"What is it, Mademoiselle Amelia?"

She recognized Henriette's voice, but she couldn't seem to lift her head from the bed. The padding of the novice's feet grew near, but Amelia had no strength to greet her. A warm, comforting hand squeezed her shoulder. She peered up from the bedcovers, finding deep anguish in Henriette's eyes.

"I am so sorry, Amelia." Henriette made the sign of the cross, then dropped down next to her. She wrapped her arms around Amelia and gently rocked her. "I know this is hard for you. We shall all miss your Menina dearly."

Henriette's touch was a soothing balm that gradually calmed Amelia's tears. She rose and sniffed in short inhales, trying to regain some composure. She turned to Henriette, but her lips trembled as she spoke. "Menina always guided me . . . and took care of me. I simply wanted to do the same for her."

"And you have. She loved you for all you did for her, and she loves you still as you assist her to her place in heaven."

Amelia looked at the lifeless body peacefully resting on the bed. "It all seems so final. She was the only mother I ever knew. And now she is gone. Gone from this world and I shall never speak to her again."

"I know you are hurting. Once you said that our loved ones who have passed live on in our hearts and minds, the way they have always lived inside us. And we can choose to keep their light alive." Henriette took Amelia's shoulders and looked into her eyes. "If you let your Menina live on inside you, she can still guide you, just as the radiant light from faraway stars guides ships through unknown waters."

"Thank you," Amelia muttered as she blotted her eyes on the sleeve of her chemise. "That is of some comfort."

A rush of shoes against the stone floor echoed out in the passageway.

"Mademoiselle, I heard someone cry out," said Griselle, eyes wide as she came through the door in haste with Jacquette at her side. "Are you injured? Or stricken with some affliction?"

Sorrow pinched Amelia's face as she cast her eyes toward Menina.

Griselle put a hand to heart and gasped.

Little Jacquette tiptoed toward the bed, then spread her small arms over the body, gently laying her little cheek upon Menina's. She looked up at Amelia with eyes as blue as the heavens. Like an angel coming to take Menina home, Jacquette's sweet face took a bit of the ache from Amelia's broken heart.

"Would you like me to lead the prayer?" Henriette asked.

Amelia found it difficult to bring the words to her lips, so she nodded several times, grateful for the offer, and wiped more tears from her cheeks.

Griselle's brow furrowed, her eyes filled with caring and devotion. "Mademoiselle. How can I be of service? I cannot relieve your suffering, but I wish to relieve your burden. Anything you ask, I shall do for you."

Amelia's mind was still reeling with sorrow, so she took a deep breath to steady herself. She knew the traditional rituals were meant to transition the soul on to God, so it was important there be no delay. "After we pray, will you help me clean her body and assist with the balming embrocation?"

"Yes, mademoiselle." Griselle's voice held a slight quiver.

Amelia stood, and the women all moved languidly into a circle around the bed. Taking each other's hands, they lowered their heads while Henriette recited the prayer.

"Saints of God, come to Menina's aid. Hasten to meet her, angels of the Lord. With God, there is mercy and fullness of redemption. Eternal rest, grant unto her, O Lord, and let perpetual light shine upon her. May she rest in peace. Amen."

"Amen," the others echoed in plaintive voices.

Amelia stared into the room, empty of Menina's laugh, empty of her wise eyes and loving smile.

The novices, one by one, wrapped their arms around Amelia, encircling her with their love and empathy. She held them close, her dear hatchlings nearly ready to take flight on their own.

"You are so kind to me," Amelia said. "And I am so proud of the women you are becoming. Menina is proud of you, too."

The prayer had moved her thoughts away from the all-consuming pain, and now the next steps in the ritual brought a purpose to occupy her mind.

"We should begin," she said, her voice still tremulous and mournful.

She poured water from the pitcher into a wash basin and took two linen towels from a drawer in the bedside table. After she dipped them in the water, she handed one to Griselle, then the two of them began gently drawing the towels over Menina's soulless body.

"When we have finished, we shall need to empty the water pitcher and beaker," said Amelia, pushing forward through her despair. "And the wash basin as well. We must clear the open water sources, for it is said the soul might fall in. Menina is still near but is needing to find her way to the other side. Henriette, the frères keep a blend of spikenard, frankincense, and lavender in the Infirmaria. Would you please bring some? And Jacquette, please fetch a jar of honey and leave it open on the night table.

'Twill attract the insects that carry the souls of those already dead, and they will show her the way."

The two sisters bobbed a curtsy, then each made haste to carry out their tasks.

Amelia paused, her eyes locked on her grandmother's withered body. She no longer recognized her. This was not the jovial, loving sage-femme who tended after all the babes and mothers in the Gorges du Tarn. This was an empty shell, hollow of everything that made her the wise woman she had been.

Amelia had done this ritual on occasion, assisted by Griselle, when a few Catholic patients had not recovered from injuries or illness. But this was not the same. She scarcely knew those people. Her attachment to her grandmother went far too deep to be the one to facilitate her departure from this earthly realm.

"I cannot bear to complete the ritual myself," Amelia lamented. "Please, Griselle, will you finish for me? You recall the process, do you not?"

Griselle took Amelia's hand. "Certainly. Perhaps you might use some rest."

Amelia nodded, every leaden muscle in her arms and legs telling her Griselle was right. Still dressed in her night chemise, she walked with unsteady movements toward the doorway, deep melancholy weighing each step.

She stopped then turned round to speak to Griselle. "Please call me when you are ready to close the shroud. I wish to see her for one last goodbye as we send her soul on its way."

A dark fog seemed to fill the passageway as Amelia moved through it, despite the morning light spilling out through the open chamber doors. She descended the grand staircase, its stone floor cold beneath her bare feet. It seemed as though she were lowering herself into some deep cavern filled with memories of Menina—of the times she struggled to ascend the staircase, but also of the gay Yuletide festivities when she stood holding the banister while the novices danced to a tin whistle tune. It was those happy times that Menina would want her to remember.

The immense oak entry door emitted a mournful creak as she opened it and moved past the guards, emerging into the most brilliant sunlight she had ever experienced. She let the warmth of it bathe her face, and envisioned her beloved Menina's soul taking flight on the radiant beams. Her grandmother seemed to call out. *Be happy for me, child, for I am going home at last.*

The chapel bells tolled—once, twice, three times—as Amelia drifted up the rise to the stables, her limbs numb and scarcely feeling the ground. Romulus and Remus burst out and ran up beside her, licking and nudging her hands. The horses brayed, ushering her into their sanctuary. When she entered Luisant's stall, the great dun Andalusian mare lowered her head. Amelia took it in her hands and nuzzled her cheek on Luisant's soft forelocks, listening to the soothing cadence of her breathing for a time. Then she settled into the soft straw, curling up between the dogs, and succumbed to exhaustion.

CHAPTER 20

LONDON CALLING

JEHAN

7 July 1699
Spittlefields, London, England

The arrival into London the previous day had immediately sparked Jehan's interest in all the wonders he might explore while he waited for Amelia to join him.

Cast in the warm glow of sunset, the intimidating Tower of London and the great London Bridge had been the first marvels to greet him as Lord Galway's ship navigated up the Thames River to the customs house quay. Lieutenant Brooks had pointed out the magnificent Saint Paul's cathedral that was under construction in the distance, whose size and costly workmanship excited attention. Jehan had never seen anything so grand and hoped, one day soon, to visit it along with the great royal palaces of Kensington and Greenwich he'd heard so much about.

By the time the refugees had made their way to the Church of Saint Jean in Spittlefields, as directed, there'd been little time to become acquainted with Monsieur De Joux, the pasteur assigned to lead their group to Carolana. He had warmly welcomed them on the doorstep of the parsonage, but had been ready to retire, already wearing a simple Banyan dressing gown and night cap. He seemed an amiable man, but the hour had been late, so he sent them on to their lodging with instructions to the French Almshouse until they could make other arrangements.

Neither Jehan nor Corbell nor Mathieu Roussel had resisted the idea, since a hot bowl of broth and a straw mattress that didn't sway throughout the night had been all they desired after disembarking the ship.

Yet once they'd had an uncomfortable night crowding into the too few beds, Jehan and Corbell had risen early and decided to find an alternate solution.

"I am sorry, friends, that I cannot join you," said Mathieu. "My savings are running quite low. Did my snoring keep you awake, or did you find something else utterly disagreeable."

Corbell clasped a hand on Mathieu's shoulder. "Oh, we are well accustomed to sleeping with you. Your snoring has become a familiar melody to our ears. 'Tis sharing a bed with yet three others that is too much to take."

"You and the others are in far greater need of free lodging," said Jehan. "So we think it only fair that we vacate the bed so the rest of you can get some sleep."

On the way out to search for other options, Jehan left a generous donation with the head trustee and thanked the staff for a hearty breakfast of oat porridge.

He and Corbell stepped out into the breaking daylight and Jehan stretched, loosening muscles still taut from the cramped sleeping arrangements.

"We should go meet with Pasteur De Joux again to learn more about the status of the resettlement project."

"Do you think he will know of other lodging?" asked Corbell.

"Surely, he knows of something." Jehan pulled off his hat and tucked back a few loose strands of hair while recalling their walk into Spittlefields. "I noticed many inns on our way from the waterfront, but therein lies the dilemma . . . how to choose the best value among them all."

After a short walk, they arrived back at the parsonage and asked the housemaid to rouse De Joux. He appeared over the woman's shoulder and greeted them with a broad smile. Already dressed for the day in black ecclesiastical robes and white linen preaching band, he had a more relaxed appearance than most pasteurs. He wore his thin, graying hair to his collar, suggesting he was no more a fan of ostentatious perruques than Jehan was.

De Joux invited them into the kitchen where they were served tea, followed by the disappointing news that he had no more information for them about the Carolana project. Though Jehan was truly relieved to find he was a kind, fatherly sort.

As they prepared to leave, De Joux offered to lead them in a prayer of thanks for the safe journey from Rotterdam, for the provisions they'd been graciously provided, and for a promising future for all.

"Thank you, monsieur," said Jehan with a gracious bow when they had finished. "Before we part ways, can you provide us with a recommendation on the foremost inn in the area?"

"One that is not too expensive," Corbell added.

"I am sorry, but I could not say," said De Joux, "since most of my congregants are permanently employed in the textile trades and have taken rooms at their employer's atelier or in boarding houses arranged by them. But concerning the Carolana project, I would suggest you meet with the French Relief Committee commissioner to see what assistance he can offer. Perhaps he knows more that he has yet to inform me of."

Corbell huffed as they left the parsonage. "*Still,* we have no answers," he said, gritting his teeth as he spoke. "No dates for our departure . . . no word on repayment. You'd best see the commissioner on your own. After all the vagaries of this venture, I may lose my patience should one more person tell me they've heard nothing."

The French Relief Committee office was located not far from the church, in the heart of the Spittlefields community. Jehan had left Corbell waiting on the portico, and had been promptly ushered in to meet with the commissioner. Though the meeting had been brief and to no avail, Jehan was glad to have it past him so he could move on to other things.

As he rushed back down the long hallway to join Corbell, he tried to formulate in his head a list of inquiries to make on this first full day in London—lodging of course, banking, employment, bookstores, grand sites. It was all a bit overwhelming, especially after the news the French commissioner shared.

The information began to settle in his mind just as he found his friend at the doorway, framed by the morning light, anxiously pacing in and out. Corbell was eager to know the outcome of the meeting and would not be too pleased to learn their fate was still very much undetermined.

They stepped out onto the portico and down to the street, Corbell shoulder to shoulder with Jehan and keeping pace. "Well, did you report De Sailly's mismanagement? And will they reimburse us for our travel?"

"I did, and they will. If we can give them an accounting of our expenses."

"And how long till we can leave for Carolana?"

"All they could tell me was that De Sailly and his employer, a Dr. Coxe, have promised to make new appeals for funding since they did not meet with success in the Swiss cantons."

Corbell scowled at their surroundings. "This sprawling, sooty city is not what I bargained for when I signed on to this venture."

Jehan surveyed the area. Although there were still gardens and small pastures here and there in this area they called by the strange name of Spittlefields, it was clear that new development was swallowing up the natural settings to make room for the surge of new French refugees. Rows of wooden-sided townhouses were set far too close for the maintenance of good health.

"It does not agree with my nature either," said Jehan. "I would much prefer the clear and pleasant air of Carolana. But have patience, my friend. We've only just arrived. Should you recall, they told us in Rotterdam not to expect to leave before next spring. Which is quite fine by me. You know I shall wait for Amelia before I depart. If De Sailly and his company do not pull through by the time she arrives, then we can always set out on our own."

Corbell wrinkled his nose and shook his head. "Na. Don't want to spend my every last denier . . . or pence as it would be here, I suppose. Not when someone else will cover the cost of my voyage."

On passing down the side streets toward the market square, Jehan became aware of an odd absence of bustle and activity, despite the density of the houses. But the clack of looms could be heard here and there, drifting out the large expanses of open leaded glass windows on the upper loft floors of the houses. It was evident at a glance that most of the houses were built expressly for weavers—three, four, or five stories high, with those loft windows providing significant light the same way they did at the ateliers in Aarau.

"So then . . . where are we headed?" asked Corbell.

"To explore. London may not be of our choosing, but does it not thrill you in some small way to know there are splendid places and people and knowledge to be discovered here?"

"Well . . . yes! Certainly. I have been so resolute on getting to Carolana, I had not considered it."

A low din grew louder as they continued toward the market. The clopping of a donkey-drawn cart piled high with potatoes drew Jehan's attention toward the field where a few weekday stalls were open. The usual arrangements of vegetables could be seen, but potatoes were apparently the staple commodity.

Jehan sighed in dismay. "The weavers' incomes must be scant here. We mostly used potatoes to feed our livestock at Cougoussac."

A peddler standing on the street corner called out in French. "Knives, combs, inkhorns, quill pens. You young gentlemen there," he said, pointing toward them. "You look to be the sort who are in need of these accoutrements."

Jehan stepped up and reached for one of the small horns in the peddler's tray.

"May I see?" He turned it in his hand, feeling the smoothness of the polished exterior. "Fine quality, indeed."

"Yes, sieur. They are quite desirable among noble travelers, such as yourself. Just two pence."

Jehan reached into his purse. "I have only French currency. Will deniers do? I am sorry for the additional trouble."

"Why, of course," said the peddler. "But you will need to get yourself to the bank to make an exchange should you plan to be here for a time."

"Most certainly. And where shall we find it?"

"Take a right after the Tenter Ground, then head into the city by way of Bishopsgate until you reach Threadneedle. 'Tis in the Grocer's Guild Hall, near the Royal Exchange. And Garraway's coffeehouse is nearby." The man shared a playful grin, then exclaimed, "The best penny university you'll find to learn all the news and make your connections. You might find someone who'll offer rooms for let. Far better than holding up in one of the inns for too long."

Jehan regarded the fine quality of the peddler's clothing. Simple, but certainly not the clothing of a pauper. "You seem to know these places well."

The man winked and nodded. "Most certainly do. If you are lucky, Fellows from the Royal Society or the College of Physicians may include you in an informal meeting, or even invite you to a lecture at Gresham College. 'Tis where I go to learn about the most lucrative investments."

A peddler with money enough to make investments? Jehan looked sidelong at Corbell, who arched his brows and feigned a smile.

The peddler huffed, seeming to catch their doubts. "You misread the situation, messieurs. They even admit sorts such as myself as long as one can afford the one-pence admission. I do a far better business selling wares and investing than working the loom. I was a weaver back in France, but the English want fine clothing at a very low cost, so they don't pay well. I had to strike out on my own. With the thousands of weavers now in London, they are France's loss and England's gain."

Jehan doffed his hat. "You are quite resourceful, monsieur. We thank you for the information. And I shall find you again when I need to refresh my supply of ink."

They set off walking along the boundary of the Tenter Ground, where lengths of wet cloth were hooked onto frames and stretched taut using hooks. Another new sight completely unfamiliar to Jehan, the system appeared to keep the cloth flat and square while it dried.

"Should we find work?" asked Corbell as they turned off toward Bishopsgate Road. "To preserve our money?"

"I was warned by the commissioner that it will not be easy to find work in the trades we are skilled at. There are plenty of locals for the apothecary and cutlery trades. And I prefer not to work for a shoemaker again."

Corbell huffed. "We'll likely go crazy, waiting for God knows how long, not knowing our fate and with nothing to occupy our time while hauled up in the almshouses and soup kitchens like fish caught in nets."

Determined to keep their hopes high, Jehan raised his brows and said, "We *shall* find something. There is no reason for us to rely on the French Committee's good hospitality. And we cannot, for much longer. There are many poor souls in much greater need. I was instructed that we should locate our own lodging forthwith, since we have the means to pay for it. And that there is an abundance of options near Bishopsgate. We may as well make the most of our itinerant living conditions . . . within reason, of course."

When they landed on Bishopsgate Road, the area was cheerfully populated with the cries of hagglers, hawkers, hucksters, colporteurs, costermongers, and chapmen bouncing off the walls.

Jehan saw that the buildings were far older than those they'd just seen around Spittlefields. Here, the late-medieval character was preserved, the street lined with both small half-timber wattle and daub houses in shambles, and grand mansions in sturdy stone or brick. And there was no shortage of reasonable lodging near the city gate with a dozen or more inns in either side of the road. One had posted a leaflet advertising theatrical performances that stirred Jehan's curiosity.

"Now there is something to add to our list of new experiences," said Jehan.

"Indeed." Corbell removed his hat and put his face near the posting. "See here. This play is about an apothecary."

Jehan peered over his shoulder and read the billet.

PHYSICK LIES A BLEEDING, OR, THE APOTHECARY TURNED DOCTOR, A COMEDY, acted every day in most apothecaries shops in London : and more especially to be seen by those who are willing to be cheated, the first of April, every year : absolutely necessary for all persons that are sick, or may be sick.

"It appears London's physicians fear the apothecaries are taking their business," Jehan surmised.

"Ha! All the more reason to get us to Carolana, where I am certain good healers, such as yourself, are in short supply."

Jehan patted Corbell's shoulder. "Let's make haste. We've much to do today." He looked up at the gathering clouds, fleecy white masses that were already spitting. "And it is about to rain."

"Why don't we stop and take a meal first," Corbell suggested. "And wait till it lets up."

"I am really wondering about you, Corbell. Have you lost your sense of adventure? We can have something at the coffeehouse where we will learn far more than at an inn. Besides, now is a good time to wander about, when the streets are not too crowded and the air is clearer."

Jehan inhaled as the light rain splattered over his face. "Ah, already smelling much better. And look ahead, see how much farther we can see down the road now that the rain is clearing out the smoke and dust. Puff up your feathers, my Raven friend!"

Just after they passed through the unguarded city gate, a carriage raced by in the opposite direction, sending mud and dung flying from a puddle in the gutter and directly at Corbell.

"Hey, there," Corbell shouted, then brushed the filth from his justaucorps and chuckled. "We've been here only a day and I'll already need to find a laundress."

Jehan followed with a long, heady laugh of his own. "Please do! You smell like one of the dead rats from Lord Galway's ship."

A smirk came across Corbell's face. "You are no sweet-smelling rose yourself, BonDurant," he goaded in return.

Just a stone's throw from the Royal Exchange, they found the bank where Jehan deposited his bill of exchange, and they both changed the money in their purses for English currency.

As they left the building, a blinding downpour threatened to soak through their already damp wool clothing, so they waited on the portico. Tremendous drops beat a percussion on the streets so loud that it drowned out the clatter of carts and horses. Several minutes had passed when the bells for half past ten rang out.

"This might never let up," said Corbell.

Jehan looked up and down the street, seeing the way was clear. "Maybe we should just take to our heels."

Corbell smirked and laughed. "This sodden raven's feathers are already too damp to fly!"

Jehan also felt the dampness seeping through the shoulders of his clothing and regretted the goading he had given Corbell earlier. Not everyone was inured to the sort of relentless rains that Cévenols were accustomed to.

"On second thought, you are the wise one here, Corbell. 'Tis for the best that we wait a few more minutes."

Still anxious to locate their lodging, Jehan tapped his foot on the stone threshold. Each moment felt as though time was dragging on. But in no more than a few minutes, the rain lightened.

"Here's our chance," said Jehan as he darted out in the direction of the coffeehouse, with Corbell following.

The labyrinth of alleys had them utterly lost at first, until they stopped a couple huddled under their waxed linen cloaks who set them on the right course.

A little further on and, at last, there it was—Gallaway's coffeehouse—a large four-story brick building, austere except for the simple adornments that were a weak attempt at recalling earlier Italian styles.

Upon entering the spacious, high-ceilinged room, each of them handed a penny to a young man stationed at the entrance. Rich aromas of coffee and pipe smoke welcomed them in.

Jehan found the place rather genial. An inviting coal fire burned in the hearth, red and blazing. A curious arrangement of dwarf spits, all armed with tempting muffins, twirled round and round on a brazier atop a counter. Guests were imbibing wine, sipping coffee, or munching toast, the warmth and good cheer having smoothed the wrinkles and painted rosy cheeks on everyone's faces.

Small groups, mostly of men, were gathered in partitioned corners, listening in to each other's conversations, interjecting or debating whenever they pleased, and reflecting upon the latest stories in newspapers with titles such as "The Tatler" and "The Spectator". Or they sat at long communal tables where every type of media imaginable was strewn—leaflets, pamphlets, more newspapers, journals, books.

Jehan tipped his hat to an older gentleman seated at the table nearest the door. "Good day, monsieur."

The man responded in French, laced with a slight English accent. "Frenchmen, eh? You two seem to be new," he said. "Come sit with me."

Jehan and Corbell looked at each other, not accustomed to so much friendliness in one day.

A powdered perruque framed the man's amiable face. "I believe you are strangers to our community establishment, but whatever your social background or political allegiances, you are always welcomed into our lively, convivial company. We are mostly noblemen, physicians, merchants, and gentlemen of quality, or apothecaries and *chirurgiens*. But we enjoy the company of all sorts. What is your interest today?"

Jehan took a seat at the bench across from the man, then Corbell joined him.

"We stopped for a bite to eat, and to see what work we can find in our trades. Apothecary," Jehan said, pointing to himself. "And my friend here is a cutler. And I, for one, would be elated to find my way to one of those medical lectures I hear of."

"The Guilds control all the trades here," said the man. "You would need to settle here, and then find work as an apprentice for some time, before you could approach the appropriate Guild Halls to be considered for entry. But I do know a doctor who offers lodging at his townhouse in exchange for assisting in his endeavors. He may be able to help you both."

Corbell beamed and nodded. "Thank you, monsieur."

Jehan sighed, grateful that all was falling into place. After all they'd been through, they deserved a fortuitous break. "That would be splendid were you to be so kind as to make an introduction."

"That I shall do, my young friends. The good Dr. Ramsdell arrives daily at ten. And should you linger a while, other Fellows of the Royal Society come here after a weekly meeting at Gresham College, and on occasion demonstrate experiments on mechanics, magnetism, and such. Should you befriend one, you might even secure an invitation to anatomical dissections or microscopical observations."

The muscles in Jehan's face lifted and a warm sensation swelled his chest. His long-held designs to learn and practice the healing arts were coming together. Perhaps the morning's humble prayers, and the vision he held of a bright future ahead, were finally setting things in motion.

CHAPTER 21

GRAND ESCAPE

AMELIA

10 July 1699 ~ Early Evening
Hospitaller Commandery, Mont Lauzère, France

Timoleon's sergeant-at-arms announced Amelia and Cavalier as they entered the commandeur's formal meeting chamber. An immense iron chandelier, set with glimmering candles, cast a warm light that danced over the tracery on the polished oak wainscot. It brought a gentle, comforting luminance to the room despite the empty hearth grate.

Of late, the hearth fires were seldom lit until long after Vespers, if at all, since even the manoir's thick stone walls did little to protect against the sweltering summer days. At least the heat and gloom inside gave Amelia another reason, aside from missing Menina, to sleep under the stars, curled next to Romulus and Remus on a straw pallet she would carry out into the garden.

As she and Cavalier approached the Commandeur, he studied a set of maps spread across an ample Gothic refectory table with such intensity that he did not look up.

"Pardon, Commandeur," said Amelia as she leaned in, trying to catch his eye.

He raised his head, his gaze keen and inquisitive. "Mademoiselle. . . Cavalier. . . I scarcely heard you come in. I've been quite intent on finding a safer pilgrimage route to Saint-Baume. How may I help?"

Amelia clasped her hands together, unsure of how Timoleon would react to her decision. "'Tis time I set a plan in motion to join Jehan, and I have come to speak to you concerning this."

"Certainly, but do you feel ready to set out so soon after Menina Elise's interment?"

"I am as ready now as I shall ever be. And I promised her I would go to Jehan. Menina is now in a better place than this harsh world we live in. And I know she is held in Divine unconditional love. 'Tis the same love we spend our lives hoping for, is it not?"

"Yes," said Timoleon. "Our very purpose in this world is to prepare for the afterlife.

"There are so many memories here . . . and threats to my safety. I believe change is for the best. I have been using teas of *millepertuis* and lemon balm as a bulwark against the grief and melancholy. They have settled my mind and renewed my courage."

Timoleon smiled and gave a relieved sigh. "I am most pleased to hear. *'All things have their season'*. There is a time to mourn, which you have done for many months while making Menina's last days comfortable and peaceful. And I hope, soon, you will have your time to dance. Please, the both of you, be seated."

Once Amelia and Cavalier settled in the high-back chairs opposite the Commandeur, she presented her concerns. "I am nearly ready to set out, however, I need your advice. I have been weighing the notion of hiring Massip, the guide Jehan used, but Cavalier tells me Du Chaila and the Intendant's dragoons are surely on the watch for him."

The Commandeur raised a brow in question.

"There is no doubt," Cavalier confirmed. "Massip is one of the best, but that's exactly why they are on the hunt for him. The daily patrols have intensified to the point that many of us only travel by night when the soldiers are occupied with debauchery in the taverns."

Amelia laid a hand on the table and leaned in as she looked to Timoleon for answers. "Moreover, I shall need to make my way to Genouillac . . . for the money Jehan instructed me to collect from his cousin, André. Yet it all seems such a risk. I say this not from a place of fear, but I want to formulate a wise strategy."

She was determined not to let this dilemma vanquish her resolve, trusting that, between the three of them and her devotional prayers for God's aid, they would find a solution.

"I have a thought," said Timoleon. His eyes fell on the map again, and he traced his finger along a circuitous path. He leaned toward Amelia on his forearms, his expression tightening. "You will be most at risk while traveling out of the Cévennes, so you are prudent to concern yourself over any attempt to meet up with Massip. Should you be prepared to leave soon, we can escort you first to Sainte-Baume for the Fête de Marie de Magdala, as we do every year. No one will think anything of it or dare confront you, as long as you are with us and wearing your Hospitaller sash. Yet that gives you merely five days to prepare."

"I had thought of that as well, but where would I go from there?" asked Amelia.

Cavalier shifted in his chair, his discomfort over the idea apparent. "It seems rather far from the usual route through Savoy to the Swiss cantons . . . the same route Jehan took."

"Precisely," said Timoleon. "And that would further confound any pursuers. Instead, we would continue the pilgrimage by staying in the low country, closer to the Mediterranean . . ." He tapped a finger on the map locations as he continued. "Through Aix and Arles, and then arrive near Saint-Gilles, where our Grande Prieuré is located on the Petit-Rhone. Not far from the port at Aigues-Morte. If we cannot locate a Dutch merchant ship heading to London, you might need to travel to Malta or Tripoli on a Knights of Malta ship first. Patience may be required at the port cities. But you should arrive in London at nearly the same time as dangerously meandering without our protection on mountainous routes known to the French soldiers."

Amelia looked at Cavalier with a smile, hoping to ease his worries. "This design feels far less dangerous, do you not agree?"

He hesitantly lifted one corner of his mouth, then nodded just once.

She realized they were likely thinking the same thing—her safety was assured as long as she traveled with the knights, but after that, she would need to keep her wits about her and use her value as a healer to negotiate the unknown that lay ahead.

14 July 1699 ~ Early Morning
Genouillac, France

As their travel party set out for Sainte-Baume, moving far beyond the protection of the commandery walls, Amelia reflected on the departure with solemnity, remaining silent and letting the sway of the saddle calm her.

There had been so many heart-rending goodbyes in only a handful of days. She had expected saying goodbye to Romulus and Remus would be exceedingly difficult, for they had comforted her when no one else could. Her salty tears had wet their muzzles for nearly an hour before she had prepared Luisant's saddle. Henriette and Jacquette had clung to her side, looking for one more hug, one more kiss, until she had passed through the commandery gates.

But seeing tears glistening in Cavalier's eyes as he stood outside the manoir, his hand raised in a reluctant adieu, had tugged twice as hard at her heart. Her young friend had grown to be an intelligent, courageous man before his time, and she would dearly miss his brotherly amity.

They had all been so much a part of her cherished homeland and she would treasure them all forever. By allowing each bittersweet moment, she embraced her sadness and then let it go, enabling her to summon the courage to leave. After nearly two hours of farewells, she climbed onto her horse, falling in line with the others as they departed.

Now only a league away and, already, regret attempted to destroy her fragile, newfound emotional armor, seeping through the cracks with a dull heaviness in her chest. Yet she knew she must cast that regret aside, or she may miss all the beautiful moments of the new life that awaited her. At least she had Griselle's company and the loving service of Jehan's mare, Luisant, for the next several weeks as they traveled with Commandeur Timoleon and four of his knights.

Amelia stayed lost in her thoughts while they descended the steep dirt roads down Mont Lauzère toward Genouillac. Dawn's light filtered through tall pines that lined each side of the road, creating a cathédrale-like canopy where dust twirled in radiant orange sunbeams. When the horses brushed past the dense understory of plants, a captivating aroma of calamint infused the air—as though a message telling her it contained the remedy for the bruises that lingered on her heart and soul.

With unwavering determination, she held that vision firmly in her mind, refusing to let it slip away, until the sudden clattering of hooves on cobblestones broke her concentration. The noise alerted her to their juncture with the old Regordane Way, signaling their arrival at the outskirts of town. The landscape gave way to open fields of waist-high amber rye where dew-heavy stalks bent in the breeze, and cicadas sang out in tiny squeaks and twitters.

Timoleon sidled up beside her and asked. "Do you remember which is the BonDurant townhouse?"

"I believe so. This old Roman road becomes la Grande Rue and we simply stay on it. 'Tis about halfway through town and has an unusual staff of Asclepius carving on the lintel above the door. 'Tis a bit different. I have seen no others like it, so we should find it easily."

Just as they entered the narrow medieval streets of the town, the bells for Prime rang out, and aromas of fresh bread teased Amelia's hungry stomach. They passed several shops and smaller homes, then approached a grand, three-storied stone townhouse. As they grew nearer, she could make out the Asclepius carving. It had three staffs, one formed in the shape of the Tau symbol. This was surely the place, so she signaled Luisant to a stop.

"Here, this is it," she said to Timoleon, then dismounted while he took hold of the bridle.

Amelia had never met Jehan's family before, but thanks to the company of the Commandeur and his knights, she was relieved of any awkwardness she might have felt if she'd arrived on her own. Still, her heart fluttered with an odd excitement about meeting the family of her beloved.

She stepped up to the large wooden entry door and tugged on the iron bell pull. After several moments, she heard voices from the upper floor and then the clicking of shoes descending what must have been a flight of stairs.

The door opened, and an elegant, dark-haired woman appeared. A charming smile spread across her face when her eyes seemed to catch sight of the cravate that Amelia wore around her neck.

"You are Amelia," said the woman.

"Yes. How did you know?"

"I recognize Jehan's cravate. And he has written to say you would be stopping. He didn't know when it would be, but I am quite pleased that it is so soon. I am Lucrèce. André's wife."

Amelia curtsied. "A pleasure."

"Please step in while I retrieve the purse André has prepared. The children are still sleeping and I see your party awaits you, so I shall only be a moment."

Amelia nodded to Timoleon, then stepped inside and pulled the door behind her as Lucrèce ascended the worn walnut stairs to the first floor. The entry hall was rustic and simple. The rough stone floor and iron sconces gave no clue to what the upper floors might be like. She glanced up to the top of the stairs and noticed a portrait hanging on the wall in a carved, gold-gilded frame, hinting that there was refinement just beyond.

While she waited, she nervously checked her hair to be sure it was tucked under her veil, adjusted the Hospitaller sash, and smoothed the skirt of her old linen gown. She had spent so little time outside of the Gorges du Tarn that it always took some adjusting to feel comfortable in the cities and towns.

Soon Lucrèce came gliding down the staircase with a small purse and a larger cloth bag embellished with a bit of embroidered trim. "I thought you may need some other clothing choices."

Amelia sensed a blush heating her cheeks when she looked at Lucrèce's fashionable summer gown of gold embroidered silk, then glanced down at her own—the linen weave so very worn, the blue woad dye so faded, that she could easily be mistaken for a vagrant.

"I know I am long past due for a new gown."

Lucrèce opened the larger bag and pointed inside. "And now you shall have this one. 'Twill help you fit in with various sorts of people, in various circumstances. 'Tis high quality fabric, yet not overly adorned."

"But I cannot accept such a fine gift."

Lucrèce smiled and hummed a melodious sigh. "Of course you can. And you will also accept this ensemble and boots," she said as she pulled out the leg of a pair of brown wool serge breeches. "'Twas my brother's before he sprouted into a man this past year."

Amelia had never considered she might need a disguise, but she was grateful that Lucrèce had. With all of Amelia's intentions to have a carefully reasoned plan, she hadn't thought of everything. It had all happened so fast, and she would be eternally grateful to each and every one of her friends who assisted her along the way.

Amelia held a hand to her heart. "God bless you, Madame Lucrèce."

"And Godspeed to you, Mademoiselle Amelia."

❧

28 July 1699 ~ Midday
The Camargue, France

After Amelia had journeyed with the Hospitallers group to Grotte de Sainte-Baume, and then on through the southern cities, they came to the vast alluvial plains of the Camargue which provided a quiet reverential atmosphere, so very different from any landscape she had traveled before. A chain of marshland and lagoons that glistened in the midday sun were strewn with tall grasses and reeds. And much of the remaining land was laced with canals skirted by ferns and trees, or cultivated fields of rice.

As they rode on, hour after hour, fatigue began to catch up with Amelia. Her limbs weakened and her hands cramped from clutching the reins. But she held on as the creak of leather and padding of horses' hooves over unfamiliar sandy roads became a cadence that easily lulled her into a deep meditation.

At times, they came upon other pilgrims, of all faiths, traveling the road. Many were lame and a few were lepers, but all were on their way to seek healing through prayers to Saint-Gilles, the patron saint of the disabled. Each time Amelia's party of travelers would steer around past the unfortunate souls, her heart ached for them. When she slowed Luisant to see if she could offer help, Timoleon assured her the Hospitallers at Saint-Gilles would tend to them.

"Best you say a prayer for them, instead. Most need no medicine once the frères pray for Saint-Gilles' intercession. 'Tis quite a miracle."

Though the healer in her wanted to do all within her power to help, she soon resolved to trust Timoleon, and let go of her fretting, placing it all in God's hands.

Her eyes adrift over the landscape, she wiped a sleeve across her damp forehead and spotted one of the renowned Camargue cattle *gardians* in the distance. Wearing leather breeches and hat, he rode a stout white horse, its long mane and tail streaking behind on the breeze as man and horse worked in unison to steer a herd of black bulls out of the water.

It was another world entirely here, and it captivated her, igniting a wayfaring urge. *How exciting it will be.* To travel the world with Jehan, exploring new cultures, new fauna and flora—especially the untried plants and herbs with medicinal properties that would expand the variety of cures in her old recipe book.

Amelia licked her parched lips, then breathed in the sweet, salty air. Finally, the weight of living such a restricted life the past two years was lifting. Her shoulders relaxed, and she sensed a lightness about her.

Although she would miss her homeland in the Cévennes, her yearning for Jehan outweighed her desire to stay. She felt certain every new location along the way would enthrall her. And discovering the passionate love she and Jehan had awaited for so long was what her heart craved most.

The very thought of Jehan's touch brought delight as she mapped his body in her mind. The enticing blue eyes, open and loving, like the heavens calling. The noble set of his jaw framed by a mane of wavy brown hair. His warm, rugged hand held against her cheek.

Closing her eyes, she lost herself in the memory of their last moments together—her fingers had rested on his strong arms as he pulled her close, pressing his firm body against hers in an embrace that had shifted her equilibrium in a strange, exquisite way. As she evoked the images, her connection with Jehan quivered through her body and flushed her cheeks, bringing a blissful smile to her lips.

Realizing she was forgetting herself, she quickly blinked and took in a deep breath to bring herself back to the here and now.

"Commandeur," she called out. "I believe the heat is affecting me. May we stop to take some water?"

Timoleon brought his horse to a stop and, as he looked around, the gray in his dark beard caught the bright sun in tiny sparkles.

"Let us rest here a bit," he said, then pointed. "There. Under that tree, next to the canal."

The dappled shade cast by the graceful willow at the foot of the canal's embankment would be a welcome relief from the hot, humid air. And he horses would also need a drink. Their coats were dark and shiny, wet with sweat—as they all were. So Amelia reined Luisant in under the protective cover, next to Griselle, who rode astride the commandery's gray Auvergne mare. They both dismounted and secured the horses to the sturdy old tree.

Timoleon did the same and signaled his knights to follow. "Wait a bit before you take the horses to the water. They will need to cool down."

The four young knights descended and stood at attention around the women with their eyes fixed on the horizons.

Griselle pulled a loaf of bread wrapped in a length of linen from her saddlebag. She removed the cloth and shook it out then laid it near the base of the tree. Tearing off several morsels from the loaf, she offered a portion to each member of their party, along with water from a costrel. It elicited a round of thanks and soft prayers from the knights as they made the sign of the cross.

Amelia placed her hand on her tender low back and stretched. "After this journey, I have a new respect for life on the road," she said to Timoleon. "The annual trip to Sainte-Baume has always been long, but the pace was much slower and not near as many leagues. God be praised, we have had no troubles."

He wriggled his shoulders, then spread his arms wide, twisting side-to-side in a stretch of his own. "You are fortunate to still have youth in your favor. But, even so, ease is not what develops our character."

"This is true," agreed Amelia. "'Tis only through trials and suffering that the soul can be strengthened."

Griselle broke her silence. "Those pilgrims we passed . . . they could teach us all something. They show great endurance and tenacity despite their misfortune."

Amelia wrapped an arm around the novice's shoulder. "Indeed. You have become so wise, little wren."

"We've not far to go now," said Timoleon. "We shall stay at a farm just outside of Saint-Gilles, where we'll not draw attention."

Griselle stepped up onto the embankment and held a hand above her eyes. "Oh my! Look, Amelia. What are those pink birds?"

"Pink birds?" Amelia scrambled up the rise to join her and gasped. On the opposite side of the canal, in an expansive shallow lagoon, she saw a flock of the most whimsical, leggy, pink birds with long, curving necks. Her heart fluttered at the thrill of it. They strutted about in water resplendent in shades of pink to magenta and edged with white crystals. "I have never seen such a sight," she exclaimed.

Timoleon stepped up beside them. "They are flamingos. Can you see there, further in the distance, there is a white mound? That is salt that has been extracted and it leaves these large ponds where pink algae thrives. The birds eat the algae and small crustaceans, so . . ."

"So they turn pink!" Griselle giggled with delight.

"Precisely. At the time of the Romans, this was the ancient Gulf of Beaucaire. But the delta of the Rhone and the Petit-Rhone have gained upon the sea ever since."

Amelia's skin tingled as she took in the wonder and magic of God's creation. So many more sights lie ahead and her freedom to explore alongside her beloved was finally within reach.

◈

Early Evening
Saint-Gilles, France

Last light streaked the endless horizon with a palette of colors as they arrived at their host's farm. A middle-aged woman, who introduced herself as Claire, motioned Amelia and Griselle through an open doorway covered with a screen of horsetail hair.

A breeze moved through the door and over the earthen floor and white plastered walls, cooling every corner of the room. Lively red geraniums filled the room—two vases on the mantel, a small potted plant on the night table, and in window boxes resting on the sills. Delicate white gauze drapery hung at the windows, diffusing the light from outside. And the same sheer fabric was suspended to make a canopy and curtains over a bed blanketed in white linen, creating a space nearly as enchanting as the nature outside.

The woman peered from under a generous white coif that had slid down over her dark eyebrows, then pointed to the gauze curtain surrounding the bed. "You should not have a problem with mosquitoes in this room if you keep the bed curtains pulled closed." She moved to the doorway, then turned around. "I shall bring you a tray with supper in a bit."

"Thank you, madame," said Amelia.

"Yes, thank you. You are so kind." Griselle said, as she curtsied deeply.

When the woman left the room, she turned to Amelia. "Everyone deserves the respect of royalty. I finally understand that if we treat others the way we wish to be treated, we are most likely to receive it in return."

"Indeed!" Amelia took Griselle's cheeks in her hands and kissed her forehead. Then she pulled back the bed curtains and sighed with contentment. "Doesn't this look absolutely heavenly?"

Griselle took her hand and they both let themselves fall backward into the plump, soft bedding at the same time, laughing like children, safe at last to express their delight.

29 July 1699 ~ Evening
Aigues-Morte, France

Timoleon had risen early to hire a salt barge to take him down the Petit-Rhone in search of a ship. Amelia and Griselle took heed of his instructions to stay indoors as much as possible until his return, and spent the day in the cool of Claire's kitchen, helping her with chores, playing with her orange tabby cat, and sharing stories.

The entire day had passed when Amelia sat down by the window to watch the sunset, holding the cat in her lap. As she stroked between its ears, enjoying its soothing purr, a rhythmic knock came at the door.

"That would be Commandeur Timoleon," said Claire, pushing open the small iron cover on the eyehole.

She opened the door, and he entered with a weary but determined look in his eyes.

He took a seat at Claire's table and looked across the room at Amelia. "There were no Dutch merchant ships in port at Aigues-Morte. But . . ." The Commandeur paused and heaved a deep breath.

Amelia's chest grew tight while she awaited the next words.

"I have negotiated an agreement with the captain of a Maltese Hospitaller's galley ship. The *Galera Padrona*. His crew is a hardened lot who spend most of their days going after Barbary corsairs, yet you should be able to trust them. However, since it is not customary to take a woman on board, the captain requires three things. Firstly, you will need to dress in the manner of a young man. Only the captain must know your true identity."

A vein in Timoleon's neck pulsed in a frenetic tempo, causing Amelia to suspect there was more he wasn't saying. Her implacable nature had already had enough of blindly following orders over the past two years—even Timoleon's, even if for her own protection. Surely, the knights on board were honorable men.

"You can be direct with me," she said. "Tell me, Commandeur, why should I dress as a man aboard this ship?"

Timoleon's mouth twisted into a nervous half-smile. "Not only is it a ship full of knights whose appetites, even with a vow of chastity, are not entirely predictable, but there are also galley slaves on board. The chances are slim that one would escape their shackles, but you can be certain that there are some you cannot trust. Not all are good Huguenots, captured for practicing the Reformed faith. Most are thieves. And there is always the danger of an attack by the corsairs."

When he stopped talking, Amelia realized that, unbidden, she had protectively wrapped her arms around herself. Her eyes swept around the room to confirm there was nothing there to threaten her.

Griselle stayed near the hearth with Claire, sweeping nonexistent dust into it, but by her astonished look, she had heard every word.

"So, should it not be clear to you yet," Timoleon said, "dressing as a man might preempt a possible assault."

He was right. This thinking through scenarios was not meant to frighten her, but simply to keep her alert and aware, and she would need to practice that skill herself from here on out.

"Very well," Amelia conceded. "I am fortunate that Madame Lucrèce shared your foresight and gave me her brother's ensemble."

Timoleon took another deep breath and gave a short, pensive sigh. "Good then," he said. "And you will be required to go by the name Monsieur Auvrey. You are the son of a physician who is now living in London and you are to return home after a Grand Tour of France."

The Commandeur's eyelids grew heavy, as though exhaustion was taking hold.

Amelia set the cat down, then took the bench across the table from Timoleon, where she could keep eye contact. "And what is the third requirement?"

"I shall explain when we arrive at port. I've returned here on the ship's *pinnace*, the tender boat, and the boatmen are taking supper at the inn while you ready. Once you reach Malta, you will easily find a merchant vessel to London, or one going straight on to the colonies. Female passengers are not such a rare occurrence aboard those vessels."

As the Commandeur's shoulders relaxed, Amelia noted some relief in his visage that had not been there for weeks.

"Thank you, Commandeur." Amelia folded her hands at her heart and bowed her head to him.

"'Tis my duty and pleasure to assist. You should prepare now. We shall leave at midnight and board the ship at dawn."

As their boat glided down the river and into the port at Aigues-Morte, the scent of briny tidal marshes and distant fires gave way to the pungent odors of freshly discarded clam shells and rotting fish bones.

Amelia's eyes scanned the clusters of warehouses that appeared as ghostly ruins, their inky black shadows likely concealing arrant thieves or kindly fishermen slipping out before the dawn. She welcomed the cloak of night, grateful for the concealment it would grant their party as they entered the city.

The boatmen moored the pinnace at a quay near the Tower of Constance—a tall, imposing structure that glowed eerily in the moonlight. It made Amelia wonder about the poor Protestant women being held there. A whispered prayer for their souls moved over her lips as she stepped from the tender boat. One of the boatmen led them quickly through the dark street to a carriage house and knocked twice on a large, arched wooden door meant for carts and carriages to pass through.

Amelia huddled close to Griselle and the knights as they waited outside. She felt certain that the disguise Lucrèce had given her would suffice to conceal her identity. Around her shoulders, she wore her cloak over the young man's ensemble, and under a black felt hat, she had tied her hair back into a queue, secured by a black ribbon she found in the bag. The brown boots were a near perfect fit and the sturdy leather covered to the knee, so she was well prepared for inclement conditions.

Now, she needed only to act the part. Her heart fluttered as she began the process of embodying a masculine persona, in a way not unlike the technique she'd heard was used by actors in the playhouses of London and Paris.

When the carriage house door creaked open to the soft light of a single candle, a face with skin was as dark and wrinkled as old leather peered out.

"Hurry in," said a gruff voice.

A burly man already dressed in work tunic and cap ushered them inside with haste. Murmured words were exchanged, and Timoleon handed the man a purse of money.

The Commandeur cleared his throat. "The stablemaster has the preparations completed for your transport."

"Transport? What do you mean?" Amelia asked.

"This is the third part of the agreement. I thought it best to wait to tell you so as not to create anxiousness. They will need you to be concealed as they take you on board."

Amelia bit her lower lip. She had never anticipated such a thing. The Commandeur was wise to not tell her earlier.

"Here . . ." He stepped inside one of the horse stalls and held his hand in the direction of a large wooden box on a workbench, then lifted the lid. "There are discreet holes throughout, so you will have no problem breathing."

Her shoulders tightened at the thought of being trapped. "But it is only for a short while, is it not? And who will let me out?"

"Yes, it will not be for long. The captain will come for you as soon as the boat leaves the port."

She needed more assurance than that. "Can he be trusted? What if something were to happen to him?"

"They will only use these small nails," Timoleon said, pointing to four short slender nails on the workbench. "All you need to do is push on the lid a bit, or kick with your foot. The nails will not hold."

Amelia raised her brow and pursed her lips, still not certain about giving herself up to this confinement.

"I see that look, Mademoiselle Amelia. They have demonstrated it to me, so I trust them. See here. . ." Timoleon said, pointing inside, "how they have fashioned it like a coffin with ample space near the shoulders."

"A coffin?" Amelia let out a small, nervous laugh. She could not let her thoughts take her hostage now, since the box would do that all on its own.

"The customs inspectors rarely ask to see inside a coffin. Should they do so, you will need to play the role of your life and hold perfectly still."

She blew out a long, soft breath. "I was just envisioning this as play acting, hoping to soothe my fears. 'Tis good that I am practiced at meditation. I can hold very still and even slow my heartbeat." She swallowed, trying to push back the trepidation and convince herself it would all be fine. But her instinctive mind, that bestial side of her human nature, was not so sure. It still resisted the idea of being caged. She needed to ask for courage to get through this, and everything that lay ahead of her.

"Commandeur, will you lead us in a prayer before I begin my performance?"

There was benevolence in his eyes as he proffered his hands. She and Griselle each took one and lowered their heads.

"Through the intercession of Saint Bona, we pray for the health and safety of Mademoiselle Amelia and all pilgrims and refugees in every corner of the world. And we pray for the intercession of our patron, Saint Jean the Baptist, that our lives and actions may be the voice of one, calling out into the desert, preparing the way for the work of our Lord."

Amelia gradually sensed the presence of the Holy Spirit resonate through her, growing stronger moment by moment. For so long, its presence had withered to a dim light, but now, with God's grace and mercy, it was replenishing her with peace and warmth and fortitude.

Yet there was one thing more. Now that the plan was becoming clearer, she needed to write to Jehan before she left. "May I be provided with a quill and paper or parchment? Jehan must know of my designs."

"Certainly," Timoleon answered, then turned to the stablemaster and raised his chin.

The man swaggered off through a doorway that seemed to go to a kitchen. They waited while they heard him speaking with a woman on inside. Moments went by that seemed an eternity, but before too long, the stablemaster returned with a rough sheet of hempen looking paper, quill, and ink, and handed them to Amelia.

"I will see to it that your letter goes through the Protestant network," said Timoleon. "It should arrive in London before you do. But there is not much time. We've got to get you on board."

Amelia spread the paper over the workbench and dipped the quill, her heart pounding like a mallet against her chest while she leaned over and wrote as fast as she could. Without wax and seal, she knew she would have to use one of her more difficult folding techniques to discourage prying eyes. Her fingers worked furiously until she finished the last tuck, then inhaled deeply and handed it to the Commandeur. Now, at last, she could fulfill her destiny in that far off Eden.

She held a hand over her pocket, where she carried the old recipe book that had brought good fortune to her family and many healers before them. To be in the service of others was not only her desire, but she felt assured it would also open the path before her—ensuring her safety by keeping her of value wherever she went.

She turned to Griselle and embraced her, holding her close for several moments before letting go. "Please take good care of Luisant. I am certain Jehan would want you to have her."

"I shall. I promise you. I shall love her as you both have."

"Let my parting words be the beginning of an amazing life for you, little wren. The Commandeur will need you now that I am leaving, and you are fully ready to step into my shoes. Though, never stop learning. Life, and the forest, and books of course, have so much to teach us."

A tear trickled down Griselle's cheek that caught the lantern light with a sparkle. The girl threw her arms around Amelia and held on so tight that she could not lift her arms to return the hug.

"Always remember you are loved, little wren. And I will miss you."

Griselle let go and slid her hands around to Amelia's. She squeezed them gently, saying, "I will always remember, and I shall be forever grateful that you pulled me out of the darkness and taught me to read." She took a breath and stood tall. "As you have said, words have power, so I shall take your words and repeat them daily. In that way, you will always be with me."

"Are you ready?" asked the Commandeur.

Amelia nodded, her lips pressed tight together.

Timoleon held out his hand and assisted her while she climbed atop the workbench and lowered herself to sit inside the coffin.

She took her satchel from her shoulder, then tucked it inside her cloak and laid down with her hat atop her chest. As the lid was being lowered above her, and the nails tapped into place, she shivered—it was as if she were moving into the realm of death. She had to rein in her thoughts quickly, so she closed her eyes and focused on the sweet, pungent odor of the newly milled pine wood. It reminded her of the forest on Mont Lauzère, where the trees soared to the sky and their shadows played against the gray stone cliffs. She told herself that, in this death of sorts, she could be reborn to a brand new life. As she let herself fall farther into the meditation, images filled her mind of joyous days roaming the meadows and exploring the streams and waterfalls. The spring days when the wildflowers were abundant and her garden flourished. She only scarcely felt the stirring as the coffin was being lifted and carried out. When the movement turned to a gentle rocking, she could hear the soft lapping of water against the tender boat and the oars dipping into the river. Jehan's face appeared in her mind, sharper and more vivid than it had for many months, and soon she was lulled deeper, deeper into an altered state of awareness.

❧

Several taps roused Amelia to sentience. She heard the calls of seabirds and the gurgling of waves, the shouting of orders for the deckhands, and the low groaning and flapping that she reckoned were the sails being hoisted.

Lantern light spilled into the coffin in a narrow shard as the lid was being lifted.

"Monsieur Auvrey. 'Tis time now."

She blinked away the spots before her eyes to see a smiling, sun-kissed face peering in at her. The man who hovered over her wore a blazing red justaucorps with gold braid trimmings—those customarily belonging to a captain. The familiar silk sash with the eight-pointed white cross draped across his chest, and a ring of white feathers adorned his black hat.

"You will want to get your sea legs above board. Follow me." He headed through the dark hull of the ship, brimming with barrels and crates, and up a steep, open staircase.

Amelia made haste to climb out of the coffin, embracing her new role with all the energy of an eager young man setting off on an adventure, and scurried up the staircase after him.

Her eyes took a few moments to adjust to the breaking dawn as she stepped outside the hold doorway. Beyond the sails, the sky was a mesmerizing canvas of striated pink hues fading upward into the deep blue of the night, still adorned with sparkling stars. The vast Mediterranean before her was another new sight to behold. The pulsing body of water was its own master until the quavering sails harnessed the winds, and countless oars cut through the white-capped waves, setting the ship on its course.

She felt the freedom of the sea breeze caressing her in a sensuous massage, and dawn broke in a burst of the most majestic sunlight she had ever seen.

CHAPTER 22

THE CALL OF FREEDOM

JEHAN

23 August 1699 ~ Morning
London, England

The day had come for the renowned Bartholomew Faire at Smithfield, and since it occurred only once a year, Jehan was determined to waste no time getting there. His new lodging in Doctor Ramsdell's Soho townhouse was nearly two miles from the field, and Jehan was eager to arrive before the heavy queues formed so he could secure a spot at one of the comedic performances.

Rising early, he tossed back the sheets then stretched his stiff limbs as he ambled to the window. He lifted the casement, and it swooshed as it glided in its tracks. Morning light was already stealing through a crack in the shutters, so he tossed them open, and when the sun burst across his face and spilled into the room, he felt certain it would be a good day. Pleasant birdsong met his ears while his nose was treated to the fragrance of summer roses wafting up from the rear courtyard.

A tap came at the chamber door, followed by Doctor Ramsdell's lilting voice in fluent French. "Are you up yet, Jehan?"

Jehan's eyes fell down along his chemise to his bare legs and he wiggled his toes. "Only just. And I haven't dressed."

"I wanted to inform you that I must run out to call on a patient. So I shall be gone for breakfast. Are you and Corbell still going to the Faire?"

"I am, but Corbell was to think on it overnight."

"Well . . . 'Tis a treat not to be missed. I shall see you for supper then."

Jehan hastily went to the basin on the bureau to wash and shave. He dressed in his blue ensemble, gave it a quick brush, and grabbed his hat on the way out of the room.

Deciding to forego breakfast, he trotted downstairs to the entry hall with a bounce in his step to wait for Corbell. With the Doctor out, the house was quiet, save a bit of rattling coming from the kitchen. Jehan listened to see if he could hear Corbell moving about upstairs. His friend was dawdling today—today of all days—but Jehan owed it to him to wait.

Corbell had been the best of comrades throughout the past few years—reliable, trustworthy, and, until recently, the more adventurous one. Jehan enjoyed his consistent companionship and was quite pleased when Doctor Ramsdell had offered the pair of them employment in exchange for room and board, plus a small stipend.

Jehan tarried to check himself in the carved wood mirror above the hall console table, brushing the wrinkles out of his ensemble. With no word yet from Amelia, he looked forward to some mirthful distractions to quell his yearning for the day she would arrive. When not assisting the good Doctor Ramsdell with blending cures, or studying the English language, he had kept himself occupied at Gresham College open lectures, exploring the latest science and medical techniques. But he'd heard the amusements and mysteries at this Faire offered something altogether different, causing his heart to pound in anticipation and his movements to feel light.

He could hear the cook pattering about on the other side of the kitchen door. Then she poked her head out, all round pudgy cheeks and white coif. "Wot? Are yer ter leave wivout eatin', eh?"

Her English was thick and muddled, but Jehan had become accustomed to it. For clarity, it was best to keep his replies in English rather brief.

"Yes, madame," he said. But it was hard to say no to her breads and jams, or to her fresh poached eggs with a pinch of Indonesian nutmeg.

"Wait. I shall bring yer some tea," she said, and scuttled off.

Jehan tossed his profusion of dark, wavy hair back over his shoulders, then patted on his hat. He proceeded to fold and secure the hat's brim on three sides, one after the other, using pins from a porcelain holder that Doctor Ramsdell kept on the console table. The cocked hat had become the accepted fashion among the coffeehouse gents, and wearing the style had helped him fit in with new contacts from both the Royal Society and the College of Physicians, making it well worth the extra effort.

The cook came back down the entry hall and set a cup and saucer on the console in front of him. "Er ya go. Some nice Chinese green," she said, then slipped back into the kitchen without another word.

Jehan sipped the warm, fragrant tea between rounds of preening until, finally, Corbell came bounding down the stairs, dressed in his somber Sunday clothes.

"Well, my friend," said Jehan, setting the cup on the console table. "Have you decided? Will you join me?"

"I shall, but after worship." Corbell stopped in front of the mirror to adjust his cravate. "I want to pay a visit to Pasteur De Joux's church in Spittlefields again."

"You, Corbell? You were the most ardent free-thinker in our group back in Aarau. What is it that appeals to you?"

"I'm enjoying the less restrictive Anglican style he preaches. I think you would also appreciate his teachings . . . and his demeanor."

"When first we met De Joux, I did sense he is altogether different from Uncle Barjon. But I have been reluctant to commit to anything new."

"De Joux's teachings stress the capacity of humankind to find salvation on their own. He encourages enlightenment by reason and by leading upright, moral lives . . . *unlike* your uncle's insistence that only those chosen by him on God's behalf, and forced into conversion, are to find salvation."

"I do hope to get better acquainted with De Joux's manner since he is to be the spiritual leader in Carolana." Jehan stepped near the entry, preparing to leave. "I should set out now but, since we head in the same direction, please, tell me more while we walk."

When Jehan opened the front door, sounds of clattering iron-shod wheels and hooves clip-clopping over brick instantly spilled into the entry. The door's glossy black surface and polished brass hardware reflected the morning light in a striking example of the modernity found around Soho Square. It glided smoothly on its hinges—such a pleasing contrast to the ancient doors on Jehan's homes in France.

He peered out to the street; it was an exciting new world out there, full of promise, even if the future still held unknowns.

Listening intently, Jehan motioned Corbell out first, his friend's warm brown eyes lively and animated as he spoke.

"De Joux's services are quite different from those at the traditional French Reformed temples in the area."

They stepped out along the broad thoroughfare lined with stately brick townhomes. An array of elegant carriages came and went, even one drawn by a team of eight great Palfrey horses. There was an occasional mule-drawn cart carrying supplies, and sedan chairs transporting elegantly plumed ladies fanning themselves against the heat.

Corbell continued, raising his voice as the rhythmic clamor enveloped them. "The Anglican church still allows both private confession and making the sign of the cross. And De Joux adds joyful singing from the French Psalter."

"Sounds as if I would, indeed, appreciate his style," Jehan said, recalling how much he enjoyed the Psalter hymns that Lucrèce and her friends always sang at their secret prayer meetings. How the songs spoke of clean hands and pure hearts and mercy. But mostly how they spoke of the majesty of God's creations in nature—seas, rivers, holy mountains—as the true heaven on earth, the true Eden. Carolana held assurance of that Eden; the place where he could finally embrace the Divine as he once had in the forests of the Gorges du Tarn. He inhaled deeply, the sweet anticipation of that place building tenacity to see the vision through.

"Perhaps I shall join you next week," Jehan suggested. "I have had quite a time over the past four years giving up the act of confession and relinquishing the habit of crossing myself. Both were so ingrained in me, having been raised by the Dominicans."

As they came upon an elderly couple strolling along the brick sidewalk in the opposite direction, Jehan and Corbell both paused and tipped their hats.

"Good morning," said Jehan, practicing his English.

"Messieurs," said the man with a polite nod.

Corbell chuckled softly. "You will need to work on that accent if you no longer want to be identified as French."

"I am not concerned. I am proud to be French, just not proud of the King and his advisors and his ruthless minions."

Jehan gazed up between the tall buildings to see a small slice of blue sky and billowy clouds, his mind still ruminating on his spiritual path.

"In truth, I feel closer to the Divine when in nature rather than in a church. And there is certainly not much of that around here. All the same, I shall endeavor to make the best of things until we reach the wild frontier in the New World. Oddly, I have realized of late that I can find communion and growth just by interacting with the diverse people of this great city . . . no matter their sort."

Corbell raised an eyebrow and smirked. "I often find it quite challenging, myself," he admitted. "Attempting to speak the language and learn the peculiar customs can be difficult at times."

"And that is how we grow," Jehan said, counseling himself as much as Corbell. "Think of the true challenges we have faced . . . watching families brutally punished for simply practicing the religion of their choice, and feeling we could do nothing to stop it . . . being hounded by dragoons until we submitted to authoritarian rule . . . and then being forced to flee our homeland in dangerous conditions." Jehan's neck tensed at his own mentioning of the atrocities. "Look at how that has changed us. I find it far easier now to quell my temper and have mercy for others than I did only a few years ago."

The bells of a nearby church chimed once, signaling half past the hour, followed by a cacophony of others in the distance, all rousing the city from its morning languor.

Jehan recognized the spot just ahead where the boulevard branched in two directions. "Here is where I head off."

"Where shall we meet then?" asked Corbell.

"There is a garden square just northeast of Smithfield. Charterhouse, I believe it is called. Find me there at half past noontide."

The Bartholomew Faire was a tawdry comparison to the Hospitallers' Fête du Saint Jean on Mont Lauzère. Rather than offering enchantment and feasting and ancient ritual dance in a tranquil setting under the stars, this Faire was so enormous that one could easily get lost amongst the cheap attractions and never find their way out. Jehan had heard the Puritans tried to have it banned, but the city authorities would do no more than to limit it from a full week to three days and ban the selling of goods during Sunday worship.

Despite the slight iniquity of it all, Jehan found it enthralling. The puppet shows, mime shows, tightrope walkers, jugglers, rope dancers, performing dogs, dancing monkeys, animal exhibitions, and cockfights were all meant to attract the masses and raise money for Saint Bartholomew Church so its clergy could feed the poor.

But Jehan was not here for all the trifles. Instead, he was here for the actors. Those ingenious people who could communicate the prevalent ideas and travails and emotions of the times. There was so much to be learned about the English culture through their entertaining performances.

The crowd was thin near the first stage Jehan came upon, so it was a good place to start. Just as he positioned himself within an arms-length of the stage, a young lad, donning a tattered red velvet cap with an arching white feather, approached with a handful of leaflets, jabbering in English.

"Awh, 'is show's a gooser. Come on over an' bring your chinkers to da only stage to offer a real screamer."

Jehan struggled to get the boy's meaning. "Goose? Stinkers?"

"No, no," said the boy, then he spoke louder as though Jehan were hard of hearing. "This show is *bad*! Bring your money to *our* show. 'Tis the only *good* show!"

It never seemed to fail—if Jehan had even the slightest difficulty understanding English, people spoke to him as though he were deaf or an imbecile. He was thankful for the patience it was teaching him, and that Doctor Ramsdell, and many in the community around Soho—French Huguenots and well-educated English alike—spoke fluent French.

Jehan followed the boy to his company's stage and stood laughing through what seemed like the entire one-act show. The boy had been right, and Jehan's cheeks ached, but he wanted more.

He went on to enjoy two other outrageously merry plays—light-hearted comedies and fast-moving farces intended as parodies, some enlivened by song and dance interludes. He made out enough English to understand the fervent messages on the pitfalls and shortcomings of London society, resolving him to begin donations to local almshouses at the earliest opportunity.

In the midst of the fourth play, the city's bell towers tolled half past noontide.

Time to meet Corbell.

Jehan darted through the crowds and along Charterhouse Lane toward the square, panting as he ran down the long block and through the main gate.

Stopping to catch his breath, he leaned his hands on his thighs, then noticed Corbell, his features smudged by the distance. He was down a long walkway surrounded by low trees, watching a pair of ducks splashing about in a fountain.

Jehan slowed his pace as he headed down the gravel walkway, the crunching of stone beneath his feet evoking memories of strolling the terrace at his château in France. Like a gentle breeze, these fragmented recollections brushed against his heart, as they often did, leaving a lasting impression.

Just as he approached Corbell, his friend turned toward him. His face lit up with brows raised and a jubilant smile.

"I have great news! Important news," he said as he hastened up to Jehan.

Had Corbell joined De Joux's congregation? Or been offered better employment than making new medical instruments for Doctor Ramsdell?

"What is your news?" Jehan asked.

"De Joux says the Carolana resettlement project can move forward!" Corbell paused to take a breath between excited words. "He has been told that King William and a few private investors will approve funding. 'Tis only a matter of going through the governmental formalities and hiring merchant ship captains who will outfit their vessels. De Joux says all should be complete by spring, in about nine months' time."

Jehan breathed a huge sigh of relief as the vision of Eden became clearer in his mind's eye. "That should allow time for Amelia's arrival. Your news is of great solace, my friend," he said, fondly clutching Corbell's shoulder.

"Indeed. And yet there is even more news to please you on this fine day," Corbell said, reaching into his pocket. "A letter . . . from Amelia." He proffered a tiny parcel of linen paper. "It came to Pasteur De Joux just yesterday."

Jehan's heart bounded with a sudden giddiness as though it were lifting him above the ground. Could it truly be that she was on her way at last? He blinked his eyes to be sure it was no dream before reaching out a hand to take the letter.

As Jehan carefully dismantled the many intricate folds, Corbell asked, "I have often wondered . . . what is it that makes Amelia so special? What makes her worth waiting for?"

Distant remembrances of time spent in her gentle company swept through Jehan; treasured keepsakes that gave him the purpose and drive to push on. The excitement that coursed through him now was palpable, the blood in his arms and chest quivering while he loosened the last few folds of the letter. He wanted to read it straight away—not wait to answer his friend—but he held it to his heart and tempered the impulse with patience, honoring Amelia with his words.

"From the moment I first met her in the forest, there has been a special light that shines around her. There is a sense of connectedness and oneness with her . . . and all of creation that . . . I have never felt with any other woman. When I am with her, I feel as if I am home." Jehan gazed toward the sky and his smile blossomed as he thought of all she brought to his life. "And . . . she is brave and compassionate and looks at the world in such a different way. With her in my life, I appreciate the world and *everything* in it."

"Ahhh . . ." said Corbell, smiling, his eyes bright with new awareness. "Although I've never been so fortunate as to have experienced that, I am beginning to understand."

"When I thought I had lost her, I became bitter and judgmental, even though I had Udine to satisfy my baser desires. With Amelia, I am a better man and..." Jehan stopped talking, his palms becoming sweaty as he pulled back the last folded corner of the letter.

"I shall give you your privacy now," Corbell said, then darted away.

Jehan's eyes fixed on the words penned on hempen paper in Amelia's beautiful hand. He lowered himself to sit on the fountain wall and began reading.

> *Tomorrow I shall be hidden inside a casket and placed on a Maltese Hospitaller ship where I shall be reborn as a joyful sojourner! Timoleon has negotiated an agreement with the captain to take me to Malta and, from there, I shall find a merchant ship and journey on to London.*

> *Through the many trials we have each faced, I know there have been times when the voice of Spirit has grown small. Yet it came to me today, as I prepared to board the ship. It has renewed my hope*

and inner strength, and I have found my bearings once again. The bearings that give me faith that I shall join you soon, and we shall thrive in the Eden we've long dreamed of. From here forward, let nothing disturb or distress us. We shall seek deep within to find perfect Wisdom. Then we can walk the narrow path ahead, fearlessly and with joy in our hearts.

The bright glow of your soul also guides me. The chivalry you possess . . . that desire you have to champion those who need raising up . . . that is your elixir of love and I long to taste it again. I have a delicious pain for you in my heart and I hope time passes quickly till we can be together again. The indigo night sky and her millions of stars have been the place where we have met for too long now. At last, we shall meet in the light of day, and it will be a day so brilliant that my heart will burst forth with joy and bliss.

All my love, always and forever,
Your Ame

Jehan held his arms wide, letter in one hand and face toward the heavens, and rejoiced aloud, "Mon Ame, the more love I hold for you, the more I have to give to the world. Praise be for all the goodness in my life."

His jubilation aroused a flock of sparrows from the gravel walkway and lifted them into flight with a fluttering and whirring of hundreds of tiny wings that excited his ears. He laughed with delight at the sight of their emancipation into the vast cloudless sky, an undulating wave of tiny specks against the most stirring, brilliant cerulean blue.

He watched until the birds disappeared from view, then looking to see where Corbell had gotten to, Jehan cast his eyes around the square and realized he stood at the center of two intersecting walkways—two paths that converged, at this place, at this moment in time, like a mysterious symbol portending the certainty of his reunion with his beloved.

After the past few years of unhappiness, their arrival in the New World would mean the end of persecutions and restrictions, the end of hiding and fleeing. No longer shackled by oppression, it would be the beginning of true liberty for them both. With the call of freedom as their compass, they would sail the great Atlantic Ocean, an open sea of endless possibilities and, guided by the same stars that bound them to each other, they would find the new land on the horizon where life could begin again.

THE END

GLOSSARY

- *Alemannisch:* a dialect of German spoken in the region of Alemannia, which covers parts of Germany, Switzerland, and Austria

- *Bleibt ruhig, Leute:* German – Stay calm, people.

- *brusc:* Occitan - beehive

- *cazelle:* Occitan - shepherd's stone shelter with a door-less opening

- *Celtae:* Latin – the name that Gauls of *Gallia Celtica* called themselves, according Julius Caesar

- *Cévennes:* French – range of mountains in south-central France; name comes from the Gaulish "Cebenna", thought to translate to "rigdeline", Latinized by Julius Caesar to Cevenna

- *chanson:* French - secular songs of medieval and Renaissance music

- *chapellerie:* French – atelier and shop for making and selling hats

- *chemise:* French - men's shirt or women's shift

- *chignon:* French - hairstyle achieved by pinning into a knot

- *chirurgien:* French – surgeon (modern English), chirgugion (16th & 17th c. English)

- *coif:* French - a close-fitting cap worn by both men and women

- *consistory* – a church tribunal or governing council

- *coquette*: French/English – a woman who trifles with men's affections and is given to flirting

- *cordonnier:* French – shoemaker

- *costrel:* French – wine skin made of leather for traveling

- *couturiers:* French – a fashion designer who manufactures and sells clothes that have been tailored to a client's specific requirements and measurements

- *cravate:* French – neckband or scarf; cravat in English

- *danke:* German – thank you

- *de amore:* French – of love

- *denier*: French – French currency used in late 17th c. worth one penny

- *dikhlo:* Romany – woman's scarf worn with hair tied in bun or two braids under it, used traditionally to signify she is married

- *dragonnade*: French – French government policy instituted by King Louis XIV in 1681 to intimidate Protestant families into converting to Catholicism; billeting of ill-disciplined dragoons in Protestant households with implied permission to abuse inhabitants and destroy or steal their possessions

- *dragoons*: French – mounted soldier or hired mercenary, often ill-behaved, named for the guns they carried, carbines or muskets called a "dragon" because they were carved with a dragon's head

- *drailles:* Occitan - trail or pathway used by livestock farmers in the mountains of southern France for the yearly sheep migration known as the "transhumance"

- *Dreikönigskuchen:* German – a version of "King Cake" or "Epiphany cake"

- *ecu*: French – a gold coin worth three livres, about three British pounds

- *épisode cévenol:* French – succession of torrential rains and floods when cold air from the Atlantic coast meets warm air from the Mediterranean

- *es gibt:* German - there are

- *féerie, fée:* French – fairy

- *frère:* French – brother/monk, at a prieuré, monastery, or convent

- *für*: German – for

- *Gabali Celtae*: Latin – Celtic tribe dwelling in the Gévaudan region in the southeast portion of the Cévennes Mountains during the Iron Age and the Roman period

- *garbarre*: French – flat-bottomed river vessel or barge meant to hold about thirty passengers and/or cargo, often with a small cabin or benches and a collapsible center mast and sail

- *gardians:* French - horse-mounted cattle herdsmen

- *Gâteau des rois:* French – "King Cake" similar to brioche flavored with orange blossom water, traditionally consumed during the Christian festival of Epiphany

- *gentilhomme:* French – gentleman

- *gewicht:* German – weight, heft

- *glockenspiel:* German – carillon bell tower

- *haute couture:* French – high fashion

- *Herr:* German – Mister, Monsieur, Sieur, Sir, Lord

- *Herren und Dame:* German – gentlemen and lady

- *Huguenot:* French Protestants, mostly Calvinists, who faced persecutions; primarily used in 16th-17th c. as derogatory name, but later became a badge of honor

- *inspiré:* French – the term originates with the Huguenot assemblers of the Cévennes, referring to a person claiming to be possessed by the Holy Spirit and who announces the end of the world and Christ's Second Coming; later referred to as "French Prophets"

- *Intendant:* French – high-ranking administrator who reported to the Controller-General of France; oversaw finance, commerce, and sovereign council (courts)

- *Ja:* German – yes

- *justaucorps:* French – long, knee-length coat worn mostly by men, but also women, in the late 17th c. -18th c., with buttons along the entire length of opening, with stiff, wide skirting that protruded in back, and fitted sleeves with deep cuffs

- *Konditorei:* German – confectionary or pastry shop

- *Kreig:* German – war

- *langue d'oc:* French /Occitan, – language of oc, known as *lenga d'òc* by its native speakers; a Romance language similar to Catalan; the original common language in southern France and of the troubadours

- *livre:* French – French currency in late 17th c. worth one livre (franc, pound, dollar)

- *mantua:* French - popular dress style mid 17th – late 18th c.; instead of a bodice and skirt cut separately, it hung from the shoulders, made from a single length of elaborately patterned silk fabric, pleated to fit with a long train; more modest than previous fashions and fussy, with bows, frills, ribbons, and other trim

- *Mélusine:* French – legendary *féerie*/fairy woman whose lower body turned into a fish tail when she bathed

- *menhirs* - a tall upright stone erected in prehistoric times in western Europe

- *Menina:* Occitan – grandmother

- *métayer:* French – peasant farmer who managed a seigneurie parcel of land in a partnership with the Seigneur who paid for stocking the land; the farmer worked it and paid rent as a percentage of the yield in crops or money

- *millepertuis*: French – *Hypericum perforatum* also known as St. John's Wort

- *mistral:* Occitan – meaning "masterly"; strong, cold, northwesterly wind, usually in winter or spring, averaging 40 mph and up to 115 mph; accompanied by clear, fresh weather

- *mon Ame:* French – Jehan's nickname for Amelia; also meaning "my friend"

- *mon Dieu:* French/Occitan – my God

- *n'ei pas bona:* Occitan – it is not good

- *nein:* German – no

- *noblesse:* French - nobility

- *nouveau converti:* Latin – (plural - *nouveaux convertis*); newly converted to the Holy Roman Catholic faith; often done only to avoid persecution while still practicing one's true faith in secret, such as the Reformed faith, Judaism, Islam, etc.

- *pasteur:* French – Pastor

- *perruque:* French – wig or periwig; common in the 17th -18th c.

- *physick:* English – multiple meanings; a term for physician or the practice of medicine; also a term for a purgative

- *pieds:* French – measurement equivalent to one foot/twelve inches

- *pinnace:* French – a small boat, with sails or oars, forming part of the equipment of larger vessel

- *posset:* French – drink made of milk curdled with wine or ale, often spiced and used as a remedy for colds or to relax for sleep

- *prieur:* French – Prior; priest in charge of a priory, convent, monastery

- *prieuré:* French – Priory; monastery or convent governed by a prior or prioress

- *Reformed:* English – *Réformé* in French; originally, people or church of several Protestant groups to distinguish them from "unreformed" Roman Catholics; after great controversy over the Lord's Supper in the mid 16th c., the name became associated with only Calvinist churches

- *sabots:* French – peasant shoe generally made from a single piece of hollowed-out wood

- *sage-femme:* Occitan/French - wise woman; a midwife healer

- *Schlösser:* German – castle, château, fortress

- *Seid ruhig, Leute:* German – be calm people

- *Seigneur / Sénher:* French / Occitan – Lord of a manor, fief, or kingdom known as a Seigneurie

- *seigneurie:* French – Land, estate, and other property owned and governed by a Seigneur or Lord, which provided certain economic, social, judicial, and honorific privileges and obligations

- *solaire:* French – room in grand houses and châteaux intended as a quiet, private place for the family, especially for women; south-facing windows were required for good sunlight since the room was used for reading, embroidering, writing, and more

- *sopar:* Occitan – supper

- *sous:* French – French currency used in late 17th c. worth 12 deniers (penny) and 20 sous was worth one livre (franc, pound, dollar)

- *spazierstock:* German – walking cane

- *stadtkirche:* German – town church

- *stapelrecht:* German – staple right or stacking right; allowed river towns along the Rhine the right to demand boats carrying commercial goods must stop for three days and offer their goods for sale at their market through a local agent. This was even imposed on goods that had already been contracted for at their destination.

- *Tanta:* Occitan – Aunt

- *toilette:* French – the process of washing oneself, dressing, and attending to one's appearance

- *transhumance:* Occitan – seasonal movement of livestock between fixed summer pastures in the lowlands and winter pastures in the mountains

- *und:* German – and

- *unzufrieden:* German – unsatisfied

- *va:* Romani – yes; ava is also used

- *valet de pied:* French – footman

- *vos prègui:* Occitan – please

- *weidling:* German – flat-bottomed boat, similar to a punt, 30 or 33 ft in length

- *zerstort:* German – during

CHARACTERS
***Indicates a Fictional Character**

CÉVENNES MOUNTAINS, FRANCE

Amelia Auvrey* (Ame, Mon Ame are Jehan's terms of endearment for her) – free-spirited holy woman, healer, and beekeeper; mother died in childbirth, a few years later father captured while participating in a Huguenot uprising, sentenced to the galleys, then died trying to escape
Luisant* - Jehan BonDurant's faithful Andulusian mare
Romulus* - Amelia's brave, loving wolf-dog
Remus* - Menina Elise's wolf-dog, brother to Romulus
Commandeur Timoleon (François Timoleon de Montaud Labat) - Commandeur de l'Ordre de Saint Jean de Jerusalem Knights Hospitaller Commandery at Gap-Francis, Mont Lauzère from 1695-1707
Menina Elise* - a *sage-femme*, (wise woman), healer and midwife for the Castelbouc area; "Menina" is Occitan for grandmother
Griselle* - novice from Causse Sauvterre
Henriette* - novice from Pont-de-Montvert
Jacquette* - novice, younger sister of Henriette
Jean Cavalier (de Ribaute) 1681-1740 - from a modest farming family; worked as shepherd, then baker; compelled by persecutions to take up the cause of protecting freedom of worship for the Reformed Calvinist Huguenot group in the Cévennes known as the Children of God; later a primary leader of the Camisards referred to as "Colonel"
Abbé du Chaila 1647-1702 - French Catholic Abbé of Chaila (or Chayla), Archpriest of the Cevennes and Inspector of Missions of the Cevennes; his brutal persecution of Huguenots by means of torture caused his assassination and sparked the War of the Camisards

André Bondurand 1664-1710 - Jehan's father's first cousin, a master apothecary in Genoüillac who had his practice and resided at the townhouse Jean Pierre Bondurant inherited from his parents
Lucrèce de Durand 1675-1702 - André Bondurand's wife

ON THE PATH TO FREEDOM

Jehan BonDurant / Jean Pierre Bondurant 1677-1735 - French refugee minor noble born in Genoüillac, France to Huguenot parents but converted by the Dominicans at about 7 yrs old; trained as an apothecary. The spelling of the family's last name has taken many forms through the years. The BonDurant spelling is rare, but used here to remind the reader that the characters have been fictionalized. Although there is no record of his using Jehan, the Occitan (*langue d'oc*) spelling of his name, some of his ancestors did. It is used in the story as a nickname, and the pronunciation is very similar.
Moyse BonDurant b.unknown-1699 - Jehan's distant cousin, a French refugee who shared a household with him in Aarau
Massip (Jean) - guide from Cannes-et-Clarian who assisted refugees to Geneva
Stéphane* - guide working alongside Massip
Syeira* - young refugee Roma woman from a *lăutari* musician family; dancer and fortune teller
Manfri* - young refugee Roma man that Syeira marries; name meaning 'man of peace'
Anne Broussard* - French refugee hatmaker for Malbois
Daniel Isnard - French refugee hatmaker for Malbois from Veine south of Lyon, although his hometown is fictionalized to somewhere in the Cévennes
Jacques Isnard - French refugee hatmaker for Malbois, brother of Daniel Isnard

AARAU
SWISS CANTON OF BERNESE AARGAU

Pasteur "Uncle" Guillaume Barjon 1635-1712 - Jehan's maternal uncle and Calvinist *pasteur* (pasteur) who led a group of refugees in Aarau and Germany.

Monsieur Brochet (Pierre) b.1662 - refugee merchant from Orange

Monsieur Malbois (Henri) b.1664 - refugee hatmaker from Aigues-Mortes

Jean Giraud - French Huguenot refugee bookseller from La Grave in the Hautes-Alpes

Madame Bernadine (de Tourtoulon) de Valobscure 1656-1729 - wife of Pasteur Barjon

Louis Barjon 1685-1698 - son of Pasteur Barjon and Madame Bernadine de Valobscure

Madame Saigne b.1655 - maidservant for the Barjons

Udine Schuler* - assistant to Monsieur Lemieux in his clothing boutique

Monsieur/Meister Lemieux* - owner of clothing atelier and boutique

Jacques Corbell - (also Corbel/Corbet) listed in records as a single man who shared a household with Jean Pierre Bondurant in Virginia; fictionalized as cutler

Luc Dodet - locksmith from Viguan in the Cévennes; French refugee on affidavit seeking aid in Rotterdam after being abandoned by Sieur de Sailly who had recruited them for a resettlement project

Elaine - wife of Luc Dodet; records do not list her name so it is fictionalized

Etienne Roussel - French refugee glovemaker from Paris; listed on affidavit seeking aid in Rotterdam

Matthieu Roussel - French refugee glovemaker from Paris, brother of Etienne Roussel; also listed on affidavit seeking aid in Rotterdam, and on ship Peter & Anthony ship with Jean Pierre Bondurant

Antoine Aigoin - French refugee hatmaker, from Ribaute in the Cévennes; also listed on affidavit seeking aid in Rotterdam

Constantin Eschalier b.1677 - French refugee stocking maker from Vivarez in the Cévennes

Frantz Ludwig Michel 1675-1717 - Swiss explorer and mapmaker from Muenster, Swiss Canton of Bern; traveled the middle colonies searching for a site for a Swiss colony

Monsieur Borel - French refugee pasteur employed by Charles de Sailly to recruit Huguenots in the Swiss Cantons for resettlement projects

Sieur de Sailly (Charles) - French nobleman refugee in the service of King William III of England and Lord Galway as an agent to organize and recruit Huguenots for resettlement schemes

BASEL-STADT
SWISS CANTON OF BASEL

Herr Vermittler* - Intermediary agent for refugees in Basel

ROTTERDAM
THE DUTCH REPUBLIC

Lieutenant Brooks* - Lieutenant aboard Lord Galway's ship

LONDON

Pasteur de Joux (Benjamin) 1637-1703 - French refugee pasteur from Lyon; joined the Church of England and became a founding minister of the London parish of Saint Jean Spitlefields (known today as Spittlefield's; appointed to minister Huguenots going to the colonies
Dr. Ramsdell* - Soho based physician who offers lodging in exchange for assistance in his practice

OTHER HISTORICAL FIGURES MENTIONED

King Louis XIV 1643-1715 - King of France 1643-1715
Marie de Magdala (Mary Magdalene) 1st century - follower of Jesus of Nazareth and "apostle to the apostles"; revered in southern France as one of the first Christians to preach there; annual pilgrimages to the Sainte-Baume cave, (where she is said to have lived her last years), have occurred since at least the 5th century
Intendant Nicolas de Lamoignon de Basville 1648-1724 - French magistrate and administrator under Louis XIV who was steward of Languedoc for thirty-three years beginning in 1685
Pasteur Claude Brousson 1647-1698 - charismatic Calvinist Reformed *pasteur* (pastor) who risked preaching in the Cévennes mountains even after being exiled. He used the alias names Paul or Olivier Beauclose.
Lord Galway - Marquis de Ruvigny, Earl of Galway, Lord Justice of Irelande; a French refugee and one of the most important diplomats in the service of King William III
King William (III) 1650-1702 - Prince of Orange, Stadtholder of the Dutch Republic, King of England, Scotland, and Ireland; a staunch protector and defender of Protestantism

OTHER CHARACTERS MENTIONED

Métayer Benat* - land steward of Château de Cougoussac; Catholic

Biatris Gasquet* - cook for Château de Cougoussac; Reformed

Marie Mathieu b. unknown – d. unknown – Huguenot prophetess from Lussan in the Cévennes known to have interacted with Jean Cavalier and the Camisards; some sources say she was Cavalier's love interest

AUTHOR'S NOTES

Both *Find Me in the Stars* and the first novel in The Cévenoles Sagas series, *The Muse of Freedom*, draw inspiration from my eighth great-grandfather and his extended family. During the late 17th century, Jean Pierre Bondurant dit Cougoussac, a French Protestant Huguenot, lived in the Cévennes mountains of southern France, a crown of natural wonders, surprises, mystery, and contrasts.

The region changes from place to place, making it a maze of winding rivers, deep gorges, caves, waterfalls, causses (plateaus rich in limestone), heather-covered moors, and aromatic plants and herbs that provide nature's medicines. The slopes are covered with a variety of trees, depending on the locale. Sweet chestnut forests, les châtaigneraies, were planted by early Benedictine monks and commonly referred to as the "bread tree" for providing sustenance. White oak, beech, Scotch pine, and spruce are used for building, and the mulberry trees were planted centuries ago for feeding silkworms. In the river gorges, life flourishes with beaver or birds of prey, such as the peregrine falcon or the Bonelli eagle nesting in the cliffs. At nightfall, bats come out of crevices in the cliff walls. The ancient woods are a refuge to many wild creatures, from the stately, agile wolf down to a multitude of rare beetles.

The relationship with stone here is ancient and sacred. The thousands of menhirs (standing stones) scattered across the causses were used by early inhabitants 4000-5000 years ago for worship, while the dolmen and barrows were for burials. From generation to generation, the ancient knowledge of stoneworking has been handed down and continues to be crucial to building homes, churches, and field walls.

The livelihood of the region's people has been diverse, since farming alone was often difficult in the rugged terrain where terraces are required. Sheep and goat herding have been common along with the keeping of magnaneries (buildings for the raising of silkworms), and chestnuts have been cultivated as a source of flour.

The mining tradition is old in the Cévennes, with a history of iron and silver mining works since the Gallic period. During the Middle Ages, the bishops of Mende and lords of Sauve-Anduze acquired much wealth from silver galena veins around Mount Lozère, and the first coal mining occurred near Alès during the 13th century.

The Cévennes are located in the area originally known as Occitània. When it became a part of France (in what was essentially a hostile takeover), it became known as Languedoc, and since 2016, as Occitànie. These terms for the region come from the name of the traditional language, Occitan, sometimes referred to Provencal. The word Occitan comes from "òc" which means "yes". This was the original language of southern France and, being the language of the Troubadours, was the primary language in Europe during the Middle Ages. Of the many dialects and subdialects, the Languedocian form of Occitan is the original language of the Cévennes mountains region. Within the novel, this language is primarily referred to as langue d'oc.

Being steadfast in their traditions, the people of the Cévennes have made for rebellious souls when others have tried to force change upon them. The Cévenol people clung to their traditional Occitan language even after the Ordinance of Villers-Cotterêts in 1539, when it was decreed that the langue d'oïl (precursor to modern French) should be used by all French administrations. Occitan's greatest decline was during the French Revolution, when diversity of language was considered a threat.

The ancestry of the Occitànie people, and the core of their religious beliefs, has been shrouded in secrecy for centuries, leaving much yet to be discovered. Thought to have melded into the culture over time are the Gabali Celtae (Gauls), Phoenicians, Romans, Essenes—the earliest Christians including Marie de Magdalen (Mary Magdalene), Lazarus, and Martha—Cathars, Francs, Moors, Sephardic and Ashkenazi Jews, Roma, Spanish, Italian, English, Scottish, and others.

Often referred to as "the Desert" by Reformist preachers, the Cévennes offered a remote place to live for those who chose to practice their own spirituality outside the strict confines of the Roman Catholic Church, begetting much diversity. The desert was a place of tribulations, temptations, and despair, but also a place to hear the word of the Lord. Over the centuries, periods of conflict and persecution were interspersed with times of limited tolerance, so living in this area kept most out of the watchful eye of the State which became the strong arm of the Roman Catholic Church.

There had been earlier conflicts in France between Catholics and Protestants during the late 16th and early 17th centuries that settled somewhat during a short period of limited tolerance when the Edict of Nantes was signed into law on 13 April, 1598 by King Henri IV, Louis XIV's grandfather. But by the late 17th century, France was once again a land deeply divided by King Louis XIV's lust for wealth, war, and tariffs and his insatiable passion for religious persecution, all driven by a goal of authoritarianism perfected.

Colbert, the Minister of Finances under Louis XIV from 1661 to 1683, was known for encouraging major public works projects, increasing France's colonial holdings, and working to create a nationalist balance of trade by instituting tariffs and regulations on goods and trade guilds. This was the beginning of Louis XIV's focus on authoritarian control and what many French perceived as the loss of their independence. The new tariffs drove prices on imported goods so high that only the wealthy could afford them. And the retaliatory tariffs from other countries restricted the export of French goods, causing many trades to take huge losses.

After the death of his first wife, Louis XIV secretly married Madame de Maintenon, who became one of his closest advisers and influencers. She and the Roman Catholic leaders pushed for edicts to force Huguenot parents to educate their children in the Catholic faith. These efforts eventually resulted in edicts that allowed the Catholic clergy to forcibly take children from their homes to be held at the priories, convents, and monasteries by Franciscans and Dominicans.

King Louis's desire for absolute control led Louvois, the French Secretary of State for War, to institute forcible military enrollment of the nobility and gentry, (unless one had the money to provide payoffs in exchange), curbing the spirit of independence Louis and his advisors sought to extinguish. Louvois's modus operandi was discipline and complete subjection to royal authority. He claimed credit for inventing the dragonnade in 1681, which was the use of mounted soldiers, referred to as dragoons, to intimidate Huguenot families into converting to Catholicism. The ill-disciplined dragoons were billeted, (troop quartering), in Protestant households with implied permission to abuse and torture the inhabitants, and destroy or steal their possessions, earning themselves the title "booted missionaries".

Then in the year 1685, Louis XIV ended the Edict of Nantes due to the pressure and influence of the Roman Catholic clergy within Louis' circle and that of Madame de Maintenon. His Edict of Fontainebleau called for the Revocation of the prior

Edict, and persecution of "heretics"—Protestants and anyone not of the Roman Catholic religion—escalated into renewed violence, causing many to seek Réfuge.

The King appointed Intendant Nicolas de Lamoignon de Basville, a friend of Madame de Maintenon, as the French magistrate and administrator for Languedoc beginning in 1685. He was extremely zealous and accused of significant cruelty in his pursuit and management of Protestants and others, not of the Catholic faith.

In 1688, Louis XIV initiated the Nine Years' War (1688–1697), often called the War of the Grand Alliance or the War of the League of Augsburg. It was a conflict between France and a European coalition fighting the aggression of France, which mainly included the Holy Roman Empire, the Dutch Republic, England, Spain, Savoy, and Portugal. Fought in Europe and the surrounding seas, North America, and India, it is sometimes considered the first global war. The war, along with Louis's extravagances at his Versailles court, drained France's coffers to the point that new taxes had to be instituted to cover the cost of the war—just as famines were occurring from the two years of cold, wet weather in 1694-1695.

Just as the poor in many parts of France were starving, the ensuing destruction and atrocities from Intendant Basville's persecutions were creating divisions between neighbors and within families. The situation had citizens questioning whether they should stay in the country, or leave to seek refuge in a new land. As a result of the persecutions and poverty, a mysterious spiritual resistance arose in the Cévennes mountains to fight the absolutism of the kingdom—both against the demand for religious unity and the new taxes that created an unfair burden on the poor and working classes. This resistance emerged into full rebellion in the year 1701 and has come to be called the Camisard War.

This is the story of the Cévenol people during that time, some who chose to live in secrecy, some who chose to rebel, and some who chose to take the path of the refugees, fleeing the country by the hundreds of thousands, stifling the French economy in a way Louis XIV never could have imagined.

Many refugees fled to the Swiss Cantons for freedom of conscience and for better opportunities in a land where peace prevailed. But, in 1699, most were required to leave due to new restrictions the government imposed on the French refugees. The Elector of Brandenburg in the Holy Roman Empire, (now a part of Germany), offered the Huguenot refugees safe haven in a town called Sieburg, (commonly called Karlshafen since 1717), and assistance in building communities.

Other refugees learned of the Carolana Floride resettlement project (shortened it to Carolana for the novel) in the New World, which was heavily promoted throughout several "refuge" countries via pamphlets and meetings. Carolana was a vast tract of land covering what is today North and South Carolina and the northern panhandle of Florida. Those interested in the project left the Swiss Cantons, traveling the Rhine River to Rotterdam, then taking ships to London to await the promised voyage to the New World.

If you have already read this novel, you will be aware of how this project took a turn for the worst, leaving the refugees abandoned in Rotterdam. Some gave up and took aid offered to them to go to Brandenburg instead. Others in the group made their way to London, where they lived for many months while the project organizers acquired funding and commissioned ships. Yet they were well-received while in this great city. Many discovered it to be a place for new knowledge and discovery, and those Huguenots who stayed on in London found opportunities that had been denied to them in their land of origin.

For further details on the Bondurant family, you'll want to read *The Muse of Freedom*, the prequel to this book. It contains copious Author's Notes on the documented history with footnotes and sources. From this, you will learn how I came to conclusions needed to fill in the gaps and develop the characters and storyline.

I hope that after reading this novel, you will hold a place in your heart for all people—past and present—who have struggled to escape persecution, oppression, violence, war, or poverty.

History teaches us that oppression comes from greed and greed comes from fear of lack—lack of food, water, land, money, attention, affection, control, power—it goes on. When fear is allowed to take over in our minds, it can result in separation and divisions that soon become hateful and often violent. The circle of fear stops with each individual. I ask that we learn from history and choose love, not fear. When we choose love, it will encourage others to do the same and give us hope for humanity.

ACKNOWLEDGEMENTS

I am grateful to my partner of sixteen years, Jon Cotham, for sharing my passion for historical fiction in books and on screen, for being a sounding board for ideas and plot twists, and for indulging me with extra support when deadlines were near. He makes it possible for me to bring my novels to fruition.

Special thanks go to Janet Wertman, who has faithfully supported me through every chapter of this journey with her expertise and enduring friendship. She has listened frequently to my laments over the "rules" to avoid adverbs—one of many grammar rule distortions created by the world of blogging. (I do not shy away from adverbs but subscribe to Matt Moore's philosophy: "*Not using adverbs is the bastard mutant off-spring of some excellent writing advice: be precise in your wording.*")

My late uncle, Jackson Larimore Snyder, instigated my stories about Jean Pierre Bondurant about twenty years ago. I may have never known about the Bondurants if he had not shared genealogical findings showing we descend from Jean Pierre on two lines—twice the DNA for channeling his character! At that time, my character of Jehan began to take form, evolving over time. Jean Pierre is actually a well-researched figure with an estimated quarter of a million progeny, many of whom have been fascinated with his story.

I am also in gratitude to Loic Breton for sharing stories and opening the old Bondurant townhome in Génolhac, France, which has belonged to his family since the 19th century. His tour up Mount Lozére was a must do, where he says Jean Pierre Bondurant "surely" spent time at the Camisard hamlet of Les Bouzèdes. During my brief visits with Loic, I experienced the warm character and generous spirit of the Cévenol people from whom he is descended.

I used many resources while writing, but I would like to call out three historians, Mary Bondurant Warren, Owen Stanwood, and Kristine Wirts, whose publications gave me a far better understanding of the Huguenot refugee diaspora in the late 17th century.

Distant cousin and dedicated historian and researcher, the late Mary Bondurant Warren, greatly contributed to my research into the Bondurant family. Her three books on the early Bondurants are filled with well-researched facts about the family.

Owen Stanwood, an associate professor of history at Boston College, brought to light all the inner workings and underbelly of the Huguenot diaspora in his book *The Global Refuge: Huguenots in an Age of Empire.* He dedicated a significant portion of his book to the refugee resettlement project that Jean Pierre Bondurant was a part of, featuring the major players who ended up in Manakintown, Virginia in their search for "Eden".

It was Kristine Wirts article "Keeping the Faith: The Story of a Seventeenth-Century Peddler and his Protestant Community" in *The Journal of The Western Society for French History* that helped me create the all-important character of Jean Giraud, the bookseller who assisted Jehan and Amelia by transporting letters and money. Although I have fictionalized some details about Giraud, it was Ms. Wirts' article that presented a real-life persona on whom I could develop this character.

Many thanks also go out to all the other researchers and scholars, past and present, who laid the groundwork for this story. A few others whose names deserve a mention are Marie-Lucy Dumas, Lionel Laborie, the various authors of the

19th century publications of *Memoirs of the Academy of Nîmes*, and curé-doyen Father César Nicolas who assembled and published primary source historical records in *The Génolhac Dominican Convent: 1298-1791*.

And, last but not least, my enduring gratitude goes out to all my family, friends, and fellow authors who gave input throughout the journey: my daughter, Megan Stone, who is a healer in her own way (and is a joy to watch blossom) as she brings wellness education to the world; the members of the Historical Novel Society who constantly inspire and educate me; members of France's Splendid Centuries writers collaborative—Ann McClellan, Keira Morgan, Rozsa Gaston, and Michèle Callard for beta reads, reviews, and amazing support; my Bondurant Family Association cousins—Eve B. Mayes, Bruce Ramsdell, Su McDonnell, David Bondurant, and Marcelle Bondurant Hoffman—who constantly offer their patronage and enthusiastic encouragement; map brush designer (and author), K.M. Alexander, who created the tiny cities and mountains you see in the inset map of the Cévennes; and to all the advanced readers and reviewers.

SELECTED BIBLIOGRAPHY

Bainton, Ronald H. *The Reformation of the Sixteenth Century.* Boston: Beacon Press, 1952.

Baird, Charles W. *History of the Huguenot Emigration to America* Vol. II. New York: Dodd, Mead & Co., 1885.

Baring-Gould, S. *A Book of the Cevennes.* London: John Long, 1907.

Beverly, Robert. *The History and Present State of Virginia, In Four Parts.* London: R. Parker at the Unicorn, under Plazza's of the Royal-Exchange, 1705.

Bouras, Alain. *Lussan: Between Sky and Scrubland.* Lussan, France: Alain Bouras Publisher. 2012

Cavallier, Jean. *Memoirs of the wars of the Cevennes, under Col. Cavallier.* London: J. Stephens, 1726.

Desel, Jochen. "Guillaume Barjon - Hugenottenpfarrer in den Cevennen und Mitbegriinder von Bad Karlshafen an der Weser." *Vereins für hessische Geschichte und Landeskunde* 1834 e.V. ZHG 98 (1993): 69-84.

Du Quesne, Henri. *Un projet de république à l'île d'Éden (l'île Bourbon) en 1689.* Paris: E. Dufossé, 1689.

Ebard, Prof. Dr. Fr. "The Huguenot community of Aarau 1685-1699". Zurich: Argovia Journal Vol. 50, (1939).

Ehrenreich, Barbara and English, Deirdre. *Witches, Midwives, and Nurses*. New York: The Feminist Press, The City University of New York, 1973.

Fogelman, Aaron Spencer. *Two Troubled Souls: An Eighteenth-Century Couple's Spiritual Journey in the Atlantic World*. Chapel Hill: Univ. of North Carolina Press. 2013.

Gordon, Bruce. "Polity and Worship in the Swiss Reformed Churches". A Companion to the Swiss Reformation. Brill. 2016.

Gwynn, Robin D. *Huguenot Heritage: The History and Contribution of the Huguenots in Britain*. Eastborne, UK: Sussex Academy Press, 2000.

Laborie, Lionel. *The French Prophets: A Cultural History of Religious Enthusiasm in Post-Toleration England (1689-1730)*. Ph.D. Thesis, University of East Anglia, School of History, 2010.

Ladurie, Emmanuel Le Roy. *The Peasants of Languedoc*: Translated with an Introduction by John Day. Urbana and Chicago: University of Illinois Press, 1978

Lagarde, Régine and Wick-Werder, Margrit. "Une colonie d'environ 200 réfugiés a vécu à Aarau". Association Chemin des Huguenots et des Valdesi General Assembly Report.

Lambert, David E. *The Protestant International and the Huguenot Migration to Virginia*. New York: Peter Lang Publisher, 2010.

Monahan, W. Gregory. *Let God Arise: The War and Rebellion of the Camisards*. Oxford: Oxford University Press, 2014.

Mortimer, Ian. *The Time Traveler's Guide to Restoration Britain*. New York: Pegasus Books, 2017.

Paspati, A.G.; Hamlin, C. *Memoir on the language of the Gypsies, as now used in the Turkish Empire*. Journal of the American Oriental Society 7:143-270, 1863.

Randall, Elizabeth. "A Special Case: London's French Protestants," *A History of the French in London*. London: Univ. of London, School of Advanced Study, Institute of Historical Research, 2013.

Reclus, Élisée. *The Universal Geography, Vol. II, France and Switzerland*. London: J.S. Virtue & Co., Limited, 1876.

Spaulding, Robert Mark. "Revolutionary France and the Transformation of the Rhine". Central European History Journal, Vol. 44, No. 2 (June 2011), pp. 203-226.

Stanwood, Owen. *The Global Refuge: Huguenots in an Age of Empire*. Oxford: Oxford University Press, 2020.

Stillman, Allison. *The Sacred Art of Anointing*. Ojai, CA: Romancing the Divine Publisher, 2008.

Warren, Mary Bondurant. *The Bondurants of Génolhac, France*. Tricentennial Edition, Athens, Georgia USA: Heritage Papers, 2000.

Wilson Bohannan Land, Mary. "The Establishment of Huguenots in Virginia". William & Mary Scholar Works, 1942.

Wirts, Kristine, "Keeping the Faith: The Story of a Seventeenth-Century Peddler and his Protestant Community".

The Journal of The Western Society for French History, Vol. 42, 2014.

Yaghoobi, Reza. Kazerouni, Afshin. Kazerouni, Ory "Evidence for Clinical Use of Honey in Wound Healing as an Anti-bacterial, Anti-inflammatory Anti-oxidant and Anti-viral Agent: A Review". Jundishapur Journal of Natural Pharmaceutical Products. NCBI/NLM/NIH. (2013 Jul 17).

Zhent, Erstes. *Geschichtsblätter des Deutschen Hugenotten-Vereins, Vol. 1.* Fabersche Buckduckrei, A & R Faber. Magdeburg, 1892.

Pharmacopoeias

Bostock, John, M.D, F.R.S. and Riley, H.T. Esq., B.A. *The Natural History of Pliny. Translated with Copious Notes and Illustrations*, London: Henry G. Bohn, 1856.

Gerard, John; Rolle, John; Islip, Adam; Norton, Joyce; Whitaker, Richard; Fisher, Sidney T.; Dodoens, Rembert; Johnson, Thomas. *The herball, or, Generall historie of plantes*, London: Adam Islip, Joice Norton and Richard Whitakers, 1636.

Salmon, William, Professor of Physick. *Pharmacopœia Londinensis. Or, the New London Dispensatory*. London: Th. Dawks, Th. Buffet, Jo. Wright, and Ri. Chiswell, 1682.

Thompson, C.J.S. *The Mystery and Art of the Apothecary*. London: John Lane The Bodley Head Limited, 1929.

THE CÉVENOLES SAGAS

Find Me in the Stars is the second novel in a trilogy that follows the life of Jehan BonDurant and his Muse in their search for "Eden" and their efforts to stand up for tolerance and compassion. From France through the "Réfuge" countries, these stories will take the reader on a journey to several intriguing locations.

To learn about future novels, receive special offers, access the Readers' Guide, and read fascinating blog posts articles, visit my website and sign up at
juleslarimore.com.

If you enjoyed this book, I would be grateful for your honest reviews on **Goodreads** and **Amazon**. Even if you have no time to write a review, a star rating of any sort to tickle the algorithms would be wonderful!

Adventure on my friends!

Jules Larimore